THE GLASS DAGGER

THE GLASS DAGGER

First in the Glass Maker Series

by

with best wishes

Peter Cooke

Peter Cooke.

Petan Publishing

Paperback ISBN 0 9553418 0 9

Sole Distributor
Petan Publishing
20 Dorchester Crescent
Baildon Shipley
West Yorkshire
BD17 7LE
petanpublishing@blueyonder.co.uk
www.petanpublishing.co.uk

Produced by Central Publishing Services
Milnsbridge Huddersfield West Yorkshire HD3 4QY
www.centralpublishing.co.uk

PROLOGUE

'**G**et out of the way, you stupid oaf!'

Like a glass falling on stone, the shout shattered Giam's reverie into myriad pieces. His startled glance revealed two pounding horses almost on top of him. The leading horse knocked out of its stride by a savage haul on the reins, reared up in front of him, its hooves flailing the air. Avoiding them by a hairsbreadth, he received a fierce blow from a fetlock that sent him crashing to the ground, where he lay too stunned to move. Opening pain-blurred eyes, he was vaguely aware of someone at his side. Lifting his head he beheld two beautiful deep brown eyes gazing anxiously at him.

'Are you hurt?' A low, musical voice enquired,

Giam tried to sit up but lay down again as pain lanced through his body.

'Are you hurt?' she repeated, but less anxiously this time, now that he'd moved.

As the pain eased, Giam opened his eyes again and studied the face carefully; afraid that if he broke the spell by speaking this vision might disappear. The lovely eyes, high cheekbones and pale complexion were framed by golden hair entwined with seed pearls; the bleached hair and the pearls around her neck signified her noble birth; by law, no courtesan was allowed to wear pearls.

'Thank you for your concern, my lady,' he replied courteously sitting up gingerly. 'It was my own fault for not looking where I was going. I'm only bruised and mostly my pride,' he said with a wry grin.

There was a rustling of silks as she stood up. 'I was afraid you would be badly hurt when we rode you down.' She threw her arms out impulsively. 'It's such a joy to ride here on Murano, where there's space to do it!' As she turned, Giam saw the horse and rider

i

motionless behind her; obviously the man who had called out before the horse hit him.

'Adrian and I were racing for the gate,' she said apologetically, indicating the other horseman. 'I was concentrating on staying in front and I didn't see you until you stepped out.'

This is no ordinary lady, Giam thought. Noble ladies don't ride out with a man without a chaperone; nor beat them in horse races! He tried to stand, but his unsteady legs let him down. As he staggered, she put an arm round his waist to support him and Giam almost collapsed again at the perfumed warmth of her body.

The rider of the second horse dismounted and strutted towards them. He was about the same age as Giam, or possibly a year or two older. He wore knee breeches and doublet, with a heavily trimmed satin and damask cloak slung carelessly across his shoulders. The hilt of his sword and scabbard were lavishly encrusted with rubies and diamonds, obviously a nobleman of some substance.

With a scowl of disapproval, he took a proprietary hold on the Lady's upper arm and tried to pull her away. 'My Lady Maria, you should not be concerning yourself with clumsy peasants. Leave me to deal with this fellow.'

The Lady resisted. 'Let go of me, Adrian!' she cried struggling to release her arm. 'I'll not be handled, or ordered about like this!'

Incensed, Giam moved forward quickly his hand on the hilt of his sword, 'Take your hands off her, 'he cried, or you'll have me to answer to.'

They confronted each other like fighting cocks and then the nobleman releasing the ladies arm, stepped back and drew his sword forcing Giam to do the same for his own protection.

'No, Adrian! You must not fight,' the Lady cried out in dismay. 'He is no common vagabond from whom I need protection.'

The nobleman ignored her and with a sneer, lunged at Giam without even the courtesy of a salute. Angered by this breach of etiquette Giam kept his temper and parried the thrust. Concentrating on defence at first, Giam parried his opponent's skilled, but overconfident lunges and ripostes with relative ease. Gaining the measure of his man he increased the tempo and direction of his thrusts, his blade flickering like a snake's tongue. Eventually, with another dazzling change of direction, Giam's sword point tore through the sleeve of his opponent's doublet, drawing blood. With a curse, his opponent withdrew, clapping a hand to his injured arm.

The Lady immediately stepped between them. 'This has gone far enough. Put up your swords!' she cried imperiously.

It was a risky move, Giam thought in admiration, but it had the desired effect. Both men obeyed, Giam with a sense of relief, his opponent, he could see, plainly furious.

'You are a very skilled swordsman, sir,' she said turning to Giam, with a warm smile. 'The first blood is yours. It was generous of you to stop when you had the advantage. Thank you too, for your earlier concern. Don't worry about Adrian; I'm used to his bullying ways. They don't intimidate me.'

She turned to the nobleman. 'Heed my warning, Adrian,' she said icily. 'Never handle me in that fashion again, or you'll regret it. I'm not a servant to be ordered around.' She bestowed on him a haughty, scornful look. 'And next time, when you draw your sword, I'd advise you to take more care in choosing your opponent. A less generous one would have spitted you, instead of merely tearing your doublet and giving you a scratch.'

Giam couldn't help grinning, but the lady had stern words for him, too. 'As for you, sir,' she said, 'perhaps it would be advisable to look where you're going in future.' Her words were censoring, but the dimpled smile took much of the sting from her words. 'What is your name, sir?'

'Giacomo Bellini at your service, my lady,' he replied with a deep formal bow.

'Bellini!' The voice of the now red-faced young man rang with contempt. 'You're the son of that fool of a nobleman who married a commoner.'

'My father, Senator Eduardo Bellini, is no fool, sir,' replied

Giam proudly. 'Have a care how you speak of him, or I'll be forced to teach you some manners, yet again.'

'I need no commoner to teach me manners. My family is one of the oldest in Venice.'

'Then you'll be familiar with the fact that my name is inscribed in the Libro d'Oro,' said Giam. 'My mother may have been the daughter of a glass-maker, but by decree of the Senate I am of noble birth.'

'In the Libro D'Oro you may be, but you will always be a commoner. Noble birth can only be bestowed by generations, not by a line in a book written by fools.'

Giam forced himself to answer calmly, out of respect for the lady. 'It is interesting that you consider your peers to be fools, for that would make you one too. In any case,' he went on, with a smile that failed to reach his eyes, 'since your breeding must have taught you the proper way of introduction, it would be appropriate to do so now. Should we fight again; at least I will know whom it is I've killed!'

There was a short pause, during which Giam and the lady exchanged amused glances. The nobleman fingering his sword, fought to check his fury, before making a very small bow and saying arrogantly, 'I am Senator Adrian Ragazoni and this is Lady Maria Morisini, my betrothed. Her father is Senator Ricardo Morisini. Even you must have heard of him,' he added scornfully.

Of course Giam had heard of Senator Morisini. He was one of the richest and most influential men in Venice, with a reputation for being somewhat unconventional. He had made his money by investing heavily in the silk trade from Cathay, which it was rumoured he now controlled. He was also an Avogador, a lawyer whose job it was to see that the Laws of Venice were used correctly.

Before he could frame a suitable reply, Lady Maria turned on Ragazoni, eyes sparkling with anger. 'You go too far, Adrian,' she stormed. 'I'm not betrothed to you! If you make such a presumption again, I will inform my father who will send you back to Venice.'

With that, she seized the reins of her horse, placed her foot in the stirrup and much to Giam's admiration, swung athletically into the saddle. Making a polite inclination of her head to Giam, she gestured imperiously at Ragazoni, and, wheeling her horse round, cantered up the drive, leaving Ragazoni open-mouthed.

Giam watched Lady Maria until she disappeared from sight. Then, hearing the hiss of a sword drawn from its scabbard, he spun around and in one fluid motion, drew his sword and was instantly en-garde. It was just as well. Snarling with rage Ragazoni lunged recklessly to the body, but Giam parried effortlessly with a riposte that required a hurried parry from Ragazoni. Wary of Giam's skill, Ragazoni now began to fence elegantly and with some élan. Equally matched at first, Giam eventually began to gain the ascendancy as his greater athleticism played its part.

He made a flying riposte as he glided back after another attack and when Ragazoni attempted a direct riposte in reply, he deflected his opponent's sword with a strong grazing action of his blade, forcing him slightly off balance. Noticing that Ragazoni was not gripping his sword as tightly as he should, Giam tried a slightly risky move he had learned only recently from his fencing master. Feinting to the left, he made a strong downward beat against Ragazoni's sword then enveloped it, sweeping it in a full circle. When Ragazoni moved to counter, Giam entangled the two swords and then, with a sinuous twist of his wrist, sent Ragazoni's weapon flying from his hand.

Giam held his point against Ragazoni's throat, as he moved towards the fallen sword. Bending down, still keeping his eyes on Ragazoni's thunderous face, he picked it up, slid it into the other's scabbard and then stepped back sheathing his own sword. He regarded Ragazoni with a stony face. 'You're lucky I didn't kill you on this occasion, Senator Ragazoni,' he said calmly at last, when Ragazoni made no move. 'I suggest you follow the Lady Maria's example and retire to the Palazzo. If you choose to draw your sword again, I will not spare you a third time.'

Ragazoni glowered at Giam; hesitated, then swung up into his saddle. Sawing at the reins so his horse, its eyes wild, reared and pawed the air, he spat out his reply. 'I'll remember this, Bellini. You can be sure of that. We'll meet again at a time and place of my choosing.' Then, thrusting his spurs cruelly into the flanks of his horse, he galloped up the drive and was soon lost to view.

Jacob stared after him in dismay. He couldn't help but remember his grandfather's words of a few hours earlier, warning him not to offend the Old Families. It seemed he'd already made an enemy of one of them, a dangerous and vindictive one at that. However, his natural optimism soon took over and his thoughts turned to a pair of flashing brown eyes. As he daydreamed about Lady Maria Morisini, he quickly forgot his misgivings. Perhaps things aren't so bad after all, he rationalised to himself. Adrian Ragazoni will forget about me when he cools down, I'm not important enough. On the other hand, I may see Lady Maria again soon, although he was not too optimistic. Noble ladies didn't usually enjoy too much freedom. Perhaps she'd inherited her fathers liking for flouting convention. He'd seen her today, in unusual circumstance, so who knows what the future might hold?

Gaining comfort from this, Jacob resumed his interrupted walk until he reached the Ponte Vivarino. Stopping for a moment, he leant on the parapet and looking out over the glassmaking district, his eyes sought out the Luciano Glasshouse. It was going to take some time to accept he was now its Fattori and Master Glassmaker and all that those titles represented. Thinking over the changes, which must inevitably follow, his thoughts drifted back to the day his grandfather first accepted him as a glassblower.

CHAPTER ONE

Giam Bellini wiped the sweat from his eyes, not for the first time that morning, and fed more alder and willow billets into the ravenous mouth of the furnace. Peering intently through a window in the furnace he examined the molten glass inside the fire clay pot for any signs of bubbling; it had been heated for several hours now and was a quiescent, brilliant mass. The dazzling surface was difficult to distinguish from the gleaming sides of the paele itself, but Giam's now experienced eyes knew the mass of liquid glass was ready for working. Signalling to the waiting feeder that the glass was ready, he moved round to the front of the furnace where it was slightly cooler, sat down on the bench against the wall and composed himself for the coming test.

Giam's real name was Giacomo, but only his tutor ever called him that; unless he was in trouble! At thirteen, he was tall for his age, with a sturdy athletic build. Brushing an unruly lock of black hair from his forehead, he thought about his coming trial. He'd been learning the art of glass making from his grandfather, Antonio Luciano, Master of the Luciano Glass-works, for the past two years. It had taken him months just to understand the language of the Works. The word 'Chair' for instance had been very confusing. It could refer to the team of workers, or to the Glass-making Chair, a wooden stool with two extended arms. The Capo used these to rotate the blow-iron while shaping the glass. When a Capo was bawling out instructions to the apprentices, it was not always easy to know which 'Chair' he meant.

Now he was about to be tested on the skills he had learned and he must satisfy his grandfather that he knew them well enough to be allowed to help the Capos. Waiting impatiently for his grandfather to arrive, he looked around the room. He loved everything about glass making and even the sweltering heat of the furnace room

1

didn't deter him. In the golden glow of the furnace, apprentices were hurrying to serve the Capos, the experienced glass blowers of the Works, and to Giam's mind the best in Murano. There were six of these at present and their job was to see that, as far as possible, each piece of glass was finished to perfection.

Luca Ridotti, an apprentice a couple of years older than himself, strolled across to Giam carrying a blow-iron. 'Best of luck in the test,' he grinned. 'I'm sure you'll pass easily.' Giam grinned back. He liked Luca, he was always friendly and he was very skilled and often acted as foot maker for the Capos.

'I wish I could be so sure,' he replied with a grimace. 'Grandfather won't show me any favouritism. I'll have to be perfect if I'm going to be allowed to make a real glass.'

'Don't worry; you'll be all right. At least you know he's fair, which is more than you can say for some,' said Luca, indicating, the Chief Capo, Marco Baffo. He was man with a short temper and long ears.

'Ridotti! Are you going to be all day getting that bowl done?' Baffo bellowed. 'Stop chattering and get on with it! As for you, Bellini, stop holding up my feeders, or you'll get my boot up your arse!'

Luca winked at Giam. 'Right on cue; I'd better get on, or his highness will bust a gut; best of luck Giam, nil desperandum!' And with a cheery wave he hurried off to the furnace.

Giam, admiring Luca's skill, watched as he rotated the blow-iron inside the mouth of one of the pot. 'Gathering a blob of molten glass on the end he rolled it across the smooth, highly polished surface of the flat piece of iron Giam had learned was a marver. The blob was quickly and expertly shaped and smoothed. Occasionally Luca blew down the tube to distend the still molten mass into the shape of a bulb. He reheated the glass and passed it to Baffo, who skilfully removed the surplus glass with a pair of pucellas. The blow-iron was then rolled along the arms of the Chair to rotate the glass, while Baffo used the pucellas with his right hand to obtain the final shape.

Giam missed the end of this process as at that moment his grandfather came striding across the room. 'Ready, young Bellini?' he asked in his usual brisk manner. When Giam replied that he was, Antonio led him to a vacant Glass-making Chair. 'Now Bellini,' he said, as if Giam was an ordinary apprentice and not his grandson, 'I'm going to ask you some questions and I expect you to answer them fully.' He picked up a pair of blunt shears. 'What are these called and what are they used for?'

'Those are pucellas and they work rather like a large pair of sugar tongs. The Capo uses them to shape the blown glass by removing the surplus from the rim and also for adjusting the diameter of the bowl.'

Next, Antonio Luciano held up an iron tube with a mouthpiece at one end and a globular shape at the other. 'What about this?'

'It's a blow-pipe used for making a rough shape of the glass.'

'How is that done?'

Giam smiled as he took the blowpipe from his grandfather and accurately demonstrated the actions that Luca had just performed. 'When he's completed it, he passes the glass to the Capo.' He looked anxiously at his grandfather searching for any sign of approval, but his face was inscrutable.

Without any comment Antonio continued. 'And how does the Capo detach the blow-iron from the bowl of the glass?'

'He touches the bowl in the right place with a moistened piece of iron,' said Giam demonstrating, 'and then he strikes the blow-iron with the iron like this, causing the bowl to crack completely round its circumference.'

Antonio nodded. 'What happens next?'

'The Capo grips the foot with a clamp, a spring clip on the end of an iron rod. He reheats the glass, shapes it and trims the bowl with the pucellas, until he's satisfied it's finished.'

Antonio just nodded. 'What happens to the completed glass?'

'It's put into an oblong fire clay tunnel in the top part of the furnace to anneal.' Giam mopped his brow. He was starting to sweat profusely as the relentless questions continued.

3

'What does anneal mean?'

'The top of the furnace is warm and allows the molten glass to cool down slowly. If it cools too quickly, stresses are formed in the glass and it cracks easily. This is called crizzling and annealing stops this happening.'

Just as Giam was thinking that the questions would never end, Antonio gave a small smile. 'That's about right,' he said in grudging approval. 'Now all we need to do is to see if your skill with words is equal to your skill with your hands. I want you to make a glass. You will act as Capo; I'll get an apprentice and he and I will act as your team.'

Looking to get a little support, Giam pleaded with his grandfather. 'Could we have my friend Luca, please, Master Antonio? I've worked with him before.'

'I don't see why not,' agreed Antonio. 'Baffo seems to have finished the batch he's making and they're just cleaning up at present.'

So it was that, shortly afterwards, Giam made his first glass as Capo of a team at the Luciano Glass-works. When it was passed to Luca to put into the fire clay tray in the top of the furnace, his grandfather turned to him and said gruffly, 'That was quite well done. I think you're just about good enough to work with one of the Chairs now.'

Luca, who had overheard this comment, looked at him in surprise. 'Begging your pardon, Master Antonio, but I can't tell the difference between the one Giam made and the ones that the Chief has just done.'

'Perhaps that's why you're not a Capo yet, young Ridotti,' Antonio Luciano said sternly, but there was no malice in his voice. Luca turned away, a broad grin on his face.

While Luca started to clear up, Antonio led Giam out into the fresh air and they sat on the billets of wood near the canal-side. It was refreshing after the heat of the furnace room and they sat in companionable silence. Eventually his grandfather broke the mood. 'I didn't say too much inside,' he confided, 'it doesn't do to praise too much. But you did well. You've also a loyal friend in Luca Ridotti. It's good to have friends at work Giam, you might be thankful for them one day.'

'I already am, grandfather,' Giam said. 'Luca's helped me a lot over the last year.' His face took on a wistful look. 'I wish I had more friends outside of work though. I don't get to meet other boys very often, especially since Lunardo Carreras moved to Venice. I only see him occasionally now.'

Lunardo was the son of his father's friend, Enzio Carreras, a shipwright. They were firm friends and were always getting into some scrape or other. Giam pushed him into the canal on their last day together, but Lunardo soon got even; when Giam offered his hand to pull Lunardo out he'd pulled him in too. Giam smiled at the memory.

'You have to study,' said his grandfather. 'There's a lot you must know as a noble.'

'But I spend so much time studying,' Giam said plaintively, 'and I don't get to meet other boys now I've had to leave the Academy San Venier. Since I became a noble, father insists I have a tutor and be educated at home.'

About a year earlier the Senate had passed a law which stated that if a nobleman married the daughter of a glass-maker, any child of the union would be treated as being of noble birth. This was to recognise the rising importance of glass making to the Venetian economy. The aristocracy, usually referred to as the Old Families, had opposed it. The Orseoli's and Cornari's and their ilk, with lines going back to the founding of Venice, saw this law as diluting their noble stock. Giam had benefited because his mother was the daughter of the glassmaker, Antonio Luciano, President of the Guild. She had died from the sweating fever five years earlier, when Giam was eight. A shadow passed over his face as he thought about her.

'It can't be easy being tutored at home since your mother died,' his grandfather agreed sadly, 'although I understand why your father insists on it. All the sons of the nobility have live-in tutors. But

Eduardo should make sure you get to mix with people of your mother's class, too.'

'It's not too bad, grandfather. I'm not bothered about meeting sons of the nobility. Those I've met are mostly very arrogant and treat me as an inferior. My tutor keeps me busy most of the day, but at least my father lets me come here in my spare time.'

Giam thought wearily of his days filled with the learning of Latin, Law, Dissertation, French, English, Seismographic, Dancing and Writing under the strict eye of Il Docente Giorgio Alessandro, but then he smiled and said, 'He does at least let me study the history of glass-making, if only to help my Latin. I also have to learn fencing - father insists. So I go to Fencing-master Enriquo Gomez once a week and it's my favourite lesson after glass-making.'

'I'm afraid all of the sons of nobility have to study these things, Giam. Having your name in the Libro D'Oro is more than just a line of handwriting in a book.' His grandfather couldn't keep the pride from his voice. 'It gives you a standing in Venice that I could never have, no matter how good a glass-maker I am.'

'I never wanted to be a noble, grandfather. I just want to be as good at glass-making as you are.'

Antonio smiled. 'You'll have to work very hard, then.'

'It won't be for lack of trying' said Giam earnestly, even though he knew his grandfather was joking. 'I just hope that being a noble doesn't prevent me from achieving it.'

'Come on then lad,' said Antonio gruffly, 'enough of this daydreaming. Go and give Luca a hand to clear up and I'll have words with you later.'

Four years later an excited Giam, holding a tall goblet in his hand, burst into his grandfather's office. 'I've done it, grandfather! I've designed my first new glass....' His voice tailed off in confusion as he realised that Antonio Luciano was not alone. Seated to one side of the desk was a pair of richly dressed visitors. The man, hawk-nosed and bald, wore a long black silk robe with wide sleeves, ornamented with a double row of buttons. A black triangular cap often worn by Senators topped his matching doublet and hose. Around his neck he had an ornate catenina d'Oro; the heavy gold chain was a sure sign he was a wealthy merchant. The woman, obviously his wife, wore an embroidered red velvet cloak over a matching red day dress. Giam made a hasty bow and placed the glass on the desk.

'Please excuse my grandson Giacomo, for his bad manners,' said Antonio before Giam could apologise. 'He's a little overexcited.' Turning to Giam, he introduced the visitors. 'Senator Dalle Fornaci and his wife Signora Foscarini-Dalle Fornaci; they are considering the purchase of some stemware from us.'

As Giam made a formal bow, the Signora began examining his new goblet with great interest. The bowl was a simple round funnel shape festooned with flowers around the rim in diamond-point engraving; the stem having a central boss engraved into a lion-mask.

She turned to her husband and held up the glass. 'This is very unusual! I like it very much.'

The Senator also examined the glass with interest. 'It is different from your other glasses, Master Luciano. We were hoping that by coming direct to you, we might obtain a style that was a little out of the ordinary. I think this glass will do very well. It's the right size for our needs and will make an excellent talking point at our next dinner. How soon can you let us have ten of them?'

Giam was flattered by this appreciation of his new glass and beamed ecstatically.

His grandfather quickly brought him down to earth. 'First of all, Giacomo Bellini,' he said sternly and Giam winced at the use of his full name. 'You will apologise to Senator and Signora Fornaci for your lack of manners. And secondly,' he held his grandson's disconcerted gaze for a long moment and then, unable to keep the pretence up any longer, he gave a broad grin, 'you'd better tell me how soon you can make ten more.'

CHAPTER TWO

Sunlight streaming through a gap in the curtains finally woke Giam. Shielding his eyes from the glare, he squinted around the room with bleary eyes. He'd not heard the Campanile bell that tolled at sunrise, but from the angle of the sun it was well past that time. Springing out of bed he washed quickly, splashing water from the jug into the bowl and over the polished surface of the toilette stand. Throwing wide the curtains he stepped out on to the balcony, blinking in the strong sunlight, fumbling with the buttons on his linen shirt and fastening his breeches.

The Canale Degli Angeli was already teeming with activity. Gondolas were plying for trade and people bustled along the Fondamenta San Venier that ran alongside the canal; Murano, the glassmakers' island of Venice, was open for business. Giam gave an appreciative sniff as the smell of burning wood mingled with the salty, brackish odour of the canal. He loved the smell; it brought back memories of a childhood spent watching his grandfather, Antonio, blowing glass.

Drinking in the busy scene he failed to notice the gondola sculling round the corner of the villa to the side steps until a familiar voice called from below. 'Ciao Giam, aren't you going to Luciano's this fine morning?'

Looking down, Giam saw Angelo Robusti, the gondolier, who often took him to the Luciano Glass-works. 'Ciao Angelo,' he called back. 'I've overslept; can you come back for me in about a half hour?'

Angelo held up a package wrapped in a cloth. 'Take your time, it looks like being busy today, so I may as well eat my breakfast now, while I have the chance.'

Giam gave a cheery wave and hurried to finish dressing. Brushing his thick, black curly hair into a more acceptable state, he

8

surveyed the results in the mirror. It's a good job Giorgio Alessandro can't see me, he thought, brushing an unruly curl away from his dark brown eyes. I'd surely get a lecture on the perils of vanity. With a mocking salute to his image, he picked up his sword, belt and scabbard and strode downstairs.

His father greeted him at the door to the kitchen. 'Buon giorno Giam! I trust you slept well?'

'Too well, thank you, father. It's a good job I don't work in the Arsenale! The half-hour after the Campanile bell is long gone.'

'No matter,' was his father's preoccupied reply. 'I've already eaten and I'm going to my study now.'

Giam made short work of his meal. As he ate, he thought about his father. For several weeks now, he had been withdrawn and aloof. This had begun shortly after an argument about Giam's future. Having completed his studies, Senator Eduardo Bellini thought it was time to discuss his proposed career. The discussion had not gone well.

It started amiably enough. After the evening meal his father suggested a stroll in the cloistered courtyard, which was pleasantly cool after the heat of the day. Eduardo raised the subject of a career and suggested that Giam should follow him into politics. Giam, intending to make a light-hearted comment, had managed to offend his father by insulting politicians in general. Before he knew it, a furious row broke out. Eventually, Giam apologised for his comments. 'I really am sorry, father. I went much too far.' True. He had never intended to make so much fuss, but things had a habit of getting out of hand when he argued with his father. Nothing further was said, but Giam knew that he must find a way to achieve an understanding.

Only a few days ago he had gone to see his father to try to resolve the distance between them. Eduardo was in his study going through some documents; probably some business for the Senate. As he waited for him to finish writing, Giam looked around at the book-lined shelves. On the small occasional table in the corner by the window stood a goblet and Giam gave a start of surprise. He recognised it immediately; it was his most recent design.

Before he could gather his thoughts, his father looked up. 'I'm rather busy at the moment, Giam, can you be brief?'

When Giam began to explain his mission, Eduardo cut him off mid-sentence, saying it was not the right time for such a discussion. He promised they would meet soon and Giam had left, having neither resolved the situation, nor found out why the glass was in his father's study.

Although Giam wanted to find out the reason for his father's distraction, he was already late, so he set off for the side entrance. Unusually, the Villa San Venier had three entrances. The front entrance on the Canale Degli Angeli was the main entrance leading to a paved inner court. This in turn led into the atrio, from which a staircase, its walls lined with family weapons and armour, mounted to the second storey. The rest of the ground floor was used as a warehouse and display room for the Luciano Glass-works. At the right-hand side was the land entrance and staircase that led to the main apartments on the first and second floors. When using a gondola Giam much preferred to use the door on the left, which led to a small staging on the side canal.

Leaving through this door, he jumped into the waiting gondola and barely had time to sit down before Angelo headed out into the Canale Degli Angeli. The gondolier chattered away about a masque that had been held at the Casa Da Mula the previous evening, but Giam was only half-listening. His thoughts were still on the goblet in his father's study. How had it got there? He knew that his grandfather had visited the villa several times recently, so perhaps he had left it; but why? Before he could come to any conclusion, Angelo pointed out the Casa Da Mula as they passed. The Morisini house was the showpiece of Venice and the venue for many lavish balls and masques; last night's masque being no exception. Its imposing façade looked over the canal, but the formal gardens at the side and rear were the talk of Murano. Only on Murano was there space for such an extensive display of the gardener's art.

Passing on, they glided under the Ponte Vivarino, the main

bridge of Murano and then turned into the Rio Dei Vetrai that led into the heart of the glass-making district. Here the air was thick with sparks as apprentices fed the insatiable furnaces their daily diet of alder and willow. Standing up for a better view, he returned the affable waves of his friendly rivals, at the Alla Sirena and Al Lion Bianca glass-works. Arriving at Luciano's, he paid Angelo, giving him a little extra for his patience and then set off to find his grandfather.

Later, sitting in Antonio's office, he was pleased to see that his grandfather's face, which had been pale and gaunt the day before, now had a much healthier glow. He had coughed a lot that day and Giam was sure he'd seen blood on his kerchief

Antonio pointed to a tall drinking goblet with a lion-head boss on the stem. 'Do you remember this glass, Giam?'

Giam examined it carefully. 'It's the first glass I designed, isn't it?

'Do you remember the day it first went on to the Luciano list?'

'Of course I do! I still remember the incredible feeling when it cooled without any crizzling. I burst into your office and interrupted your meeting with a Senator and his wife.'

They laughed together at the memory and then Antonio became serious. 'Do you know, Giam, that over the last few years you've created eight of our best-selling pieces?'

'Was it as many as that?' Still, spread over four years, I suppose it's not so many.' He regarded his grandfather thoughtfully; it wasn't like him to reminisce like this, he usually got straight down to the business at hand. Giam placed the glass on the desk. 'I don't imagine for one minute that this glass is the real point behind this conversation,' he said studying his grandfather shrewdly. 'What's on your mind?'

Antonio smiled sheepishly. 'You know me too well! I do have something else on my mind, and this glass is part of it.' He fidgeted with his jerkin for a moment, pulled on his beard and then continued. 'As you know, I was fifty-four last April and my health has been poor lately. I'm thinking of retiring and handing the

11

business over to someone else.'

Not Marco Baffo, Giam thought, I doubt whether he has grandfather's business acumen and he's not popular with the men.

Antonio continued. 'Your father told me some time ago he was hoping you would follow in his footsteps and join the Senate. I have no doubt, my dear Giam that you would make a good career in politics, but politicians are two a penny. Anyone can hold forth about the price of bread; not many are given the skill to work in glass. In my opinion, there's only one career for you: Fattori and Master Glass-blower of the Luciano Glass-works.'

Giam was dumbfounded. 'What about Marco Baffo? He said at last, despite his earlier misgiving. 'He's been your senior glass blower for over ten years! Wouldn't he expect to be next in line?'

Antonio snorted. 'He's had every chance to show his worth. He's not the man for the job.' He put an arm round Giam's shoulders and regarded him proudly. 'I believed you had glass making in your blood from the very first time you blew a glass. It was as natural as breathing. Then, when you started creating new glassware, I knew it for sure.'

'I wish I was so sure,' Giam said longingly, 'but won't being a noble make it impossible?'

'Impossible, no – difficult, yes. Even if it's only by the power of the Senate that you're a nobleman; noblemen don't work in trade. To be Fattori will to be difficult, certainly, but you're more qualified than anyone to be Fattori of Luciano's. Please give it some serious thought.'

His grandfather's praise gave Giam immense pleasure; but more than this; the idea itself was gathering momentum. He rehearsed the title in his mind; Giacomo Bellini, Fattori and Master Glass blower of one of the most influential Glass-works in Murano; no, in the whole of Venice. He'd been wondering what to do with his life and now he was being offered the thing he most wanted. He knew that now. More than anything he wanted to work with glass, that strange malleable substance that could be blown into such fantastic shapes. But persuading his father to accept the idea was another matter entirely.

'What about my father? He's never going to accept me being Fattori.'

Antonio had another surprise for him. 'That's where you're wrong, my boy. Your father and I have come to an understanding. Surely you must have realised I wouldn't have made this offer without discussing it with him? You know, he owns the half share in the Luciano Glass-works that came from your mother.'

Realisation flooded over Giam - his father's moods; no wonder he'd been distracted and didn't want to talk about a career. 'So that's why you've had all those meetings with father,' said Giam and then gasped as another thought struck him. 'The glass! Of course! That's what it was doing in father's study! You took it to show him my latest design.'

A smile crossed Antonio's face. 'That was the thing that tipped the balance. He still has misgivings, but he'll tell you about them himself tonight. I'll be joining you for dinner and we'll thrash the whole thing out. Be prepared, though. Your father will only agree to you becoming Fattori for a trial period, of say, six months. You may think this isn't fair, but you'd be wise to accept it, or he'll not agree to it at all.'

Later that evening, after a splendid meal, Giam, his father and grandfather sat in the main sitting room, its walls decorated with silken tapestries brocaded with silver, weapons, armour, and family relics. Eduardo explained his fears to Giam. 'The Old Families have never accepted the law which gave you noble status. We had quite a battle last year getting the Senate to agree to the addition of your name in the Libro d'Oro. The Orseoli's, Cornari's and Ragazoni's all opposed it and tried to get the law changed. Even well known moderates such as the Morisini and Dalle Fornaci's were known to have serious doubts. None of the Old family members have ever worked. The opponents of this law could use the fact you work as sign you're not a noble and therefore, an excuse to lobby the Senate for your removal from the Libro d'Oro. I've spent the last few weeks going through the detail of the law and while it doesn't say you can't work as a Fattori, it doesn't say you can either.'

'I thought you were still angry that I didn't want to take up politics,' Giam exclaimed.

Eduardo nodded. 'I can see that's how it might have seemed. But I haven't given up on you entering politics, you know.' He pursed his lips and smiled. 'Your grandfather and I have gone over this idea many times in the last few weeks. In fairness I must tell you that I still have a lot of reservations, but your grandfather has the highest opinion of your ability and I have been very impressed with your designs. Against my better judgement, but out of respect for your grandfather's wishes, I'm prepared to let you act as Fattori. But only for a trial period of six months mind,' he continued quickly, holding up a hand to stop Giam's expressions of gratitude. 'I must have your promise that if you can't make a success of it in that time, you'll accept the legal path to the Senate I've mapped out for you.' He held out his hand and grinned. 'I told you I hadn't given up on politics. Do we have an agreement?'

Without hesitation Giam grasped the hand and shook it enthusiastically. 'We have indeed, father,' he said, as Antonio looked on in delight. 'If I can't make a success of Luciano's in six months, I'll give politics my best try. You have my word on it.'

Later, as they walked in the cloister of the inner courtyard to take some air, Eduardo gave Giam one final warning. 'You must understand what this will mean. There will be many nobles who'll despise you, not for who you are, but for what you represent. The nobility owe a considerable part of their wealth to glass making, if only as investors. Money and the power it buys is what they most admire. Beware of these people. Take great care in your dealings with them. They wield great power and make very bad enemies. And to them, anyone who's different is an enemy.'

With this warning ringing in his ears, Giam said goodnight and hurried off to his room with his mind spinning with ideas to promote the Luciano Glass-works.

The following morning was sunny and humid. Giam arose early, too excited to stay in bed any longer; he felt like a child looking forward to a treat. After a small serving of bread washed down with a glass of wine, he hurried down to the Glass-works.

His grandfather insisted he must make the announcement to the workers, not Jacob. 'I know them better than you and I want them to accept my decision willingly. However, I expect Marco Baffo will have a lot to say and it will be better if he says it to me.'

As Giam had expected, the men were stunned by the announcement. For the most part though, they accepted Antonio Luciano's decision and agreed to give Giam the benefit of the doubt. The one exception, as expected, was Marco Baffo. He'd always assumed that he would be Luciano's successor. Giam had once heard him bragging about it to his friends; enjoying the prestige his prospective elevation to Master had given him.

'Why have you done this to me, Antonio?' he burst out, his face twisted with anger. 'Haven't I served you faithfully for the last ten years? You made me your Chief Capi because I'm the best. Isn't that right?' He turned to the other Capos for support and became further incensed when they failed to spring to his defence.

He turned back to Antonio and shouted, 'you chose Bellini because he's your own flesh and blood. Bellini's too young and inexperienced. At the first sign of trouble he'll go running back to his father.'

'I don't deny that you're good,' Antonio said quietly, after Baffo's tirade had ended, 'but you don't have the skill to design new styles. Giam is exceptional at this and his best is yet to come. I believe he'll become one of the finest glass-makers that Murano has ever produced.'

There were loud murmurs of agreement among the men at this statement. Looking significantly towards Marco, Antonio made a final telling point. 'Without Giam's skill we will stand still. If we stand still, we stagnate; if we stagnate, we die. The glass industry needs new young blood. That's the way of things and why I tell you with all my heart,' here he paused dramatically to let the full weight of his words sink in. 'Giam is the only one qualified to be Fattori, so Fattori he will be from this day forth.'

Luca Ridotti, Giam's friend from his apprentice days and now a Capo in his own right, came forward to show his loyalty. Several of the others, taking their lead from Luca, wished Giam success and assured him of their full co-operation. But Marco Baffo was full of anger and resentment. He stormed back into the Works with a final furious scowl at Giam, who resolved to do all he could to have a good working relationship with him. The last thing he needed at this stage was a feud. It was a daunting prospect to have so many men and their families dependent on him, Giam now realised. The Fattori not only controlled the Glass-works, he controlled the lives and fortunes of the workers too.

Seeing his hesitation, Antonio put a reassuring arm round his shoulder. 'Come on, Fattori, there's much work to be done. You can't stand around here all day. You've a business to run.' He led him into the office and handed him a well-thumbed official looking document. This is my copy of the Matricola of 1441, issued by the Council of Ten. It contains all the rules for the running of a Glass-works, from production to selling and taxes to relations between glassmakers and other workers. Learn it well, for if you follow the rules it lays down, you can't go wrong.'

Giam took the document and glanced at it quickly. 'At least it's written in plain language and not full of official verbiage,'

Antonio smiled. 'It's not too bad. The original was so difficult to follow that this was written in the vernacular so that people could use it properly,' he grimaced, 'not that the rules aren't difficult to stick to at times. However, that's up to you now. As for the rest, there are documents to be read and signed before you have a legal title. You'll also need to go over the order books and make decisions about production. So, the sooner we start, the sooner we'll be done.'

Later that evening, Giam strolled along through the narrow alleys of the glass-making district. Even the pungent smell of burning wood and the occasional shower of sparks rising from the chimneys like fireflies, bright against the evening sky, failed to attract his attention. At the end of the most eventful day of his life and now Fattori of the Luciano Glass-works, he'd been too restless to accept his grandfather's offer to join him for the evening meal and had decided to walk home. Now, deep in contemplation, only vaguely aware of the rough cobbles under his feet, he pondered the recent events that had plunged his hitherto comfortable life into a maelstrom of change.

Ignoring the jostling homeward – bound workers, he left the glass-making area and turned down the pathway at the rear of the Casa Da Mula. In the high wall, an ornate arch led to a beautiful formal garden with lines of fruit trees, but Giam passed without a single glance. Deep in thought he strolled towards the path, leading to the Ponte Vivarino, the main bridge over the Grand Canal. This path bordered the largest open grassy space in Murano, which on holidays would be crowded with people enjoying the open air. Now there were only a few people on the canal side path heading for the bridge. Immersed in his thoughts, he approached the impressive wrought iron gates of the Casa Da Mula. Wandering carelessly across the gateway he was startled out of his reverie by a man's angry shout.

Giam came back to reality with a start and realised he was standing on the Ponte Vivarino in the gathering gloom. His memories had been so vivid; it was as though he'd lived them again. With a shake of his head, Giam straightened up and with determined strides set off for home. Tomorrow he took up his new role as Fattori of Luciano's Glass-works and there was much to do.

CHAPTER THREE

Giam's first task on becoming Fattori was to learn all he could about the Luciano Glass-works. How it was organised; the purchase of raw materials; the way the glass was sold. Of course, he already knew a lot, but not in the same detail as his grandfather. Antonio was willing to help, but his health had deteriorated rapidly after the handover. He was suffering from the early stage of consumption and so Giam was left to his own resources. Marco Baffo was no help at all. Any questions were met with a shrug and a surly reply. Fortunately, Antonio had kept meticulous records, which were a mine of information. Giam's father also gave him an insight into the sales side of the business and introduced him to the suppliers of the quartz pebbles, seaweed ash and soda used in the glass mixture.

Once Giam had established his credentials with his suppliers, he turned his attention to the Works. All was not as it should be. The apprentices were no strangers to punishment: a clip around the ear for misdemeanours, or a kick to encourage the idle, was all part of daily life. But many of them had bruises and black eyes that spoke of a much harsher regime. The Capos were always grumbling and production of glass was well down on what Giam knew it could be. The cause of their low morale soon became apparent. Marco Baffo was taking out his anger on everyone who worked on his Chair. Matters came to a head when he beat Jacopo Doti, the oldest of the apprentices, into a senseless heap. As soon as Giam heard about this, he sent for Baffo.

As soon as the Capo entered Giam's office, he started to justify what had happened. Giam stopped him immediately. 'I don't want to hear your so-called reasons, or justifications, Baffo,' he said angrily. 'I just want you to listen. I know you've still not accepted me as Fattori, but that is who I am. In the Luciano works while I am Fattori, there will be no beatings like the one given to Jacopo Doti. Should it happen again, you or anyone else responsible will be dismissed immediately. In addition, I will ensure that the other glassmakers on Murano know the reason for the dismissal. Do I make myself clear?'

Baffo glared. 'You need to keep them in line,' he blustered. 'They won't do anything if you don't give them a lick or two.'

'I was an apprentice too,' Giam reminded him, 'and a clip or a kick was what I deserved at times. It's the beatings that must stop and it's you who must stop it. You know the price of failure, so let's hear no more about it.'

Word soon spread that Baffo had been threatened with dismissal and morale improved dramatically. Production soared, banter resumed and everyone was on their toes. Giam Bellini was Fattori!

He now began to stamp his own personality on the Works. Sure that sales could be improved, he completed several new glassware designs. Bowing to the rising popularity of ornate stems, he produced his own variants. His earlier success with the lion-mask stem led him to produce two similar goblets. Two weeks later, all were ready.

With the new designs in place, Giam turned his attention to the glass making itself. Each piece of hand-blown glass was individual and there was too much disparity between glasses of the same design for his liking. The range of variation depended on the skill of each Capo. If they put their mind to it, they could produce a glass that differed only very slightly from a pattern. Murano Patronis were happy as long as the glasses looked fairly similar, so the Capos had become lazy.

Giam changed this. He produced carefully worked-out pattern masters, sketches and instructions for the Capos. In future, they must take extra care to make the glass as near to design as possible. To prove it could be done, he demonstrated by making five glasses to a pattern, while all the other Capos made five of the same design in their usual way. When the six sets of glasses were put side by side, it was clear that Giam's were almost identical, while the others varied widely. The Capos were convinced. Giam had proved his method worked, so they all agreed to follow the pattern – except Marco Baffo. A few rejected glasses soon brought him into line.

Giam was now ready for the next part of his plan. Traditionally, Murano glassmakers relied on their clients to visit one of the neighbourhood warehouses, or the Glass-works itself. Giam wanted to try another way. His first task was to convince his father of the merit of his plan, since it involved the Casa San Venier warehouse. Using the new designs, together with the best of the old, he would set up an attractive display in the large area near the atrio. The range of designs would be called 'Andrea', after his mother. The name would feature widely in the display. All the nobility and prominent Families would be invited to attend; an orchestra would play sweet music and refreshments would be served. Although never attempted before, Giam hoped this original approach would galvanise sales of Luciano glass. Eduardo was less enthusiastic, but even though he thought it was an expensive venture, he agreed it was worth a try.

The exhibition was to take place in a weeks' time - a tight schedule, but with hard work on the part of all the workers, the whole project was ready a few hours early.

As opening time drew near, only a handful of guests had arrived. Giam began pacing up and down the lantern bedecked canal side. 'It's going to be a failure,' he thought despairingly. 'I should never have suggested it.' A short while later, just as he was about to go into the atrio to find his father, he saw a cluster of lights appear from under the Ponte Vivarino. As they came nearer, Giam could make out a small flotilla of gondolas approaching. Soon a constant stream of people were alighting from gondolas and entering the Casa. The nobility, always keen to make a grand entrance, had arrived late as of right.

After his welcoming speech, Giam mingled with the crowds as they examined the exhibits of gleaming glass. Approaching the entrance to the atrio, a party of latecomers entered the room. His heart leaped as he recognised Lady Maria Morisini and Senator Adrian Ragazoni, with an older man whose resemblance to Lady Maria marked him out as her father. Lady Maria lifted her gaze from the exhibits and glanced across the room. Their eyes met. She acknowledged him with a slight inclination of her head. Giam replied with an expansive bow.

Ragazoni who had seen this little byplay picked up one of the glasses and made a remark to Lady Maria. Giam was too far away to hear Ragazoni's words, but their effect on Lady Maria was immediate. Taking hold of her father's arm she stalked away, leaving the angry Ragazoni on his own. Giam wondered if Ragazoni had made a disparaging remark about the glassware, and hoped that Lady Maria had stood up for him. He realised her good opinion of his new designs meant a lot to him.

Giam lost sight of Lady Maria's group, as his attention was needed elsewhere. By the time he was free, they had already left. Giam was disappointed to have missed her. He longed to know if she liked his new designs. His father proclaimed the exhibition a triumph and sales of the new range were excellent. Giam would have exchanged all of it for one favourable comment from Lady Maria.

A week later, sales of the 'Andrea' range were continuing to rise. The Capos at Luciano's were coping well with the new regime and production was only slightly down on previous levels. Within a short time, variations in the pattern settled down to a satisfactory standard and even Marco Baffo dropped his objections. Not of course that this had anything to do with the fact that Baffo was trying to prove he was better than Giam! Giam was elated with the progress and reasonably confident he would not have to contemplate making politics his career.

At the beginning of May, he had an unexpected visit from Enriquo Gomez his friend and fencing master with a comrade he introduced as Miguel Santini, formerly master gunner of the galleass 'Galliano'.

'To what do I owe the pleasure of this visit, Enriquo? Do you want to buy some glass from me?'

'Not at your prices,' Enriquo joked. 'I'm retired now, you know.'

Giam laughed. Enriquo was a wealthy man, thanks to investing his money wisely on the advice of his former pupils. 'How can I be of service?'

'It's a long story, so please hear me out before you make any comments.' Giam agreed so Enriquo continued. 'As you know in May each year the Doge makes a state visit to the Arsenale as a compliment and homage to the service. It is usual on these occasions for the Patroni of the Arsenale to put on some sort of spectacle. Have you ever attended one of these?'

Giam shook his head. 'I've heard of them of course. I believe they can be quite spectacular, but I've never been.'

'In that case, my friend, how would you like attend this months spectacle and play a major role in it?'

Giam was puzzled. He couldn't for the life of him think how a glassmaker could have anything in common with the Arsenale, the armament and ship building works. 'I don't see how I can be of help, but please enlighten me.'

'What I have to say must be confidential. The Patroni like to make sure that the event is a total surprise to the guests.' When Giam agreed he continued. 'This year, the Arsenale will not only build, rig and fit out a war galley while the Doge dines; afterwards, he will name the galley and there will be a gunnery contest using culverins, cast and mounted during the meal.'

Giam was still puzzled. 'It sounds a very spectacular event, but I can't see what part you want me to play.'

'I was just coming to that,' said Enriquo with a grin. 'Miguel is an old friend of mine, going back to the campaigns in Dalmatia in the fifties. He has retired from the service and is now setting up as a teacher of gunnery. Unfortunately, he is not well known for his diplomacy. He was very critical of the training of gunners at the Arsenale when applying to be the new master gunner. The Patroni of the Armoury took exception to this and the result was a bet that

Miguel can't train a gunner in ten days to beat the best of the Arsenale trained gunners in front of the Doge.'

Before Giam could say he was still not sure where he came in, Enriquo gave a wide grin. 'I forgot to tell you one thing. Miguel said he could train anyone better than the Arsenale, even a nobleman, which is where you come in. If he's right, he gets the job, if he's wrong, he loses a thousand ducats!'

'Let me see if I have this correctly,' Giam said in disbelief. 'You want me to learn to fire a culverin in ten days and beat the best gunner in the Arsenale!'

'Best two gunners.' said Enriquo, with a chuckle.

'You must be mad!'

Miguel Santini who had looked on silently during this exchange stood up and suddenly threw an orange at Giam, which despite his surprise, he caught deftly.

With a nod of satisfaction Miguel turned to Enriquo. 'He'll do. He has quick hands and eyes. I will supply the rest.'

Despite Giam's protests that he was far too busy, the following day he started his instruction. Ten days later, he sat in the flag – festooned enclosure on the quayside of the inner lagoon of the Arsenale watching the arrival of the Doge, the Chief Magistrate and Leader of the Republic. He was preceded by eight silver trumpets to herald his approach and at his side, noble youths, sumptuously clad in robes of cloth of gold, walked with waxen tapers in their hands, as a representation of his purifying influence.

Before him was carried the Sword of State and officers of the household supported a silken canopy over his head. The Doge was magnificently dressed in a red doublet with a high collar and tapering sleeves that were partly hidden by the long outer mantle with its border of gold fringe and a circular clasp of gold. A sable cape, red stockings and shoes completed his attire.

The speeches were long and Giam found his attention wandering. Looking around at the seated Patricians, he felt a thrill pass through him as he spied Lady Maria Morisini with her father. He tried to catch her eye, but failed to do so by the time the meal was announced and the construction of the galley began. Giam wasn't present for the meal; Miguel wanted him to help in the preparations for the contest. There was powder to be checked for smoothness, balls to be selected as near perfect as possible and wadding to be approved. Throughout the preparations, Giam watched in admiration as the hugely efficient Arsenale sprang into action. A hull, one of a one hundred held in readiness, was towed along a narrow canal and at regular points, standardised decking, row locks, oars, masts, rigging, cannons and provisions were added; in less than three hours the galley was ready for launching. By the time the elaborate meal had finished all was ready.

The Doge, replete after the meal, made a speech expressing his pride in the work of the Arsenale and their amazing feat in fitting out a galley and casting its culverins in such a short time. He named the galley 'La Liona' and at his signal, the galley, now fully manned with the gunners on board, was launched out into the main basin to be moored stern in to the quayside in front of the admiring audience.

To Giam, the spectacle was a matter of huge pride at the accomplishments of Venice his home. The gunnery contest itself was an anti-climax. Miguel had taught him well and even the difficult two hundred yard target, at the extreme accurate range was hit.

Giam stepped forward to the applause to receive his reward from the Doge, a fine miniature painting of the Arsenale by Veronese. The first to congratulate him was Enriquo, although Miguel's 'not bad' seemed less than fulsome in the circumstances. His father, Senator Morisini and Lady Maria joined the circle to add their congratulations. As the two Senator's chatted Lady Maria said rather icily, or so Giam thought, 'I think you quite enjoy fighting, Master Bellini, despite your talent for glass-making.'

'I'm not sure if that is meant as a compliment,' said Giam. 'But yes, I enjoyed the whole atmosphere today; it was very different to my normal day.' Before she could respond her father took her by the arm, bowed and led her away. Giam was disappointed; he'd hoped that Lady Maria's response to his triumph would be more enthusiastic but, despite her rather barbed comment, he had thoroughly enjoyed the day.

CHAPTER FOUR

Giam pushed his platter away with a contented sigh. The evening meal had been most enjoyable, particularly the cavassoi, a kind of mullet, fresh from the sea that morning. Giam was dining alone; his father was out on some Senate business. The stress of the working day was starting to ease now and Giam was extremely happy. He now felt truly in charge of the Luciano Glass-works. With less than a month of his trial period left, Giam was confident that politics was not to be his lot. Indeed his father had hinted so only that morning.

On a whim, he decided to take a walk. Draining the last of his malmsey, his favourite wine, imported from La Palma in the Canaries, he headed for the door. The evening was pleasant, cool after the heat of the day, and less humid. He strolled aimlessly along the narrow streets bordering the canals, with no real idea of where he was heading, just enjoying the fresh air.

Eventually he found himself outside one of the many taverns that flourished in that part of Murano. Lured by the sounds of merriment from within, he decided to investigate. Alessandro, his tutor, had issued many dire warnings about the moral danger he would face if he were to enter one of these dens of iniquity; the loose women, the drinking and gambling. It was a sign of his growing independence that he entered the Luna Tavern without a single qualm.

Pushing open the door, a gush of warm air regaled his senses with a confusion of intriguing smells of wine, spices, pasta and oil from the many flickering lamps. The noise of revellers smote his ears like a physical blow. Three street musicians were playing a rousing song, which seemed popular, although Giam had never heard it before. Competing with them, the raucous voices of the customers threatened to lift the roof from its rafters.

At the far end of the room were a number of tables set in alcoves where groups of men sat drinking, playing cards, talking, or joining in the singing. Scurrying in between, were cameriera, flirting, dodging the occasional groping hand on their rumps or down their low cut bodices, keeping up a lively banter.

In a corner, Giam recognised Luca Ridotti among a group of men from the Glass-works playing cards. Not wishing to intrude he turned to leave, but Luca called him over. 'Ciao Master Giam, what are you doing here?'

Giam went over, intending to have a quick word and leave. 'So this is where you get to after work. And Luca, please call me Giam in here.'

'Thank you Giam I will. Come and join us and I'll introduce you to the others.'

Before he could think up an excuse to leave, Giam had a glass of ale in his hand and was embraced by their high-spirits. Sitting back, enjoying his drink, Giam experienced for the first time the pleasure of the company of ordinary young men of his own age. Luca, Jacopo and Vittore Albertini worked in the Luciano Glass-works. The brothers Filipo and Tommaso Miotti were also glass-workers in the Al Lion Bianco Works a little way down the Canale Dei Vetrai.

He looked around, greedily drinking in the atmosphere. He was so intrigued by the sheer exuberance of the scene that he only paid attention to the conversation when he heard the words, 'Mendosa Glass-works', spoken by Vittore to Luca. Giam had heard this rival factory was in trouble and Vittore seemed to have some information, which might prove valuable.

'You remember that cousin of mine who works for Mendosa,' Vittore was saying. 'Well, last night he told me old man Mendosa is selling out. The rumour is that he's lost a lot of money on a trading venture. He needs to sell to pay off his debts. They're all worried to death about it at the Mendosa Works. Who knows what will happen now.'

'It worked out alright for us,' said Luca with a conspiratorial wink at Giam. 'We're doing better than ever, since Antonio Luciano retired.'

Giam blushed and the three lads from Luciano's roared with laughter. As he looked away, a cameriera delivering glasses of foaming ale to a nearby table caught Giam's eye. Her long black hair cascaded over her bare shoulders and she had the sultry look of the East about her. Turning to go back to the bar, she gave him a bold glance, at the same time skilfully avoiding a groping hand and then, with a flick of her head, walked away with hips swinging.

Giam watched her until she disappeared in the throng. She was quite the most attractive cameriera he'd seen that night. Luca smiled. 'Watch out for that one, she has claws like a tiger.'

'And I suppose you've got the scars to prove it,' Giam quipped, drawing a laugh from the others.

The rest of the evening flew by and Giam was amazed when he realised it was nine o clock. Reluctantly he said goodnight and left for home. The next morning in the Glass-works, he was Master Giam as usual. None of the young men even mentioned the previous evening, or tried to take any advantage of the fact that he'd been included in their number. It was as if there were two Giam's: Master Giam who ran the Luciano Glass-works, and plain, ordinary Giam who shared the fellowship of the workers. Enjoying the company of men of his own age for the first time in his life, Giam became a frequent visitor to the Luna Tavern.

Like all his newfound friends, Giam fell easily into the routine of flirting with the cameriera. They in turn reacted with their usual mock anger and affronted modesty that fooled no one. He rapidly became a favourite for their attention; except for Consuela, the girl he had noticed on his first visit, whose sultry looks and lithe body made her a target for many amorous advances. She continued to avoid him, brushing aside his overtures with an infectious laugh, sweet words, and a swift retreat.

One night some weeks later, Luca told him that one of the other girls thought Consuela was 'sweet' on him. Giam reacted with surprise. She hadn't given him the least encouragement. Later that evening he began to receive a lot of attention from Consuela. This time, when he put an arm round her waist, she allowed him to pull her on to his knee. To cries of encouragement from Luca, Jacopo and the others, she threw her arm round his neck and gave him a quick hug. Then sprang up, flouncing away with a flash of her eyes. Giam found it hard to endure the ribald comments from his friends without blushing. Consuela didn't come near him again that evening but as he was leaving, a little earlier than usual, she appeared by the door.

'Are you leaving without saying goodnight, Giam?'

He was flustered. 'Err - yes, I'm rather tired.' And as Consuela pressed herself close to him, he was conscious of his rising desire.

'Will I see you tomorrow then?'

He mumbled something incomprehensible, backing away towards the door.

Consuela gave him a smouldering look from under her lashes. 'Tomorrow then,' she whispered. Standing on tiptoe, she put her arms round his neck and kissed him full on the mouth. With cheeks burning, Giam turned away, blundered into the door and then looked back, cursing himself for his clumsiness and timidity. With head held high she was walking away, but turning her head to see if he was watching, she gave a smile of satisfaction, and then sashayed towards the rear of the tavern.

Giam made his escape into the night. Out of sight of the tavern, he leant against the canal-side railings and took deep breaths, remembering the sweet taste of her lips. Women had been an unknown quantity to him up till now – he had been too busy with his fencing lessons and learning the techniques of glass making. But recently his thoughts had been turning towards the charms of the opposite sex, ever since that day beside the Casa Da Mula. Lady Maria was too high born for him, even though he was a nobleman and Fattori of the Luciano Glass-works. Consuela on the other hand certainly seemed to be available. Tomorrow he was going to find out.

The next night the tavern was busy. A number of sailors were getting determinedly drunk and the cameriera were having a difficult time. One, a short, thickset fellow was paying particular attention to Consuela. 'Never mind these common sailors,' he mouthed drunkenly, 'come and sit on the lap of a real man. I'll show you what I've got for you.'

Consuela ignored him and stalked off. The fellow stared after her and scowled. 'I'll have her next time,' he bragged to his friends. 'You see if I don't.'

He made good his threat. As soon as Consuela came within range, he grabbed her round the waist. Helpless in his grasp she was dragged on to his knee, while he groped at her breasts. Consuela did not struggle, but raised her hands to the back of her head, thrusting her breasts forward as she did so. With his companions egging him on, he made to slip his hand inside her bodice. Like a cobra striking, Consuela whipped a slim bodkin out of the bun at the nape of her neck and stuck it deep into the back of his hand. Loosening his grip, he clapped his wounded hand to his mouth with a vile oath, sucking the blood from the freely bleeding wound. Consuela made good her escape.

Giam sprang to his feet, hand on his sword, but Luca put a restraining hand on his arm. 'Leave it to the Patroni,' he counselled. 'He'll not stand for this. But if you get involved, there'll be a riot.'

Even as he spoke, the Patroni and three of his men appeared behind the sailors, hefting heavy clubs. When the thickset sailor made to draw a knife, he was immediately clubbed senseless. The others sobering up quickly offered no resistance. Picking up the motionless sailor, they were escorted out of the tavern with a warning not to come back.

Later that night Giam left the tavern as it was closing. He was annoyed because there'd been no opportunity to speak to Consuela. He stood for a while hoping that Consuela would come out, but after ten minutes or so, started walking back to the Villa San Venier.

Turning the corner, he heard a woman cry out. The sound came from the alley, at the rear of the tavern. Drawing his sword he ran swiftly into the dark mouth of the alley, nearly running full tilt into a stack of beer barrels. Consuela was struggling with the short, stocky sailor whose drunken antics had ended when the Patroni laid him out. The sailor had one hand over Consuela's mouth; the other was bunching up her skirts, revealing a slender white thigh. Consuela was fighting him off as best she could and obviously managed to bite the hand over her mouth. The man jerked it away with an oath, then, recovering, struck her hard across the face. She fell backwards, her skirts flying up to expose tender white thighs. Leering, the sailor fell on top her, his hand fumbling to untie her linen drawers.

At Giam's roar of anger the sailor sprang to his feet with a curse, drawing a large knife. But in his drunken state, he staggered and almost lost his balance. Giam was upon him at once, and although the sailor warded off the first lunge of Giam's sword, he was wide open to the second. About to run him through, Giam changed his mind and dealt him a thunderous blow to the head with the hilt of his sword. It would not do for the Fattori of the Luciano Glass-works to be indicted on charges of affray in a dark alley behind a Murano tavern. The man staggered, but to Giam's amazement, he didn't fall. Instead, he shook his head; sneered as if to say, 'Is that the best you can do?' and aimed a murderous slash at Giam's face.

Giam did well to avoid the knife, but fell heavily against the wall. His adversary heaved up a barrel of ale from the stack and, with a snarl of triumph, hurled it at him. With a desperate roll, Giam managed to avoid its trajectory and the barrel splintered against the wall, its contents flooding out and soaking them both. Giam sprang to his feet, sword at the ready, only to discover that the sailor was running drunkenly along the alley, his malevolent curses hanging in the air. About to give chase, Giam heard a low groan behind him and turned to see Consuela staggering to her feet. Quickly sheathing his sword, he ran to her side, just in time to catch her as she collapsed. As he held her close, shudders racked her trembling body and she began to sob.

It was some time before she was able to speak. 'Oh Giam,' she sobbed. He's been pestering me all night! I saw you talking to your friends outside the front door. I wanted to see you alone, so I went out of the back door to wait for you at the corner. He was waiting at the end and dragged me into the alley.'

Taking his cloak, he wrapped it round her shoulders to cover her torn bodice, which she was ineffectively trying to pull together. He held her until she quietened. 'Come now, Consuela,' he said quietly, 'it's late. I'll see you get home safely.'

Clutching his arm tightly, she directed him to her lodgings a few streets away. It was little more than a bedroom with a small area for cooking. 'Please don't leave me, Giam,' she said with a sob. 'I couldn't bear to be alone. Promise me you'll stay.'

Cradling the apparently terrified girl in his arms again, Giam sat on the bed. Eventually she snuggled up close to him and fell asleep with her head on his chest. Gently, so as not to disturb her, he laid her head on the pillow and lay down beside her. He thought how vulnerable she was and how easy it would be to take advantage of her in her present state. At first, his feelings had simply been protective, but the stirring in his groin as Consuela clung to him made him anxious. The glimpses of her full breasts through her torn bodice only made his anxiety worse. He couldn't help thinking about Maria Morisini and what it would be like to stroke the swell of her breasts, explore the deep valley between and then further down, the stiffening point of her nipples.

He almost jumped out of his skin as Consuela caught hold of his traitorous hand and held it tightly. She gave a throaty laugh at the stricken look on Giam's face, and then pulled his mouth to hers. They kissed, gently at first. Casting off their clothes, they explored each other with Consuela encouraging and leading him. Rubbing her body against his and caressing him until he forgot his anxiety, she guided him into her with practised ease. Wrapping her legs around him she matched his thrusts. As the tempo increased she gave little gasps of pleasure and moved her hips to draw him in deeper. He gave a final thrust, shuddering at the explosive release, soaring on wings of pleasure and then plunged into gasping lassitude.

Some time later, he woke from a deep untroubled sleep. Consuela's arm was flung across his chest and he was aware of the gentle pressure of her breast against his side. As he stirred, she opened her eyes and smiled at him. Arching her back like a cat, she stretched her lithe body in a gesture, which he would come to know well.

He leaned on his elbow and gazed at her. 'My friends told me you were sweet on me, but at first I thought it was a joke.'

Springing on top of him, she moulded her body to his. 'It seems to me,' she chuckled, 'the joke is on you.' Giam laughed with her and hugged her fiercely to his chest. She gasped and begged for mercy. 'You're cracking my ribs.'

He eased his grip a little. 'Very well then, I will stop, but only if you give me a kiss.'

With a sigh of resignation, Consuela did so, but with so much enthusiasm that one kiss led to another. She sat with her hips astride him and he reached up to fondle her breasts. She responded immediately and rising up, she mounted him and stayed still for a while, biting her lip in pleasure. Then, slowly at first, they made love; moving in perfect harmony as the rhythm gradually increased. Swept up on a tidal wave of ecstasy they reached a climatic peak, and were dashed down like so much flotsam, lying exhausted, but content.

Giam cradled Consuela in his arms, ashamed that at the final instant he had almost cried out the name Maria. It was she, not Consuela, who was in his thoughts at that moment. An overwhelming wave of guilt swept over him. He felt he'd betrayed Lady Maria by making love to Consuela. 'It will be dawn soon,' he said rising quickly. 'I must go. If I stay with you any longer, I won't have the willpower to leave. I will spend the time making love to you instead.'

Consuela gave a wicked smile. 'Am I of so little importance that you can't wait to get back to your hot and filthy Glass-works? You men are all the same.'

'You know that's not true, but I do have responsibilities to...'

He trailed of as Consuela rocked with laughter. Picking up a pillow, he hurled it at her. 'I suppose I was being a bit pompous.'

'A bit pompous! You should run for the Senate.'

'My father suggested that,' he grinned, 'but I hardly think it was for the same reason.'

This set them both laughing. Eventually, Giam sat up and regarding her earnestly said, 'I have to leave you now. I have some commissions I must finish. If I don't leave now, I won't be back in time to see you home safely.'

Consuela said mock sulkily. 'Is that all you want to do?'

'Of course not, I want to make love to you again.'

Consuela hugged him. 'You've been very good for me Giam, but I know you must go. I'll sleep soundly now with only good thoughts for company. You mustn't feel you have to see me tonight. I'll understand if you don't come.'

He did of course and gave her many gifts during the time they were together. Inevitably they moved on to other conquests without any recriminations, but Giam always had a soft spot for her.

CHAPTER FIVE

Giam was now enjoying a fuller life than at any previous time in his life. His leisure time was largely spent at the Luna Tavern. The Miotti brothers were usually there when he called and were a mine of gossip and information about the other Glass-works. Only the previous night he had learned from Vittore that Mendosa had sold the Glass-works, but had disappeared after another bout of gambling. Tommaso said there was a rumour that he'd been arrested on a charge of treason. 'That's the last we'll see of him if it's true. The Court of the Council of Ten takes a dim view of that. Someone may have denounced him through the Lion's Mouth off the Giant's staircase at the Doges Palace. I hear that if the accused can't prove their innocence they're strangled and dropped into the lagoon.'

Filipo leaned forward conspiratorially. 'That's if they don't send the assassins with their glass daggers.'

Vittore sounded very sceptical. 'What's this about glass daggers Filipo?'

'You must have heard about them,' said Filipo, looking round anxiously to see if anyone else was listening. 'They stab you under the ribs to the heart and then snap the blade off,' he said demonstrating with an imaginary dagger. 'It only leaves a little mark when the flesh closes over the blade.'

Giam thought this was a very fanciful tale, but he knew from what his father had told him that the Ten seemed to err on the side of caution when treason was involved. Kill first and apologise later if wrong, seemed to be the way they worked!

His father had also explained about the Lion's Mouth. Anyone could be denounced in a letter posted through the Mouth. The letter went straight to the Council of Ten, but the denunciation would be ignored unless the informer signed it, along with two

35

witnesses. The name of the informer would then be kept secret.

The most interesting point from all of the conversation was that Mendosa had sold his Glass-works, but sadly Vittore didn't know who had bought it.

Unfortunately Giam was not able to set aside as much leisure time as he would have liked. His days were hectic now that he'd been formally recognised as Fattori by his father. Not only that, but he'd insisted on transferring his half-share in the Glass-works to Giam.

'I want you to have these shares in the Luciano Glass-works,' Eduardo said. 'They were part of your mother's dowry. She would be proud of the way you've built it up.' He smiled. 'And in case you're wondering, I've torn up my plans to put you into a political career!'

When the equally well liked 'Senator' and 'Serisima' ranges followed the 'Andrea' range the Luciano Glass-works became the most popular supplier of stemware in Venice. This put a lot of strain on the supply and storage of raw materials and before Giam could make suitable arrangements, a serious problem arose.

One morning in July, Baffo informed Giam that two of the fireclay pots needed recharging with a glass mixture. Finding that they were short of soda, Giam called over to Roberto Rosso, a young apprentice. 'Go and fetch some more Barilla soda, and be quick about it.' Rosso hurried away and came back looking scared. 'Master, there's no more left.'

Giam clapped a hand to his head. 'What about the old stuff, Rosso? We had quite a few sacks of the old Roquetta soda, I seem to remember.'

The lad dashed away again, and came back with one of the sacks that had been stacked away in a corner since production had changed over to Barilla soda. When Giam examined its contents, to his dismay, the soda, was caked into a solid mass and badly contaminated with soil. Giam knew that production would have to stop unless he could obtain a new supply - and quickly. He set Rosso and the other apprentices to carefully sift the soda to remove as much of the contamination as they could, but this achieved little more than half a day's supply. Urgent embassies to his suppliers yielded nothing. No more Barilla or Roquetta soda was available for at least a week, or possibly two. Baffo was told to start the process of shutting down. But first, Giam asked him if he had any experience of cleaning soda. As usual, Baffo was singularly unhelpful. 'It's for you to decide if it's worth trying, Master Giam.' Giam had come to expect little else from Baffo these days.

He wracked his brains for a way out to his dilemma. The only thing he could think of was that soda was soluble in water and dirt and soil were not, otherwise they would wash away in the rain. His face brightened. He had an idea. 'Go to the Villa San Venier,' he ordered the apprentice. 'Tell the cook to give you all of the muslin she can lay her hands on.' He handed him some money for a gondola. 'Go at once, and quickly.'

When the boy returned with a large supply of muslin used for cheese making, Giam tried out his idea. Picking some of the most contaminated soda, he added very hot water and stirred until all the soda had disappeared. Covering the top of another clean pot with some of the cheesecloth, he poured the mixture through it. To his relief, the dirt and soil did not pass through the cloth and the liquid ran clear. He put the pot and solution carefully into the glory hole in the furnace and allowed the heat to boil away the water. Once the water had gone, there was what seemed to be dry soda left behind. Not only that, but it was a good white colour and showed no sign of contamination. Breaking up the caked mass, he found it was more powdery than usual, but otherwise looked the same, as far as he could tell.

Before he risked treating the whole batch, he quickly made up a standard mix with the cleaned soda and tried it out. To his great delight, it not only worked, but the glass produced was clearer than usual and appeared to be satisfactory in all other respects. This took quite a while and by the time Giam was sure of the result, it was already well after midday. He lost no time in organising the cleaning of the whole batch of contaminated soda in the large boiler in the yard. With several of the men helping, they eventually had all of the sieved soda solution into the boiler with a good fire burning away underneath.

By now, it was late in the afternoon and Giam remembered that he'd promised to see his father after work to arrange for the reorganisation of the warehouse at the Villa San Venier. He instructed Roberto to stay behind to watch the boiler until he returned.

The meeting went on later than he expected and several hours elapsed before Giam returned. As he strode into the yard, he was angry to see that the fire under the boiler was out. There was no sign of Roberto.

'Roberto,' he called loudly, and immediately the lad scurried out of the furnace room, rubbing his face, looking scared. 'I'm very sorry. Master Giam. You were such a long time. It was cold outside so I went into the furnace room to get warm. I must have fallen asleep.'

Motioning the lad to accompany him, Giam examined the boiler. To his intense disappointment, only half of the water had boiled away. He realised that unless they stayed for half the night, there was little more that could be done. He turned to Roberto, intending to remonstrate with him, but saw he was yawning widely and rubbing his eyes. His flash of temper subsided immediately. 'Come on, sleepy head, we may as well go home.' His tone was resigned, but friendly. 'There's nothing more we can do tonight that won't be better done in the morning. I'll get the gondolier to drop you off near your house; your mother will be worrying about you.'

'It's all right, Master Giam, she won't be worried,' he said sleepily. 'I asked one of the men to tell her I had to work late.' He yawned again. 'I'll be glad to get home though.'

By the time they arrived at the landing near his home, the lad was fast asleep. They were in the poorest district, close to the Jewry. Giam was looking around, unsure which house was Roberto's when a small plump woman came bustling up. She curtsied to Giam and shaking Roberto awake sent him into a small house nearby. 'It was kind of you to bring him home, Master Bellini. I've been watching out for him. He's all I have now.'

'How long have you been a widow?' Giam enquired. 'It must be difficult, bringing up a boy on your own.'

'My husband was bosun on a fleet galley, but he was killed five years ago by Turkish pirates off the coast of Cyprus.' She grimaced and pointed to a small wooden, two-storey building that was in a poor state of repair and in need of a coat of paint. 'We only just have enough money to rent this little house, it's not much, but at least it's a roof, although the landlord is a pig. He threatened me once, but Roberto frightened him off with his throwing knives.'

She smiled at the memory. The landlord was a bully and had demanded his rent although it wasn't due for several days. He'd forced the door open when she refused and raised his arm to hit her. Suddenly, a knife pinned his sleeve to the door and another stuck in the door right in front of his nose. Roberto appeared and pulling out the knife by his nose told him that the next time he wouldn't be so lucky.

'He hasn't tried that trick again and with Roberto working, we are able to pay on time. The money left over after the funeral was just enough to send Roberto to the Academy of Signor Tagliente for his schooling. He's a good boy and he loves his work. His ambition is to be a glassblower like you Master Bellini.'

Giam returned her smile. 'You may tell Roberto he needn't come in until late tomorrow morning. Now I must be away to my bed.'

He was at work early next morning. Going straight to the boiler he examined the soda solution. Expecting to see a clear solution, he was amazed to see a small clump of crystals at the bottom of the boiler. Somehow, they'd been formed from the soda solution, but he had never heard of such a thing happening before. The crystals were regular in shape and slightly opaque, but gave an impression of purity. Quite what they were Giam didn't know. Working quickly, he broke up the hard mass and sieved it all through some more cheesecloth. The crystals stayed on the cheesecloth and a clear solution was in the pot. Pouring this solution back into the boiler, he lit a fire and started to boil away the water as before.

Going into his workroom, he examined the crystals. As far as he could tell they appeared to be crystals of soda, but in a very translucent form. Carefully wrapping them in a cloth, he hid them at the back of a cupboard in his working area. He then went back to keep a vigil by the boiler until, by the time the rest of the men came in, the water had boiled away and there was a large amount of soda powder in the bottom.

Calling Marco Baffo, he told him to put the soda into use straight away. Baffo himself was the first to use the cleaned material and called Giam over to see the result. 'This is the best soda we've ever had,' he said excitedly, sounding more enthusiastic than he had for a long time. 'Look at the cristallo, it's the clearest I've ever seen. If this is what boiling the soda does, we must always do it.'

Giam agreed. The cristallo was excellent and although he knew it would be a lot of extra work to treat soda in the same way in future, the end result might well be worth the effort. Curious to examine the crystals he'd found, he went to his office and took out the bag from its hiding place. Carefully weighing out the crystals, he ground them up and added them to a standard glass mix, instead of the usual soda. He was about to go into the furnace room to make the batch, when caution made him hesitate. He couldn't explain this hesitation even to himself; perhaps it was the fear of ridicule if his experiments proved worthless, or perhaps they might turn out to be really special. In either case, it seemed sensible to find out in private, when everyone had gone home.

During the mid-day break, Giam found time to have a word with Roberto Rosso. The boy was already involved in this experiment to some extent, and Giam would need some help if he was going to take it further. That night after work, Roberto found Giam in his workroom.

'Are you going to make one of your special designs, Master Giam?' he enquired eagerly.

Giam regarded the young man gravely. The anxious words,

eager expression and longing look in his eyes – Giam himself must have looked and sounded much the same when Antonio had first started to teach him. 'Can you keep a secret, Roberto? From everyone: even your mother?'

Roberto looked rather alarmed. 'What sort of secret, Master Giam?'

Giam laughed. 'Don't worry, I'm not asking you to break the law. It's simply that what we find out tonight might be an important discovery.' He gave a wry smile. 'On the other hand it might be a complete disaster, which I definitely wouldn't want anyone to know about. Can you give me that sort of loyalty, Roberto?'

Roberto, with hero-worship in his eyes, breathed, 'I'd never betray you. I'd rather die first.'

Resolving to make sure the boy's loyalty was not misplaced; Giam placed his hands on his shoulders and looked squarely into his eyes. 'I don't think you need to go quite that far tonight,' he said with a grin, 'but I'll see that you don't regret your decision.' Then he said briskly, 'Right lad, we're going to make a glass from this mix. You'll be my feeder while I take the Chair. Put this mix in the glory hole and let's get to it.'

At first, the design that took shape under Giam's skilled hands puzzled Roberto. He obviously couldn't see any difference between this glass and dozens of others he'd seen Giam make. When it was finished, they waited impatiently for the glass to anneal in the top of the furnace and it was still warm when Giam told Roberto to remove it.

'We'll have a look at it now Roberto,' said Giam, his patience at an end. 'I know it needs to cool properly, but we can still see what it's like.'

When he placed it on the bench Roberto couldn't hide his disappointment. 'What's special about it, Master Giam? It looks just like any one of those over there.' He pointed to the stack of glassware from the afternoon production.

Giam smiled. 'Bring me the best one you can find, put it next to this one and tell me what you see.'

Roberto examined the two glasses carefully. 'Well, the first thing I can see is that you've blown the new glass a lot thinner on the bowl. The stems are the same, but they look different somehow.' He sounded puzzled. 'I'm not sure why, but this one does look different.'

Giam regarded him patiently, like a teacher schooling a willing pupil. 'Look at it again, Roberto, forget about the design,' he urged. 'Look at the material, what do you see now?'

Roberto studied them again, but finding no answer turned to look at Giam for some sign. Receiving none, he turned back, and gasped. The two glasses were identical no longer! 'I can't believe it!' he cried. 'Why didn't I see it at once? Your glass is so clear and bright compared to the other. Even in this dark place it reflects the glow from the furnace like…like the lagoon at sunset,' he said blushing with embarrassment.

Giam clapped him on the shoulder. 'Well done lad, I couldn't have put it better myself. You're right, the clarity and colour are superb. This glass is the best I have ever seen, or heard about. The reason you couldn't see the difference before,' he explained, 'was because glass doesn't develop its true colour until it's cooled to nearly room temperature.' He held it out for Roberto to touch. 'This is still a little warm even now.' He walked to the door and held the cristallo glass up to the setting sun. It glowed with pulsing light as if carved from a huge diamond, its serpentine stem taking on a life of its own. There were some small faults in the material, which was normal, but the glass itself was superb.

'There isn't another glass like this in the whole world, Roberto. The clarity of the material is unique, as far as I know. I think this is as important as when Angelo Barovier first discovered cristallo or cristallino as he called it in fourteen hundred and fifty. If I'm right, it could make Luciano's the most important Glass-works in Venice.' He walked back to the table and put it down carefully. 'I don't have enough of the crystals to make another mixture. We must keep the glass safe until I find out if I can make some more. In the meantime, you mustn't mention this to a soul.'

CHAPTER SIX

Lady Maria Morisini came down the stairs intent on seeing her father. About half way down, she stopped as the door of his study opened and he appeared with Pietro Ragazoni, Adrian's father. Neither of them noticed Maria on the stairs as they paused for a moment.

'I will give what you asked a lot of thought,' her father was saying, 'but not without involving Maria.'

Pietro Ragazoni shrugged. 'As you wish, of course, but I'm sure that a dutiful daughter will do as you say.'

'I'm not sure the same is true of your son,' Ricardo Morisini said dryly. 'From what you've said in the past, he tends to go his own way.'

'That has been true on occasions,' admitted Pietro, 'but I can tell you that we are both of a mind on this matter.'

With that, the two men shook hands and her father watched as a servant escorted Ragazoni down the main staircase. Then, with a shake of his head, he turned on his heel and vanished into the study.

Maria was intrigued. I wonder what that was about, she thought, I'm not sure I like the sound of it. When she went into the study, her father was looking serious. 'I'm glad you came down now, there's something I want to discuss with you. But it can wait. What did you want to see me about?'

'Oh it's nothing important, father. You go first.'

Ricardo leaned back in his well-worn leather chair, resting his elbows on the arms. His hands were clasped together, fingers extended and he tapped his bottom lip thoughtfully. 'I can't think of an easy way to say this,' he said with a sigh, 'so I'll tell it plainly. I've just had a visit from Secretary Pietro Ragazoni. He suggested that a marriage should be arranged between you and his son Adrian.'

'Marry Adrian Ragazoni! Surely you are jesting, father!'

Ricardo smiled wearily. 'This is not a jest at all, but before you dismiss it lightly, it would be well if you considered all the implications.'

'What implications, father?' she enquired.

'Marriage into the Ragazoni family would give you enormous status in Venice.'

'But you have a lot of status too father.'

'Not exactly status my dear; respect for my money and political influence. I am not from one of the original founding families even though my ancestors arrived shortly afterwards. My money and position as an Avogador make up the difference.' He shrugged and gave Maria a searching look. 'It is far from simple to reject such a suitor out of hand.'

'It seems simple to me,' she said. 'I don't love Adrian Ragazoni. In fact, after his recent behaviour, I'm not even sure that I like him any more. He's arrogant, rude and dictatorial. Oh! I could go on, but what's the use. I don't want to marry him.'

Ricardo smiled ruefully. 'I think I understand that! However, perhaps you ought to consider the alternative.'

Maria was puzzled. 'The alternative? Please explain.'

'Simply this dear, in recent years, daughters of the founding families have only married sons from other such families. Because of the lack of available men many women are finding that impossible. More and more of them are entering a convent. Almost half of them have to make this choice.'

'Half,' Maria said faintly, 'as many as that?' Of course she was aware that several of her friends had married into Old Families and one acquaintance had entered a convent, but she had not realised the extent of this trend. Her father was a lot more tolerant than most parents, but there was no such freedom for daughters of the Old Families, they were kept very close to home.

Ricardo nodded. 'Perhaps the thought of Adrian Ragazoni is not so terrible now you are aware of that fact?'

Maria was quiet for a moment, and then her face took on a determined look. 'It doesn't change anything, father. Marriage to

Adrian Ragazoni is not possible. I won't entertain it.'

Ricardo gave a delighted smile. 'I'm very pleased to hear it, my dear,' he said. 'I don't think he's at all suitable. However, I knew that if I forbade it, you might want to marry him just to prove me wrong.'

Maria groaned. 'Am I really so perverse?'

'I could always send you to a convent if you were!'

Maria could see that he was joking, but she knew that he had the power to do it if he chose to exercise it. She put on a downcast expression. 'I know father and I will of course, as always, be a dutiful daughter.'

Ricardo chuckled. 'I'm sure you will,' he said. 'However, I feel that I owe you an explanation. Venice is one of the most liberal and enlightened of cities, but despite this, I am regarded as being still more so. The Old Families are not so liberal in their outlook. They wield a lot of power and are extremely anxious to keep it that way. You seem to have inherited my rebellious nature, for which I praise God. I would not have it any different.'

'I know, father,' she replied, 'and I'm grateful that you've allowed me to be more of a free spirit than any of my friends.'

'That is why I have my doubts about Adrian Ragazoni as a suitable husband,' he said. 'He would expect you to conform to the Old Families idea of convention, which would be slow death for you.' He took her hands in his and drew her on to the nearby settle. 'There are also my own doubts to consider,' he went on. 'I don't agree with those who believe that the only way to preserve the heritage of the Old Families is for their children to intermarry. In my view it only weakens the line. Strong young blood is needed to strengthen it.'

'In that case, why did you vote against the Bill allowing the offspring of a glass-maker's daughter to be entered into the Libro D'Oro?'

Ricardo gave a broad grin. 'Whatever gave you the idea that I voted against it?'

'It's well known that you had serious doubts.'

The grin became wider. 'Of course it was,' said Ricardo. 'I made sure of that. But I voted for it, not against.'

'I don't understand you at all sometimes,' Maria sighed.

Ricardo smiled. 'Perhaps that's as well. But on the matter of this proposed marriage, I do not wish to reject it out of hand. Despite the reservations I have just expressed, the advantages could still outweigh them.' He smiled indulgently at her grimace. 'Whatever you feel now Maria, I want you to consider this offer of marriage calmly and dispassionately. Do not dismiss it without careful thought.' He kissed her fondly on the forehead and held her at arms length. 'Use your intelligence my dear, then we will talk again.'

A little while later Maria sat in her favourite window seat looking out over the gardens. Her first realisation was that she there was going to be a profound change in her life. Adrian Ragazoni had been her companion on many occasions. He was solicitous and friendly at first, ever willing to indulge her whims. Lately he'd become more possessive and dictatorial. His assumption that they were engaged had been a real shock. To Maria theirs was simply a friendship.

Whatever the advantages might be for her in marrying into an Old Family, Maria knew Ragazoni was not interested in her as a person, but in the extremely large dowry that her father would provide. With no Morisini male heir, Adrian would also gain her father's empire after his death. Lately, his unprovoked attack on Giacomo Bellini and his insulting remarks about his revolutionary glass designs had made her revise her opinion of him.

This set her thinking about Giacomo. He'd sprung to her defence when Adrian was being a bully; he was athletic and a superb swordsman. He was also not too bad looking. Unfortunately their last meeting had not finished as she had intended. After the gunnery contest at the Arsenale, she had made a light-hearted comment, which had been misunderstood. Unfortunately, she had been whisked away by her father before she could explain. At least Giacomo had been polite about it. In comparison, Adrian Ragazoni fared very badly.

Maria gave a start. She was sitting here daydreaming about Giacomo Bellini as if he were... Oh no! That was definitely not an avenue to pursue. She'd just finished with Adrian Ragazoni and now she was thinking of Giacomo Bellini in more than terms of friendship. Still, she rationalised, it wasn't as if thinking about him was committing her to anything, was it!

A few days after the meeting with her father, Maria developed a severe chill and was confined to bed. Miserable with its effects, she mulled over her father's warning. Eventually after her father had given her a soothing potion of honey and lemon and she fell into a feverish doze. Her dreams were beset by nightmares of marrying Adrian Ragazoni and being locked her in her room while he laughed at her pleas to be let out.

A soothing cold compress on her hot forehead woke her. 'Is that really you father?' she said clutching his hand and being reassured by the squeeze she received in return. 'I've had such terrible dreams. Adrian locked me in a room and wouldn't let me out.'

'Shush my dear,' he said stroking her hand. 'Don't distress yourself it was only a nightmare brought on by the chill.'

Maria sank back on to the pillow with a sigh of relief as she came fully awake. It was all a bad dream after all, but even as she thought this, the realisation that it could happen in life came to her. She resolved to make sure that she didn't marry Adrian Ragazoni, whatever the circumstances. Sipping a little more of the honey and lemon her father had brought her, she gave him a smile. 'I think I could sleep more peacefully now father,' she said and snuggled down in the bed.

Ricardo stroked her hair and kissed her tenderly on the forehead. 'I will look in on you a little later. Sleep well now my dear.' As she fell into a gentle sleep, he tucked the sheet in around her and quietly left the room.

By Ascension Day Maria was feeling a lot better and was allowed to go to Mass. The church of Santa Maria Degli Angeli was crowded. Leaving the church after the service, they met Eduardo and Giam Bellini talking to the priest outside the main door. After shaking hands with the priest themselves, they walked with the Bellini's through the churchyard towards the San Venier main landing, which was close to the Casa San Venier, the Bellini's home. Her father walked along behind chatting to Eduardo Bellini, while Giam offered Maria his arm, for which she was grateful, since she was feeling a little faint. They walked along making polite conversation, but after a little way Maria became dizzy, staggered and would have fallen without Giam's support. Giam swept her up into his arms; she lay quietly, eyes closed and her cheek resting on his shoulder. With the fathers fussing around, Giam carried her the short distance to the Casa San Venier.

By the time they approached the door Maria was already starting to feel better, but made no move to show it. She rather liked the feel of Giam's strong arms around her and snuggled against him. When Giam laid her gently on a settle in the cool atrio, Maria was conscious of a strong feeling of disappointment.

Eduardo, who had hurried off, while her father sat by her and rubbed her hands, came back with a glass of brandy. 'Sip this slowly my dear, it's strong, but it will help you to feel better.'

Maria did as she was told, gasping a little as the strong spirit burned her throat. Her pallid face soon took on a healthier glow and after a short while she sat up and smiled weakly at them. 'I'm sorry for causing you so much trouble, but I feel a lot better now.' Indeed she was starting to feel much stronger. She turned to Giam with a pretty smile. 'And thank you too for your strong arms. I doubt if I could have walked very far at the time.'

'I was glad to help Lady Maria,' he said. 'I'm delighted to see you looking stronger.'

'So am I,' Ricardo said. 'If you feel you are strong enough my dear, I suggest we go home. I think you've had quite enough excitement for one day.'

A short while later, Eduardo and Giam escorted the Morisini's to a waiting gondola, with Giam once more offering his arm for support. This did not go un-noticed by Ricardo and Eduardo who were saying their farewells. So engrossed were they, that none of them noticed the scowling face of Pietro Ragazoni surveying the scene from a passing gondola.

That same gentleman was even more incensed a few days later when at the Annual Murano Glass-makers Fair in the Campo San Stefano he saw Ricardo Morisini and Lady Maria enjoying an animated discussion with Giacomo Bellini at the Luciano stall. Being on the opposite side of the Canale de Vetrai, he couldn't hear what was being said, but his thunderous face reflected his feelings.

Later that afternoon, Pietro Ragazoni arrived at the Casa San Venier and demanded to see Ricardo. When he was told that he was busy with some clients in the Luciano showroom, he remonstrated angrily with the servant and made so much fuss, that Eduardo came out of the showroom to discover the cause of the commotion.

'Senator Ragazoni, what is the meaning of this unseemly behaviour?'

'That is exactly the same question I came to ask of you,' shouted Pietro. 'What are you and that son of yours up to with Lady Maria Morisini?'

Ricardo was amazed. 'With Lady Maria? I have no idea what you mean.'

This reply only seemed to incense Pietro further. 'I know what it is you're about; you're trying to marry off that commoner son of yours to a member of the real nobility to give him some legitimacy. I saw you outside the Casa San Venier on Ascension Day and at the fair. It was plain to see what was going on. Well I'm here to tell you, that Lady Maria is engaged to my son Adrian and you have no right to try and steal her away from him.'

Eduardo gaped at him in surprise, but before he could frame a reply, Ricardo Morisini stepped out of the showroom and confronted the thoroughly disconcerted Pietro Ragazoni. 'What was that you were saying about a betrothal Senator Ragazoni?' Without waiting for a reply, he turned to Lady Maria who was behind him and gave a broad smile. 'Do you know anything about being betrothed to Adrian Ragazoni my dear?'

'Nothing father,' she said sweetly. 'Oh, there was that suggestion that the Senator made a few weeks ago, but as I told you at the time, I have no interest in marrying Adrian Ragazoni.'

'So you did my dear. I confess that I've had no time to reply to the Senator's kind proposal, but I suppose I won't have to after this conversation. Will I Senator Ragazoni?' Abruptly turning his back on the discomfited Senator, he smiled at Eduardo. 'Oh and by the way Eduardo, will you thank your son for the glass we ordered from the Luciano's stall at the fair I am very pleased with it. I hope he'll be able to deliver the new order I've just given you fairly quickly, I'd like to the glass when next I entertain.' He grinned at the look of surprise on Senator Ragazoni's face. 'Will you also thank Giacomo for the help he gave us on Ascension Day when Maria was taken ill,' he said looking pointedly at Ragazoni. 'Without his help, Maria would have had a nasty fall when she fainted.'

As Ragazoni listened to this last revelation a mortified expression crossed his face at the extent of his blunder. Spinning around he stalked out of the Casa without a word of apology.

CHAPTER SEVEN

After the easygoing atmosphere of the Ascension Fair, which went on for two weeks, it was back to normal routine for Giam. On the first day back, he made his usual daily inspection of the Luciano Glass-works; stopping from time to time to have a word with the Capos; checking the latest glasses in the stack; generally keeping an eye on things. As he went out into the fresh air, Jacopo Doti came hurrying up. Giam had put him in charge of the raw materials warehouse after the debacle with the contaminated soda that led to the discovery of the Cristallo transparente. Although it that had turned out to be a blessing, it could so easily have been a disaster.

'I need you to check the latest stock of soda, Master Giam. A number of the bags are quite badly damaged. I think we should ask the supplier to replace them.'

'I assume we'll have enough stock without them?'

'Oh yes, Master Giam. In any case, I won't send them back until they bring the new ones.'

'In that case, I agree. Well done.'

Giam went back to his office and sat thinking about the last few months. He was firmly established as the Fattori and Master of the Glass-works. In fact, things seemed to be going along very smoothly. He guessed it wouldn't last; things always went wrong on occasions. He was confident, though, that the Works was now in good shape to handle most problems. For now he was just going to enjoy life and make some glass.

Later that morning Giam received a message to say that a client was waiting to see him in the outer office. He sent a message saying he would be along shortly and finished the last of the glasses in the batch. Setting the apprentices to clear up, he set off to the office wiping the sweat from his face as he went.

Assuming it was a merchant he was expecting, he didn't take the time to change the shirt and breeches he wore when working. He was both surprised and discomfited to discover a lady of the nobility, dressed in a beautiful green day gown with a pearl encrusted ruff, her face obscured by the fan she was using. His heart gave a lurch when, on lowering the fan, the beautiful face of Lady Maria Morisini came into view.

She smiled prettily at him. 'Buon giorno, Master Bellini. Am I so unwelcome that all you can do is to stand there with your mouth open like a fish?'

By a supreme act of will Giam controlled his furiously pounding heart and offered her a chair. While she was seating herself, Giam composed himself and studied his visitor out of the corner of his eye. She was even prettier than he remembered. 'Please excuse my appearance, my lady,' he said making a deep bow then mopped his brow and tried to tidy up a little. 'I was expecting one of the merchants otherwise I would have taken the time to change.'

She smiled. 'Please don't worry Master Bellini, it is of no consequence.'

'Then how can I be of service Lady Maria?'

'Well, since you are now one of the most sought-after glass-makers in Murano,' she responded, flirting a little with her eyes, 'where else would I go to buy a present for my father's birthday?'

Giam was doing his best to keep his feelings in check. She was a beautiful young woman and he began to feel giddy and light headed. It was only by a great effort he was able to ask about the present. 'What sort of present did you have in mind, my lady?' Even to him it sounded pompous. 'Perhaps I could interest you in a set of drinking glasses, or you might prefer a more ornate presentation bowl?' That's even worse thought Giam with a mental groan.

The fan fluttered at Lady Maria's throat. 'I'm sorry, Jacob Bellini, I can't take you seriously when you're behaving like a pompous tradesman,' she said tartly. 'I much prefer you when you're rushing to the aid of damsels in distress.' Having teased him enough, her tone became friendly. 'I would like to thank you for looking after me so well on Ascension Day, I wanted to tell you before, but you were busy with the Fair. I could so easily have fallen in the canal or hit my head.'

Giam smiled as the memory of carrying her in his arms gave him a warm glow. 'I'm glad I was able to help. I understand from my father that I missed a rather interesting conversation with Senator Pietro Ragazoni.'

'I'm afraid we were rather hard on him,' Maria said with not a trace of sympathy in her voice, 'but it was very wrong of him to jump to conclusions on several counts.'

Giam nodded, he'd been delighted to hear about the spat from his father. It meant Lady Maria was free after all! Seeing that Lady Maria was looking expectantly at him, he invited her to tell him her ideas for her father's present. When she had finished he asked, 'what did you think of the 'Andrea' range? Would one of the designs from that range or the 'Senator' and 'Serisima' ranges be suitable?'

'I thought the designs were excellent and fresh and I was pleased to hear you had done so well. The exhibition was a very exciting idea and your new designs at the Fair impressed father. He has used the glasses he bought already. Several of his friends liked them very much. However, I don't think there was anything quite suitable for this occasion.'

He then showed Maria several of his special presentation pieces; a goblet vase from a two piece mould with dragon relief's; a latticinio vase with its distinctive coloured banding and even a salver with a gilded and etched border. None of them was quite what she was looking for. Reluctantly, he decided to try the glass in Cristallo transparente he had finished only the previous day. 'I've been working on a new kind of cristallo for some time,' he said, 'and although I've not offered it for sale yet, I'm confident I've solved all the major problems. Let me show you my latest effort. You can judge whether it will be suitable.'

Excusing himself, Giam went into his workroom and came back

with a glass wrapped in cloth. Removing the covering with great care, he held the glass up for Lady Maria's inspection. She caught her breath in surprise. This was unlike anything she had seen before. The trumpet bowl was extremely delicate, as was the intricate serpentine stem, but these were not so different from other Murano designs. But when Giam placed it on the desk in a shaft of sunlight streaming through the window, it acquired a life of its own, glistening like a drop of water caught in a spider's web.

Maria was entranced. 'Oh Giacomo, it's beautiful. However did you come to make such a marvellous thing?'

Excited by her use of his first name, Giam forgot his natural caution. 'It's not a new process, Lady Maria. I've just been able to make some improvements. I've found a new way to make it. The metal is clearer and stronger, so it can be blown much thinner.'

'Metal?' Maria enquired. 'I thought it was glass!'

Giam smiled. 'I'm sorry, Lady Maria; it's just a term glass-blowers use for the material that makes up the glass.'

'Oh I see! Do please continue.'

'Well as I was saying, blowing the glass thinner improves the clarity of the glass beyond anything that's been done before.'

Maria favoured him with a dazzling smile. 'Have you made many others like this one?'

'A few,' he said cautiously, 'but this is the only one left at present. All the others had faults and they've been broken up as cullet.' He gave a rueful smile. 'Another glassmaker's term,' he said apologetically. 'We use it for broken glass.' In case she might think that this was a setback, he hurried to reassure her. 'Don't worry; I'm sure I've sorted out the problems now. When is your father's birthday?'

'It's in three weeks' time, and there will be a masque and Ball at the Casa Da Mula.' She paused and gave him a brilliant smile. 'I'll see you get an invitation.'

Giam gave a delighted smile. 'I'll look forward to it,' he said trying to keep the excitement from his voice.

A smile lit up Maria's face. 'I knew you'd have something

54

special for me. One of my friends advised me to go to Mendoza's now that Adrian Ragazoni owns it. However, after the little contretemps with his father at the Casa San Venier I didn't think it was a good idea.'

'So it was Adrian Ragazoni who bought out Mendosa,' Giam said taken aback at the news. 'I knew Mendosa was selling, but that is a surprise. Since when has Ragazoni been involved in glass-making?'

'His father owned a half share in the Mendosa Works, which he gave to Adrian on his coming of age. Then Mendosa recently sold his remaining shares to Adrian, so he effectively owns the whole Works.' Her eyes sparkled. 'You seem to have started a fashion amongst the nobility. Not that Adrian will actually work in the Glass-works. He'll engage a Master to run the place.'

Before she could continue, a servant dressed in the distinctive blue and red Morisini livery appeared at the door and bowed. 'Pardon my lady, but Sigisbei Vercelline asked me to remind you of your other appointment.'

Lady Maria rose at once. 'Please excuse me! I hadn't realised that time had passed so quickly.' Instructing the servant to advise the Sigisbei she would be there directly, she gave Giam a dazzling smile. 'I promised to meet my father and he is sure to ask me where I've been if I'm late. It is well that Sigisbei Vercelline reminded me. You will make sure that my father doesn't learn about his present.'

'Your secret is safe with me,' Giam promised, 'but who is this Sigisbei?'

'He's the master of the household, advisor, general factotum and my chaperone when I go out without my father.'

'I didn't see him when we first met.'

Maria laughed. 'I'm afraid I gave him the slip that day. He lectured me for a half-hour afterwards. Doesn't your father employ one?'

'I'm afraid he probably thinks it's a waste of money and rather pretentious,' said Giam as he escorted her to the door. As for the present for your father don't worry, I'll make a very special glass and have it ready in time for his birthday.'

'I think you're the best glass-maker in Murano, Giacomo,' she said impulsively touching his arm. 'I'll look forward to seeing you again when the glass is finished.' She held out her hand and Giam took it, bringing it slowly to his lips. She made no move to stop him; then suddenly snatched her hand away and swept out of the office, leaving behind only the heady aroma of her perfume.

Giam was surprised and delighted by her small show of affection. He told himself that she was simply pleased about her father's present, but as he put the glass away, he was so distracted by his thoughts he almost dropped it. When he returned to the office, he thought about his promise to make a glass from Cristallo transparente. He was appalled at his lack of caution and the enormity of the task he'd set himself. Despite his confident predictions to Lady Maria, Cristallo transparente was still very much an untried process.

To add to his worries, the glass he'd shown Lady Maria contained the last of the special metal. As if that were not enough, he'd promised to supply an untried glass to one of the most prominent citizens of Venice; in front of the whole of Venetian society, or at least all of it that mattered. Only the sick or dying missed the chance to attend a masque at the Casa Da Mula. His reputation would be at stake. Fail to impress Senator Morisini and the whole of society and his standing and that of Luciano's would suffer terribly. He could even be ruined!

CHAPTER EIGHT

B y next morning he was regretting ever having promised Lady Maria a special glass, but there was nothing for it, but to go ahead; it was far too late to back out. And the nub of the problem was he couldn't decide what form the design should take. The one Maria had seen was the first successful design he'd made from the special crystals. The most recent glasses were clearer in colour and thinner than ever, thus improving their delicate looks and clarity. Giam discussed his dilemma with Roberto. 'Do I make a completely new design for Lady Maria, or do I alter one from the 'Andrea', 'Senator' or 'Serisima' ranges?'

Roberto thought carefully before answering. 'I can't tell you anything about design, Master Giam. You're the expert. I just think you should make a design that shows the material at its best. Cristallo transparente isn't conventional, so why use a conventional design?' The simplicity of this argument struck Giam with some force and he smiled ruefully. 'You're absolutely right, of course. I should have trusted my instincts.' His thoughts started to race as he visualised a design. A giant lidded goblet, over ten inches high, with a simple plain foot slightly wider in diameter than the bowl - the stem, two hollow blown knops, separated by bladed knops to give the whole thing balance. For decoration, he'd use the Morisini Coat of Arms. No, that was too formal; a cartouche with Senator Morisini's initials in gold leaf would be more personal. He'd need to preserve the balance; it was a large goblet. Perhaps he could use an engraved mask of the Lion of St. Mark on the reverse side of the bowl? Giam's mind raced on as he visualised the glass taking shape. Emerging from his trance-like state, he began to draw furiously on a fresh piece of paper and Roberto gave a satisfied smile and crept quietly away.

Five days later, Giam put the finished glass on his desk,

leaned back and regarded it with awe. It was the best thing he'd ever produced, even better than he'd envisaged. He knew he couldn't improve on it, so wrapping it carefully in several layers of cloth he locked it away in his cupboard.

Now that the presentation glass was finished, Giam immersed himself in the business again and tried hard to achieve reconciliation with Marco Baffo. All his attempts were met with a solid rebuff. The fact that Roberto was Giam's assistant had not made matters any easier. In recent days, Baffo had been acting out of character, offering to stay behind and help him, when he learned that Giam was making a new glass. At first, Giam had thought that it was the first signs of a thaw in their relationship. But when Giam said he was experimenting with a new design and there was no need for Baffo to help, he was obviously furious and Giam braced himself for the usual explosion. To his great surprise, Baffo gave him a look that would have melted glass, but said no more.

Later in the evening when the men had left; Giam and Roberto were about to start on the new design, when they discovered Baffo in the furnace room trying to look busy and obviously looking for an excuse to be present. When Giam told him to go home, he was furious, but again he didn't make a scene, but walked out muttering to himself. For the first time, Giam began to think seriously of replacing Baffo, but he would be difficult to replace, so in the end he decided to try and put up with his moods.

He couldn't get over the feeling that Baffo was spying on him though. He always seemed to pop up at unexpected times. Things had still not improved when a couple of weeks later, Roberto informed him that Lady Maria Morisini had arrived. Taking off his dusty apron and straightening his hair, Giam hurried out to meet her. She returned his greeting warmly and offered her hand, which he bowed over politely. Ushering her into his office, he invited her to sit down and offered her a drink of the freshly squeezed orange that he kept in the office. Nervous of her reaction to her father's present, he put off the decisive moment.

'May I compliment you on your gown, Lady Maria? It's a most

attractive shade of yellow.'

Maria smiled politely. 'It's the first time I've worn it. I'm glad you like it. I understand that your business is becoming very popular. You must be pleased.'

Giam cleared his throat as Lady Maria began to fidget with her fan. 'Yes, I am, my lady; it has exceeded my expectations. I hope the preparations for your father's birthday are going well?'

Maria rose to her feet, snapping her fan shut against the palm of her hand. 'Giacomo Bellini, you're the most infuriating man I know. Have you made a glass for my father? Have you finished it? Can I see it?' She regarded Giam with an expression of extreme exasperation. 'Why don't you answer me?'

'Because, my Lady,' he said with great courtesy, 'you've not given me any time to do so.' He bowed and grinned. 'I'll go and fetch the glass immediately.'

Maria was entranced when it was unveiled with a flourish. 'Oh, Giacomo, it's even better than I expected! There can't be another glass like this in the whole world. I love the simple style and the clarity; my father will be delighted to own a glass so unique.'

Giam felt himself blushing. 'I hope you're right, Lady Maria. It's so difficult to judge your own work. I just hope other people feel that way.'

Maria sighed happily. 'I know they will,' then flushing becomingly she said, 'and please, call me Maria when we're alone. After the ball your glass will be the sensation of Venice and you'll be famous.'

Giam was optimistic about its reception, but a 'sensation' - that was another matter. In any case, the glass wasn't the main thing on his mind. Maria's invitation to use her given name had made his mind suddenly go blank. Then he became aware that Maria had been talking and he'd no idea what she had said. 'My apologies, Lady - err - Maria, I'm afraid I was miles away. Would you mind repeating what you've just said?'

Maria smiled sweetly at him. 'I said you'll need these,' she said, holding out two ornate rolls of parchment.

Giam accepted them with a puzzled frown. 'What are they?'

'Your invitation to the masque and ball of course; you will come won't you? She said eagerly, 'I promise to save a dance for you.' She gave a delighted smile when Giam nodded and then seeing Giam looking at the other roll she went on, 'Oh and the other one is for your father.'

'For my father?' he said in amazement. 'He doesn't go to masques, or balls for that matter.'

'I think he'll come to this one. Our fathers are old friends. They've served together in the Senate for years.'

'Perhaps you're right; I'll see he gets it.'

'You will come to the ball Giacomo, won't you?' she said insistently, putting her hand on his arm and gazing intently into his eyes.

Giam was lost. 'Of course,' he said earnestly. 'I can't think of anything I'd rather do than dance with you, Maria and please call me Giam, all my friends do.' He took her hand and squeezed it gently.

Maria hurriedly snatched it away. 'I'll look forward to seeing you at the masque then, Master Bellini.' she said formally. 'Will you please arrange to have the glass delivered to the Casa Da Mula tomorrow morning? My father will be out and I'll be making arrangements for the presentation. I want to make sure it's a surprise.'

Giam could see she was flustered and said just as formally. 'I'll send my assistant at about ten o'clock, my lady,' he replied. 'He'll be instructed to give the glass to you personally.'

'Thank you. I'll make sure the servants know he's coming and that he's to see me in person.' With that she rose to her feet and with a cool inclination of the head, but with a much warmer smile, she swept out of the office.

Giam sighed and shook his head in mock despair. He was sure Maria was attracted to him, but her constant changes in attitude from primness to boldness to formality confused him. It felt so right when he held her hand; it gave him such a warm feeling and he was sure she felt it too. Ah well! Life was far too short to find an answer now. He'd have to wait until the masque. Calling for Roberto, he made arrangements for the glass to be packed and delivered to Lady Maria.

That evening he told his father about the visit of Lady Maria and passed on Eduardo's invitation. To Giam's amazement, not only did his father agree to go to the masque, but seemed positively enthusiastic about the prospect.

'Why was Lady Maria visiting you, by the way?' he enquired.

Warily, Giam told him about Maria's visits, the present for her father and about the Cristallo transparente he'd used to make it, but leaving out the technical details.

Eduardo smiled. 'As I recall from Ascension Day, she's grown up to be a rather attractive young lady. Was that your impression?'

Giam blushed furiously. 'I suppose she's quite attractive in a haughty sort of way. But our meetings were simply on a professional basis.' Much to Giam's relief, Eduardo changed the subject and asked about the new glass. Feeling on safer ground, Giam told him in general terms about his discovery and of his hopes for the process. He also told him about his problems with Marco Baffo and the surprising news that Adrian Ragazoni now owned Mendoza's Glass-works.

Eduardo was concerned. 'Be very wary of young Ragazoni, Giam, he's not to be trusted. Even his father admits he's become too headstrong and wild. Take my advice and steer clear of him. I believe he's also keen on Lady Maria,' he went on with a wide smile. 'He was almost betrothed to her once I seem to recall; I'm sure Ricardo Morisini mentioned it. He didn't seem too happy with the idea for some reason.' They laughed at this allusion to the confrontation with Pietro Ragazoni. Giam thought of telling his father about his first meeting with Adrian and their duel, but decided against it. Nothing had come of it and he couldn't see any reason for causing his father further alarm.

In the days before the masque and ball, Giam became more and more tense. It was not only the fact that his professional skill was at stake; it was his anticipation of meeting Lady Maria. He daydreamed about taking her in his arms. Did she really have feelings for him, or was she simply flirting? He must find out!

The day of the ball dawned at last and he'd still not come to any conclusions about Maria; he was simply glad it was here at last. He had planned to leave early to get changed, but a crisis with the main furnace meant he would have to work late. He sent for the new clothes he'd put out ready at home, gritted his teeth and got on with it. By the time the furnace lining had been replaced it was late and he was filthy. Sending the men home with his thanks for their hard work, he hurriedly washed and changed and was just about to leave when Marco Baffo burst into his office. His manner was strained and truculent, yet strangely hesitant.

'I'm leaving Luciano's,' he announced, 'and there's nothing you can do to stop me, so don't try.' His voice became strident as Giam looked at him in astonishment. 'I'm going to work for Senator Ragazoni at Mendoza's. At least he recognises my ability. I'm to be the new Master.' Giam remained silent. He could see that Baffo was in a very unstable state. Marco reacted angrily. 'Well, aren't you going to say anything at all?' he demanded, leaning over the desk and glowering. 'Tell me I'm wrong and that you really do appreciate my work.'

Giam stood up without a word, and came round the side of the desk. Baffo backed away a little uncertainly. To his obvious surprise, Giam held out his hand. 'It may surprise you to know, Marco, but I think you're one of the best glassblowers in Murano. I wish you luck in your new job, I really do.'

He put his hand down when Marco ignored it, but still tried to make his peace. 'I wish we could have worked together to build up this business, but it's been obvious, in the last few weeks, that there's too much bad feeling and lack of trust between us for that. I'm sorry you feel I've wronged you; I've tried to settle our differences, but it's not been possible. It's probably for the best that you leave. We'll both be happier and you'll get the chance to be Master of your own Glass-works.'

Baffo was totally lost for words. Whatever he'd expected, he obviously hadn't foreseen such a reasonable response. 'The fact the Giam had not blustered seemed to puzzle him. He hesitated, as though about to speak, paused, shook his head, then muttered that he was going to collect his things and dashed out of the room as though the devil was after him.

Following his departure, Giam sat for a time to come to terms with this new development. These disputes with Marco had affected him deeply, as had his failure to find a solution. He realised he'd been foolish not to bring matters to a head before now. He made a mental note not to let things lie in future. It was another valuable lesson learned. With a start, he realised that he was now very late for the masque. Locking up he hailed a passing gondola and offering him a double fare to get to the Casa Da Mula as quickly as possible, he settled back to control his jangling nerves ready for the judgement of his peers.

CHAPTER NINE

The masque, a Greek tragedy, had finished by the time Giam arrived at the Casa Da Mula. When he entered the superbly decorated salon, with its tapestries, ornate mirrors and splendidly gilded pillars, his senses were assailed from all sides by the sights and sounds of Venetian society at play. In the minstrel gallery, an orchestra was in full swing. Men in rich cloaks and accoutrements, with swords and hats clasped firmly in their left hands, were strutting to the insistent strains of a galliard. Ladies in long ornate dresses, hair piled high in pearl-bedecked swirls, swayed around them, holding ornate masks lightly to their faces in a formalised ploy of anonymity.

Around the outside of the salon were groups of more people just as opulently dressed, striving to hear each other over the music as they exchanged the latest society gossip with unrestrained glee.

Giam surveying the scene for Maria spotted her dancing with a young aristocrat. On their previous encounters, Maria had worn formal riding habit, or day clothes. Tonight the sumptuous white dress she wore had a tight bodice richly decorated with pearls and had pleated panels at the front down to the waist. At the hips, a full skirt was gathered up at the sides then swept down to floor level. Her hair was piled up in an elaborate style decorated with several large pearl drops; while matching, single drop pearl earrings complimented the single strand of large matching pearls around her neck. She carried an ornate silver mask, but made no attempt to cover her face. She was so beautiful! A strange feeling gripped Giam's throat and his heart pounded as he tried to catch her eye.

Her partner meanwhile was obviously trying to impress her, whilst she in turn was fluttering her fan and flirting with him. Giam told himself that this was all part of normal society behaviour, but he knew he was jealous.

Moving to a better vantage point, Giam observed Lady Maria and her partners for some time. As soon as one dance was finished, she became the centre of a circle of young bloods all trying to claim a dance. On one occasion, he was sure that Lady Maria had seen him, but she didn't acknowledge his bow and continued to flirt outrageously with partner after partner. He began to get angry. Recognising that it was jealousy didn't help at all and he decided it was up to him to make the next move.

Examining the crowd around Lady Maria, he was pleased to see no sign of Adrian Ragazoni. Nor could he see any sign of him in any of the groups of people clustered around the room. Perhaps he had not been invited, although that was unlikely. All of Venetian society was present.

Spying his father in a small group to his left, he went over to join him and saw that the man speaking with him was his host, Senator Ricardo Morisini, Maria's father. Giam bowed and offered his apologies for missing the masque and they made polite conversation for a few minutes. Then, after a respectful interruption from Sigisbei Vercelline, Senator Morisini excused himself and set off up the nearby staircase. Giam looked around for Lady Maria, but to his disappointment she was nowhere in sight.

Just then the music ended with a flourish and a loud and prolonged fanfare of trumpets stilled conversation all round the room. Sigisbei Vercelline called for the floor to be cleared and at his signal; two servants appeared carrying a table covered with a blue velvet cloth. They placed the table on a raised section of the floor at the bottom of the main staircase. Two more servants appeared carrying lighted candelabra and set them at either end.

Another fanfare rang out and down the stairs came a servant carrying a large box, which he set in the middle. A final fanfare and all eyes turned to the beautiful young woman gliding down the stairs on the arm of her proud father. As they moved serenely down the stairs to stand at the table, her beauty held him spellbound. He'd never felt like this about anyone before, not even Consuela. He'd been attracted to Maria from the first, but seeing her tonight was a revelation. It was like watching a beautiful butterfly emerge from its chrysalis, spreading its wings in the warming sun for the first time. He was still angry about her flirting, but he was in love with Maria and wouldn't rest until he found out if she shared his feelings.

Maria smiled at her father and then turning to face her rapt audience she began to speak. 'As you know, today is my father's fiftieth birthday and it also marks twenty-five years of his service as a Senator,' she announced, pausing while the crowd applauded enthusiastically. 'To mark the occasion, I have arranged for Master Giacomo Bellini of the Luciano Glass-works to make a very special glass in his new Cristallo transparente.' She opened the box with a theatrical flourish. 'I would now like to present this glass to my father.'

Before she could do so, a man burst through the crowd. It was Adrian Ragazoni, carrying a wooden box beneath his arm. Bowing to the Senator, he pointed an accusing finger at Giam. 'A thousand pardons for this intrusion, Senator Morisini, but I cannot stand by and allow that thief Bellini to steal my company's Cristallo transparente.'

Giam stepped forward at once. 'How dare Senator Ragazoni make such an accusation,' he cried angrily. 'Cristallo transparente is my discovery and not his.'

Ragazoni scoffed and marched forward. 'I have here a glass made in the Mendosa Glass-works some weeks ago,' he said placing the box on the table beside the one Maria had just opened and turned to Senator Morisini. 'If you will just consent to compare them, it will prove that what I say is true'

'This is hardly the time, or place for a dispute of this sort,' said Ricardo, angrily. 'It would have been better made in the civil court. However, since you've chosen to accuse Master Bellini of being a thief in front of everyone, you had better explain if Master Bellini agrees.'

The Senator's intervention gave Giam a little time to think. Had Ragazoni somehow learned of the secret process and used it to make a similar glass? That was impossible. Only Roberto knew of the process beside himself and he trusted him implicitly. The sudden departure of Marco Baffo on the eve of the presentation now became apparent. He must have passed on the information about the sieved soda to gain the Master's place at Mendoza's. He had presumably stayed on to see if he could discover anything else about Giam's developments. His strange behaviour was now explained; aware of Ragazoni's intention to steal his discovery he'd left before Giam found out. Relief flooded through him. By the time he was asked for his reaction, he was in complete control of himself, confident of the outcome and angrily determined that Adrian would rue this night's work.

Giam glared at Ragazoni. 'I would suggest that Senator Ragazoni would be well advised to withdraw this infamous accusation, before he is exposed as the liar.'

Ragazoni's hand flew to his sword, but just in time he recovered his composure and sneered at Giam. 'Some months ago I took over the ownership of the Mendosa Glass-works and I was informed that they had devised a new form of cristallo, which was going to be sold in the near future. There were a few problems, which delayed the launch. Four weeks ago I engaged a senior glassblower from Luciano's, one Marco Baffo, to be my new Master. He was made to stay on by Bellini until a replacement was found. Earlier this evening he informed me that Bellini had somehow learned of my process and made a glass for the Senator,' he said indicating his host, 'intending to take credit for its discovery. Accordingly, I picked up one of the glasses we have for sale and came straight round to confront him.'

Giam who had been listening in astonishment to this tissue of lies stepped forward. 'My apologies Senator,' he said angrily, 'but I cannot allow such a deliberate attempt at character assassination to go unchallenged. This whole thing is a charade.'

Ragazoni smirked. 'You notice how carefully he refrains from denying the charges. He does himself no credit by not admitting his fault.'

The two men confronted each other, hands on swords, and it

seemed that they were likely to duel. Senator Morisini stepped forward and motioned the two angry men to step back. Ragazoni tried to speak, but was silenced with a gesture. 'I'll be the judge of it for myself,' he said decisively. 'I hope for your sake Senator Ragazoni that what you say is true, otherwise the consequences for you will be most serious.'

Turning towards Giam, the Senator asked him to join them and bade him stand at his right hand side and Ragazoni on his left. The crowd, spellbound by the drama, edged forward to get a closer look at proceedings. The Senator turned and addressed Giam. 'Have you anything to add Master Bellini.

Giam fought to control his temper – he was convinced that Ragazoni was only aware of the sieved soda method now and that his own glass would be superior. Deciding to toy a little, he deliberately made his reply seem weak. 'How dare Senor Ragazoni make such an accusation? Cristallo transparente is my process and I've been working on it for some time. I can only imagine we've both been working on a similar process.'

Adrian snorted loudly in disbelief. 'You hear for yourselves that once again he does not deny the charges,' he cried in ringing tones. 'Who can believe his claim that we were both working on a similar process? I am already taking steps to obtain a patent. The man is a thief and a liar; I'll prove he lies and I shall demand that the Senate and the Council of Ten prosecute him to the full extent of the law.'

At that moment, Giam realised his mistake. Ragazoni was not trying to make him look a fool in front of Maria and society; but was intent on destroying him completely. Ragazoni was unstable and dangerous and losing face in front of all of society would give him every reason to hate Giam, but there was no time for regrets; the die was cast. They must play out the scene to the end, whatever the consequences.

Turning to Senator Morisini, Giam bowed and spoke in a firm and carrying voice. 'Senator, you have my apologies for my unwitting part in this intrusion, on what should have been a happy occasion. Senator Ragazoni has chosen to make certain accusations against my honesty and integrity. We've heard his words, now let's see his so-called proof. I'll be happy to stand by your judgement, if you are willing. Compare the two glasses and decide for yourself if the same process made them.'

The Senator's reluctance was obvious. 'It would seem I have little option, especially as it is my present which has caused this furore.' There was a buzz of anticipation from the onlookers as they crowded forward. 'I must state from the outset that I don't claim to be an expert on glass. I may not be able to determine if there is a difference between the two glasses.'

Ragazoni seized on this point immediately. 'In that case, Senator, my case is proven. There are workers at Mendoza's who will swear that they've been working on this process before I took over the firm and I've applied to patent the process. By his own admission, Bellini has only been working on this for some weeks.'

Before Giam could reply, the Senator held up his hand and called for silence, then turned back to Giam. 'Since you have been challenged, you should choose whether your glass shall be the first, or the last to be seen. What is your wish?'

Giam turned to face his accuser. He felt very calm and his voice was firm and strong. 'I'll go last, not that it will alter the outcome one jot. You will not need to be an expert; the truth of this matter will be plain to see.'

For the first time, there was a sign of doubt in Ragazoni's eyes. Giam's calm bearing was obviously sending the first twinges of alarm through his mind.

Giam pressed home his advantage. 'Come, Senor Ragazoni, why do you hesitate? Perhaps you are not quite so sure of your claim after all?'

Ragazoni glared and started to unpack the glass, wrapped in blue velvet, which he laid down with a flourish. The crowd, craning their necks to get a better view, showed their approval immediately. The glass was made from clear cristallo and its serpentine stem was a fine example of the latest design.

Giam let out the breath he'd been holding, despite his

confidence in the outcome. Ragazoni's glass was made of fine cristallo, but to the recipe that the Luciano Glass-works had been using for some weeks, not his Cristallo transparente. Before he could reply, a peal of laughter broke through the hubbub; it was Lady Maria. All through the exchanges she'd remained silent. Now her laughter stilled the chatter as she stepped forward. When she unveiled Giam's glass, a gasp of amazement rose from the crowd.

She turned on Ragazoni with stinging rebuke. 'You're a fool, Adrian Ragazoni, and a vindictive one at that. My father doesn't need to judge the glass; the difference is there for all to see.'

Giam's goblet had an ethereal quality. The simple design of the stem, the plain initials, and the shimmering presence of the glass as it caught the candlelight combined to give an effect the other couldn't match. All round the room, there were gasps of awe and people began applauding and calling for Ragazoni to withdraw his accusations. Giam stood impassively, trying not to show his emotion. He was elated by Maria's support, not with his victory.

As the clamour grew, Maria said quietly to Ragazoni, 'I think you should apologise to Master Bellini immediately. It is he who should take this matter to the Council of Ten; I would in his position. As for myself, I'm ashamed of your actions. You are no longer welcome here as my friend.' She turned to the other guests. 'I tell you all that I've seen Master Bellini develop this glass over many weeks. Both the glasses he showed me during that time were superior to the one Adrian Ragazoni claims as his Cristallo transparente. There is only one true Cristallo transparente and it is Master Giacomo Bellini of Luciano's who discovered it.'

As the crowd acclaimed her words, Ricardo held Giam's glass aloft for all to see. 'Thank you, Maria, for such a splendid present.' He put the glass down carefully and embraced Giam warmly. 'My thanks to you too, Master Bellini. This is the most superb glass I have ever seen and I'm proud to own it. I congratulate you on the discovery of this Cristallo transparente. It is in the finest tradition of the Murano Glassmakers and the reason why they are pre-eminent in glass-making the world over. I believe this discovery will prove to be every bit as important as that of Angelo Barovier when he made cristallino glass for the first time.'

At his words the crowd surged forward, anxious to see the glass more closely. Senator Morisini stood with his arm around his daughter. A crowd of admirers imploring him to make them a glass from his Cristallo transparente surrounded Giam. As for Ragazoni, he was totally ignored and jostled as people surged past. Spinning on his heel without a backward glance, he strode from the salon.

CHAPTER TEN

Adrian's departure marked a change in the whole atmosphere of the room. Sensing this, Senator Morisini strode to the centre of the floor. 'Come, my friends, this is a celebration. Let us forget all this unpleasantness and enjoy ourselves.' He held out his hand to Maria, and, turning to the musicians, called out, 'Play on, maestro, my daughter and I wish to dance the galliard!' The conductor bowed and turning to the orchestra raised his baton and the strains of a lively tune in triple time filled the room. Maria and her father led off and were quickly joined by other couples.

Standing to one side, Giam watched Maria intently; oblivious to what was going on around him. He gave a start when his father put an arm round his shoulders and looked at him blankly, realising he had not heard what Eduardo had said. 'I'm sorry, father; my thoughts were elsewhere.'

Eduardo laughed. 'I'm not surprised! Maria was very vehement in defence of your honour, wouldn't you say?' Grinning with affection at the blushing Giam, he slapped him playfully on the back. 'You're a lucky man. Maria reminds me a great deal of your mother. There's a strength of character and spirit there that's so important. Take my advice, son; don't let her slip through your fingers. You'll have to go a long way to find her equal.'

Giam was thrilled by his words. His father's tone had been teasing at first, but there was no mistaking his sincerity and genuine regard for Maria. 'Don't worry, father, I'll make sure she doesn't. Tonight has opened my eyes to a lot of things.' He grimaced at the recollection of his negligence. 'I've been foolish, arrogant, and blind for too long. I only thought about what I wanted and ignored the sound advice you gave me about Ragazoni. It's another mistake I don't intend to make again. In fact, it has been quite a day for finding out my mistakes,' he said with feeling. 'As for Maria, I very much hope that she'll play a large part in my plans for the future, if that is what she wants.'

His father hugged him with an unusual show of affection and then held him at arms' length. 'I don't think there's any doubt about that,' he said, 'and before you ask, I don't think defending you was just duty. It was far more than that.' He turned to watch Maria dancing with her father and said teasingly, 'But why are you telling me? It's Maria you should be talking...'

He didn't finish. Giam was already striding across the floor towards Maria and her father, who had just finished their dance. Paying no heed to the admirers who tried to draw him into their circles, he headed purposefully towards the group forming around her. Despite the protests of her admirers he pushed his way to the front and made a deep bow. 'I believe this is the dance you promised me, my lady.'

She gave him a dazzling smile and a curtsy in acknowledgement. Taking her hand, he swept her out on to the floor. As they paraded around to the music, oblivious to everyone else, Giam gazed into her eyes. Although they didn't speak, the tenderness he saw there blew away his doubts. 'We must go somewhere quiet so we can talk,' he whispered hoarsely. 'Will you come out on the terrace with me?'

'Of course I will.'

As they went out on the terrace, the Sigisbei made to follow, but Senator Morisini talking animatedly with Eduardo Bellini gestured for him to remain. Once out on the terrace, Maria took Giam's hand and, with a quick glance to make sure they were alone, led him out into the garden. Following a series of paths, they came at last to a secluded bower. Maria sat down and drew Giam to her side, asking in a low, breathless voice, 'What was it you wanted to tell me, Giam?'

'You must know how I feel about you, Maria. I'm in love with you and I think I have been from the moment we met.'

She didn't answer, but threw herself into his arms, kissing him with a passion that astounded him. Time passed. They were oblivious to everything except each other. Eventually it was Giam who pulled away a little and regarded her fondly. 'We must talk. We'll have to tell our parents about us and how we feel about each other.'

Before she could reply there was a delighted chuckle from the path. 'I think we understand very well from what we've just seen Giacomo Bellini, but we'd be interested to hear your explanation,' said Senator Morisini.

They sprang apart guiltily and looked up to see their fathers standing there with large grins all over their faces. Maria was the first to recover. 'Father, you gave us such a start. How long have you been there?'

'Long enough, I believe.'

Maria blushed deeply and Giam sprang to her defence. 'I'm sorry Senator it was entirely my fault. We shouldn't have come away from the dance like that, but we had a lot to talk about.'

Eduardo and Ricardo laughed loud and long. 'You didn't seem to be doing much talking as far as I could see, Giam,' said his father when he regained his control. 'But enough of this banter, we have more serious things to discuss. Maria, your father and I think that your betrothal should be announced at the earliest opportunity,' he looked enquiringly at them. 'I take it that neither of you have any objection?'

The stunned couple just nodded in amazement at this declaration and Ricardo turned Maria's father. 'I think that was a yes, don't you? We'd better get them inside and get on with it.

When Senator Morisini announced to the whole gathering that Maria was to marry Giam Bellini at a date yet to be decided, the news was universally acclaimed. Well-wishers surrounded Maria and Giam and they had little time to enjoy each other's company. At the end of the ball, they did manage to snatch a few minutes together, but not without the Sigisbei in attendance.

'I'm afraid we'll not have much chance to see each other alone before we are married.' Maria said wistfully. 'Francesco Vercelline, the Sigisbei will always have to chaperone us.'

Giam was not used to the idea of a Sigisbei, as only the Patrician households, the richer ones at that, felt it necessary to employ one. 'I'm not happy about that at all,' he announced, 'but I suppose it is necessary.'

'I'm sure we'll be able to escape his attention, if only for a short while,' said Maria. 'We must think of ways, after all, lots of Patrician ladies have lovers, so there must be ways to do it.'

Giam frowned. 'I trust you won't be taking a lover when we're married.'

'You'll have to make sure I have no cause to want to,' said Maria with a laugh.

Giam was spared the need to follow this up by the Sigisbei who informed them that Senator Bellini was about to leave. Giam and Maria joined the two Senators and then, having said their farewells, Giam and his father left for home.

True to Maria's prediction, they did indeed find it difficult to escape the presence of Sigisbei Vercelline whenever they tried to be alone. Not that he was intrusive; he was just always in the background. He was scrupulously polite; he was also persistent and try as they might, they were unable to escape him.

Giam had never had such a hectic social life, but a few snatched kisses were all they managed to arrange. Despite this, their affection grew daily and they longed for the chance to be alone together.

As the celebrations of Candlemas gave way to the New Year, Giam began to formulate a plan how he and Maria might be together. It was Maria who first thought of the idea, when she mentioned the annual Regatta that took place every January the twenty-fifth. 'It's always immensely crowded during Regatta, can't we find a way to get lost in the crowds?' she said longingly.

Giam thought this was an excellent idea and began to make plans to bring it about. A few days before the Regatta, he sent Anna Rosso to Lady Maria with detailed instructions in a letter and by the twenty-fifth everything was prepared.

The Doge and all of the Senators were to assemble at the

Doge's palace ready for the signal for the opening ceremony, so Maria and her Sigisbei set off alone for the Piazza San Marco - in a gondola sculled by none other than Angelo Robusti, the gondolier that Giam knew so well. Like many of his trade, he had a lucrative sideline using his gondola for assignations. The day cabin with its curtains closed was private and largely anonymous as it progressed along the canals.

Maria wore a distinctive red cloak over her day-dress and a very ornate mask with large plumes that were easy to see even amongst the crowds. At least that was her explanation to Sigisbei Vercelline. When they approached the landing at San Marco, Angelo informed them that the quayside was too crowded and that he would have to find a place for them to alight little way along the Riva Schiavoni.

They were forced to wait for a place at the jetty and the Sigisbei paid Angelo while they waited. As soon as they alighted, Maria set off for the Piazza San Marco. The narrow walkways were seething with people hurrying to reach San Marco before the opening ceremony, so Maria walked in front and the Sigisbei following close behind. Dodging lithely through the crowd Maria quickly managed to get some distance in front forcing the Sigisbei to rely on the plumed mask and red cloak to keep her in sight.

Crossing the Ponte Vin, Maria dodged into the mouth of an alley a few yards further on. Quickly exchanging masks and cloak with the waiting Anna. Maria fastened the blue cloak around her shoulders and donned the plain mask: Anna set off in Maria's place towards the Piazza San Marco. Maria waited in the alley until the unsuspecting Sigisbei had passed, following the distinctive plumes and cloak. Once he was out of sight, Maria hurried to where Angelo was waiting. He took her hand and steadied her as she stepped aboard the gondola and Maria ducked into the day cabin; straight into the waiting arms of Giam. Angelo carefully closed the curtains and then set off for the lagoon opposite the Piazzetto San Marco.

Oblivious to the passage of time and that the gondola had moored on its mud weight, Giam and Maria made up for lost time. It was a discreet cough and a knock on the roof that roused them from their exuberant embrace some time later.

'The ceremony is about to start,' Angelo informed them apologetically. 'You will be able to see quite well from here.'

A large platform had been set up in front of the Doge's palace and three bulls were tethered close together in the centre. As they watched, a huge member of the palace guard mounted the platform and standing in front of the bulls, bowed to the balcony where the Doge was acknowledging the cheers from the people crowded into the piazza. Turning to face the expectant revellers, the guard drew a large scimitar from his waistband and saluted them and then, to a great roar of approval, with one long, continuous swing, he severed the heads from all three bulls.

Maria shuddered at this gory sight and Giam put a protective arm around her shoulders. The sacrifice of the bulls was the traditional opening of the Carnival and Giam had seen it many times, but for Maria it was the first time. A little way to one side Giam noticed some activity in the water by the side of a galley. A rope led from the galley up to the gallery of the Tower of San Marco. Where the rope dipped into the water, a man dressed in silver robes could be seen. As Giam drew Maria's attention to him, the galley backed away a little causing the rope to tighten. Now they could see that the man was mounted on the back of a spectacular silver dragon, which, when the men on the galley hauled on their ropes, flew along the rope over the heads of the crowd. As the man passed overhead, he showered the crowd with small silver sonate coins causing a mad scramble to gather the bounty.

Reaching the gallery of the Tower, the man dismounted from the dragon and by means of another rope rapidly reached the Doge's balcony where he presented a nosegay and read some verses in the Doges honour. When these had been delivered he bowed, returned to the cupola and thence back into the sea on the dragon, to the rapturous acclaim of the milling crowd.

The Doge held up his hands and the crowd hushed, until at his signal, twenty trumpeters played a triumphant anthem and a mighty roar came from the watching throng. The regatta was open.

As was custom, the people split into two factions the Nicolotti and the Castellani; a throwback to a dispute of the fourteenth century. Their claim had long been settled, but remained as an annual formalised conflict, with the population of Venice choosing a side to support. Giam had been a Castellani for as long as he could remember.

Only the previous year he had taken part in the yearly struggle on the Ponte dei Carmini, where the opposing forces struggled to cross the bridge. As was inevitable on a bridge lacking parapets, a certain number on either side received a ducking, Giam amongst them. This year he was content to watch the two factions amusing the crowds with feats of balancing, traditional dancing and a competition of wrestling. Maria had never taken part, so she chose to support Giam's side. The young couple joined in the cheers for the Castellani and booed when the Nicolotti gained the ascendancy.

All too soon, they were reminded of the reality of their situation, when another gondola pulled alongside and Anna passed the red cloak and plumed mask to Angelo. Once in the crowded Piazza San Marco, she had removed them and vanished as far as the Sigisbei was concerned. Realising that they would soon have to return to face the wrath of her father, Maria and Giam closed the curtain of the day cabin again.

'We can only shut the world out for a short time longer, my love,' said Maria sadly. 'I don't wish to cause Sigisbei Vercelline too much grief, he doesn't deserve it.'

'I understand Maria, of course I do, but just a little while longer please,' Giam pleaded.

Maria flew into his arms and when at last they parted, they were both breathlessly happy. Knowing they could delay no longer, they ordered Angelo to take them to the quayside. Together with Anna, they set off through the throng for the Doges Palace.

Senator Morisini had been none too pleased at being called away from the celebrations by a dismayed Sigisbei who had admitted losing his daughter in the crowded piazza. The Senator was just about to organise a search, when Maria arrived with Giam and

Anna. Whatever suspicions he might have felt that the meeting had been arranged none was ever voiced. The Senator returned to the reception and for the rest of the afternoon, they all watched the games and galley races together with the Sigisbei in close attendance. Anna did her best to distract him by asking for explanations of the various events and the young couple were able to talk a little more freely than otherwise would have been the case. When at last it was time to go home, they both agreed it had been a wonderful day.

CHAPTER ELEVEN

In the months following the dramatic events of the Masque at the Casa Da Mula, Giam became one of the most talked-about men in Venice. His clash with Adrian Ragazoni and his betrothal to Lady Maria Morisini was endlessly discussed whenever and wherever people met. Demand for his glass reached new heights. Cristallo transparente would have been popular even without Adrian's false accusations, but the drama of that event ensured that the story reached the widest possible audience. As the tale was passed on by word of mouth, it improved in the telling until everyone in society felt obliged to have at least one glass made from Cristallo transparente.

This huge demand posed a serious dilemma for Giam. To cope with the orders, all of the glass he made would have to be in the Cristallo transparente; to maintain secrecy, the vital soda crystals had to be made by Giam in private. This imposed impossible demands on his time.

Following the defection of Baffo and the information on the sieved soda method acquired by Ragazoni, Giam was sure that there'd be other attempts to find out the formula for Cristallo transparente. He needed to ensure that, apart from Roberto, none of the other workers knew how the crystals were made. For the time being, he couldn't make enough crystals for all his orders, so a waiting list was introduced. Production of Cristallo transparente was limited to one-half of the total production and a strict first come, first served policy was enforced. Cristallo transparente was sold at a high premium rate and all other production, using sieved soda, was sold at a small discount.

At first, Giam dealt with all the customers, but as demand grew he was forced to help the other Capos and spend more time making glass. Roberto found himself left to deal with customers on his own. He proved to be a natural. He was polite but firm with everyone, irrespective of his or her place in society. Some of the older noblemen believed they should have preference over younger customers, or those of lower rank. Roberto remained unmoved by their blandishments and even their bribes. Within weeks the system was working smoothly and Roberto's unfailing courtesy earned the respect of all Luciano's customers.

Although Giam had been released to concentrate on production, he still had to solve the problems of making enough of the soda crystals. He and Roberto had fallen into a routine of starting work early and leaving late, manufacturing the crystals when the workforce had gone home and finishing them early next morning. They managed to keep making enough crystals, but on several occasions their work was nearly discovered by one of the other Capos and Giam knew it was only a matter of time before his secret process was revealed.

Giam's desire to live nearer to Luciano's in a villa where he could meet Maria in private provided the answer. He was making large sums of money and demand for his glass was still rising. As a result, he had a great deal of spare money at his disposal. A large building across the street from the Glass-works was for sale and Giam made discreet enquiries. The building was self contained, but part of the outbuildings of a villa, which had its main entrance in a street that ran parallel to the Glass-works. Giam acquired the keys from the owner and was allowed free access to the whole estate.

After careful study, Giam decided that it with a few modifications, it would be perfect for his needs. The building opposite Luciano's was separated from the rest of the villa by a high wall. The villa itself was not too large, but there was a large garden at the rear. Although the price was high, he was able to negotiate and complete the sale quickly.

He was now ready to put the second part of his plan into action. A building firm from Verona was engaged to make certain alterations and paid a large bonus to ensure secrecy. A door was made through the wall emerging on the inside of the building

81

opposite Luciano's. On the villa side, the door was concealed behind dense bushes and on the other it was hidden behind a set of shelves in a locked room. Only Giam and Roberto had keys to this room, which was used for storing the secret crystals.

In addition, Giam had a large single-storey sala giardino built quite close to the hidden door. It would serve as a study where he could work away from distractions. There was a veranda for sitting outside in the cool of the evening, and also a bedroom. One evening after work, when everything had been completed to his satisfaction, he invited Roberto and his mother to visit him. When he had shown them around, he asked them both to move in. Anna was to organise the domestic and Roberto the business arrangements.

When she'd recovered from the shock of this announcement, Anna was the first to speak. 'I'm extremely grateful, Master Bellini. I'll be pleased to come and look after your household and I promise you my complete loyalty.'

Roberto too pledged his loyalty and tried to thank Giam. 'There's no need, Roberto,' Giam said with absolute honesty. 'It is I who should be grateful to you. In the last few months, you've dealt with customers in a manner that reflects great credit on you. As soon as you have completed your apprenticeship I've decided to make you a junior partner.'

Roberto stammered his thanks. 'You've earned it by your own efforts and discretion,' Giam said kindly. 'But now it's time we got on,' he said briskly. 'I want to move into the villa quickly. I'd be grateful if you could you make arrangements for the move, with the assistance of my father's servants.' One week later, they were installed in the Villa Bertolini.

Roberto and Anna took to their new responsibilities as though they'd been doing them all their lives. Anna had at Giam's insistence taken on two servants and within days they'd established a routine that left Giam free to concentrate on his complicated life. Certain tasks became part of the pattern. Two evenings each week, Giam and Roberto slipped through the secret door and prepared a batch of the special soda crystals. They would set them to dry overnight and early next morning Roberto would bag up the crystals and add them to the store.

After a few weeks had passed, things at the Glass-works improved to the point where he felt he could at last pay a visit to Enriquo Gomez for fencing practice. Dusk was falling as he left Gomez's house to go home. Against the dark swell of water by the quayside, the lamps of the gondolas moored on the opposite side bobbed and swayed like fireflies in a courting ritual. Giam stood on the steps and called for a gondola. One of the gondoliers, untied his craft and, manoeuvring with consummate ease, sculled across. As he pulled in to moor, Giam became aware of two men emerging from a nearby archway. The taller of the two wore a dark cloak over what looked like chain mail, although in the dim light from the nearest lantern it was impossible to be sure. The other man was small and roughly dressed and wore a gauntlet on his right hand, which was fingering a stiletto stuck into his belt. Giam recognised the dress as being typical of the sort of uniform worn by the Bravi, a band of knaves who preyed on unsuspecting travellers, often around quaysides. Instantly alert, he watched their approach for any sign of aggression.

'Thanks for calling the gondola; we'll take it and that fat purse on your belt,' said the small one, 'unless you want to fight us for it, of course?' The other man said nothing, but slowly eased his sword in its sheath as he waited for Giam's reaction.

Giam smiled disarmingly. 'This is my gondola,' he said calmly, fully alive to danger. 'There are many more across the way.' He turned to face them and stood with his arms at his sides in a deceptively casual stance. 'As for my purse, take it from me, if you can!'

With a shout of rage, the small man drew his stiletto and lunged at Giam. At this signal, the taller man drew his sword and made to engage him as well. Had Giam been unprepared, the encounter would have ended at that point, but Enriquo's training now showed its worth. In one fluid movement, Giam drew his sword, parried the knife thrust, and swivelling struck the man a buffet to the side of the head with the hilt of his sword. His assailant stumbled off balance and with a thrust of his foot, Giam sent him sprawling into the canal with a mighty splash.

Baulked for a vital moment by his partner's fall, the other man, launched into a ferocious attack and under the flurry of blows Giam retreated, his own sword a blur as he countered every move, patiently waiting for an opening. The man was a skilled swordsman and tried trick after trick, but Giam parried them all, content to play the waiting game.

Finding his attacks rebuffed with such ease, Giam's opponent became desperate. Launching himself wildly at Giam, he presented him with the perfect opportunity. With a series of dazzling moves, Giam drove the man back to the edge of the canal, disarming him with a sinuous flick that sent his sword spinning into the water. Finally, to hoots of derision from the watching gondoliers, he sent him tumbling into the canal to join his companion.

Giam stood on the steps, to check if they would try again, but his assailants were only interested in saving their own skins and were struggling to get out of the water further along the quay. Sheathing his sword, Giam seeing that the gondola he had hailed was still waiting by the quayside, stepped nimbly into it. The gondolier regarded him with undisguised admiration. 'You certainly taught those Bravi ruffians a lesson they won't forget! They're getting bolder by the day; they usually attack later at night. Only last week they stabbed a man near here and stole his purse and rings. Do you want me to call the Watchmen?'

'No, don't bother,' he said, 'they'll be long gone before they can get here. They're never around when you want them.'

'That's for sure,' said the gondolier, poling his craft away from the steps. As they approached the Grande Canal, Giam looked back to see two bedraggled figures gesturing angrily at the departing gondola. He gave them a cheery wave and then as the gondola turned into the main canal to the sound of the gondolier's eerie warning cry, they were lost to view.

Giam would not have been so cheerful if he'd known what transpired at a meeting in Ragazoni's sumptuous reception room a few hours later. Standing in front of the two would-be assassins, Ragazoni berated them with a black expression on his face.

'You idiots,' he raged. 'How could you fail to kill one unsuspecting man? You're supposed to be professional assassins; not complete incompetents. I don't know why I put my trust in such fools. It seems I'll have to take charge myself, if I'm ever to get rid of this upstart Bellini.'

'We dressed up as Bravi to make it look like a robbery,' said the taller man, 'just like you said, but you didn't tell us he was a master swordsman. We thought he was just a glassmaker, or we'd have used the folding crossbows on him; they're lethal at twenty yards.'

Ragazoni cut him short with peremptory gesture. 'Just get out of my sight, and leave me to think this through. Tell Baffo I want to see him immediately he's finished his discussions with the Frenchman he's meeting and then wait next door. There'll be a job for you to do later, which even you two will find difficult to mess up.'

When they'd left, Ragazoni poured himself a glass of wine and sat down in his favourite chair. Taking a deep draught, he considered the situation. I'm glad they've failed, he thought. Killing Bellini quickly was far too simple a punishment. I'll make him suffer in the same way I have. But it won't just be humiliation. I'll ruin him. And then I'll have him killed! As for Maria Morisini, she'll rue the day she rejected me in favour of that upstart. She'll pay too, but in a different way.

He laughed as a new thought struck him. The Frenchman, Thieré, what was it Baffo had said about him earlier when he'd called at the Glass-works? Oh yes, it was dangerous talking to a man who'd asked for help in making glass in London. Smiling to himself, he leaned back in the chair, considering a plan of action. As a Senator and a member of the Council of Ten, the body that ruled on matters of treason against the State, he was aware of the Capitulary that made selling secrets to foreigners, or setting up glass-making in another country, an act of treason. Maybe he could use this law for his own ends.

Deep in thought he only became aware that Baffo had arrived when he gave a discreet cough from the doorway. Looking up, he saw the Master of Mendoza's standing there with a worried expression on his face. He studied him in silence, until Baffo began to shuffle his feet nervously.

'You sent for me, sir. I trust nothing is wrong?'

Ragazoni leaned forward in the chair. 'Wrong! Of course there's something wrong! Thanks to you and your false information, I'm now a pariah in Venetian society. Meanwhile, Bellini has stolen my fiancée and gets richer every day.'

Baffo turned pale and took an involuntary step backwards. 'I told you I wasn't sure if my information was the complete process, sir. I don't know how he gets his glass so thin and clear. I'm sure he hadn't reached that point in the process when I brought you the information on the sieved soda method, Patroni.'

Ragazoni scoffed. 'A lot of good that did me.'

'I stayed at Luciano's for three weeks trying to find out if there was more,' whined Baffo visibly shaken by the virulence in Ragazoni's voice. 'I even stayed on until the night of the presentation to see if I could find out about Bellini's presentation glass, but he kept that hidden away. There must be some secret additions to the glass mixture that nobody else knows about.'

Ragazoni's mood changed abruptly. He leaned back in his chair and smiled serenely at Baffo, motioning him to sit down. 'I have thought about my challenge at the masque and perhaps I was too eager to put Bellini in his place. However, if you had given me the right formula, I would have prevailed.' He let his words hang in the air for a few moments then continued. 'However, you can make amends,' he said, leaning forward again, fingers drumming on the arm of the chair. With a cold smile on his face he studied Baffo intently. 'You do want to make amends, don't you, Baffo?'

'Oh yes, Patroni, I'll do anything I can to help you beat Bellini. Anything!'

Ragazoni smiled bleakly. 'Good, good, now listen carefully. I want you to tell me the exact truth and not what you think I'd like to hear, do you understand?'

'I'm not sure, sir. What do you want me to tell you about?'

'That French merchant you mentioned earlier, I believe you said his name was Thiéré. Is he still at the works?

Baffo looked relieved at first, and then a worried expression came over his face. 'No he's left for another meeting, but he didn't say where. No doubt he'll return to his lodgings later. I certainly don't intend to see him again. He's a fool and a dangerous one at that. He's no idea what trouble he can cause asking for information about how we make glass and help with his Glass-works. If the Council get to hear that someone has helped him, they'll be thrown in prison and never see the light of day again.' He shuddered as a new thought crossed his mind. 'That's if the Council of Ten don't send the assassins with their glass knives!'

'Quite right, Baffo, that's exactly why I want you to set up a secret meeting with him,' Ragazoni said with a wolfish smile.

'Set up a meeting with him?' Baffo was appalled. 'I might as well cut my own throat!'

Ragazoni laughed. 'I thought you said you'd do anything to get even with Bellini?'

'What has Bellini to do with it? If I meet the Frenchman, as Patroni, you could be in trouble as well, I can't see...' Baffo's voice trailed off as realisation of Ragazoni's meaning sank in. 'Oh, I see. You want me to arrange for him to meet Bellini, not me.' His relief was obvious. 'I could send one of your servants to his lodgings with a note and arrange to set up a meeting,' he said eagerly. 'With a bit of luck, Bellini might agree to go to London and run his Glass-works and we could make sure the authorities get to know about it.'

Ragazoni's voice dripped with irony as he congratulated Baffo on his insight. 'That's right, Baffo; you must make sure the Frenchman thinks Bellini has set up the meeting. You're just a go-between, doing a favour for your old employer. It has nothing to do with me and Mendoza's; do you get my meaning?'

Baffo nodded and willingly agreed to set up the meeting, he was too relieved at getting off the hook to notice the patronising tone of Ragazoni's words. Ragazoni barely nodded at his agreement; he'd planned for nothing else.

'Good. I was sure you'd see things my way. With the right timing, you might even get Bellini to say something incriminating about his damned Cristallo transparente in front of you as a witness. Do you think you could manage that?' His voice was heavy with sarcasm. 'That would be really splendid.'

Rising from his chair, he came round the table and putting an arm round Baffo's shoulder led him towards the door. 'Do this for me, Marco, and I'll see you get the reward you deserve.'

He watched Baffo leave and then called for his two servants from next door. He spoke with them at length, until he was sure they understood his instructions. Then, sending them on their way with a final warning not to fail him this time, he sat down in his chair and poured himself another glass of wine. He raised it in mock salute. 'Here's to revenge! May it be as sweet as this wine.' Taking a deep drink, he sat back in his chair, at peace for the first time in many weeks.

CHAPTER TWELVE

Ricardo Morisini sat back in his chair and sipped his wine as he studied his visitor thoughtfully. Coming to a decision he sat up. 'Monsieur Thieré you have asked a difficult question. Before I can advise you, it is important that you understand a little more of the background to the peculiar situation that Venice finds itself in at present.'

Thieré nodded. 'I too think it would be better for me, that I understand,' he said in his accented English.

'First and foremost, Venice is a nation that must trade for its food, since it does not have the means to produce enough food for itself. There is plenty of fish of course, Venice was built on a series of islands, but flour for bread is another matter.' He leaned forward. 'What I am about to tell you is my opinion only and one I would deny if questioned.' He smiled at Thieré's puzzled expression. 'In some quarters it is considered treason to think that Venice is not the most powerful nation in the world. I myself know that for hundreds of years the Republic has been the most powerful influence in the region, but events have occurred which will change this and Venice I believe will go into a slow decline, as is the fate of all Empires.'

Thieré shrugged. 'I am not sure to what events you refer. For myself, I believe Venice is a very strong Republic.'

'This is true,' said the Senator, 'but the rise of the Portuguese and English navies and the merchant adventurers, with their powerful sailing caravels and frigates has changed the balance of power. Their discovery of the route to the Levant around Africa means that we will eventually lose a lot of our trade in silks and spices. The overland route is much slower and even the great galleys that go to England and France with the Galley to Flanders, as it is called, cannot survive the sea route around Africa.'

'This is all very interesting, but if you will forgive my ignorance,

I cannot see how this affects my problem in setting up a trading partnership for shipping glass to England,' said Thieré.

'It is very simple, monsieur. After this year, there will be no more Galley to Flanders. The Mude or summer convoy to England and France will cease, because Venice will be at war with the Ottoman Empire over the islands of Malta and Cyprus. In my view, we may be able to keep Malta, since it is so far from the Ottoman's nearest port it will be difficult to supply. But we can never defend Cyprus for exactly the same reason. It is too far for us to supply the garrison, but close to Ottoman ports.'

'Does this mean that Venice will cease to trade with England?'

'No, but it will be down to individual merchants to take the risk of shipping alone. As you know, the risks are already great in a convoy, but a single ship and with Cyprus and possibly Malta too in the hands of the Ottoman the risks will be unacceptable.'

Thieré looked thoughtful. 'I see what you mean. This puts a totally different complexion on the whole matter. I think that I must revise my ideas and try to take as much glass back to England this year as I can afford. Maybe I will have to turn my attentions to the Glass-works in Antwerp, although if the truth be known, the political situation there is far from stable.'

'I entirely agree,' said the senator. 'As you know my silk and spice business to Antwerp has been very lucrative; no little thanks to your warehousing facilities and the financial arrangements we have been able to make. It is very useful to have finance available in Antwerp; it saves me the high risk of sending money by sea. My agent in Antwerp has been warning me for some time that Spain's argument with the Huguenots could lead to a serious crisis in the city and that is why I have been happy to run down my stocks.'

While they had been talking, Thieré's attention had been drawn to a goblet in a special display case behind the Senator's desk. 'Pardon my curiosity, Senator Morisini, but that glass goblet behind your desk looks rather unusual. Do you mind if I examine it?'

'Not at all,' said the Senator lifting it carefully from its case and handing it to Thieré who examined it with great care.

'This is a truly remarkable piece of work,' said Thieré in admiration. 'I have never seen glass so transparent. It's nothing like the Façon de Venice styles I have seen before. Was it made here in Venice?'

'Indeed it was,' said the Senator proudly. 'It was made at the Luciano Glass-works in Murano by Master Giacomo Bellini, who is engaged to my daughter.'

'Indeed,' said Thieré with interest. 'Do you think he will sell me some goblets like this to take back to England?'

'You will have to ask him for yourself. His Glass-works is extremely busy since he made this present for my birthday. It has been quite a sensation.'

'I can see why that would be,' said Thieré. 'I wish I had a Glass-maker of such talent at the Crouched Friars Glass-works in London.'

The Senator laughed. 'You can forget about this one, Monsieur Thieré, there is only one Glassmaker of that sort of talent and he would never leave Venice, even if he could. He has every reason to stay here, love, money, acclaim what more could he want? In any case, the authorities do not allow Glass-makers to set up in other countries, it is against the law.'

He stood up and walked with the Frenchman to the door. 'I regret that I could be of so little help to you, but I think you should carry out your idea of taking as much glass as possible back with you.'

Before they parted he made one final caution to Thieré. 'Please remember that we in Venice take great pride in our Glassmakers and reward them well. However, they are restricted by law from passing information to outsiders on glass making, or from setting up a Glass-works outside of Venice. Please be discreet about this and with the personal views I have expressed. Otherwise I wish you great success with the Murano glass and bid you good day. Fare you well, Monsieur Thieré.'

'Look lively there, Roberto! I need the foot blob now, not next week, ' chided Giam with a grin as Roberto scurried to the furnace with a fresh blowpipe to attach some molten glass for making the foot. 'You're out of practice. I'll have to make sure you don't spend too much of your time dealing with clients, or you'll be useless if I need you for my Chair.'

The recipient of this threat smiled broadly as he deftly picked up a molten blob of glass; he quickly shaped it on the marver, twirling the blowpipe as he did so and then returned to the Chair. He held up the foot so that it could be joined to the stem of the goblet Giam was making. 'I don't know about that, Master Giam, but I'd much rather be working here than in the showroom. The stories people tell to get their hands on Cristallo transparente drive me crazy.'

Giam laughed as he rolled the pontil backwards and forwards along the arms of the Chair to keep the soft stem from drooping out of shape. 'I bet some of them offer you money to get what they want?' His broad smile robbed the words of any malice.

'Give me money!' exclaimed Roberto in mock anger. 'Those stingy noblemen think they can get round me with a few coins,' he sniffed dismissively, 'I keep telling them it's first come, first served, but they never believe me.'

Giam laughed at the righteous expression on the face of his assistant. As Roberto held the now cooling stem gently in some tongs, he removed the goblet from the pontil and Roberto whisked it away to cool on the racks at the side of the furnace room.

Giam stood up and stretched. They'd been working steadily for two hours now and he was getting stiff. I don't know about Roberto, he thought wryly to himself, but I'm certainly getting out of practice. At one time, I'd have thought nothing of a two-hour session in the Chair. Now I'm as stiff as a board. 'Clear up now please, Roberto,' he said as the boy came back. 'Join me in the showroom when you've finished. I want to go through the order book with you.'

The heat of the afternoon struck cool after the searing temperature of the furnace room. Giam entered the small room at the back of the office where he kept a basin and towel and a change of clothes. As he finished dressing, he heard someone calling and went through to the showroom to see Marco Baffo standing there with an obsequious smile on his face.

'Ah, Master Bellini, I was told you were here,' he said in a too-friendly tone that surprised Giam. 'My goodness, this place has changed a lot since I was last here. You must be doing well out of your Cristallo transparente.'

'Quite well, thank you,' Giam said politely. 'What can I do for you?'

'It's more what I can do for you. You see, a Frenchman, Monsieur Jean Thieré, came to see me the other day. He's a merchant, living in London. He wants to buy some of your Cristallo transparente to ship back with the summer convoy.'

'Why didn't he come straight to me?' Giam said, puzzled. 'Well, it's like this,' said Baffo, 'he'd bought some of Mendoza's designs, but when he went to Senator Morisini's on another matter, he saw your birthday goblet and wouldn't look at anything else we had to offer. He asked me to arrange a meeting with you, in secret. He's worried other London merchants will get wind of the new Cristallo transparente first. I think he's hoping to buy up all you have available.'

Giam listened to Baffo with some scepticism. In view of the manner of their parting, he was surprised that he should want to help Luciano's in any way. Still perhaps the last bit about seeing Senator Morisini's goblet explained it, or maybe he was just trying to get back into favour.

'I don't know if I can help him at all,' he said noncommittally. 'The order book is very full and we always operate on a first come, first served basis.'

Giam thought for a moment. 'You'd better make an appointment for him to see me and in the meantime, I'll see what we can do.'

'Oh no,' said Baffo hurriedly, 'that won't do. He must see you now. The Galley to Flanders sails soon, so there isn't much time left. He's outside in a gondola; it won't take a minute to fetch him, if that's all right?'

Giam was not keen to see the Frenchman on such short notice. He was busy enough as it was. *Still he's come such a long way I suppose I might as well.*

'All right, but I can only spare a short time. Make sure he understands.'

Just after he left, Roberto came in. 'What did Baffo want? He's up to no good, I'll be bound.'

'Don't be so suspicious, Roberto! He's only brought a Frenchman to see me who wants to buy some Cristallo transparente.'

'Cheat us, more likely,' said Roberto darkly. 'I don't like it. Why would he be doing you a favour? Don't trust him, Master Giam.'

'If it makes you happier, I promise I'll be very careful in my dealings with this Frenchman.' Giam assured him. 'Now, go and get me the order book. I need to check if we can spare any of our Cristallo transparente. We have never sold any glass to London and I'd like to let him have some, even if we can only spare a few items. Check the latest batch as well, while you're doing it. They're not on the stock list yet and we'll need to consider everything.'

Roberto went off with a resigned look. Shortly after, there was a knock on the door and Baffo came in, followed by a man wearing a cowled cloak, which almost completely concealed his face.

Baffo bowed. 'Allow me to present Monsieur Jean Thieré, formerly of Antwerp, but who now owns a Glass-works in London.'

The stranger threw back his cowl, brushed his black hair away from his face and bowed to Giam. 'I am honoured to meet you, Master Bellini. I have heard a lot about you from Senator Morisini. Thank you for seeing me. I hope this will be the beginning of a long and profitable relationship.' Turning to Baffo, he bowed again. 'Thank you too, Master Baffo. If you will be so kind as to wait in the gondola, I will join you in a little while.'

Noting Baffo's reluctance to leave, Giam enquired if there was anything he wanted. Obviously unable to think of any reasonable excuse, he reluctantly left the office.

Turning to Giam the Frenchman bowed. 'I am afraid my Italian is somewhat poor,' he apologised, 'but I am told by Senator Morisini that you speak very good English,' he said. 'I have been in England for some time now, so I am reasonably fluent.

Giam nodded. 'I have studied English and have a good knowledge of it, but since I seldom speak it, I am a lacking in practice.' He invited the Frenchman to sit down and offered him a glass of freshly squeezed orange juice. 'I can recommend the juice; I keep a fresh supply here when I'm working in the Glass-works. The heat dries you out in no time and there's nothing I like better when I finish. We're a bit short staffed today, so Roberto and I have been working a Chair to clear up some of the backlog.'

'Roberto?' questioned Jean.

'My assistant and keeper of the order books; you can trust him implicitly.'

As his visitor sipped his drink with obvious relish, Giam perched himself on the edge of his desk and studied him. He was of average height, slim, with a swarthy complexion and short black hair with a moustache and pointed beard. His doublet and hose were a rich blue, with the sleeves of his doublet slashed to reveal paler blue silk linings. Round his neck he wore a stiff, white-ruffed collar. The hilt of his fine sword was studded with emeralds and diamonds, as was its scabbard. He was obviously a man of taste and some wealth.

When Thieré put his glass down with a sigh of contentment, Giam asked what he could do to help and why there was the need for such secrecy.

'You should understand that there is more to this meeting than a simple buying mission,' the Frenchman began. 'This is not all of my doing, although I admit that I am extremely anxious to stop my competitors learning of my interest in your glass. I am hoping that it is so new, they will not have heard of it. It was only by chance that I saw your glass at the home of Senator Morisini. He is rightly proud of his present. During my visit to discuss a legal matter, he told me of your betrothal to his daughter, although I did not have the honour to meet her. I assume that Senator Morisini has advised you about my interest in your glass; how do you call it?'

'Cristallo transparente,' replied Giam looking puzzled, 'but I received no message from the senator.'

'This is a mystery then,' said Thieré, 'since the other reason for the secrecy is at the request of Master Baffo, for reasons which puzzle me. He told me that this meeting was at your request, but from your reactions, I am sure that this is not so.'

Giam smiled his apology. 'I'm afraid I'd not heard of you until a short while ago.'

Thieré nodded. 'I am also sure now that Master Baffo is not exactly your friend as he has led me to believe, n'est-ce pas?'

Giam agreed this was also true.

'In that case, I think I know why Master Baffo was so anxious that we meet. Let me explain,' Thieré said, leaning forward. 'I came to Venice to buy some of the superb glass being made in Murano. My wealthy patrons in London are keen to buy Façon de Venice glassware. I also had a second reason. My Glass-works is not doing well. I am ashamed to say that my compatriots have been a grave disappointment to me in the running of the business. Therefore, I hoped to find someone in Venice who I could trust, to come to London and run the Works more satisfactorily.'

He smiled when he saw the alarm in Giam's face. 'Do not be alarmed Môn ami, Senator Morisini has explained to me the law in the Republic and I would not dream of making such a request of you. When I explained my quest to Master Baffo before I met the senator, he probably thought that this would be a good way to get rid of you from Venice, as I think he is jealous of you.'

As Jean Thieré unfolded his story, Giam, remembering Roberto's warning began to wonder if that was Baffo's motive for bringing Thieré. Perhaps Thieré was right and Baffo hoped Giam would leave Murano. If so it was a vain hope.

'I am not sure what the senator has told you of the law,' said Giam. 'It's a treasonable offence to pass on information, or for a glassmaker to leave Murano and set up business elsewhere. Even minor infringements of the law have very severe penalties.' Giam laughed at Thieré's expression. 'It's as well you haven't asked me then, isn't it? In any case, I've no reason to leave Murano even if you did. In fact, the opposite is true. I'm engaged to the most wonderful woman. I'm well thought of by my fellow glassmakers and I'm making more money than ever before in my life. No, Monsieur Thieré, you did not ask me to go to London, nor did you ask me how to make Cristallo transparente. In fact we only discussed how much Cristallo transparente I was prepared to sell you.' He found himself liking this Frenchman so to soften the effect of his words he added, 'Please call me Giam.'

'Only on condition that you call me Jean,' the Frenchman said, 'and I hope we can do business on a continuing basis. I'm sure your glass will be a sensation in London, particularly with the court. They love Venetian glass, despite the fact that it's so expensive.' He gave an expressive sigh. 'You've no idea how much façon de Venice glass gets broken in shipping, even from Antwerp. I hope we can do a lot better shipping straight from Venice this year, or I'll only be able to sell to the aristocracy.'

'What about the Queen? Won't she buy from you?'

'The Queen seldom buys anything,' said Jean with a smile. 'She only has to hint to one of her suitors, admirers, or social climbers at court, and they fall over themselves to buy whatever she wants. She's brilliant at playing one against the other and is a remarkable diplomat. I tell you this Giam, England is going to be the next major power in the world. Not even Spain can stop this happening while Elizabeth is Queen of England.'

Giam was surprised to see the rapt look on Jean's face as he spoke. This Elizabeth must be very special if she can make a Frenchman feel this way, he thought to himself.

'Your pride in the English Queen does you great credit, Jean,' he said. 'I will have to come to London one day to see for myself,' he smiled broadly, 'and to sell some more glass, of course.'

'Naturellement môn ami. For myself, I would wish that you would be coming to run my Glass-works, but I will be happy to be your agent and to introduce you to Court. Assuming that I'm still in favour, of course. The Queen has a rare temper and the wrong approach to her can lead to dismissal from the court at best, and a visit to the Tower at worst.'

'The Tower?'

'The Tower of London is the place where all traitors are sent, before they're beheaded. It's a fortress and prison, complete with torturers and gallows. A place to avoid, Giam,' he said with a shudder. There was a discreet knock on the door and Roberto entered on Giam's invitation.

'Ah, Roberto; let me introduce you to Monsieur Jean Thiéré from London. He's going to buy some of our glass to sell to the Queen of England. What do you think of that?'

Roberto was singularly unimpressed. 'Our Cristallo transparente is the best in the world. Everyone wants to buy it. The Doge bought fifty pieces for his official engagements only last week.'

'I can see your assistant is proud of your Cristallo transparente Giam; would that my workers had the same pride in their work. I envy you such an assistant.'

'Please don't say any more, Jean,' Giam laughed, 'or he'll expect me to pay him more money.'

Roberto grinned and handed Giam the books he was carrying. 'I've added the latest batch on to the stock figures, Master Giam. They're right up to date now. If you can do another day in the Chair tomorrow, we could spare twenty of the Cristallo transparente in two styles and thirty of the ordinary production, but those will have to be all the one style. Doing it that way will cause least trouble with our other customers.'

'What did I tell you, Jean? I don't know what I'd do without Roberto. He knows exactly what I want and runs me efficiently too. I trust his judgement on matters like these. I'm sorry we can't do any better, at such short notice.'

Jean nodded. 'And now, Môn ami, I have taken up enough of your time. When may I arrange for the glass to be picked up? The Galley to Flanders sails in a few days' time and I have arranged space on a galleass for the goods I am taking. I want to make sure it's safely stowed before we sail.'

Giam turned to Roberto. 'How soon can we pack it for shipment?'

'I can have it crated and ready to ship in three days.'

'Excellant,' beamed Jean. 'That will give me ample time to arrange everything. Now I shall take my leave of you. Rest assured that I would let you know how well your glass sells in London. As for the future, well we must see.'

As they walked into the courtyard Jean embraced Giam in the French manner, kissing him on both cheeks, and bowed to Roberto. 'Au revoir, Giam, and to you too, Roberto; until we meet again, fare you well.' He strode to the quayside and jumped lightly into the waiting gondola. Then he turned, waved and disappeared under the canopy.

CHAPTER THIRTEEN

Later that same afternoon, Baffo reported to Adrian Ragazoni on Jean Thiéré's visit to Giam. Adrian was in an expansive mood. 'Come in Baffo, sit down, have a glass of wine and tell me the good news. The Frenchman went to see Bellini, did he not?'

'Yes,' said Baffo cautiously, 'he went to see him as planned.'

'Excellent, excellent.' Adrian rubbed his hands together in high hopes of a satisfactory outcome. 'Well, come on then. What happened?'

Baffo began to speak hesitatingly, 'The Frenchman saw Bellini, just as you planned, but ...err Bellini wouldn't let me stay for their discussion.' Seeing the frown on Adrian's face he went on hurriedly. 'He told me about it when he came back though.'

Adrian's frown turned to a scowl. 'It depends what he told you. Tell me exactly what he said from the beginning. I'll decide what's important.'

'Thieré told me he'd bought some of the new Cristallo transparente, but said he'd not discussed anything else with Bellini.'

'What!' snarled Adrian. 'He didn't ask him to go to London to run his Glass-works?'

Baffo spread his hands resignedly. 'He said Bellini was obviously doing very well; he was engaged to the daughter of one of the richest men in Venice and running a successful Glass-works. There didn't seem to be any point in asking him to give all that up and go to London.' He made a grimace of apology. 'I'm afraid it's all been a waste of time.'

'Didn't he say anything at all about offering him a position,' Adrian said in disbelief.

Baffo frowned. 'Well he did say he was hoping to act as agent for Bellini and that he would introduce him at the English Court if he came to London, but that's all.'

'All!' screeched Adrian. 'All...!' He shook his head in mock sorrow at Baffo's lack of understanding. The fact that Bellini was planning to go to London could easily be interpreted as an intention to run the Frenchman's Glass-works. 'You don't have any idea at all, do you Baffo? All, indeed!' He paced up and down the room, and then turned to Baffo again. 'Go down to Mendoza's and make sure everything's in order. When you've done that, come in the back way and report to me. Make sure you're not seen, it's better if we are not seen together.' 'He gave a grotesque smile. 'We wouldn't want people to think we were plotting now would we?' He ushered Baffo to the door. 'Now, get on with it and make sure you're back here within the hour.'

When Baffo had left the room Adrian sat down thinking furiously. When he had his thoughts straight, he signalled for two assassins to join him. 'Do you know the Lion's Mouth at the top of the Giant's staircase by the Scala D'Oro?' he said to the taller man.

'Yes Patroni, are you going to denounce that fool Baffo?'

'Not Baffo,' Adrian said maliciously, 'and I'm not denouncing anyone.'

He sat down at his desk and took out some writing paper. 'I want you to make sure Baffo is not seen coming in the back way to the villa. When you take him to post this letter, make sure he's not seen leaving here either. Remember, if you're asked, the last time you saw him was when he went to the Mendosa Glass-works. 'One more thing,' he said, his voice falling to a conspiratorial whisper. 'When he's posted the letter, Signor Baffo is to disappear completely. Do you understand? Completely!'

The two assassins looked at each other and smiled evilly. 'We understand,' they chorused. 'Completely.'

When the two men left, Adrian sat down and composed a letter to the Council of Ten denouncing Giacomo Bellini for selling secrets to the Frenchman Thiéré, and planning to go to London to make glass at his Glass-works. Having checked it through, he put out the materials for Baffo to copy the letter and waited.

Later that evening Marco Baffo sat in the back of a gondola, a hooded cloak shielding his face from prying eyes, grumbling continuously to the two men. They took no notice. As the taller one steered them out across the lagoon and the other coiled up the thick mooring rope around the mud weight in the bows, Baffo asked yet again where they were taking him and why it was necessary to hide now that he'd posted the denunciation letter. 'The Council of Ten are bound to want to question me,' he whined. 'I can't hide forever.'

'That's where you're wrong, Signor Baffo,' said the smaller one with a quick look around. Seeing they were totally alone he gestured to Baffo. 'Please come and hold this rope for a moment and I'll explain.' Grumbling at having to help, Baffo took the proffered rope in both hands. He had no inkling of what was to come. With practised ease, the tall man who had come up to his side took a glass dagger from under his doublet, slid it up under his ribcage and into his heart, before snapping the blade off at the hilt. With one stifled gasp, Baffo slumped to the deck and lay still.

With another cautious look around, the smaller man helped to wrap the thick ropes tightly round Baffo's body. It was not easy to secure, but finally they attached the mud weight from the bows, taking great care to see it was securely fastened. After a final look around for prying eyes, they slid the body over the side into the cold waters of the lagoon. As Baffo sank out of sight they looked at each other with the satisfaction of a job well done.

The tall one gave a satisfied smile. 'Ragazoni will have no cause to call us fools this time,' he said. 'We should get a good bonus for this. Mind you,' he advised the other. 'He's too arrogant for his own good, is that one. We'll need to watch him carefully. If he thinks we're no longer of use, or dangerous to him, it'll be us feeding the fishes.' With this stark warning, they turned the gondola round towards the lights of Murano once more.

In his villa on Murano, Giam sat back in his chair with a sigh of contentment and studied the remnants of his evening meal. I'll have to cut back on the food, he thought, or take more exercise. At least the order for Jean Thieré is finished and I can get back into my routine again. Perhaps an extra bout of fencing will do the trick. He rose from the table and was about to go to the sala giardino when there was a knock on the door and Roberto came in. He announced that a servant with a message from Lady Maria was asking to see Giam. 'The lad won't give me the message; he says he's strict instructions to give it to you, in private.'

'In that case, you'd better show him into the sala giardino I was just on my way there.'

Giam waited with some curiosity. Maria often made fun of him, but this message was more intriguing. When the servant came in Giam saw he was quite young. There was something familiar about him, but he couldn't decide what it was. The servant bowed, then stood and looked at him without saying a word.

After a little while, Giam became impatient. 'Come on then, lad, out with it. What is the message from Lady Morisini?' To his amazement, the lad said nothing, but doubled up, his shoulders shaking. Jumping to his feet, Giam hurried over to him. Strangled sounds were coming from his mouth, although he had pressed both hands against it.

Taking hold of him by the shoulders, Giam gave him a shake. 'Calm yourself lad and tell me what ails you.'

To his amazement the lad swung round and threw both hands around his neck. Before he could say a word, the lad swept off his wig and giggled. 'Oh Giam, I hoped I could fool my Sigisbei, but I never thought I'd fool you, too.' To his utter amazement, Giam found himself looking into the lovely smiling face of Maria.

Recovering his wits, Giam kissed her soundly and then, sweeping her of her feet, carried her to the settle by the window. As he released her and she snuggled in to his side, he remonstrated with her, albeit with little real conviction. 'You little minx, what do you think you're playing at? If you had been discovered, you'd be in real trouble. You must leave at once,' he said unconvincingly.

She gave a pouting smile. 'You don't really want me to go, do you? Especially since I've taken so much trouble to see that we spend some time together.'

Giam was a little shocked by the desire he saw in her eyes, but not for long. 'Are you sure you'll not be missed.' He said, his resolve crumbling by the second. What about Sigisbei Vercelline?'

'He's visiting a relative in Verona until tomorrow and when I retired for the night, I left strict instructions with the servants that I was very tired was not to be disturbed. It was easy to change into a spare livery, slip out of my room and hire a gondola to bring me here.'

'What if the servants have to disturb you for some reason, there'll be hell to pay.'

Maria smiled in satisfaction. 'I thought of that. I left a note saying I woke early and have gone for a walk. It will hold them for a while and I will be back by then.' She grinned. 'Besides, they'll be reluctant to wake me at all; I'm not at my best when I'm tired.'

Jacob grinned. 'I'd better make a note of that.' He pretended to write it down. 'Maria is a crosspatch in the mornings,' he recited and received a buffet with a cushion for his pains. There was a short wrestling match, which quickly turned into a passionate embrace. Until Giam detached himself and said, 'I'd better tell Roberto not to disturb us then.'

Maria laughed. 'I might have fooled you, Giam Bellini, but Roberto saw through the disguise almost straight away. That young man's a treasure. All he said was that it was about time we had a little time to ourselves. I hope you'll find him a place in our household when we're married.'

Giam held her at arms length and studied her seriously. He found himself in a strange position. This lovely woman, whom he adored and his body ached for, had made arrangements to stay the night and here he was hesitating about it. He was sure that she was a virgin and her honour was at stake. He had to be sure it was what she really wanted. 'Are you sure about this Maria? I know we want to be together, but it is a big step for you to sleep with me before we're married.'

'Of course it's what I want and don't think I haven't thought about the possible consequences. She threw her arms round Giam's neck and kissed him soundly. Despite his qualms Giam responded, gently at first, but soon their rising ardour swept aside all other considerations and they kissed passionately.

Divested of their clothes, they lay together on the bed and explored the wonder of each other. Maria was a little hesitant, but soon began to respond lustily as Giam showered her breasts with kisses and stroked the inside of her thighs. Soon she abandoned herself completely. 'I want to feel you inside me Giam,' she cried wrapping her legs around him.

That first time, Giam would still have drawn back despite his own eagerness, but Maria thrust herself to him and his gallantry was swiftly overcome by rising passion*s* sweeping towards the final climax. At last, unable to wait any longer, they joined together in a furious, rhythmic coupling that swept them to an ecstatic pinnacle and left them lying entwined in each other's arms, worn out but very happy. Lying in exhausted sleep, they were rudely awakened by Roberto.

'Wake up Master Giam! Wake up!'

He shook Giam's shoulders until he sat up, sleep dulling his senses. 'What's the matter, Roberto?'

Roberto shook him harder and Maria woke too, as Giam struggled to sit up. She drew the sheets round her modestly. Giam, who was now more alert, asked Roberto to tell them what was so urgent.

'I went to the market early as usual,' Roberto said breathlessly. 'On the way back, I noticed a squad of soldiers at the end of the street. I didn't think anything of it at first, and then as I went past I heard the officer mention your name. I ducked into a doorway and listened.' He paused, reluctant to tell them the worst. 'Someone has denounced you to the Council of Ten,' he burst out at last, 'and they're coming to arrest you for treason. They're only waiting for the Secretary with the official Order.'

'There must be some mistake. Are you sure you heard correctly,

Roberto?' Maria asked faintly.

'Begging your pardon, my Lady, there's no mistake. They'll be here any minute and it wouldn't look good for you to be found here.'

'Quite right, Roberto,' said Giam, rapidly coming to his senses. 'We must get Maria away. Go to the front window and keep watch. Make sure the door is secure and give the warning as soon as you see them.'

As Roberto ran off, Giam turned to Maria who was hurriedly dressing in her boy's disguise. 'Listen carefully, my love, for you can make all the difference to me. I swear to you that I've done nothing that would make me be called a traitor, but we both know that the Ten seldom acquit anyone so accused. You must go to your father and ask him to intercede in the Senate on my behalf. Even if he can't get the case thrown out, he can see that I'm properly heard when I come before the Ten.'

'Oh, Giam, I'm sure he'll want to help. I'll go to him at once, but I don't know how I'll get past the soldiers. I can only go that way and they will stop me if they think I've been to your villa.'

Before Giam could say any more, Roberto burst in shouting that the official had arrived and the soldiers were forming up. Giam gave a key to Roberto and said hurriedly. 'This is my key to the secret door, which leads to the Glass-works. Show Lady Maria where to find it and see here out of the warehouse. When you've done that, come back here as quickly as possible.'

Roberto nodded. 'I'll see Lady Maria safely away while you get dressed and then I'll answer the door when the soldiers arrive. Please hurry though, Master Giam, we have very little time.'

Maria kissed Giam fiercely. 'Have no fear, my love, my father will see that you are given a fair hearing. I'll also let your father know of your plight. Now I must go before it's too late. Goodbye my love, God be with you. I love you so much my darling.'

She touched his cheek tenderly, and then hurried off with Roberto into the shrubs that concealed the secret door.

Giam watched her go with a heavy heart. He feared for the

future and what it would hold before they could be together again. He thought about Thieré's visit and Baffo's part in it. Could one of them be behind the denunciation? Then setting aside his fears and thoughts, he hurried to dress in his finest clothes. As he finished dressing, Roberto arrived back and said that Lady Maria had left the Glass-works store without any problems.

At that moment there was a deafening knocking at the door and a loud cry was heard.

'Open in the name of the Ten!'

CHAPTER FOURTEEN

Giam drew himself to his full height and motioned to Roberto to open the door. A colonel stepped inside, followed by a squad of soldiers who surrounded him. Two seized Roberto by the arms and two more made to do the same to Giam, but Giam addressed the colonel in peremptory tones.

'I am Master Glassmaker Giacomo Bellini, son of Senator Eduardo Bellini. By what right do you intrude in my home at this early hour and seize my assistant? I demand that you release him immediately and explain your actions.'

Before the colonel could reply, a small, well-dressed man entered. With an imperious gesture, he pushed aside the soldiers and marched importantly up to Giam, waving a scroll. 'I am Signor Nicolosi, secretary to the Council of Ten. I have here an Order of Council for your arrest and arraignment on a charge of treason against the State. You will be taken to the Piombi and brought before the Inquisitori tomorrow.'

'Who has made such a charge?' Giam demanded angrily. 'I would never do anything against the Republic! Tell me at once so that I can bring this liar to account.'

'All you are required to know is that a witnessed denunciation has been made through the proper legal channel, a Lion's Mouth. You will be given the opportunity to refute this charge when you come before the Inquisitori.' He gestured at Roberto. 'Your assistant must collect the things you will need, bedding, personal requirements and reading material. You are not allowed to have scissors, knives, or razors, nor are you allowed writing implements or a lamp. If you have not broken fast, you should also bring some food, since the gaoler will have paid his daily visit by the time you reach the Piombi. It is...'

'Enough of your lists!' interrupted Giam furiously. 'I insist you treat me according to my rank as a noble and tell me who is responsible for this gross lie.'

'Signor Bellini...'

'Master Bellini, if you please.'

'Pardon, Master Bellini.' Signor Nicolosi made a slight bow. 'You must know that persons who make a witnessed statement are never disclosed. Should you be unhappy about your treatment, you must take it up with the Council.'

Turning to the colonel, he said, 'Escort the prisoner to the Piombi. See that he is treated according to his rank, but you let him escape at your peril.'

The colonel, turned towards his men, muttering under his breath, visibly angry at this slur on his competence and rattled out orders, which they scurried to obey. Giam sat down and watched the activity around him with studied indifference. When Roberto returned, he pretended to show Giam what provisions he had brought, and Giam whispered, 'Make sure my father knows what has happened. Ask him to see the Frenchman Thieré, to back up my story. Get together as much money as you can. Sell all the glass that's available and chase up the debtors I ...'

Before he could continue, one of the soldiers roughly pulled Roberto away saying rudely, 'Outside you, and stop the whispering.' Turning to Giam, he gave a mocking bow. 'The colonel requests you join him. It's time to leave.'

With an exaggerated expression of haughty nobility, Giam inclined his head and gave the slightest nod of acknowledgement. 'My respects to the colonel, inform him I will join him directly.'

Rising to his feet, he walked steadily through the door. The troops fell in around them and he and Roberto set off for the Piombi and whatever fate awaited them.

About the time that Giam was arriving at the Piombi, Maria reached the Casa Da Mula and slipped in by the servant's entrance. Taking care to avoid being seen, she made her way to her room. She passed the Sigisbei's room without incident, but to her dismay, as she opened the door of her bedroom, he came round the corner of the passage, heading straight for her.

For a moment Maria froze, then thinking furiously, she stepped over the threshold and said in the countrified tones of a servant, 'A message from Master Bellini, my Lady. The boy who brought said it was most urgent.'

In her own voice, she replied, 'Come in and close the door Alberto,' while rushing to the screen at the side of her room. Divesting herself of the Morisini livery she put on her nightgown and had barely completed this when there was an urgent knocking at the door and Sigisbei Vercelline called out to enquire if she was all right.

With a cry of dismay, she rushed to the door and pulled it open just a little, taking care to obscure his view of the room, so he would not remark on the absence of a servant. She embraced him in pretended terror and begged him to fetch her father immediately, as she had received some terrible news from her betrothed.

Maria closed the door and leaned against it as Sigisbei Vercelline hurried away as quickly as he could. Her heart was beating wildly and panic threatened to engulf her. Forcing herself to ignore her trembling limbs, she hurriedly dressed then carefully combing her hair and pinching some colour into her cheeks, she sat at her dressing table removed the note she had left and tried to compose herself. When her father arrived, she clung to him in distress as she poured out the news of Giam's arrest and the charge of treason.

Senator Morisini was horrified. 'This is dreadful news! I can't believe Giam would betray the Republic, it's not in his nature. He has the world at his feet and he's obviously very much in love with you, Maria. No!' He said emphatically, shaking his head, 'it can't be true.'

Maria hugged her father and thanked him profusely for his faith in Giam. Eventually he told her he was going to the Piombi to see what he could find out.

'I leave the hardest job to you, Maria. You must stay here and wait. I'll keep you informed as best I can. You mustn't despair.'

Her father put his arm around her shoulders, trying to comfort her. 'You must have courage, my dear. All is not lost. Knowing the Inquisitori in cases like this, they tend to work very fast and I suspect that by tomorrow it would have been too late to save him, but at least time is still on our side.' He smiled encouragingly. You must be strong for Giam's sake. I'll go to the Piombi and see what can be done to throw out this ridiculous case. I'll also try to find out who has denounced him, I'm not without influence, but it is usual to grant anonymity to the accuser.'

'Do you have any idea who might do such a thing?'

'I'm afraid I don't, I know he probably had a visit from a Frenchman called Jean Thiéré, I met him yesterday and he intended to buy some glass from Luciano's. It might be that someone has misinterpreted the reason for his visit. I have done business with Thiéré before and he's an honourable man who would have no reason for denouncing Giam.'

'What about that glass blower Marco Baffo, he left Luciano's recently and had cause to hate Giam.'

Her father gave a shrug. 'It's possible I suppose, I'm not sure he would go to those lengths, after all, he's the Master of Mendoza's now so he's achieved his ambition. Maybe it was one of the other Masters jealous of his success. I think the best thing I can do is to be at the Council chambers where I have more chance of discovering what's going on.'

With that, he gave her a final hug and left the room calling for the Sigisbei Vercelline to go to Maria immediately. Shortly after he'd left, Senator Bellini and a companion were announced having arrived to see her father. She instructed the servant to show them into the drawing room and arranged for some refreshments. She composed herself as the Senator entered with Giam's young assistant, Roberto. The Senator bowed over her hand, then sat down at Maria's invitation.

'You too, Roberto,' she said, seeing the young man hesitate. 'I take it you've told the Senator of Master Bellini's situation?'

'Yes my lady. He told me to send a messenger to inform you.'

Maria inclined her head, hoping it would indicate her gratitude to Roberto that he had kept her assignation with Giam a secret. 'My thanks to you, Master Rosso, I was informed of events an hour ago.'

Senator Bellini stood up impatiently and interrupted at this point. 'I understand your father is out. Does he know what has transpired, Maria? I hope you'll excuse my familiarity, but I regard you as almost one of the family now, and this is not the time for formality. Please feel free to call me Eduardo.'

Maria was touched by his words and hurried across and embraced him warmly. 'My father has gone to the Piombi to see what can be done.'

'I hoped that would be the case. Your father has more chance than most people of discovering what's going on. Although it will be difficult to avoid being accused of a vested interest when his prospective son-in-law is involved.'

He held her at arms' length and studied her gravely. 'I told Giam he'd be a fool to let you get away! You remind me so much of his mother. She was beautiful too and had real strength of character. I know this is a terrible situation, but he'll need your strength and courage to help him to get through.'

Maria was touched and a little embarrassed by his praise and busied herself with handing round the refreshments. When they were seated again Roberto asked Maria if there was anything he could do for her. 'I would like to go to Luciano's to carry out Master Giam's instructions to sell as much of the Cristallo transparente as possible, to raise money.'

'By all means, Roberto,' cried Maria. 'You must look after the Glass-works in Giam's absence. I'm sure Giam will be happy to know you've taken charge, but as for money, I'm sure my father would be willing to help if there's a problem.'

Eduardo clapped Roberto on the shoulder in a friendly gesture. 'As will I. I agree with Maria, you are the one who knows how to run Luciano's and I know you have Giam's full trust. I'll try to see Giam and get a written letter of authority as soon as I can.'

'That young man has an old head on his shoulders,' Eduardo

remarked after Roberto had left. 'Giam is lucky to have someone so loyal. Wouldn't you agree, Maria?'

'I would indeed, Eduardo; I have every reason to trust that young man.' Remembering her night of passion with Giam. Maria quickly changed the subject and asked Eduardo what he thought was best to do.

'I'm inclined to agree with your father. It's important to have someone outside the Senate who can take action if needed. Your father is using his powers in the right place. There'll be a battle to be fought with the Council and he and I together can bring to bear more influence.'

Maria placed her hand on his arm as they walked towards the hall. Eduardo gave her a warm smile that reminded Maria so much of Giam that she trembled.

He paused to bow over her hand and prepared to leave. 'I must go now. I have some favours to call in and some information to gather. I'll try to get word to you if there are any developments, as no doubt will your father. Goodbye for now and I hope that next time we meet it will be in happier circumstances.'

At the Piombi, the cell in which Giam now found himself was one of four built for the Council of Ten over the chamber of the Capi, the Chiefs of the Wards. It was low and narrow, about ten feet wide and seven feet high and unpleasantly warm. It was right up under the lead roof of the chambers, with only two small iron-barred apertures to let in light and fresh air. From these windows, Giam had views of the adjoining courtyard and a section of a canal beyond.

Soon tiring of this limited view he sat down on his palliase. It was the coolest place in the cell, although as the day progressed the term 'cool' was only relative. Now he was over the initial shock of his arrest, he could think about his situation. He tried to think who could have denounced him. It was a puzzle. Jean Thieré, had no motive; Marco Baffo had a motive, but this was the work of a more subtle and devious mind; a person with a deep desire to do more

113

than humiliate him and one who would plan his downfall.

It had to be Adrian Ragazoni, the only person with reason to hate him and devious and cunning enough to plan revenge in this way. Giam cursed his foolishness in underestimating Adrian a second time. For Giam was in no doubt what this denunciation meant. The Council of Ten had a reputation for swift and permanent actions. Anyone who couldn't prove they were innocent simply disappeared. Rumour had it that the assassins of the secret service garrotted them, or quietly drowned them in the deepest parts of the lagoon. They reserved the glass daggers for secret assassinations.

Giam marshalled his thoughts. He must counter the accusations against him and avoid such a fate. But how? Luckily, there was one thing his betrayer could not have foreseen and that was the presence of Maria at the time of his arrest. Thanks to Roberto's warning, she'd been able to get away and alert both the Senator and his father to his fate. With any luck they should be able to find out what was happening and perhaps devise some sort of defence.

There was the sound of a key in the massive lock. The door was flung open and two guards entered with Signor Nicolosi the Secretary to the Ten. 'Master Bellini, you are summoned to appear before a Tribunal of Three - the Inquisitors chosen from the Ten to adjudicate on matters relating to improper revelation of state secrets,' he announced.

Giam was appalled; the Three had a reputation for even more summary decisions than the Ten. He was escorted down the stairs, across a wooden bridge over the canal and into the Council chamber where the Three were in session. The Secretary motioned him to sit in a chair placed in front of a table, behind which were three high-backed and ornately carved chairs. The guards took their places at each side of him and stood silent and impassive as they waited for the arrival of the Inquisitors.

Despite his predicament, Giam found himself awaiting the arrival of the Three with some anticipation. The identity of the

Three and those of the Council of Ten were never announced publicly; it was the subject of considerable gossip. The Chamber was magnificently decorated with the paintings by some of the foremost artists of Venice, including the 'Battle of Cadore' by Titian and an unnamed masterpiece by Tintoretto. A door behind the table opened and the Three entered.

The delegate from the Privy Council was president of the Inquisitors and was called the Rossi, after his distinctive red robes. Flanking him on either side, in black robes, were the two representatives from the Ten, the Neri. The Rossi was the Secretary to the Grand Council, Pietro Ragazoni; the father of the man Giam believed was behind the plot! Before he could consider this development further he was told to stand.

Secretary Nicolosi read out the charge:- 'By order of the Grand Council, Master Glassblower Giam Bellini is charged that he did pass on details of his Cristallo transparente to a Frenchmen, Monsieur Jean Thieré and that he intends leaving Venice to take charge of the said Frenchman's Glass-works in London. This is in direct contravention of the Capituary of the sixteenth of May fifteen hundred and sixty-three, issued by the Grand Council to protect the pre-eminent position of the Venetian glassmakers. The maximum penalty for this offence is death.'

The Rossi leafed through some papers in front of him and then regarded Giam with intense distaste that he failed to keep from his voice. 'Do you know this Frenchman, Thieré mentioned in the charge?'

'I have met him once at my Glass-works on Murano.' replied Giam evenly.

'When was this?

'The thirteenth of June this year: I agreed to supply him with glass to go to London on the Galley to Flanders. My assistant has dealt with the matter since then.'

'Your famous Cristallo transparente, no doubt?' said Senator Orseoli one of the Neri. 'I suppose you made a large profit from it at the expense of the local merchants?'

Giam tried hard to keep his temper. 'Thieré was treated exactly the same as the local merchants. He only received part of his order in Cristallo transparente; I don't yet have the capacity to meet demand. And yes, I did make some extra profit, but no more than any other Murano Glass-works would have done for sending glass abroad. My books will show the truth of that.'

'Books are frequently doctored,' retorted Senator Orseoli. 'Can you offer any other proof of what you say?'

'My assistant, Roberto was the only other person present during my dealings with Thieré. He can confirm our conversations and the arrangements I made with him. Monsieur Thieré will also tell you the same thing when you interview him,'

'We've already taken a statement from Robert Rosso. His statement was similar to yours, but then it would be,' sneered the Rossi. 'You'd make sure that he told the same tale.'

'Where is the Frenchman?' queried Senator Orseoli. 'I'll be interested to hear what he's got to say.'

'That will not be possible,' said the Rossi. 'Monsieur Thieré has already been deported as an enemy of the State. He's been informed his life is forfeit if he returns to Venice.'

'By whose orders? This Frenchman should have been arrested and brought before us.'

'The Advocate General and myself decided he was too dangerous to have him corrupt others. Venice is in delicate negotiations with the French. We couldn't put him to the torture without creating an incident with the French Ambassador, so the Doge signed the order to extradite him. Of course,' he said with a grim smile, 'you can tell the Doge he was wrong, if it pleases you. It certainly won't please him.'

Giam protested that he was not being allowed to present witnesses in his defence. He jumped to his feet and to try to argue the point, but the Rossi motioned to the guards who roughly slammed him down on the chair.

Secretary Nicolosi, standing at his side, leaned over him. 'Be quiet, Master Bellini,' he advised in a low voice. 'It will go against you to argue.'

For the next hour, Giam was questioned on all aspects of his business life and his dealings with other merchants as well as Thieré. Then after a brief private conference, the Rossi announced an adjournment. Giam bowed as the Three left the room. He was then hustled through the lobby and up the stairs to his cell once more.

'When do you think I'll be called again?' said Giam to the gaoler, as he made to close the door.

'It won't be until later today or even tomorrow. It depends if they reach a decision.'

Giam was aghast. 'You mean I won't be allowed to present a defence?'

'You don't have many rights where the Three are concerned. And you won't get far trying to tell the Three how to adjudicate,' he said emphatically as he dragged the door shut.

CHAPTER FIFTEEN

Senator Morisini walked briskly across the Piazzetto Saint Marco. Oblivious to the splendid white Gothic arches of the Doges Palace, he hurried through the lobby to find the Senior Avogador. As an Avogador, the lawyers who acted as guardians of the Constitution there were aspects of Giam's arrest that concerned him. Being a noble, Giam should have been advised of his rights to representation and ordered to appear before the Council of Ten to defend himself against the charges. Only a direct threat against the Republic and an order from the Doge could justify arresting him like a commoner. It was the sort of misuse of the law for which the Avogador's were created. Their veto ensured that decisions of the Great Councils, Senate and Council of Ten accorded with the Laws of Venice.

The Senior Avogador was not at the Palace, but was expected shortly, so summoning the Secretary of the Ten; Morisini put on his official grey striped robes and waited impatiently for him to arrive. When at last the Secretary did so, Morisini was dismayed at the swift way things had proceeded. The Three was already trying Giam; the order for Giam's arrest having come from the Advocate General. On questioning the secretary further, he discovered that in direct contravention of the Law, the Rossi had instructed him that it was not necessary to inform the Avogador that the Three were in session.

Learning that the Three were now in recess, he dismissed the secretary and set off for the Rossi's room to demand an explanation. As he approached the door, which was slightly ajar, he was about to knock when he heard a voice he recognised, 'I told you Bellini would deny everything,' Adrian Ragazoni was saying, 'I was not surprised to hear that Baffo has denounced him. Apparently Thieré was offering to present him at the court of the Queen of England.'

In the circumstances, despite his distaste of eve droppers, Senator Morisini had no qualms about listening.

'Perhaps we ought to get this Thieré back from exile,' Pietro Ragazoni was saying. 'Senator Orseoli is complaining about not having him available for questioning.'

'Then show him these statements,' said Adrian.

'They're signed letters from two workers from Mendoza's who delivered glass to Thieré at the Rialto quayside. Thieré mentioned he was expecting Bellini to join him shortly for the trip to London and wanted the glass loaded as quickly as possible.'

'Are you sure that these are genuine? It seems odd that Bellini should join him so early.'

'I can assure you father, I would not have brought this to your attention if I was not convinced that they are telling the truth. You must ensure that this upstart Bellini does not get away with his peasant money grabbing. Persuade Orseoli and the other Neri. We have failed to get Bellini removed from the Libro D'Oro, but now we can wipe out this stain on the noble blood of the Republic.'

Morisini listened to this last bigoted appeal in horror. What he had heard left no doubt in his mind. Adrian Ragazoni was behind the plot to have Giam found guilty of Treason. What seemed also clear was that Pietro Ragazoni was not directly involved, but had been persuaded by his son that Giam Bellini was a traitor.

There was the sound of a chair being pushed back and Morisini was about to leave when Adrian spoke again. 'I will leave it to you father, but one final thought. I can't find Baffo, he didn't report to the Glass-works this morning and he's not at home. He set off for work, but he's not been seen since. Ask Bellini what he knows about it. Perhaps he found out about Baffo's denunciation and tried to silence him.'

'Unless my colleagues think that the statements are sufficient to convict him, I may well do that,' said Pietro. 'I have already made up my mind.'

Morisini moved quickly away from the door and around the corner. Peering cautiously round, he saw them give a brief embrace then walk away down the corridor towards the Council chamber.

Morisini was aghast. He'd come to know Giam well in recent weeks and would stake his life that Giam was no traitor, or, if Adrian Ragazoni's thinly disguised accusation was to be believed, involved in abduction, or even murder. How he could stop the Ragazoni's was another matter. With Pietro probably convinced that Giam was a traitor, he might use his influence to convince the Neri as well and persuade them to reach a unanimous decision against Giam. In that event, the Senate would simply accept the verdict of the Three and Morisini could do little to stop events from running their inevitable course.

Fear clouded his mind and he strove to overcome it. His daughter's happiness was at stake. These dark thoughts must be put to one side and he must act logically. Only the Avogador's could save Giam if the verdict was unanimous. The Chief Avogador must be told and quickly. Released from his indecision, he strode off to find him.

Three hours later, Secretary Nicolosi announced to a hastily convened Council of Ten that the Three had found Giacomo Bellini guilty of Treason against the State and the sentence was death. The President called for silence above the hubbub, which greeted the news and asked the Council for their unanimous support for the decision.

Before this could be proposed, Senator Morisini and Jacapo Massola the Chief Avogador entered the Chamber and requested to be heard.

The President of the Council yielded the floor to the Chief Avogador and a hush fell on the chamber. Senator Morisini stepped back while his colleague bowed and read out a statement.

'In accordance with the laws of Venice, the Avogador inform the Council of Ten that they consider the verdict of the Inquisitori to be unsound and in contravention of the laws of Venice. The accused, Master Glass-maker Bellini, is a noble of Venice and is so recorded in the Libro D'Oro. As a nobleman he has the inalienable right to summon witnesses and to question them before the Council of Ten; the Inquisitori has denied this right. The most important witness has been banished from Venice on the instigation of the Rossi, the person responsible for the denunciation, has disappeared and in a further contravention of the Law, the Avogador were not informed that the Inquisitori were in session on the direct orders of the Rossi. In view of these circumstances the sentence cannot be upheld as safe.'

In the uproar that followed this announcement Pietro Ragazoni, who had been standing at the back of the Chamber, came storming to the front and, dramatically pointing a finger at Senator Morisini, accused him of perverting justice to save his daughter's betrothed.

Before Senator Morisini could reply, the Chief Avogador called for order in the chamber. The President joined in and the Council settled down once more. The Chief Avogador turned to the Rossi. 'Your accusation does you little credit Senator Ragazoni. Senator Morisini is only present at my insistence as he quite properly stated his conflict of interest in this matter and was not involved the decision I have just read out. In contrast, you as the Rossi have been involved in banishing the main defence witness and failed to notify the Avogador that the Three were in session. Perhaps your own motives should be considered. Had it not been for information from other sources, the Avogador would have been unable to perform their function, namely ensuring that the laws of Venice are upheld. I must further say to you, Rossi that information in my possession leads me to conclude, that you yourself should have declared an interest in the case and stood down as president.'

The Chief Avogador then turned and addressed the Council. 'As laid down in the constitution, the decision of the Inquisitori cannot be ratified at this time. I will take advice from leading constitutional experts and announce my verdict at midday tomorrow to a meeting of the full Giunta.' The two Avogador turned, bowed to the president, and left the Chamber, leaving behind pandemonium.

Later that evening, the meal at the Morisini household was a gloomy affair, and sparsely attended. Maria and her Sigisbei were the only ones present. Maria's eyes were red -rimmed with crying and she found it difficult to control her emotions when she spoke.

Maria could contain her impatience no longer. 'It's taking so long,' she cried, 'surely father has been able to find a way to reprieve Giam. He can't let him be killed. He can't!' She began to sob uncontrollably.

Just at that moment, a servant entered bringing a message for Maria. Drying her eyes, she opened it, although her hands were difficult to control. The note inside simply said that if she wanted to save Giacomo Bellini from the death sentence, she must go to the main gate at six o clock and wait for further instructions. She must come alone and was not to tell anyone where she was going, or why.

Realising that Sigisbei Vercelline was looking at her expectantly, she just said the note was from a friend who'd heard about Giam and was pledging any help they could give. She then excused herself. Safe in the privacy of her room she read the letter again. It gave no clue as to the writer and Maria couldn't think who'd sent it, or why there was a need for all the secrecy. However, willing to clutch at any straw to help Giam, she determined to keep the appointment. Since it only lacked a little before the appointed time, she hastily put on a hooded cloak over her dress and, slipping out of the villa, made her way to the main gate.

Hiding in the shadow by the gate, she waited impatiently and eventually she heard a carriage approaching. It stopped opposite her and a hoarse voice called her by name. Stepping out of the shadows, she was told to get into the carriage. As she hesitated the voice called out harshly. 'Get in if you want to save Bellini's life.'

Maria thought the muffled voice sounded familiar. The message in contrast, was very clear; she hesitated no longer and climbed into the carriage.

Before she could make out the figure of a man inside, the carriage sped away, throwing her into the seat beside him. A mocking voice, which she recognised instantly said, 'You always seem to be throwing yourself at men, my dear, it is not a good habit for one so young.'

'Adrian!' she exclaimed in astonishment. 'It was you who sent the note. What game are you playing now?'

It was indeed Adrian Ragazoni, but a very different person from the man she'd known just a few short months ago. Now he ignored her imperious tone.

'This is no game Maria. Be quiet and listen to what I have to say without interruption, unless that is you want your precious Bellini to be throttled by the secret police and dumped into the lagoon.'

Maria slumped back into her seat listening in mounting horror and disbelief.

'The only way you can save Bellini from his fate, is to marry me.' His smile was one of pure pleasure. 'I'm the only one who can save his life now.'

'Never.' she cried in loathing. 'I'll never marry you; my father and the Avogador's will find a way to save Giam.'

Adrian laughed evilly. 'If you really thought that Maria you wouldn't be here, either you agree to marry me and sign a paper to that effect, or I'll go straight to my father. I'll make sure he gets the Doge to ratify the decision. He can do it you know; he's the Rossi for the Three.'

As she started in surprise, he smiled evilly. 'Your father didn't tell you that did he? The Rossi's already got that fool of a Frenchman thrown out of Venice.' He thrust the paper towards her. 'Sign the paper, Maria, and I'll make sure he lives Sign it now and save everyone a lot of trouble.'

He thrust the paper towards Maria, but she pushed it away, 'I don't trust you Adrian. You swore to get even with me as well as Giam. What's to stop you from letting Giam die as well as getting a written promise from me?'

Adrian looked thoughtful, and then produced his trump card. 'If I speak out in public tomorrow and get the Giunta to reprieve Bellini, I'll expect the signed paper straight away. I won't show it to anyone, unless you fail to keep your promise. You'll call off your engagement to Bellini and in due course we'll be married. You'll not be blamed; it will be natural for you to marry a noble from the Old Families and a pillar of society. Bellini won't be able to stay in Venice; at the very least he'll be deported or imprisoned, but at least he'll be alive. Make no mistake about this Maria; I'll only do this if you give me your sworn word. I'll put my trust in your honour. Now it's up to you to decide. You have until we reach your father's villa. After that, it'll be too late.' Leaning out of the window he shouted. 'Coachman, return to the Casa Da Mula with all speed.'

The coach swung round violently throwing them roughly in a tangled heap in the corner. Maria recoiled as Adrian fondled her breast and struggling upright, she moved as far away from him as she could. Meanwhile, the coach sped quickly back the way it had come and Maria realised that she only had a few minutes to decide. She racked her brains for an alternative, but Adrian had done his work well. She could see no other way of helping Giam.

As the coach slowed to a halt by the gate of her home she cried out. 'I'll sign your paper Adrian Ragazoni; you have my word on it. But only when you speak in public and save Giam from death. Should my father or anyone else do this, I'll not sign the paper. Only on those conditions will I do as you want. Is that agreed?'

'Of course it is my dear Maria; no one but me can help Bellini. Until tomorrow then!'

Maria climbed out of the now stationary coach and fled sobbing into the Casa while the coach sped away into the night.

Maria arrived back in her room without anyone being aware that she'd been out. Throwing herself on the bed she lay numbly, clutching a pillow to her breast. She lay there for some time in abject misery, until at last she fell into a disturbed sleep, haunted by nightmares of Giam being drowned in the lagoon by a laughing Adrian.

The following morning, it was late when she woke. She felt tired and listless, but forced herself to wash and dress. She didn't feel like eating, but contented herself with a glass of fresh orange juice. Her father had left a message to say he was going to the

Piombi and that there was to be a meeting of the full Giunta around noon.

Maria was in a confused state of mind. She was very aware of the bargain she'd made with Adrian and couldn't come to terms with what it would mean. The more she thought about it, the more she realised that whatever happened today, she was going to lose Giam. The realisation came, that in keeping her word, Giam would be completely lost to her, even though he would still be alive.

CHAPTER SIXTEEN

Giam slept badly the night following his arraignment. The cell was hot and stuffy and it was not until the cool of the early morning that he fell into a fitful sleep. He was wakened when the door was opened and the gaoler showed in a tall man dressed in grey ceremonial robes. Motioning to the gaoler to leave them the man studied Giam gravely. 'Master Bellini I am Jacapo Massola, Chief Avogador of the Great Council and I have taken the unusual step of visiting you because your case is unique in the history of Venice. I regret to tell you that you have been found Guilty of treason by the Inquisitori and sentenced to death.'

Although Giam had been expecting the worst, nevertheless, to have it confirmed was a huge shock. The Avogador regarded him kindly. 'You must have many questions, but please hear me out first.' When Giam just nodded numbly, he continued. 'I have told the Senate of my strong misgivings about this case in many of its aspects. To my mind there is enough evidence to show that you have been the victim of a plot, although I lack the proof.'

'Adrian Ragazoni is behind this affair,' Giam blurted out. 'I'm sure of it. He hates me for showing him up over Cristallo transparente on Senator Morisini's birthday.'

'I fear you are right, but this is not proof. The reason for my visit is to try to get you to understand the peril you are in. The Three have reached a unanimous verdict and at any other time that verdict would have been ratified immediately by the Senate and sentence carried out by now.'

He paused to allow the import of his words to sink in. Giam was too shocked by this revelation to ask any questions.

With a reassuring smile the Chief Avogador continued. 'Do not despair, Master Bellini, all is not yet lost. There is a chance that we can overturn this verdict. A slim one I must admit, since no unanimous verdict has ever been overturned in the history of the rule of law in Venice. You can plead that your rights as a nobleman have not been upheld. That is indisputable. You can further plead your innocence and try to get some evidence to support it, but with the Frenchman deported and your accuser missing, it will be well nigh impossible.'

'What has been going on?' cried Giam. 'You say my accuser has disappeared? You must know who it is then? It's Marco Baffo isn't it? He's the only one who could have supplied the information the Three were questioning me about yesterday.'

The Advocate nodded, 'I should not tell you this, but much of this case is irregular. Marco Baffo sent an accusation via a Lion's Mouth and has not been seen since. There has even been a suggestion, that you are responsible for this. It seems to be yet another attempt to condemn you by hearsay, rather than fact.'

Giam nodded and pointed out that he'd had no communication with anyone since his arrest and had only been told of the charge against him and nothing else. 'What can be done to get this ridiculous case dismissed?'

'I'm very much afraid that we might not be able to do that.' said the Avogador. 'The reason my post exists is to prevent cases like this, but I confess that the speed and thoroughness of the plot have left little room for manoeuvre. I'm confident however that we can rescind the death sentence. There's too much doubt for that to stand, of that I'm sure. How much we can reduce the sentence is another matter. If I'm right, the Senate will uphold the Guilty verdict, but may consider a plea for mercy in a favourable light. I'm afraid that at the very least you'll be sent to the galleys and perhaps your assets seized by the state.'

'This is monstrous,' raged Giam. 'I've always supported the rule of law, so has my father and now the law is being twisted by Ragazoni for the purpose of revenge.'

'I assure you that I will use every iota of my power and influence prevent that and to expose the perpetrator. There is one thing I can do for you and that is to arrange for Senator Morisini to see you. I wish that I could let your father see you, but the law only allows Avogador to question you, not even the Senate can prevent this.'

As the Chief Avogador prepared to take his leave, he told Giam not to give up hope and then hurried away.

Left on his own again, Giam began to think of ways in which he could try to alleviate his likely sentence. He was over the shock and at least he was not likely to die, if the Chief Avogador was to be believed. On the other hand, there were still some very severe sentences they could impose like sending him to the galleys for life - a terrible fate.

To avoid brooding, Giam tried to think about other things. He'd hardly thought about Maria during his imprisonment. She had obviously raised the alarm and in so doing had probably saved his life. The matter of his assets now came to his mind. He was not going to accept the state seizing the Glass-works without a fight.

As the day wore on the heat in the room became unbearable. Being right up under the roof with only the small narrow windows high up, there was little air circulation. Having thought of all the possibilities on his idea Giam could only wait. He tried to sleep but found it impossible. By mid afternoon, or as near as he could tell from the position of the sun, he was very dehydrated and feeling quite faint. He closed his eyes and tried to sleep.

Some time later, the sound of the key in the lock brought him out of a fitful doze. The gaoler opened the door and spoke in a querulous voice to someone behind him. 'You can only stay for a short time or I'll be in trouble with the Three.'

Senator Morisini pushed past him handing him a small leather pouch. 'I am an Avogador and we are investigating this case on behalf of the Great Council. Take the purse for your trouble and don't hurry back.' With that he waved the gaoler away and embraced Giam warmly. 'How are you my boy, I hope you are bearing up well. Maria sends you her love.'

Giam was overwhelmed by the warmth of the greeting, but responded in kind. 'I'm as well as can be expected, Senator, and feeling all the better for seeing a friendly face.'

'I know how you must feel my boy and please call me Ricardo. I'm sorry to rush you, but we must get down to business. I know the Chief Avogador has told you how things stand and I'm afraid little has changed since this morning.'

'Please don't be afraid to tell me the worst.'

'I fear we will not be able to persuade the Senate to clear you completely. You'll be sick of hearing it, but no unanimous decision of the Three has ever been overturned. However, I do believe we will be able persuade them that you were not given a proper chance to present witnesses and to question them. Most of the case is built on the accusations of Marco Baffo and despite a rigorous search he has not been found.'

Giam shook his head in disgust. 'What about Jean Thieré? Has anyone been able to speak to him yet?'

Ricardo shook his head sadly. 'I'm still trying to find out which galley he's being held on. The Doge will not reconsider his deportation for fear of seeming weak, but we are trying to locate him so that he can be interviewed.'

'He'll confirm that he did not ask me to go to London, nor did I give him any secret information on my Cristallo transparente. I simply sold him some glass.'

'I'm sorry to ask you these things Giam, but in my role as Avogador, I needed to hear you deny these accusations in person. I believe that you're innocent of these charges and the victim of a cunning plot by Adrian Ragazoni.'

He told Giam about the conversation between Adrian and his father. 'I'm sure that this whole thing was hatched by Ragazoni for revenge, and that his father is a bigoted, but unwitting tool in his machinations. Proving it is another matter entirely. There's only my word for the conversation he had with his father. It would be easy to discredit what I said and I would be labelled as an anxious father in law clutching at straws. That's not so very far from the truth.'

Giam thanked him for his trust. 'I'd like you to be brutally frank. Tell me what you think you'll be able to achieve with the Senate.'

'Very well my boy, but you must understand that I'm only guessing. I doubt if anyone can predict the outcome of this trial, but I'll try. I fear the Senate will uphold the verdict, accept a plea for mercy and reduce the sentence. Should our arguments hold sway, it could be a token fine. If not, you could be sentenced to the galleys, or even have your assets seized.'

Giam contemplated this summary in silence for a while. The thought of being sent to the galleys sent shudders down his spine, but at least he'd still be alive. Many men in need of money enlisted in the galleys to clear their debt of taxes. Venetian galley men were neither slaves, nor badly treated. They were only chained when in port. In time of war, or against pirates, they were armed and were part of the fighting force. Nevertheless, it was a hard and austere life and many died before completing their term.

Ricardo interrupted his thoughts. 'I know this is a difficult for you, Giam, but I fear we have little time left and I need to discuss your affairs before I leave. This is probably the only chance before tomorrow.'

'Tell me what you suggest.'

Pulling some papers from inside his doublet, Ricardo handed them to Giam. 'Your father and I worked late into the night and discussed possible outcomes. We drew these up for you to sign if you agree with what we've suggested. Only sign them if you feel they will help.'

Listening to Ricardo's words as he read the papers Giam could see the sense in what they'd drawn up. The documents were essentially deeds for transfer of title and articles of partnership. They transferred half of the shares in Luciano's to his father and the rest to Ricardo in return for sums of money to finance his coming wedding and the building of a new villa for Maria. Giam insisted that his villa should be in Maria's name, and that Roberto and his mother must stay employed. Anna would make a good companion for Maria and Roberto was to be made a junior partner in the Glass-works.

Asking for a short time to consider he thought about the

choices the papers gave him. Of course, he wasn't worried about Ricardo and his father stealing from him. Just not happy with some of the dispositions they'd made.

With a slightly rueful smile he turned to Ricardo and congratulated him on his foresight. 'I can see that there are some devious minds working for me as well as against me. I'd like to make a few changes. I hope you have pen and ink; I'm not allowed to have them.'

Ricardo made the necessary adjustments took the signed documents and blew on them to dry the ink before hiding them in his doublet again. 'I promise you that these will only be used in the event of the state trying to seize your property. If they do these papers will protect the main ones and you will get everything back as soon as it's safe,' he said his voice husky with emotion, 'All my resources will be available to you and Maria once you are free again.'

Giam took his proffered hand and shook it warmly. 'Look after Maria for me Senator and give her my love. Make sure she knows that I'll always love her. Try to reassure her that we will be together again as soon as this affair is over.'

Ricardo embraced him and banged on the door to call the gaoler. 'I couldn't have wished for a better and more courageous son in law. I will support your cause to the full extent of my resources. Even if we can't free you immediately, we'll keep on pursuing the case until we find out the truth. God be with you, my boy.'

'And with you too Ricardo,' said Giam, close to tears.

CHAPTER SEVENTEEN

Maria sat in the main reception room at the Casa Da Mula, impatiently waiting for some news. Since early morning there had been a steady flow of visitors to her father's study where he had been ensconced with Senator Bellini for almost three hours. She was about to send the Sigisbei with a message when the door opened and her father, Eduardo and Roberto came in, with a man who from his dress, was obviously a sea captain.

'Maria my dear, allow me to present Captain Lunardo Carerras, of the Galleass 'Galliano.' He has brought us some interesting news, which I have asked him to share with you.'

Captain Carreras bowed over Maria's hand and regarded her gravely. 'I regret we meet in such difficult times. I am an old friend of Giam's and I was delighted to hear of his success and betrothal. I only heard of his trial yesterday afternoon quite by chance. Let me explain. Two days ago a Frenchman called Thieré was deported from Venice by order of the Doge. He is being held on the Galliano. I have passed on his story to your father, but he believes that a glass-maker called Marco Baffo has denounced Giacomo for treason against the Republic by planning to set up a Glass-works in London to make Cristallo transparente.'

'That is totally absurd.' stormed Maria. 'Giam is in love with me and wouldn't leave Venice. He's one of the most respected and sought after glassmakers in Murano. What possible incentive could this Frenchman offer him to leave all that behind?'

Captain Carreras smiled bleakly and nodded in agreement. 'That's exactly what Thieré said to me. He told me he'd only bought some glass from Giam and talked about a possible partnership to sell glass to England next year, if his Cristallo transparente was well received in London. Anything else is sheer fabrication. Regrettably, I couldn't leave the galleass until the morning tide, but I came straight away to see your father.'

Maria turned to her father excitedly. 'Surely the Senate will accept the word of Captain Carreras and it will be enough to throw out the case.'

'I'm afraid it's too late for that. The unanimous decision of the Three has made it impossible to make any move to throw out the case.' Ricardo shook his head sadly. 'This is the predicament we've been battling against since yesterday. The Giunta will never reverse the decision of the Three; it's against all precedent. They may however, be convinced that there were enough irregularities in the handling of the case to agree to rescind the death sentence. It depends how many Senators support us and how many vote to uphold the power of the Three.' He turned to Eduardo. 'What do you think Eduardo?'

Eduardo thought carefully before he replied. 'Unfortunately it has ceased to be about the rights and wrongs of the case, it's now all about politics. Many of the Old Families do not accept Giam as a member of the aristocracy and may use this opportunity to get rid of him.'

'I'm fairly sure that we can discredit the trial on the grounds that neither the accuser nor the chief participant was available for Giam to question,' Ricardo said smiling reassuringly at his daughter. 'As a noble he should have been given those rights. We can also try to present Captain Carreras's testimony, but I am afraid it may be too late.

Unfortunately, we don't have any real evidence to prove the whole thing is a fabrication either. I agree with Eduardo, it has become a political matter, but knowing what the Giunta will do about it is another matter. Both Eduardo and I have called in a lot of favours and we can count on considerable support.' He grimaced. 'Whether it will be enough, I'm not sure.'

'Father surely there's more that can be done to save Giam?'

'We're doing everything we can to get Giam freed. We've also made certain other arrangements in case he's given a term in the galleys,' he glanced across at Captain Carreras. 'I think it most unlikely that the Giunta will consider deporting him; he'd be free to pass on his secrets, which would defeat the whole object of the trial. My main fear is that the Senate will simply uphold the original death sentence of the Three. The matter is very much in the balance and even now, our friends are trying to drum up some more support.' He shrugged his shoulders and muttered. 'We're going to need all the help we can get.'

On hearing this Maria realised that the intervention of Adrian Ragazoni could be vital, but the consequences of agreeing to his terms filled her with dread. Whatever the outcome, she thought; I'm going to lose Giam. A shudder passed through her as the inevitability of the situation stuck home. Her father reacted with concern and felt her forehead. 'Are you all right Maria? You've gone so cold? Sit down and I'll send a servant to fetch a wrap for you.'

Maria shook her head. 'It's nothing father, just a passing chill. Don't worry about me. I think you'd better be leaving for the meeting of the Giunta, it's getting close to midday.'

He held her at arms length. 'Try not to worry too much. We will not rest until we have saved Giam from this diabolical plot. Come Eduardo.' Together they made their farewells and hurried out. Less than half an hour later, Maria too was seated in the public gallery of the Senate chamber looking down on the crowded floor below.

News of the intervention of the Avogador in a decision of the Three had ensured a full attendance and the Debating Chamber was crowded. Looking around, Maria searched for sight of Adrian Ragazoni, but could only make out the tall form of her father. He was at the centre of a large group of Senators. At that moment a hush descended on the Chamber as the two Neri in their black robes and the Rossi in his red robe came into the room. The Leader of the Giunta, who'd been talking to a messenger, called the Giunta to order and announced that the Chief Avogador had just informed him that there would be a delay in delivering their verdict. 'They have received a letter from a member of the Senate,' he announced, 'which appears to throw new light on the case. The Avogador send their apologies, but they must study this information as it could affect their decision.'

An excited hubbub broke out at this announcement. Standing unnoticed at the back of the chamber where he had slipped in, Adrian Ragazoni smiled in satisfaction as his father the Rossi, leaned across and whisper urgently to the Leader. After a short conversation, the Leader nodded, rose to his feet and addressed the Giunta. 'I have received a request from the Rossi asking to make a short statement to the Giunta and since the Avogador are not ready, I have agreed to this request.'

An expectant hush fell as the Rossi rose to his feet and looked around at the gathered nobility. He cleared his throat then began. 'As you all know my colleagues and I have recently passed a death sentence on Giam Bellini for the crime of Treason.' He paused and gestured to the Neri. 'My colleagues are unaware of the information I am about to give. I apologise to them, but due to lack of time I was unable to inform them before the meeting.' He bowed to them then turned to the Giunta again. 'A short time ago, Senator Adrian Ragazoni, my son, informed me of some facts that had come to light only this morning. The Avogador is studying them as we speak. My son knows the facts far better than I, so the Leader has agreed that he should apprise you of the details himself.'

The Leader motioned to Adrian Ragazoni who strode purposefully from the back of the Chamber. The eyes of everyone followed him, none more closely than Maria's, who had leaned forward for a better view. Reaching the platform, he turned to face the chamber.

Maria became dizzy with tension as the enormity of the moment gripped her. Should Adrian succeed in persuading the Giunta to reprieve Giam, she would have to keep her word and agree to marry him. She sank back in despair. How could she keep such a bargain? Before the heartsick Maria could come to terms with this, Ragazoni began his address. In spite of her fears, Maria roused herself to listen.

'Members of the Giunta, I stand before you today with the object of persuading you that the verdict against Master Giacomo Bellini is a mistake.' He smiled. 'I can see that many of you are surprised; none more so than myself in view of our recent err... difference of opinion.' There were a few laughs at this oblique reference to the Cristallo fiasco. This subsided as Adrian continued. 'The Master of Mendoza's, Marco Baffo, formerly at the Luciano Glass-works, has made little attempt to hide his hatred of Master Bellini. I offer no opinion on the rights or wrongs of this matter, but simply offer it in explanation of what follows.'

He looked around. 'Two evenings ago, Baffo went into my glass-works to check the afternoon work. He'd been out on some errand of his own apparently. He was in a very belligerent mood and several of the men thought he'd been drinking. One of them mentioned Bellini's Cristallo transparente and Baffo flew into a rage. He began a tirade against Bellini, which went on for some time and then rushed out of the works and was last seen heading towards the quayside. He has not been seen since, despite a most intensive search by the authorities.'

As this statement was ending, there were restless mutterings from some of the members. A more vociferous individual shouted out asking what bearing this had on the verdict. Adrian ignored him and continued. 'Concerned about Baffo's disappearance, I questioned the employees individually. What they told me is contained in the signed depositions I have passed on to the Rossi and to the Avogador. During his tirade, Baffo said he was going to denounce Bellini as a traitor. He told them that Bellini had held a meeting with a Frenchman in the pay of the English and had passed on the secret of his cristallo.

When one of the men questioned if he was at the meeting, Baffo admitted he wasn't, but the Frenchman had told him he was going to introduce Bellini to the Queen of England when he came to London.'

After yet another dramatic pause Ragazoni continued. 'Now comes the crucial point. When one of the men laughed and said no one would accept that as proof, Baffo flew into a rage. He told them that in that case he would have to say he was a witness to the Frenchman admitting Bellini was going to take his Cristallo transparente and make it in London.

Realising what he'd admitted Baffo threatened that if they spoke a word of it he would see they never worked in the glass industry again. No idle threat coming from a Master. I have of course told the men that their jobs are safe and they have given sworn affidavits to the truth of their statements.'

In the ensuing uproar, the Leader could be heard calling for quiet. It was several minutes before he could regain order as members argued the merits of the new evidence. Finally achieving calm, he asked if either Adrian or his father had any more to add.

Adrian Ragazoni indicated he had. 'I have passed on this information to you, since no matter what my personal feelings are about Bellini, the rule of Law in Venice is more important.' There were numerous cries of support and acclaim for this and Adrian smiling went on. 'I'm certain that something has gone on between Bellini and this mysterious Frenchman. However, I'm also sure that Marco Baffo has exaggerated what he knows and has not told the complete truth. This fact alone puts some doubt as to how far Bellini has transgressed the Laws of Murano. However, the Rule of Law must be sacrosanct. A unanimous verdict has been given and must be upheld. I firmly believe that in view of these new facts, the death sentence against Bellini should be commuted to whatever the Senate deems appropriate for his crimes.'

CHAPTER EIGHTEEN

While Adrian Ragazoni was making his speech, the Chief Avogador and a colleague slipped virtually unnoticed on to the rear of the platform. When Ragazoni damned Giam by implication, the Chief Avogador spoke angrily to his colleague, but did not interrupt. Only when Adrian and his father, the Rossi, had finished their speeches did he stand up and walk to the front of the platform.

There was an expectant silence as, with a bow to the Leader, he turned and addressed the members. 'My fellow Avogador and I have studied the whole of the trial of Giacomo Bellini by the Three and their death sentence given after a unanimous verdict of guilty. Even before the evidence you have just heard, this verdict 'was unsafe.'

As several cries of disagreement rang out he called for silence and when this was achieved, he continued. 'Our reasons are as follows. Firstly, there can be no doubt whatsoever, that this trial was not conducted according to the Laws of Venice. Master Giacomo Bellini was denied his rights as a nobleman and those rights are inalienable and apply to all whose names are inscribed in the Libro d'Oro.

'Secondly, the hasty deportation of the Frenchman Thieré and the failure to obtain a written statement meant that the whole case against Bellini rested solely on the testimony of Marco Baffo. No other evidence was offered and since Baffo has disappeared, he was not available to be questioned.

'As we have just heard from Adrian Ragazoni and his father, the Rossi, this testimony must now be considered to be incorrect, seriously flawed, or possibly a complete fabrication; based on little more than Baffo's hatred of Bellini.

Roberto Rosso, Bellini's assistant, was the only other person at the meeting with Thieré and he confirms Bellini's statement. He swears that Baffo was not present at the meeting and that Thieré only discussed buying glass and nothing else. The only other so-called evidence was a mixture of innuendo and half-truths based on little more than prejudice against the defendant.' The Avogador turned towards the Three who had sat dispassionately throughout the judgement and addressed them directly. 'Had Bellini been allowed to question these witnesses as laid down in the Capituary, the Avogador of Venice believe that the sentence of death could never have been justified. The trial was a travesty of justice on a scale unheard of in Venice.'

This statement provoked a storm of comment and protest and it was some little time before the Chief Avogador could continue. 'Despite what I have already stated, nevertheless a unanimous guilty verdict was given. We have consulted the highest authorities on the Law who advise us that there is no provision in the penal code to overturn a unanimous verdict by the Inquisitori. We conclude therefore that it must be for the Giunta to decide, either by changing the law, or deciding on a more appropriate sentence.'

Before he could continue, uproar broke out in the chamber. There were loud cries denouncing the judgement from various parts of the chamber and calls for the Giunta to ratify the death sentence. From the platform, the Leader called vainly for silence so the Avogador could complete their summation. This only spurred more vociferous shouts and Adrian Ragazoni smiled smugly as his friends did there work.

Joining other members of the platform party at the front he supported the call for calm. At this signal, the shouting from his friends slowly died away and the Chamber became quiet once more. When the furore died down, the Chief Avogador stepped forward. 'There seems to be a misunderstanding of the role of the Avogador in some quarters of the Giunta. We play no part in the trial process, but simply exist to ensure that the Laws of Venice are strictly observed in complex cases like that against Giacomo Bellini.

At no time is it our role to set a sentence; that is the role of the

Ten, or the Giunta.' At this point he turned to his fellow Avogador producing a scroll from his doublet as he did so. Receiving a nod of confirmation he turned to the Senate and read from the scroll.

'We the Avogador of Venice being in receipt of certain information and evidence, do advise the Senate that in the case of the trial of Master Giacomo Bellini, we conclude that an organised attempt has been made by certain individuals to pervert the course of justice.'

There was a concerted gasp from many parts of the chamber at this announcement. On the platform, Adrian Ragazoni sat stunned. He sat upright and an apprehensive look crossed his face. On the balcony, Maria sat up with a hopeful expression as she waited for the Avogador to continue.

'From a personal viewpoint this case has disturbed me more than any other during my term as Chief Avogador,' he went on. 'I am firmly convinced that on the evidence, Marco Baffo, out of hatred for Bellini, lied in his letter of denunciation. I do not however, believe that he is the person who has orchestrated this affair.'

Turning so that he was part facing the Ragazonis, he launched his final comments in their direction. 'As I have indicated the Avogador have received evidence that implicates members of the Senate in a conspiracy against Giacomo Bellini. Unfortunately, this evidence does not constitute certain proof, but rest assured that our investigations will continue until that proof is obtained and the proper authorities will be informed of their names along with the proof of their guilt.'

Maria, with disappointment on her face at this final admission, did not miss the sudden exhalation of breath and the look of relief that flashed briefly across Adrian Ragazoni's face at this last comment and neither did the Chief Avogador. Adrian quickly recovered his control and turned to talk to his father, only turning round as the Avogador finished his speech with an appeal to the Giunta.

'Members of the Giunta, I leave you to decide on an

appropriate sentence for Bellini. The Laws of Venice may have no precedent to allow a unanimous verdict of guilty to be overturned, but they do however have a provision for you to impose a different sentence. You could grant a free pardon, a token fine, deportation and confiscation of property, imprisonment, or a term in the galleys; you could also ratify the original sentence as well. We make no recommendation; that is not the role of the Avogador. The decision is yours, gentlemen, and yours alone. I do not envy you your choice, but I do urge you to ensure that justice is not the loser. The Republic of Venice has rightly earned an enviable reputation for fairness in its justice system. It is up to you to uphold it.'

Throughout the proceedings Maria's whole body had felt numb and her mind was somehow detached from the events enfolding below. She realised that Adrian had trapped her in his web of deceit as thoroughly as he'd enmeshed Giam. Try as she would, she couldn't find a way she could accept for breaking her promise to Adrian. He'd carried out his part of the bargain and delivered what he'd promised. Now she too must deliver, but not until she knew for certain what Giam's fate was to be. She was hopeful now that Giam would be spared, but there was no way of telling what the Giunta would decide.

Realising that she'd been locked in her thoughts for some time, she looked down to see what was happening. On the platform, Adrian was involved in what seemed to be a furious argument with his father. The Rossi was shaking his head in disagreement and Adrian, looking round to see if he was being observed, leaned over and whispered urgently in his father's ear. Whatever Adrian said produced a look of shocked surprise on his father's face and a vehement response. Adrian then leaned over and spoke angrily to his father with several emphatic gestures from a pointed finger.

Maria wished she could hear what was passing between the two of them. She could see that the Rossi was visibly shaken, but was now nodding in agreement, albeit with obvious reluctance. Intent on this by-play, Maria had not noticed the Chamber had gone quiet and that the Leader was putting a proposition to them. As she listened anxiously, he asked the Giunta to vote on whether they wished to ratify the death sentence, or change it. Maria held her breath. The vote was in favour of changing the sentence! She slumped back in her chair, her whole body shaking with relief at the easing of tension following the verdict.

At that moment she became aware of a servant in the Ragazoni livery trying to attract her attention. He apologised for interrupting her and handed her a note. Before she'd even read it, Maria guessed that Adrian was calling in her promise. It was indeed so and as she read Adrian's note; she also knew how thoroughly he'd read her character. She'd made a bargain and Adrian had done his part. Sick at heart, but unable to see any other course she simply signed the note. The thought came to her that when you make a bargain with the devil; the price was your immortal soul. She'd signed away her future, but she didn't regret the sacrifice.

Meanwhile, the Rossi was addressing the members. Rousing herself, she listened intently to the end of his statement. With mounting dread she heard him sum up by suggesting that Giam should be sent to the galleys for a period of ten years as a warning to anyone else who might consider betraying commercial secrets to a foreign power, or seek to set up glass-making in another country.

She was very relieved to hear a lot of opposition to this idea. Eduardo Bellini leapt to his feet and addressed the Chamber. 'It seems to me that my son is being condemned, not for any supposed crimes, but for having been born to a commoner mother. The Rossi is only calling for a harsh sentence to justify the original trial. As we've heard, that was a mockery of justice and but for the unanimous verdict would have been set aside altogether.' There were many calls of support, but Adrian's puppets barracked him loudly. Ignoring their shouts Eduardo called for the sentence to be a token fine to show the Senate did not agree with the trial verdict. Before he finished he made a plea directly to the older Ragazoni.

'You have heard the Avogador denounce the plot against my son. I challenge you to give all the information you have to help them identify the man behind this plot. No matter who he is,' he said pointedly. 'You must have some idea who has fed the Three with misinformation and has led you all to make a false verdict. Help the Avogador bring him to account before he does something even worse.' With this final appeal he sat down to many shouts of support.

Throughout this speech the Rossi sat with a white, stony face, refusing to be drawn, totally ignoring Eduardo's appeal. Maria listened to the debate that raged on for some time, her fears rising by the minute as the debate swung backwards and forwards and motion and counter-motion were debated. Eventually a decision was reached. Giam was sentenced to three years in the galleys, sentence to begin immediately. Maria with the realisation that she had lost Giam searing into her soul slumped to the floor into the welcoming abyss.

CHAPTER NINETEEN

iam was seated in his usual place with his back against the wall beneath the two high windows. It was mid afternoon and the heat in the cell was stultifying his mind and body. Slumped in an apathetic daze, he waited for news of his sentence. The grating of the key in the lock penetrated his mood and he waited anxiously to see who would enter.

The gaoler opened the door wide and the Chief Avogador and Senator Morisini entered. He could see from their grim faces that all was not well, so he bade them to tell him the worst without any further preamble. Ricardo embraced him warmly. 'The death sentence has been quashed, but I'm sorry to say we've failed in our bid for a light sentence. The Giunta have decreed you must serve three years in the galleys.'

Giam, who'd been expecting the worst, was strangely relieved by the sentence. Of course he'd been hoping for a free pardon or a fine, but he hadn't really expected to get it. His laughter startled them. 'I haven't lost my mind; it's just such a relief I'm not going to be executed. I know that three years in the galleys will be hard, but at least when I finish the sentence, I can start again.'

He knew that many men volunteered to serve for that length of time in the galleys. It paid their taxes, which they couldn't pay in any other way. Galley-men of Venice were not slaves like those in Ottoman galleys. But it was a hard life, particularly in the War galleys that relied almost entirely on their oars.'

The Chief Avogador smiled. 'I'm glad you're taking it so well. My main regret is that our supporters could not win the day and secure a complete pardon. I would have liked to bring Ragazoni to account, but there's no doubt he's been clever and covered his tracks almost completely. I have no doubt he's involved in the disappearance and possible murder of Marco Baffo. Unfortunately,

I can't prove it, but I promise you I will not rest until I get to the bottom of this plot. When I do, I will see the Authorities take appropriate action. At least when you complete your sentence, you will still have all of your assets. The Giunta made no order to seize them as part of your sentence.'

Giam was grateful for small mercies, but he really wanted to know if he would get the chance to see Maria before he began his sentence.

'I'm afraid not,' said Senator Morisini sadly. 'In a short while the guards will come to escort you to the Arsenale; there you will be assigned to a galley. Unfortunately, you are not allowed to see anyone except the Avogador. Maria sends her love and said to tell you that she will wait for your return with impatience.'

'Please tell her I will count the days until we are together again. And now there are one or two points to settle. I want Maria to have the Villa Bertolini as we arranged.' Giam was adamant on that point. 'Leave all the arrangements we made as they are. There'll be time enough to change them when I return.' He asked Senator Morisini if he had brought paper and a pen and when these were produced, he sat down and wrote a short letter to Maria, pledging his undying love and bidding her to be of good cheer. He handed it over and then they said their farewells. Giam embraced Ricardo warmly and bade him to look after Maria. The Chief Avogador shook his hand and wished him the best of luck and then they departed leaving Giam to wait for his escort.

A short distance away in his father's room, Adrian Ragazoni was full of elation. The sentence of three years in the galleys was less than he'd planned for, but still long enough to ensure that Bellini would rue the day when he'd crossed him. He looked again at the paper in his hand and his smile became even broader. Maria Morisini had signed the marriage agreement and his triumph was complete. His stock would rise after his performance in the Chamber. Bellini would spend three years of hell in the galleys then he would have a fatal accident. In a few months time, Adrian would marry Maria

Morisini to ensure his place at the very top of Venetian society.

With these triumphant thoughts, he went across to his father and urged him to expedite the order for Bellini to be taken to the Arsenale for allocation to a galley. The large bribe given to the allocation clerk would ensure that Bellini was sent to the right galley. The bosun in Adrian's employ would be waiting to carry out the final part of his plans for Bellini.

Had he been privy to the conversation, which was at that moment taking place in Senator Morisini's room, he would not have been so confident. Eduardo and Ricardo were deep in conversation with Captain Carreras and had just given him an official document. Eduardo urged him to get to the Arsenale as soon as possible and present the document to the Chief Armourer. 'This will take precedent over all other orders and allow you to take your pick of any prisoners, who are available. You are three men short and the Arsenale is so short of men that they'll probably not have any at all until Giam arrives. He'll be much safer in your galleass than in a fleet galley. Who knows what mischief Ragazoni may have planned?'

Ricardo nodded in agreement. 'I agree entirely. The sooner Giam is away from Ragazoni's sphere of influence, the better. At least this way, Giam will be spared some of the worst aspects of his sentence with the arrangements we've made.'

The Captain shook them both by the hand. 'I will do as you bid, because Giam is my friend as well. I think it's best that he's not aware of my involvement until we're safely at sea. I intend to sail at the earliest opportunity to prevent any possible countermove.'

'There's no fear of that, Captain. That order is signed by the Doge and he's not likely to change it for Ragazoni after the Chief Avogador finishes briefing him on the trial and the Ragazoni's part in it.'

'My regards then Senators, I must be on my way,' said Captain Carerras. 'Rest assured, I will take good care of Giam.'

Giam meanwhile had been packing his meagre belongings and had barely finished this when the gaoler announced that the escort soldiers had arrived. Giam, sick at heart at his sudden fall from grace, called on all his reserves of strength and squaring his shoulders, went out to meet his escort.

On his arrival at the Arsenale with his bosun, Captain Carreras was shown straight in to see the Chief Armourer, who, seeing the bottle the Captain was carrying, broke into a broad smile. 'I see you've come to pay your debt, Captain Carreras.'

'Of course chief and well earned it is too. I promised you one of my finest bottles of French Brandy if you could complete the installation of the new guns in time. I'm most grateful to you and your men and there will be a more tangible sign of my gratitude when I return with the Galley to Flanders.'

'I hear you've been appointed as the main escort ship.'

'Yes, and I'm in need of three men. What can you do for me?'

The Chief gave a dismissive laugh. 'You and half the galleys in the fleet; I've two bosons here now, looking for men. We're short of good oarsmen and the situation can only get worse.' He pointed to the slipways where the hulls of galleys could be plainly seen. 'Between you and me, I've got a hundred hulls waiting to be built and there's likely to be a need for them if the situation with the Ottoman gets any worse. The big question is whether we'll be able to man them; building them is the least of my worries. We can turn out one a day with our standard building plan, but where are we to get the oarsmen?'

Captain Carreras nodded his agreement, 'It's a problem that will have to be addressed if it comes to war with the Ottoman, as I think it must.' He pulled from his doublet the document that Eduardo had given him. 'This is an order signed by the Doge relating to my appointment to escort duty. It gives me first choice of any men who may be available. I'd like my bosun to have a look at the men you have. Then perhaps you and I could share a toast to a successful voyage.'

The Chief Armourer went down to see the clerk and told him to give the bosun of the Galliano the pick of the men available. Seeing a chained prisoner waiting on the quayside with an escort two soldiers, the Armourer had words with the clerk. 'What prisoner is this? I was not expecting anyone today.

The clerk, a small shifty-eyed individual nervously shuffled some papers. 'His name is Giacomo Bellini and he's been sentence to three years in the galleys. I've just allocated him to a fleet galley. There is only one other and I was just allocating him to the other bosun.'

'Then you can just reallocate them,' said the Armourer with finality. 'The Galliano is the new chief escort for the Galley to Flanders, which sails tonight. The Captain has an order from the Doge himself giving him priority over all other galleys.'

Despite the protests of the clerk, the two men went with Captain Carreras's bosun and he hurried them off to the Rialto, where the galleass was moored. Despite his predicament, Giam studied the great galley with interest as they came to the dockside. The Galley to Flanders was the longest voyage undertaken. Only new built great galleys were used, due to the arduous nature of the voyage. They were much larger than standard galleys.

Once on board the Galliano the bosun chained Giam and the other man, to an oar bench on the main deck of the galleass. He explained that it was a rule of the fleet that oarsmen must be chained whilst the galleass was in port, but that they would be unchained once they put to sea. He assigned them to an experienced oarsman who would show them the correct way to row.

'This is Alexius. Listen carefully to what he says.' he warned them. 'We'll be putting to sea as soon as the Captain comes on board so you'd better learn quickly, or it'll be the worse for you.' He strode away and left them to it and for the next hour, they were introduced to the tricks of using the oars without tangling. Three oars were assigned to each bench and only careful handling and rhythm could avoid a clash of oars. Giam sat on the bench and examined the oar, which was to be his workplace for three years. Although daunted by the prospect, he listened carefully to what the oarsman was saying. It could be vital to his survival.

The oar was about thirty-two feet long and he was told it weighed about 120 pounds. Each of the three oars passed through a separate outrigger built out over the side of the galleass.

'You're lucky,' said Alexius. 'These new oars are better counterbalanced than those on my last galley. They've weighted them with lead. The main trick is to make sure that we avoid obstructing each other. After that, it's simply a matter of getting used to the hard work. You're lucky to be in a galleass. We only have to row getting in and out of port, or if there's no wind. On a war galley, you row most of the time.'

During a moment's pause, Giam looked around at the three huge lateen sails, currently neatly furled on the long spars. He had been on a merchant cog and a war galley before, but never on a galleass. As far as he could tell, it was much wider than a galley, being about twenty-eight feet across and a lot higher out of the water. There was no more time to look around as Alexius made them practice some more. 'You'd better work hard to get the rhythm, or you'll be punished by the bosun. We're leaving port as soon as the Captain comes aboard.'

When the galleass finally put to sea, Giam, fit as he was, found the task of rowing physically overwhelming. He tried his best to get a rhythm as he'd been shown, but he was exhausted by the time they were told to rest.

He asked Alexius what was happening. 'They're hoisting the sails now we're clear of the city and we'll have a chance to rest'. Sure enough, the order came to ship the oars in-board and he slumped over it, as sailors unfurled the huge sails. Not long afterwards, the bosun came along and unchained all one hundred and twenty oarsmen. Motioning for Giam to follow him, he led him to a door in the stern. Cutting short Giam's questions with a curt reply, he hustled him to the door of a cabin and knocked. A curt voice answered and he motioned Giam forward. Following him into the cabin, he announced. 'Here's the oarsman sentenced to three years in the galleys, as you ordered, Captain.'

Giam stood blinking his eyes, adjusting them to the dim light after the glare on deck. The Captains cabin was by galley standards very spacious. A man in the uniform of a Captain came striding towards him and seizing Giam in a bear hug, he pounded his back unmercifully. 'Giam Bellini, you rogue, it's good to see you. Welcome on board the Galliano.'

Giam was stunned as his old friend Lunardo greeted him. Then Jean Thieré shook him by the hand and led him to a chair. Giam looked around the cabin. At the back, were the shrouded shapes of the two cannons. To the left of them, was a curtained alcove containing the Captain's bunk, whilst to the right was a musket rack, secured by a chain and padlock. A splendidly carved table with eight chairs dominated the centre of the cabin.

'Will someone please tell me what's going on? He said in bewilderment. 'What are you all doing here and where are we going?

Lunardo took pity on him. 'We are all here, partly by chance and partly by design,' he explained. 'Jean Thieré booked some shipping space on the Galliano, which is the main escort of the Galley to Flanders. When he was expelled post-haste from Venice, he was confined to the galleass until we took him back to England. You are here thanks to some excellent planning by your father and Senator Morisini.' He looked around at Jean. 'Will you do the honours with that excellent wine Jean, while I bring Giam up to date with what's been happening whilst he's been incarcerated.'

Giam sipped his wine and listened intently as Lunardo explained about the intense activity that had been going on behind the scenes. He asked a few questions, but mostly followed the events in silence. He realised how lucky he'd been to have so many people working hard on his behalf.

'Maria, what has happened to Maria? He asked anxiously. 'Is she all right?

Lunardo hesitated slightly and then told him she was well.

Giam was not deceived. 'I know you too well Lunardo, you're hiding something. Come on tell me what's happened.'

'She collapsed after you were sentenced to the galleys,' said Lunardo, 'but it was only a faint due to the stress of the trial,' he added quickly. 'Her father took her home and sent a message to say she was just overcome by the events at the trial, but would soon recover. He sends his respect and regards and also asked me to tell you that he would make sure she was safe until you returned.' He accepted a glass from Jean and took a sip.

'Don't worry my friend, Maria will be well looked after and I'm sure the faint is nothing to worry about.'

He motioned Giam to a chair and regarded him seriously. 'Now, to more pressing matters: I've arranged things so that you will be released from oarsman duties except at certain times. Unfortunately, I can't free you altogether, or it would be bad for the morale of the other men. They will be aware that you have a three year sentence and quite rightly, they would be very resentful if you are given too many privileges.' He grinned as Giam grimaced. 'I do have an idea that will give you a little more freedom. We are short of gunners and there is room to sleep in their quarters. As of now, I am transferring you under the orders of Carlos Basadona the master gunner. You will take instructions from him under all normal situations.'

Giam was grateful for small mercies in the circumstances. 'Thank you, Lunardo, although I suppose I ought to call you Captain from now on,' he said with a tired grin. 'I'll try to make sure that I don't cause you any trouble with the authorities because of our friendship.'

When finally he turned in to sleep, he slept soundly until the early hours of the morning. The furious motion of the galleass and the howling of the storm, which had suddenly sprung up, wakened him. The galleass was running before the wind with bare masts and a sea anchor deployed. Along with the other gunners he was rousted out to help secure the guns. It was dangerous work and by the time that Carlos was satisfied, they were all soaked and exhausted.

The storm raged unabated throughout the day and Giam feared that at any minute they'd be drowned as the ship pitched violently in the huge seas. Fortunately, the wind direction was not likely to drive them ashore for a long time, or so Carlos informed them. Giam thought this was only a small consolation for the way he felt; the motion of the ship was making him feel very ill.

By late evening on the following day, the storm abated a little, but the ship was still running before the wind. When dawn broke, to leaden skies and a heavy swell, there was no sign of any of the other ships of the convoy. With the wind now blowing more favourably, the galleass was able to hoist its sails and make some progress on its journey. Fortunately, the galleass had not sustained too much damage and the crew spent most of the next day making good.

In the late afternoon, Captain Carreras called a meeting in his cabin. Giam was told to attend with Carlos. When they were all assembled, Captain Carreras told them what he had discovered. 'I have been able to establish our position and we have been blown a long way off course. We are already south of our first port of call at Zara. It seems likely that the other galleasses will have been similarly affected and will head for Corfu. With the weather improving we should make good progress through the night. I hope to round the heel of Italy tomorrow morning; although we are too far west for my liking. I want the watch doubled and soundings taken every watch. At the first sign of shelving, I must be informed immediately. For now, I suggest you all get good night sleep and we'll continue this meeting in the morning.'

CHAPTER TWENTY

The following morning the weather was much calmer and the galleass, although forced to run close to the wind, was making good progress. The resumed meeting had only been in progress for a short while, when a lookout's call rang out.

'Deck ahoy. Four galleys off the port bow.'

'What ships are they?' queried the Watch Officer, shading his eyes as he scanned the horizon.

In his cabin the Captain awaited the answer with a feeling of inevitability.

'They look like Ottoman galleys, sir.'

'Damnation!' exclaimed Captain Carreras, as his fears were confirmed, and then with the others at his heels he hurried on deck

'This is the last thing we need.' he said as they reached the stern platform. 'I was hoping to get clean through the Straits of Messina without meeting any Ottoman patrols.' Looking up, he formed a trumpet with his cupped hands and shouted. 'What course do they steer?'

'They're turning to meet us, Captain.'

He cursed again then turned to Giam who was straining to catch a glimpse of the galleys. 'They'll probably think we're a merchant ship, separated from the summer fleet by the storm. No doubt, they're looking for some easy pickings. They tend to keep away from the great galleys in convoy, but they must feel that odds of four to one are in their favour.'

'Can't we outrun them?' said Giam. 'We must carry a lot more sail than the galleys.'

'Ottoman war galleys can out-sail us in some conditions and move faster under oars,' he replied. 'We carry far more weight than they do. There's not a chance we can outrun them. Our best speed is when the wind is almost directly behind us. The wind is in the wrong quarter for both of us. They're forced to use oars since its blowing across them,' he pointed to the headland that was just visible off the starboard bow, 'and we don't have enough sea room to get by that headland if we run with it. We can steer a course to clear the headland, but they will be able to cut us off before we reach the open sea.'

He pointed towards the galleys. 'They know we can't get away without a fight, but we may be able to surprise them. They don't know how well armed we are. They will be wary of the firepower of a galleass at close range, but the new cannons fitted by the Arsenale before we left, will give us an important edge if we can make it a running battle. Mind you,' he said ruefully, 'I would have preferred the odds to be a little more in our favour.'

Giam was intrigued. Although the galleass appeared to be well armed, taking on four galleys was another thing entirely. 'How good are these new cannons?' he asked. 'I've fired culverins, but they've only a range of about 200 yards. From what I hear, the Ottoman guns aren't any better. What difference will it make if we do have a running battle?'

Just then he noticed the sly expression on Lunardo's face. 'You've not told us everything, have you?' Giam accused. 'What's so special about these new cannons?'

The captain's smile became broader. 'I bought some English long guns last summer,' he said smugly. 'They're the best in the world. I've five of them in the bow and two more in the stern. The Ottoman won't have seen anything like them. They've an effective range of almost five hundred yards and can be reloaded quicker. They're more accurate than culverins at long range too and pack a greater punch. They can cripple a galley with one solid hit in the right place. In a running fight, we should be able to disable, or sink one or two of them before we're in range of their guns. What say you to that, Giam?'

'That'll still leave the odds against us. Is there anything else we can do?'

'Be of good cheer my friend, we've other advantages which I'll explain to you shortly,' Lunardo said.

Glancing across at the galleys, Giam was surprised to see how close they had come since the first sighting. 'How long will it be before they're in range? They seem to be closing on us rather quickly.'

'About twenty minutes if we stay on the present course I'd guess,' said the captain,' but I'm going to delay meeting them as long as possible. Go to my cabin now and I'll join you in a few minutes. We must plan our tactics. '

Turning to his officers he issued a stream of orders. 'Helmsman, steer a course as close to the wind as you can and keep angling away from the galleys, but watch your sea room. Lieutenant; clear the ship for battle, but don't run out the guns. We must play the merchantman a little while longer. Be ready to change course, but only on my command. Call me if there's any change in the situation, or if they close to within about a half a mile, I'm going below now; you have the deck.'

As the Captain strode away the Lieutenant turned, his orders ringing out crisply.

'Clear the decks for action! Man all battle stations! Gunners to their posts! Load all guns, but no guns to be run out.'

Springing to their places with the smoothness of long hours of practice the crew prepared the ship for battle.

In his cabin, the Captain held a council of war with Carlos his master gunner, the first mate, his two other officers and Giam. Without any preamble, he turned to Carlos and demanded, 'How are the guns, Carlos? Have we got enough trained men to man them?'

In his usual thoughtful way, Carlos pondered carefully before replying. 'Well sir, we're pretty good in most places. We can man all of the swivels, the seven sacres and the four half sacres. We've good men on the eight pedreros and the four culverins. It's the English long guns that are the problem, sir. I've only had time to train four crews so we're a gunner short since Antonio broke his leg. There wasn't time to find another gunner; we left in so much of a hurry.'

'We'll just have to use one of the best we've got in that case.'

155

said Captain Carreras grimly. 'Use your four best crews on the bow guns and leave the stern chasers unmanned. We can always send some crews back if we need to use them. What about a gunner and crew for the other long gun? Who do you suggest?'

Carlos scratched his head thoughtfully, 'My next best crews are on the bow culverins sir, they're good enough for close quarters, but if it comes to long range I can't see them doing too well, we need a gunner to lead them.'

There was a long pause. Then Captain Carreras turned to Giam. 'Those long guns are going to be vital to our plans. A little while ago, you said you had fired a culverin and you seemed to know a bit about them. This is no time for heroics, Giam, I have to be sure. Where on earth did you learn to use a culverin?'

'At the Arsenale with a Master gunner you will know, called Miguel Santini.'

'Miguel Santini, eh, he was a legend until he retired,' said Lunardo. 'What say you Carlos?'

'Miguel Santini, sir? He was the best. I served as one of his gunners on the summer convoys of sixty-three and sixty-four. As I recall we had quite a skirmish with pirates on the way home in sixty-four. It was after that he retired and recommended me as master gunner.'

'That's the man.' said Giam. 'He came to live on Murano. He earns his money by training gunners for the Arsenale. He made a bet with the Chief Armourer that he could train anyone to be a good gunner, even a nobleman. He knew my fencing tutor and before I really knew what was happening he was training me. He told me I wasn't too bad after I was lucky enough to beat the best two gunners from the Arsenale in a contest.'

Giam's droll account of how he came to be trained provoked laughter. Carlos in particular thought it was hilarious, but managed to stammer out a comment before he burst out laughing again.

'Not too bad eh, that sounds like Miguel all right and it's just like him to make a silly bet like that and win.' When he calmed down, he turned to Giam. 'If Miguel said that you were not too bad, you'll do for me. He was never one for praise. Said it made you over confident. Captain, I reckon he'll do the job better than most if Miguel Santini taught him.'

'Then it's settled,' replied Captain Carreras after a moment's thought. 'I heard about the contest from the Chief Armourer. I'd no idea it was you as he never mentioned a name, just that it was the son of a nobleman. Giam will man the other long gun then, but mind you Carlos,' he cautioned, 'he'll take your orders just like any other gunner. Now that we have the gun crews sorted, I must decide how best to use the long guns in the present circumstances.'

The galleass had evolved from the large merchant galleys and was essentially a floating gun platform, but much of its firepower was designed for use at close quarters. At close range, its many swivel guns could decimate the crew of a galley trying to board. It did have five culverins mounted on the bow platform and a couple of stern chasers located in the rear cabin used by the Captain. With its higher, stronger sides and fighting platforms at the bow and stern, plus the extra armaments, it was more than a match for any galley. The Galliano with its English long guns was an even more powerful opponent.

He sat down and looked round the table at the expectant faces. 'My friends,' he said solemnly, 'our options are very limited. We can't out - run them with sail; the wind is in the wrong quarter. We can't out - row them for all our superior numbers of oarsmen, the galleass is just too heavy and slow. The nearest clear beach for mooring up as a fixed gun platform is too far away. Which really only leaves us with one course of action, we must fight them; so this is what I propose. We'll steer away from the galleys as long as we can. This gives us time to prepare. When they're about seven hundred yards away we'll turn in towards them, run out the guns and at five hundred yards, all forward guns will fire as they bear.'

He paused for a moment and when there were no comments, he continued. 'As soon as the guns have fired we'll turn back to our original course, which will keep us well out of range of their culverins. In any case, they seldom fire at long range. Their usual tactic is to fire at point blank range using grapeshot. They try to kill as many of the crew as they can, before they board. They might try chain shot and try for the masts. We would be in real trouble then. With these odds, I think they will try to ram and board from both sides.'

Carlos and the other officers nodded their agreement and Captain Carreras continued. 'Were not going to give them the chance if all goes to plan, as soon as we've reloaded, we'll run out the guns, turn and fire again, but this time we'll only use three of the long guns. With any luck, the two volleys will put at least the two leading galleys out of action. We will repeat the tactic once more if we have the time before the others can get to close quarters.'

'Suppose we don't get the leading galley what then?' The First officer smiled weakly. 'Ah, the other long guns and the culverins: the lead galley will have to turn towards us, or he's in trouble. We'll try and out gun him at close range.'

'That's right,' said Captain Carreras, 'there'll be no choice if it comes to close quarters. We'd give him far too much advantage if we did anything else.'

He gave an emphatic gesture, 'Get the lead two galleys though and we'll be out of their trap. We can continue on our course and keep the other two galleys away with our stern chasers. With a steady wind behind us, they won't be able to keep up the oar speed. They'll be pushing very hard just to get into contact in the first place and will have little stamina, or stomach left for a long chase, especially when they realise we've got long guns in the stern as well. A few shots will soon convince them we can sink them at long range and make them sheer away. Are there any questions?' He said looking round the table. 'No? That's the plan then, gentleman, let's get to it.'

'God be with us.' said Carlos, crossing himself.

'Amen to that!' said the mate as they filed out on deck.

'It could be an interesting morning,' said Giam as he regarded the Ottoman galleys. 'They obviously seem to think that they have us in a trap. We'll have to teach them differently, wont we?'

Captain Carreras smiled. 'Quite right Giam; now off with you to your post and may God be with you.'

At the bows, Carlos went over the procedures with Giam. There was just time for one practice before a warning from the Lieutenant sent them hurrying to their places. Giam could see the galleys clearly. They were angling closer, their oars making twin parallel lines of white foam in their wake. As the galleass ploughed its steady path, Captain Carreras turned to the helmsman. 'How far away are they now helmsman?'

'About eight hundred yards I make it, sir.'

'Make ready to turn into them. All stations report in.'

'Bow guns primed and ready to run out,' reported Carlos.

'Standing by to repel boarders,' roared the bosun.

'Galleass ready for action,' said the first lieutenant calmly.

Captain Carreras drew his sword and held it high. All eyes turned towards him. 'Right lads give them a cheer and then show them how Venetians can fight. The crew let out a mighty roar and turned to their posts.

'Run out all forward guns. Prepare to go about. Now, Mister Helmsman, if you please.'

Hardly had the guns been manhandled forward the galleass sprang forward on to her new course. With the wind fully behind the sails her speed increased rapidly.

Giam stood ready on the second gun, next to Carlos. He turned to look for instructions.

'Don't forget to fire on the up roll Giam.'

All forward guns get ready to fire as you bear,' roared Carlos.

'On my command... FIRE!'

The guns roared one after the other in a rippling pattern and Giam was aware that his gun had fired slightly after he expected. The galleass had swung back on to her previous course, but Giam was busy urging his crew to sponge down, reload and run out ready to fire. Glancing across, he saw the Galliano was noticeably nearer the galleys. He could even pick out figures in the stern.

Giam's gun was the last to run out. Just then a rousing cheer came from Carlos, 'Well done lads, we got the second galley with two hits. It looks as though she's done for. I don't think that one will worry us any more. Now all guns get ready for the next turn.'

Above the noise he shouted to Giam again. 'I forgot to warn you; the long guns take a little longer to fire the primer. Touch on the up roll next time, not at the top of it. Right lads, guns three, four and five make ready to fire on my command.

Guns one and two and the other forward guns make ready in case we need to engage another target straight away. You all know what you have to do. Good shooting everyone.'

By the wheel Captain Carreras surveyed the scene. The galleys were now strung out in an untidy line. The ship hit during the first volley was straggling well behind and sinking by the stern. The fourth galley was also some way behind the other two and obviously feeling the pace.

The leading two galleys would soon be able to turn and engage. To spring the trap the galleass needed to sink, or cripple, both of these galleys. If one or both survived the volley, they would meet them at close quarters. No sooner was his analysis complete, than the wheelman gave a shout and the Captain gave the order to come about. To a cheer from the crew, the galleass responded.

In the bows, Giam stood by his gun while the gun crew crouched in their places, ready to reload. The atmosphere was tense and Giam tried to make a joke, 'I'll buy everyone a drink in the first tavern in Corfu after we've given the Ottomans a taste of our shot.' The crew grinned and Angelo, a veteran of many campaigns laughed and said, 'We'll hold you to that Giam.'

Hardly had he finished speaking when the ship swung on to her new course. The gunners crouched over their sights and waited anxiously for the order to fire. 'Steady now lads,' shouted Carlos as the ship's bow swung towards the galleys.

'Guns three, four and five on the up roll ...FIRE!'

Giam watched in fascination as the shots roared out. The first shot raised a large spout by the stern of the first galley, but the next two balls struck the second amidships with devastating effect. The galley was almost cut in two and started to sink immediately. Giam tore his eyes from this scene as he realised the implications. The leading galley had not been hit and now it was up to Carlos and himself, with the remaining forward guns to try to stop her.

The leading galley swung round to face her enemy. Not the helpless merchant they had thought to capture without much of a fight, but a deadly, dangerous aggressor. The relentless beat of the stroke man drove her oars to greater effort as she struggled to engage at close quarters.

Giam was shocked to see how near the galley had come. The glistening beak of the galleys ram bore down on him, the bows cleaving the waves as the galley drove forward at maximum speed.

Realising that he'd have to adjust his aim he turned to the gun crew, but before he could give any orders, Carlos shouted urgently above the noise,' On the down roll Giam. Fire on the down roll as you bear.'

Giam swung round again and squinted down the long barrel of the gun, willing the helmsman to swing to starboard so that he could get in a shot. Suddenly the galley changed course and Carlos's gun roared its message of death. The ball tore through the front platform causing little damage, and then screamed through the rear rank of rowers like a scythe through corn. Almost at the same instant, the galley's forward guns discharged their reply at less than fifty yards.

Giam threw himself down as the port bow castle disintegrated into bloody ruin and grapeshot whistled its deadly tune as it screamed through the rigging and sails of the galleass.

Springing to his post again, Giam saw the galley slipping away from his sights as its depleted oarsmen tried to bring it back on course. Before it was lost to view altogether, Giam fired and gave an exultant cry when he saw the stern platform of the galley shattered into matchwood by the heavy ball.

At that moment the air was rent as the Ottoman's other guns roared out their deadly message. Giam hurled himself down again as the front platform was pounded. Splinters flew everywhere and an involuntary cry was wrenched from him as a splinter slashed a bloody trail across his forehead.

There was a brief lull then the swivel guns of the galleass roared out their defiant reply. Wiping away the blood from his eyes with his hand he sprang to his feet to give the order to repel boarders. A scene of destruction met his horrified gaze. Angelo lay half across the gun carriage with a huge splinter in his side and two others lay dead with terrible injuries.

Stunned by the swift change in fortune, but realising that there might be boarders any moment, he leapt to help his team. As he reached Angelo there was a resounding crash from behind him.

Turning to see what it was he saw the forward mast sheer away and tumble towards him in a tangle of trailing shrouds. Cursing, he tried desperately to lift Angelo, but just as he lifted him away from the gun carriage, the mast fell across it and he was smashed down into oblivion.

PART TWO

LONDON 1567 – 1569

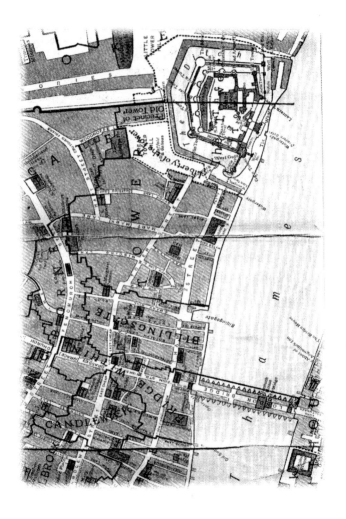

CHAPTER TWENTY-ONE

'Near twelve o' clock of a fine summer's night; give ear to the clock; beware your lock, your fire and your light and God give you good night. Near twelve o'clock, Goodnight.'

The night watchman's voice rang out in the quiet streets of the Great City of London, a city of almost two hundred and fifty thousand inhabitants in this year of fifteen hundred and sixty-seven. Throughout the night, he trudged the streets of his beat, passing through Barnard Castle, via Carter Lane and Paul's Wharf Hill. Little light shone there, for few people bothered to light a lamp by their door. Those that were lit cast only a small glow from their single candle on to the street below. The light from the watchman's lantern did little to help and at times, he stumbled on the stinking debris of daily life cast unceremoniously into the centre of the street from the overhangs above.

Turning now into Thames Street he passed Bygot House and carried on until he reached Salt Wharf. As he turned north along Trinity Lane, he passed the splendours of Cornwall House without a single glance and his weary cry was heard. 'Past three o'clock of a fine summer's morning and all's well.' Plodding on with only the silent shutters to note his passing he huddled down into his collar and thought longingly of his lodgings in Hosier Lane, near the market at Smithfield.

Finally, he found himself in Bread Street and so into West Cheape. Here the bustling activity of the bakers and the aromatic smell of fresh baked bread made him feel much more cheerful. 'Near five o'clock of a fine summer's morning and all's well.' His voice rang out and his lively step showed that his duty was nearly finished.

About this time, a new sound was to be heard as the metallic tongue of one of London's many churches started its clanging clatter to herald another day. Soon others joined in, swelling the noise, until all of London was filled with their clamorous voices making sleep impossible. There were nearly a hundred churches crammed within the City walls and as the sound of their sonorous song increased, the watchman quickened his pace again. He hurried past St. Paul's, massing hugely against the brightening sky, heading towards the postern gate at Ludgate; he was finished for the night and could hand in his halberd and lantern.

Some way to the east in Candlewick Street, Giam was abruptly awakened from his fitful slumber by the unfamiliar noise. He sat up, his heart beating wildly, pain lancing through his head. Confused by the sound of the bells and still drugged with sleep, he imagined he could hear again the pounding of fists on the door and the dreaded cry of, 'Open in the name of the Council.'

Sitting up in bed with a start, he shook his aching head to clear the ringing noise in his ears. With a wry smile, he laughed ruefully as he realised the source of his alarm. What a fool I am he thought, the noise is church bells and I'm not in Venice, I'm in London. I suppose I ought to be grateful I can still hear the bells he mused to himself. Considering I am supposed to be dead, that is.

He felt his arms and chest and then pinched his arm and winced. Well, I seem to have plenty of feeling for a corpse; perhaps there's hope for me yet. Before he could continue with this rather macabre line of thought, there was a knock on the door.

'Are you awake Giam? I've brought you some clothes.'

Giam considered the question carefully for a moment and then deciding he really was awake after all, invited the visitor in. Sitting up in bed, he surveyed his friend with a smile. 'I thought it was you Lunardo, although I'm having a little difficulty deciding what's real and what isn't at the moment. It's like being on the galley and calling you Captain Carreras. I found that very strange.' He grimaced as a nearby church added its bell to the noise. 'I must say though, those church bells don't let you sleep very well.'

'There are rather a lot of them,' Lunardo chuckled. 'The one that's just started is Saint Swithin's, I believe. It's just across the road. In fact I believe there are over a hundred churches within the city walls so they do make a lot of noise. They seem to compete with each other to see who can be the loudest.' He put the clothes down on a chair and sat down on the end of the bed and studied his friend.

'I'm glad to see you're looking better Giam. The crack you received from the mast all but killed you and it really was touch and go for a time. Mind you, it provided a very good reason for your official demise.'

Giam shook his head as this information finally sank in. He remembered discussing about playing dead, but the details were a bit vague. He was having difficulty sorting out what was real and what was a dream. He'd had so many nightmares recently it was difficult to separate fact from fiction.

'Was I badly hurt by the mast, Lunardo?'

'You were covered in blood from a deep wound on the back of your head that was the most serious. A splinter wound on the forehead looked worse than it was and a lot of the blood on your body was from the gunner you tried to save. Those who saw you after the mast was cleared away weren't surprised to hear that you'd died from your injuries.'

Giam saw in his mind the torn body he'd been trying to move when the mast fell and shuddered at the image.

Lunardo noted his reaction. 'I'm afraid Angelo died from his wounds shortly after we pulled you out. As for you, your head wound was bad enough. Fortunately you have a hard head, but you caught a fever and were delirious for almost three weeks. It looked at one point as though you would die. It was touch and go, but once the fever broke, you started to recover, but very slowly. You slept a lot and although you had periods of lucidity, you were also delirious quite a lot of the time until we got to Palermo.'

'Palermo? I seem to remember we were going to Corfu.'

'We couldn't make Corfu because of the prevailing winds and the damage to the foremast, so we headed through the Straits of

Messina. We made our repairs at Palermo and the rest of the convoy caught up with us there.'

Giam tried hard, but he couldn't remember any of it. He had a vague picture of someone by his bedside cooling his forehead and feeding him some broth, but everything else was simply flashes of conversation and faces peering down at him.

'Whose idea was it for me to die and stay in London?' He had a shrewd suspicion.

Lunardo confirmed his guess. 'It was Jean Thieré who first suggested it and then we discussed it with you. You were having one of your lucid times.'

Giam nodded slowly. 'I have a vague recollection, but I suppose it was for the best,' he said doubtfully.

At the time it had seemed, to be the best solution to his situation. Even if he had completed his sentence he would not be able to resume his place as Fattori of Luciano's; the Council of Ten would never allow it. This way he could make a new life for himself in London, with nobody the wiser and no assassins coming to haunt him.

He regarded Lunardo with a quizzical expression. 'Was it difficult convincing the crew that I was dead?'

'Seeing you when we dragged you out from under the mast, it didn't surprise anyone when we announced you had died,' said Lunardo. 'We lost five men altogether in the galley fight and your 'body' was switched using sacks of ballast sand. Those that know have been sworn to secrecy and you can trust them.'

'I can't say I was pleased at first,' said Giam, 'but I can see the sense of it now. There is nothing left for me in Venice; that accursed Ragazoni has seen to that. Rest assured of one thing though, I'll be revenged on Adrian Ragazoni. You have my solemn promise on that. For now I'll bide my time, but he'll rue the day he worked his evil tricks on me and the people I care about most.'

He turned away for a moment deep in thought. Then coming to a decision, he squared his shoulders, turned and regarded Lunardo with a quizzical smile. 'What now my friend? I think it's time I took control of my life again. Where do we begin? Any ideas?'

'I have more than ideas Giam. While you were sleeping last night, Jean Thieré and I had a long talk. As you know, Thieré wants you to run his Glass-works here in London. It's up near the Tower of London.'

'The Tower of London? Hmm, I seem to remember Jean Thieré telling me about it.'

'The Tower's the place where the traitors and major criminals are imprisoned, tortured and have other diabolical things done to them. It has quite a nasty reputation, which however, does not do it justice at all. I'd recommend you keep well away from the Tower and its torturers and other delights.'

Giam shuddered. 'I remember now and you can be sure I'll take your advice. It sounds like a place to avoid.'

'It certainly is, but as I was saying before you asked for the guided tour of the Tower, Jean Thieré wants you to take charge of his Glass-works and that's exactly what I think you should do. When I get back to Venice with the rest of the convoy, I will report your heroic demise to the authorities with a graphic account of how you saved the galleass and died trying to save another crewmember. That's near enough to the truth, except the dying part of course. It will go down well with the authorities.'

'You'll let Maria and my father know the truth though, won't you?' said Giam with concern. Seeing the others hesitation, he pressed the point emphatically.

'You must tell them. They'll suffer if you don't.'

Lunardo shook his heads sadly. 'I know it'll be hard, but it's too dangerous for them to know. They would give the game away to Ragazoni. He's sure to try and find out from them and he'll have the assassins on your trail in a flash if he's not convinced.' He looked sadly at his friend and shook his head in sorrow. 'Not only that, but he'll be able to use your family to get back at you. They could be imprisoned, or worse, if you didn't give yourself up. No Giam, they can't be told at first. Perhaps in a few months it will be safe. You'll have to trust me to decide. I promise you, I'll let them know as soon as it's safe to do so.'

Saddened by the distress he was causing, Lunardo nevertheless continued with his argument. 'I know it's hard my friend, but your family is very vulnerable. That swine Ragazoni would not hesitate to use them if he had any inkling that you're alive.'

Giam, distraught at the thought of the anguish he would cause, considered this advice for some time before replying. He tried to escape the logic of his friend's words, but he was well aware of how far Ragazoni would go if he knew he was alive and free. The Council of Ten would also use his family to force him back, so there wasn't any real option.

Lunardo tried to reassure him it wouldn't be for long, but they both knew it could well be a very long time. Eventually, with many misgivings, he was persuaded that they couldn't be told.

'I know you're not happy with this Giam, but it is for the best. There's something else too. We think that you should adopt a new name. Giam Bellini is too well known to anyone from Venice.'

Jacob was horrified. 'It's a lot to ask Lunardo,' he cried. 'I'm giving up so much already. Is it really necessary?'

'I wouldn't have suggested otherwise. You're too good a glassmaker to remain anonymous and if good quality glass is made in London with the name Giacomo Bellini attached, it will soon get to the ears of Venice.'

Giam realised at once that this was true. He wouldn't be content to make poor quality glass. Sooner, or later, he would make the sort of glass that would come to the attention of Venice. There were plenty of good glassmakers in Europe and different name would have no connection with Giacomo Bellini. Much as he disliked the idea, it was probably for the best. Giam sighed. It was time to let the past go and make a new life in London. He was not sure how he was going to forget Maria, but perhaps if he threw himself headlong into work, who knows!

Taking a deep breath, and then letting it out audibly, he stood up straight. 'You're right Lunardo. Let's decide on a new name.

Any suggestions?'

'Well, I believe the English equivalent of Giacomo is Jacob. As for Bellini,' he thought for a moment and then grinned as another church bell started its clamour. Perhaps the bells are giving you a message. How do you feel about the name Jacob Bell?'

'Jacob Bell, hmm.' Giam said the words a few times in his mind, comparing it with Giam Bellini. He looked at Lunardo who had been studying him in silence and gave a lopsided grin. 'I suppose Jacob Bell has a ring to it, so Jacob Bell I will be.'

CHAPTER TWENTY-TWO

While Jacob dressed, Lunardo chatted away about London. Jacob was not happy with the clothes. The doublet and hose in browns and gold were much more colourful than those he usually wore, but Lunardo assured him that for London, they were quite subdued. Jacob felt uneasy when he saw his reflection in the mirror. He only had one set of clothes on the galley and they were buried at sea, so these would have to do. 'They must dress like peacocks if these aren't bright. It'll be interesting to see what people are wearing,' said Jacob. 'Where are we going?'

'We'll not be going to the fashionable places today I am afraid, Jacob. The Crouched Friars is at the top of Tower Hill and I'll be taking you along the back ways. It's fortunate I know London quite well.'

He explained that the previous year, on leaving Plymouth, the first port of call in England, the Galliano had been caught in a storm on the way to London and considerable damage was done to the spars and superstructure. Forced to refit at London docks, they found that there were none of the standard parts that typified the Arsenale in Venice. All of the spars, rigging and replacements had to be made specially. It was almost eight weeks before we were ready to leave. Lunardo had spent his enforced spare time exploring London's streets and alleyways.

'This time, with the galleass still in port, some of the crew will be out on the Town, although I don't suppose for one minute that anyone would recognise you,' Lunardo grinned and stroked his chin. 'Especially with that beard you've grown over the last few weeks.'

'I've not decided whether to keep it yet,' said Jacob. 'There do seem to be more people with beards here, than in Murano.' He stood in front of the mirror and studied his reflection. 'What do you think,' he said turning around.

172

'I don't think you'd be recognised by any of the crew. They'll not expect a corpse to be walking about, in clothes like these,' he said. As for the beard, if you must keep it, at least have it trimmed. You look like a hermit.' He smiled as Jacob tried on the matching bonnet and pulled it down at a rakish angle. 'It's better to err on the side of caution though. Let's go down and eat and then we'll go and meet Jean Thieré at his Glass-works.'

The meal consisted of some fresh bread, honey and a large joint of carving ham. It was washed down with a pewter tankard full of ale, which Jacob found to be strong and rather bitter to his taste. Once he started eating, he was amazed how hungry he was. Eventually he sat back with a sigh and suggested they should get on their way.

Stepping out into the street, the hustle and bustle and the noisy cries of the apprentices as they advertised their wares startled Jacob. People were hurrying along the crowded narrow streets with little time for others. A short distance above, the overhangs from the buildings on each side nearly touched each other in the centre of the street and people were hanging out of windows and carrying on noisy conversations across the street, or with others below, while the occasional cart lumbering through the streets was a danger to all.

'Watch out for your purse Giam,' came the warning from Lunardo. 'There are a lot of rogues and cutpurses about.' Then a servant emptied a pot into the street ahead of them and he smiled. 'You'd better watch your head as well. The servants are not fussy what they throw into the street; you might get the contents of a chamber pot on your head.'

Jacob kept a wary eye above him after that comment. He kept his hand on his sword too as they joined the milling crowds. Outside every shop, the apprentices were calling out their wares, trying to attract people in.

'What do you lack Gentles, what do you lack? A watch Sir! To run as long as a Lawsuit, Sir! Be as steady and true as your own eloquent self, Sir! A watch Sir! That shall not lose thirteen minutes in thirteen years span, Sir! What do you lack gentles?'

As they turned the corner into yet another busy street, they were forced to take shelter in a doorway while a cart laden with vegetables lumbered past, with very little room to spare. No sooner had it passed than the cries started again.

'What do you lack Mistris? Mirrors for your toilet pretty lady!'

'What do you lack Sir? Clocks watches or Barnacles! What do you lack Sir?'

'Buy Rue! Buy Sage! Buy Mint! All fresh! All fresh!'

The sights and sounds of London smote his ears every bit as forcibly as the bells had done earlier. After his recent illness, he found it hard to cope with the constant jostling and the noise.

Lunardo linked arms with him and assured him it would get quieter soon. Sure enough, when they turned the next corner, it was into a quiet lane with only a few people about. 'It's a bit overwhelming at times Jacob. I found the same last year until I became used to it. It's not a lot like Murano, is it?'

Jacob smiled at the thought. 'Not really, the streets in Murano get crowded, but not like this. I suppose I'll get used to it in time, but I'll miss being able to take a gondola though.'

'There is always the River Thames, Jacob. It's used a lot and they have a sort of two-oared rowing boat, called a wherry. I went on one once from London to Greenwich. It was with the tide, so they only charged me six of their pence,' he smiled. 'It would have been twelve against the tide.'

Just then, they passed a large imposing town house and Lunardo pointed it out to him. 'Walsingham the Spy catcher lives there, or so I'm told. He is really the assistant to William Cecil the Queen's Secretary, but he acts as his eyes and ears. London's full of spies of one sort or another so they say.'

In fifteen hundred and fifty-eight when Queen Elizabeth ascended the throne of England, she was beset by religious problems. Her predecessor and sister, Mary Tudor was Catholic, but Elizabeth herself was Protestant like her father Henry VIII. After Mary married Philip of Spain, the Protestants were persecuted and the Inquisition burnt many at the stake. Elizabeth survived, despite indictment and ruthless questioning, thanks to her intelligence and will to survive.

Her own attitude to religion was much more liberal and involved none of the excesses of her predecessor. The Catholics declared the marriage of her mother Anne Boleyn, to King Henry VIII to be void. The Pope had never ratified his divorce from Catherine of Aragon. The Catholics regarded Elizabeth as illegitimate and the daughter of Mary of Guise, now Queen Mary of Scotland, was declared to be the rightful Queen of England. Despite Elizabeth's liberal attitude to religion, Catholic nobles such as the Duke of Norfolk were striving to put Mary Queen of Scots on the English throne, aided and abetted by the Spanish and French. Mary Stuart would always be a catalyst for plots against Elizabeth and her main advisors Cecil and Walsingham were in favour of a permanent solution to the problem.

Jacob was unaware of this as the two of them made their way through the streets. Turning a corner, Lunardo said they were nearly at the Glass-works. A short distance along Harte Street they came to a large gate in a massive wall. Lunardo explained that the Glass-works was built in part of a monastery once belonging to the Crouched Friar Order, disbanded during the Reformation carried out by King Henry Tudor. 'Jean Thiéré has his Glass-works in what used to be the refectory and there's also a place to play the game they call Tennis in the grounds.'

Jacob was puzzled. 'Tennis, what's that? I've never heard of it.'

Lunardo smiled broadly. 'I wouldn't worry about it Jacob, the English are always playing some game, or other that no one else has heard about. Although I believe that King Henry was keen on this one and that the Queen herself sometimes plays.'

As they passed into the courtyard the first thing Jacob noticed were the billets of wood stacked in neat rows against the walls of the building. There was a huge stack; much more than they kept at Luciano's. Jacob questioned why there were so many.

'I don't know too much about them, but I believe Jean keeps a large stock because many of the local woods are now exhausted. He told me he has to bring them in from some considerable distance.'

'It was the same in Murano except we had to bring the wood in by boat. At least they don't have that problem.'

'I wouldn't be too sure of that Jacob, a lot of the supplies for London come in boats on the River Thames. It's a very busy waterway.'

Just then, Jean Thiéré appeared and shook Jacob's hand vigorously then with arms spread wide said, 'Why are we standing out here talking? Come along into the Glass-works and I'll show you around. We can go to my office afterwards, there's so much we need to discuss.'

The tour of the Glass-works didn't take too long and soon they were sitting in the office. Lunardo explained about the new name for Giam and Jean agreed it was the most sensible course of action.

'What are your first impressions Giam, or rather Jacob, I'll have to watch my tongue on that one,' said Jean Thiéré eagerly.

Jacob hesitated. In truth, he was very disappointed by the Glass-works. There was a general air of slackness about the place and none of the ordered activity he was used to in Murano. The furnace too was very poor. It had originally been used for making window glass and was unsuited for producing fine glassware. His heart sank. He was giving up everything for this!

Seeing that Jean Thiéré was looking increasingly alarmed at his silence, he decided he must explain. 'I'm sorry Jean, but I can't hide how I feel. Your Glass-works is a shambles!' He struggled to find the right words to describe his feelings. 'You told me that it wasn't working well and I can see that is true. Your furnace is poor and the men have, what seems to me, to be a 'couldn't care less' attitude.' He smiled grimly as Jean gave a grimace. 'I will tell you what I feel must happen in the long term, and then you must tell me if you still want me to do it.'

'Go ahead, Jacob. Tell me the worst.'

'Very well. The furnace will need to be replaced, sooner rather than later. It's only suitable for making window glass. I would like to have a furnace like those commonly in use in Murano. Without seeing this one when it's cool, I can't be sure, but I think it might be possible to convert it.'

Jacob had in mind a modification of the standard type of furnace used in Murano. 'Make no mistake, Jean,' he warned. 'Converting the existing furnace will not be cheap, but if you want to make good stemware, it must be done.'

'What else?'

'I will try to train your men,' Jacob said. 'But my first impression about their attitude makes me feel that they will never be suitable. Good glassmakers care about the glass. It is a matter of pride that they produce the very best of their capability. Your people have none of this. They expect little and give little. If I am correct and that is the case, they must be replaced.'

He sighed. 'I just wish that Roberto was here. He is very good with people and would be invaluable with the customers. He'd be able to look after the every-day side and leave me free to sort out these problems and train the men properly. Ah well, it's a nice thought, but not possible.'

Before he could continue, Jean interrupted excitedly. 'I'm glad you brought that up Jacob,' he said. 'Why couldn't Roberto come here?'

Lunardo joined in enthusiastically. 'Yes Jacob, why couldn't he,' he said. 'I could take a message for you. I'd have to explain about your supposed demise, of course. And he'd have to be sworn to secrecy, but I can't see that would be a problem. What do you think? Do you think he'd come?'

Jacob began to warm to the idea. Inviting Roberto to England to work at the Crouched Friars would help him such a lot, both in the Glass-works and on a personal level. It would be difficult for the lad. Jacob's secret would need to be kept from everyone. It was asking a lot of him to leave everything he knew to follow Jacob into exile. He mulled over the idea. Am I just being selfish he thought? I promised I'd never take advantage of Roberto's hero worship.

For the next hour there was an animated discussion as they went through all the reasons for and against inviting Roberto. At last they were agreed. Lunardo would take a letter from Jean offering Roberto the chance to be involved in building up the Crouched Friars. Nothing would be mentioned about Jacob in the letter, but Lunardo would explain everything in private and swear him to secrecy. If he agreed to come, Lunardo would give Roberto sufficient money, provided by Jean, to buy passage to London on the fastest available vessel.

Two days later, Lunardo sailed for France and then home to Venice. Jacob would have liked to have seen him off, but there was too much possibility that he would be recognised. All Jacob could do now was to immerse himself in sorting out the Crouched Friars and to wait for news.

CHAPTER TWENTY-THREE

Some months later, Jacob was seated in a comfortable chair in the living room of Jean Thieré's house in Harte Street. It was evening and the room was full of flickering shadows from the log fire, which glowed brightly in the large fireplace. As he sat watching the bright sparks from the burning logs fly up the chimney, Jacob was reminded of the evening view in Murano as the furnaces sent sparks rising into the evening sky.

His face grew sad as he thought of Murano and all the people he'd left behind. This was the first time he'd allowed himself to dwell on them, preferring to immerse himself in the problems of the Crouched Friars Glass-works.

Before he could become too maudlin, the door opened and Roberto came in carrying a tray with three tankards. 'I've brought you a tankard of mulled wine Master Jacob; it's just the thing for relaxing you after a hard days work. Jean Thieré will join us directly and he wants to have a discussion.'

'Thank you Roberto,' said Jacob taking a tankard. 'You've come just in time to stop me brooding about home. I've not allowed myself to think too much about it since I decided to stay in London; it was too painful. I suppose it was the news from Lunardo that set me off. You've read his letter, what do you think about it?'

'I think that things are as well as could be hoped for. Your father seems to be holding up well, but I wish I could have let Lady Maria into the secret before I left. She took it so badly when I told her about going to London. It was if she was losing her last link with you. I'm not sure my mother understood either.'

'I wish I hadn't asked you Roberto,' said Jacob sadly. 'It was selfish of me.'

'You mustn't think that Master Jacob, once I knew you were alive, nothing would have stopped me coming.' He gave Jacob a long look. 'I know the news from Murano is distressing, but as for my part, I'm here, because I want to be, so I think we ought to leave it at that, Master Jacob.'

Jacob nodded in agreement and sipped his mulled wine in silence. He wished that the people close to him had been told he was alive, but Lunardo was still advising against it. He wouldn't keep it from them for a minute longer than necessary.

Just then, Jean Thiéré entered the room and drawing up a chair, took the proffered tankard with a sigh of contentment. 'I do enjoy evenings like this.' he said sipping his drink. 'I miss the boulevards of Paris, but I've grown to like my home here in London and the company of good friends.'

He raised his tankard in salute. 'To my very good friends,' he toasted and took a long drink. With a sigh of contentment, he put down the tankard and regarded them both. 'And now to business: as you know, I've been having discussions with William Cecil about obtaining Letters Patent for Glassmaking. He tells me that the Queen is very keen to encourage the right sort of enterprise, but the Council hasn't made a decision as yet.'

He took another long sip at his wine before continuing. 'I'm assured by Cecil that he favours our case, but he's warned me that the Glass-Sellers Guild is trying to get the Letters Patent for themselves. Not that they have the means, or the skill to make the glass. They simply want to import it from Antwerp, or Murano, and take the profits. The Queen is very much in favour of the glass being made in England and that is to our advantage. What say you to that my friends?'

Jacob was sure that Jean was right. Three weeks ago, Jean had taken him along to St Paul's Cross and introduced him to its wonderful source of gossip about the Court and London business. Several thousand people attended the sermons on Sundays and Holy days. If you were one of the great and the good, you had a seat in the covered galleries built on the exterior wall of the north transept and the choir of the huge Norman Cathedral looking down on the preacher who stood in the ground level pulpit.

Otherwise, you stood, or squashed together on the wooden benches in the space between the pulpit and the cathedral walls. It was a great occasion for everyone. Women would check on the latest fashions worn by the ladies of the nobility and merchants who occupied the galleries; men would exchange the latest commercial and other gossip in undertones.

Jean introduced Jacob to some of the other merchants and they were delighted to bring him up to date with all the latest news in the business life of London. There was often discrepancy between the stories. Jean had warned him not to believe all he heard, but to see which people were the most reliable. He listened a lot and soon began to sort fact from fiction. The sermon itself was often the provider of the official government line on matters of state and almost always the latest report on current affairs.

The news on everyone's lips was the return of John Hawkins from his voyage to Nombre de Dios and the gross betrayal by the Spaniards who had broken a signed contract not to attack Hawkins in return for letting them into the harbour during a violent storm. Anti-Spanish feeling was running high, as the tale was spread about. Government opposition to Catholicism was constantly hammered home.

Despite the length of the service, which often ran to more than two hours, Jacob enjoyed the exchange of views with the other merchants. One thing was very plain to him. England was a rapidly expanding power in the world, but suffered from a lack of a good manufacturing base except in the field of textiles. The Queen and her ministers were trying to alter this by encouraging manufacturers to train native English workers in new skills. He was sure that a manufacturer was more likely to find favour over someone wanting to import goods from manufacturers overseas; especially if he was employing English workers.

'I think you're right Jean. If we can make a really strong case, we might be able to get the sole rights to make and import glass in England.'

'What about these Glass sellers?' retorted Roberto? 'I can't see them being very happy with that situation; especially if they're not allowed to import Façon de Venice.'

Jean nodded in agreement. 'You're quite right Roberto. They have good contacts in court and are sure to know I'm trying to get the Letters Patent. They've already made one offer to buy me out. That's what I want to talk to you about. But before I tell you what is on my mind, I think another glass of this excellent mulled wine is in order. Will you do the honours please Roberto.'

As Roberto busied himself replenishing the glasses, Jacob mischievously suggested that Jean was getting too fond of mulled wine and that the French usually regarded it as sacrilege to add anything to their wine.

'Not at all, my friend, last week it was you who had too much. As for French wine, there's nothing to compare with it.'

After these pleasantries, Jean began to explain. 'What I am about to say to you is not simply on the spur of the moment.' He paused to take a drink of wine then continued. 'About five years ago I was living in Antwerp and running an import/export business, part of which was selling Venetian style glass to England. Despite the restrictions put on them by Venice, quite a large number of Venetians are working in the glass business in that city.'

'I know about them and I've an idea to put to you,' Jacob replied. 'However, since you obviously have more to discuss, it can wait until you've finished.'

Jean nodded. 'I was married at that time and had a six year old son. There was an accident on a coach ride and both of them were killed. There was nothing left for me in Antwerp so I decided to come to England. I knew that the Crouched Friars Glass-works was up for sale, so I sold my estate in Antwerp and here I am.'

He brushed aside the commiserations. 'Thank you for your concern, but life has to go on, as Jacob knows only too well. I don't want to sell the Crouched Friars, so I have the following proposition for you.' He drained his glass in one swallow then leaned forward, speaking quickly and excitedly, with many accompanying gestures. 'I want you to be my partner Jacob and if you agree, I would like

Roberto to become a junior partner.' He smiled at the stunned expressions on their faces. 'I will look after the sales side and imports/exports; Jacob will run the Glass-works and handle all technical matters. Roberto will do the same job he did at Luciano's. I know he's young, but in the short time he's been here, the Crouched Friars has improved a lot.' He looked anxiously at them.

'What do you think? Will you join me as partners? I can't think of a better combination of talents to run a Glass-works, so what do you say?'

There could only be one answer to such a generous offer and first Jacob and then Roberto stammered out their thanks and accepted with gratitude. After they had embraced each other warmly and toasted the success of the new partnership, Jean enquired about the idea that Jacob had mentioned earlier.

Jacob hesitated before he began. 'I hope you'll not think me ungenerous Jean, when I say your French workers are not up to the task of working in a good Glass-works. They've improved, but they don't have the skills, or the right attitude to help us make it a success.'

'I'm sad to say this, but I'm afraid you're right,' said Jean with a deep sigh. 'My fellow countrymen have been a big disappointment. What did you have in mind?'

'You mentioned earlier about the Venetian glassmakers in Antwerp. I hear that a lot of people in Antwerp are very worried that the Spanish will attack the Huguenots. A number of artisans have already fled to other countries including England. I'd like to see if we can get about ten good glassmakers, to come to England to make Façon de Venice glass.'

There was excited approval for this idea and Jacob explained how he would organise them. 'I'd like to see them working three chairs, with a fourth for myself. I would also suggest we take on three, or four English workers, and train them to make good glass. This I believe would go down well with the Queen and her advisors and help our efforts to secure the Letters Patent.'

'That's an excellent idea Jacob,' said Jean enthusiastically. 'I'll

183

arrange a trip to Antwerp as soon as possible and we must also see about recruiting the Englishmen. We might even pick up some that have worked in a Glass-works. There used to be several in the City, but they've all closed down, or moved away to where they can get a supply of beech wood for the furnaces. I was lucky to have a good source and a very healthy stock.'

'It's still a serious problem though,' said Jacob. 'If anything should happen to the stock, or our supplies dry up, we'd be in a difficult position.'

'I couldn't agree more and I'm pleased to say that I think I may have found a new supply. It will mean quite heavy cartage costs, but providing we get the Letters Patent, it will not be a problem. Should we not get them, it won't matter a great deal, as we won't have a business.' On that rather sombre note, the meeting ended and they retired to bed.

By the end of January, the Glass-works was ready for its reopening with its new staff. The furnace too was new. Fortunately, Jean had been able to obtain a copy of Giorgii Agricola's book *De Re Metallica,* in which there was a detailed drawing of the three-tier furnace widely used in Murano. Because there were no restrictions as in Murano, Jacob had increased the number of openings in the wall of the middle chamber of the three, to six instead of four. This would enable more chairs to work without getting in each other's way. He had often wished they had been allowed to do it at the Luciano Glass-works, but the Matricola specified four, so four it had to be. Luckily they had been able to modify the old furnace, but it had still been an expensive and time-consuming exercise.

There had been little difficulty in recruiting the Venetian workers from Antwerp. They were all delighted to get away from the city and its looming religious crisis. Finding four suitable recruits from the English workers proved to be much more difficult. Jacob interviewed dozens and rejected them all. One evening a few days later, he went to the Three Stars Tavern with Jean, for a drink after work. Getting into conversation with one of the men on the next table, he discovered that all three of them had worked in a Glass-works, which had left the area to set up in Norfolk. He invited them to come to the Crouched Friars the following morning.

None of them possessed the right skills having worked on window and bottle glass, but Jacob had expected that. So long as they were keen to learn, that was what mattered. 'I'll expect you to learn the right way to make glass,' he warned them, 'the Murano way. It's the best in the world. You'll have to work very hard just to learn the basic skills of the Venetians coming from Antwerp next week. I'll expect you to learn everything about glass blowing. You won't get a chance to make a complete glass, until you've learned all the jobs of the 'chair'.

He paused to see how his message was being understood. 'You must start by doing the menial tasks for the others then you'll be given the chance to learn each part of the job. By showing you can master these; you will have the opportunity to learn more. If you're lazy and don't bother to learn, you will be sent away for good. There'll be no second chance! I will oversee your progress and I alone will decide when you're ready to progress. And remember this, only the best is good enough.'

Having laid out the main rules, he relaxed and smiled warmly at them. 'One more thing, I don't expect you to be perfect, and you will all make mistakes. You will not be judged on your mistakes, but on how well you learn from them. I started the same way in Murano. Do you all understand?'

They all agreed that he'd been most fair and that they wanted to work for him. Jacob thanked them all and agreed an annual wage of twelve pounds. This sent them away in delight, for it was more than any of them had ever earned. Jacob had deliberately made it high to motivate them even more. In any case Jean had agreed fifteen pounds for the Venetian's and the presence of the English workers should help in the quest for the Letters Patent. It would be worth every penny if their presence helped them to this goal.

In the following weeks, Jacob's intuition proved to be right. The Glass-works was working well and there was a real sense of teamwork and pride in producing glass of a high standard. The English workers were doing well and had even found another former work-mate of theirs to fill the other vacancy.

One thing that the partners had agreed was that they should not make Jacob's Cristallo transparente. It was too distinctive and certain to be reported to Murano, sooner or later. They would know only one man could have made it. Instead they concentrated on making the standard Façon de Venice glass that was also being produced in Antwerp, although they arranged to sieve the soda to make the metal purer.

Within a few weeks, the Glass-works was working well and starting to produce a profit. Jean was delighted with the progress they had made and was busy lobbying at Court. After yet another visit to see Sir William Cecil he was in very high spirits when he returned. 'I'm certain we have a very good chance now,' he confided to Jacob and Roberto that evening.

'Cecil has suggested we produce some glasses for the Queen and he'll see that she's aware they've been made in London with the help of English workers. The donation will be made under the name of 'Mr West' to avoid any suggestion later that we made a bribe. The Queen will be told who 'Mr West' is in reality. What do you think of that?'

Jacob felt sure it would be better to send them in the name of the Crouched Friars Glass-works, but if Sir William Cecil felt that secrecy was necessary they would have to take his advice. He was more worried about making the glasses for the Queen. After all, she must have hundreds of glasses, so what could he do to make them special? When he confided his fears to Roberto the following day in the Glass-works, he was surprised at his answer.

'I know we've said we mustn't make any Cristallo transparente for fear of it getting back to Murano, but if the glasses are going into the Queen's private collection, no one would be any the wiser. The Queen would surely be impressed by the glasses and might well give you the Letters Patent on the strength of them.'

After some heart searching, Jacob began to warm to the idea. 'I think you could be right,' he confided to Roberto later that day. 'Jean said it should be beer glasses and it's difficult to make them different. We could make them with a serpentine stem, but use the new cristallo. That should do the trick and make them special enough. Personally, I confess I am not keen on the fancy serpentine style, but it has become more and more popular, particularly in England and France, so we must use it.'

Having made the decision, he set about making them and a few days later, the Queen received a gift from Mr. West of some 'little beer glasses'. The following day, Jean came bursting in to the office waving a very ornate message that had just been delivered. He could hardly speak for excitement, but when he did, the words came gushing out in a breathless stream. 'It's for you Jacob; you're to be presented to the Queen at her next audience, which will be in two weeks time. Sir William Cecil sent the invitation and he says that the Queen was very impressed with the glasses. She wants to meet the man who made them especially as she has been told you are training English workers. He also said that depending on how much public business there was to get through, you might get a private audience. What do you think of that then my friend?'

To say that Jacob was astonished was to put it mildly. He had not expected such a favourable response to the beer glasses. At the same time, he was somewhat apprehensive at the thought of going to court. He had heard a lot about the Queen's court. The courtiers bankrupted themselves vying with each other in wearing ornate and bejewelled clothes, which had to be more impressive every time they came to court.

When he mentioned his thoughts to Jean, he just laughed. 'Do not worry about it Jacob. We'll see you have some new clothes after you've been to see Walsingham.'

'Walsingham?' Jacob asked in surprise. 'What has Walsingham to do with it? He's the Queen's spy catcher, or so Marco told me. Why have I to go and see him?'

Jean laughed heartily at Jacob's expression. 'It's nothing to do with catching spies,' he spluttered. 'He's Sir William Cecil's assistant and he's agreed to meet you to advise you how to present yourself at court. They want you to give a good account of yourself, not least because they will be sponsoring you.

Walsingham will help you to avoid some of the more obvious pitfalls. Believe me, court can be most enjoyable, but the Queen is renowned for her quick temper and if anyone upsets her it can be absolute hell. Accept all the help you can get, you will need it. From what I've seen of Walsingham in action, he knows how to keep on the right side of the Queen better than most.

CHAPTER TWENTY-FOUR

Two days later dressed in his finest clothes and wearing his sword, he set off for the short walk to Walsingham's house in Seething Lane. When he turned the corner of into Seething Lane, a carriage drawn by four horses followed by four armed men on horseback passed him and drew up outside Jacob's destination. Carriages were not a common sight and he guessed that it was probably Walsingham arriving for his appointment. Curious to get a glimpse of him, Jacob hurriedly crossed the lane and moved to where he could see the occupant as he alighted.

A man walking towards the house from the opposite direction suddenly ran towards the front of the carriage. Drawing a pair of pistols from beneath his cloak he shot the lead horse in the head at point-blank range. As it collapsed bringing the other lead horse to its knees he turned, fired at the coachman then ran swiftly back down the Lane.

The coachman was hit hard and slumped down in his seat without a sound. Two of the horsemen at the rear spurred their horses to give chase. As they did so several men emerged from a nearby garden. One group rushed towards the horsemen firing pistols as they ran. A horseman was hit and fell screaming from his horse clutching his shoulder; another, his horse shot from beneath him, crashed to the ground with a sickening thud, and lay still.

Meanwhile a second group ran towards the remaining horsemen at the rear of the coach firing pistols as they came. The horsemen, momentarily thrown into confusion, gathered their wits and returned fire, shouting to a servant at the door to fetch help. Two of the attackers fell to the ground and lay inert, but the others having discharged their pistols, raced forward with hoarse cries, brandishing their swords.

Drawing his own sword, Jacob ran towards the carriage to help.

Just as he arrived a tall, well-dressed man jumped down with a sword in one hand and a pistol in the other. He fired the pistol at the attackers, without any apparent effect and within seconds he was being hard pressed by two men, with only oaths and hoarse breathing punctuating the ringing clash of sword against sword.

Walsingham, for indeed it was he, would have been overwhelmed in a very short time, but for Jacob's arrival. Ignoring any niceties, Jacob ran one man through and quickly withdrawing his sword engaged the other. His flashing blade quickly beat aside the others defence and with a practised lunge he wounded him in the side. He slumped to the ground holding his side as blood spread its scarlet stain across his white shirt.

Jacob shouted to Walsingham as the man fell down. 'Get back in the coach, sir, and reload if you can. I'll try and hold them.' Before he could do so, several more men joined the fray having dealt with the riders. Jacob and Walsingham were forced to stand back to back against the coach, defending themselves desperately against an increasingly frenzied attack.

Things were becoming desperate and sweat blinded Jacob for a moment. Wiping it away on his sleeve, he battled on grimly, determined to sell his life dearly. His sword weaved a glittering, complex web of moves, which frustrated his attackers leading them to become impetuous. Despite their superiority in numbers none of them had Jacob's skill, which was fortunate in the circumstances.

Eventually, despairing at their lack of success one of the attackers overreached and seizing the opening, Jacob dealt him the 'coup de grace'. As he turned to meet his other opponent, armed servants dashed out of the house and ran towards them. The leader now engaging Jacob broke away from the attack and called for his men to retreat. Mouthing a furious oath he threw a knife straight at the back of the unsuspecting Walsingham.

Without a thought for his own safety, Jacob pushed him out of the way, desperately parrying at the knife with his sword. It struck the hilt with a vicious clang and that was the last thing he remembered until he woke up some time later and sat up. He immediately wished he hadn't and lay back with a groan.

'Take your time my young friend, you've had a nasty blow on the temple and it's fortunate it was the hilt of the knife and not the blade, or this would be an entirely different scene.'

Jacob opened his eyes and studied the speaker, recognising him as the well-dressed man he had rushed to help. His long thin face, dark hair, moustache and beard, together with his unsmiling expression, and sombre clothes, gave him a stern appearance. He favoured Jacob with a thin smile, which completely failed to reach his eyes and studied Jacob intently. He felt like a specimen, being studied by a professor.

'My name is Francis Walsingham' he said by way of introduction, 'Assistant Secretary to the Queen and you, if I'm not mistaken, are Jacob Bell of the Crouched Friars Glass-works. I have heard much, which impressed me about your talents as a glassmaker, but I must confess that I am even more impressed with your skill as a swordsman. I have no doubt that without your intervention; the Queen would be looking for a new Assistant Secretary.'

Jacob sat up more gingerly this time and studied his surroundings. The room was richly furnished with fine tapestries on the wall, but from the arrow slits, he was undoubtedly in some sort of castle.

'What is this place?' He enquired of Walsingham. 'It seems to be a castle.'

'Quite right Master Bell, you're in my apartment in the Tower of London.' He smiled grimly as Jacob's face registered alarm at that information and he gave a short barking laugh. 'I see you've heard of its reputation. Have no fear Jacob Bell, you are here at my pleasure and not the Queen's, which is a very different matter altogether.' He didn't bother to explain, but Jacob could guess from the rumours he'd heard.

Seeing that Jacob was feeling stronger, Walsingham offered him a glass of wine. He sniffed the bouquet of the wine and commended it to Jacob. 'It's not common knowledge yet, but I am about to be appointed French Ambassador. I'm trying to get used to the idea by drinking French wines. I'm told that this is one of their better ones, so I hope you enjoy it.'

While his manner was not exactly friendly, at least he's making an effort to be civil thought Jacob. Sipping the wine, which was very acceptable, Jacob enquired why the men had attacked the carriage.

'I'm not sure whether it was simply an attempt on my life by malcontents, or something more sinister to do with Count Maldini.'

The name meant nothing to Jacob and he asked who he was.

'He's a very foolish Spanish count, who's been plotting with the Spanish Ambassador, against the Queen. Unfortunately, there was insufficient proof of his involvement so I questioned him at my house. He repeatedly denied everything and I let him go a few days ago.' There was that cold smile again. 'You know the old saying about giving a man enough rope to hang himself. I suspect that when I find out who is behind this attack, the saying might prove to be a little too prophetic for the Count.'

'What happened to the men who were wounded? Did they get away?'

'Yes, apart from one. The rest of the gang helped them to get away. There were five men left at the scene, two killed by the outriders, two you killed and one wounded and captured by the servants.'

That smile again! Jacob had the feeling that this was a man with little warmth.

'He's now telling my helpers all he knows about the affair.'

The coldness of his words and expression made Jacob shudder. He had no doubt that somewhere below them the man had been, or was being tortured. He had no sympathy for him. He would have killed him without a qualm during the fight by the carriage, but the thought of using torture was repugnant to him.

Walsingham must have guessed from his expression what was going through his mind. 'I can see that the thought of torture doesn't sit well with you Master Bell, but I must use all my resources in the fight against the Queen's enemies.' His eyes glowed with the ardour of a zealot as he went on. Jacob impressed by the loyalty the Queen commanded, listened carefully to his words

'She's a young Queen, but has inherited the fire and kingly qualities of her father. She is no weak woman mind you, as many men have already found to their cost, even though she does use a woman's wiles at times. It is my firm belief that she will make England one of the strongest powers in the World. I intend to ensure that both she and I live to see that day.' He coughed a little and looked slyly at Jacob. 'You may have heard that one of the tasks I do for the Queen is to protect her from Catholic plotters.' Jacob nodded and agreed he had heard that Walsingham was the Queen's Spy catcher. Walsingham laughed at Jacob's forthright reply. 'I can see that you're no diplomat. I'll have to instruct you in some of the finer arts of being a courtier.'

He sat down opposite to Jacob and studied him intently for several minutes until Jacob became uncomfortable. 'I'm very grateful to you Jacob Bell,' Walsingham said at last. 'I owe you my life and I will not forget it. You can rest assured that I will do everything in my power to see that the Queen grants you the Letters Patent for glass-making.'

True to his word, when Jacob had recovered, Walsingham gave him the benefit of his experience in dealing with the Queen and her court. Despite his protests, he also arranged for his tailor to make Jacob some clothes for his court appearance. The tailor, waiting in an anteroom, came in with a flourish with his three apprentices carrying, what seemed to Jacob, to be a whole shop full of cloth. After making very careful measurements, the tailor began to discuss with Walsingham what style and colour the clothes should be. They argued back and forth, completely ignoring Jacob. Finally Walsingham said he was satisfied and the tailor began to pack away his wares. Jacob who had become more than a little exasperated by the whole proceedings enquired if he was to be let into the secret.

For the first time since they'd met, Walsingham gave a smile, which lit up his face. 'Certainly not,' he replied, enjoying the moment. 'I'm giving you the clothes as a token of my gratitude to you for saving my life. I've chosen the Queen's favourite colour of the moment, but in a style, which is more in keeping with your circumstance than some of the elaborate concoctions worn in court. Have no fear that I'll dress you like a peacock, but you'll have to wait until the fitting for the rest.' He would say no more on the matter just smiling enigmatically when he was pressed for further information and Jacob gave up.

Later in the day when he returned to his friends, he was made to go over his eventful day, time and time again until he protested loudly that enough was enough. 'Whatever else you can say about the day I have to admit that it hasn't done any harm to our chances of gaining the Letters Patent.'

Roberto who had listened with awe to Jacob's modest description of the fight looked at him with pride. 'I don't know about that Master Jacob, but I do know that there are few people who could fight so many and walk away without a scratch.'

Jacob fingered the tender lump on his head. 'I wouldn't say that Roberto. After all, I had to be carried away from the scene of the fight.'

CHAPTER TWENTY-FIVE

A few days later a messenger brought an invitation for Jacob to visit Walsingham. The message was short and to the point.

To Master Jacob Bell, by hand,

Greetings, I bid you to attend my house at Seething Lane at ten in the morning on the morrow. Your new clothes will be available for viewing and a fitting. I will also have words with you on the matter we discussed at the Tower. It was simply signed 'Walsingham'.

Jacob was looking forward to seeing the clothes with some anticipation and not a little apprehension. Supposing he didn't like them? How was he going to tell Walsingham and get him to change them? He also wondered what it was that Walsingham wanted to discuss with him.

Arriving at Walsingham's house promptly at ten of the clock he was greeted like a hero by the servants. His exploits during the attack on the carriage had been witnessed by several of the staff and he was treated with great respect. It had been arranged for him to see the tailor in one of the reception rooms and then he was to join Walsingham in his study.

When Jacob saw the clothes for the first time, he was stunned. The colour was totally unexpected, being a very dark bluish violet which appeared almost black, but which glowed with violet highlights.

'We call it Raven's Wing,' the tailor proudly informed him. 'After the famous ravens at the Tower you know?' When Jacob said he didn't, the tailor explained about the legend that as long as the ravens where living at the Tower, England was safe from invasion. Jacob thought it was an interesting tale, but was more interested in the clothes.

The cut of the doublet was very fashionable with deep slashes showing a lighter shade of the 'Raven's Wing', but there was none of the jewellery, which was common in court clothes: it was a very simple style.

They were a superb fit, but the tailor fussed about until Jacob had convinced him that he was delighted with them. Jacob buckled on his sword and examined his reflection in the mirror that the tailor held for him. He was not sure about the large winged collar and the ruff, but the tailor assured him that the collar was very fashionable and the ruff, although smaller than those commonly worn, balanced the doublet perfectly, as did the hat.

When he joined Walsingham in his study, he scrutinised the clothes carefully. 'They'll catch the eye of the Queen who loves that colour and will draw you to her attention. What happens after that will depend on how well you listen to my advice? Don't be afraid to speak out, be bold and use a little flattery: flirt with her a little, it'll work wonders.'

He studied Jacob shrewdly looking for a reaction, then seeing none, gave him some further advice. 'A word of caution about that Master Bell; have a care not to flirt too much with the Queen and not at all if Robert Dudley, the Earl of Leicester is present. He's the Queen's favourite at present and an influential member of the Council. Should the Earl be in attendance just use a little flattery: that would be quite normal. However, if you overdo it and he saw you as a rival it could become very difficult.'

Jacob listened carefully to Walsingham's advice. He wasn't sure that flirting with the Queen of England was a good idea, but if that was his advice, well, so be it. He was about to ask Walsingham a question when they were interrupted by a knock at the door and a servant entered. Apologising for his intrusion, he proffered an urgent summons from the Queen.

Walsingham read the note then muttering under his breath he rose and began to put on his cloak. 'You must excuse me Master Bell, but I am required to attend the Queen immediately. There has been a missive from France, which has incurred the royal wrath.

From the tone of her summons I suspect that I'll be heading for the French Court somewhat earlier than I'd anticipated. If that should be the case, I will arrange for Monsieur Thieré to receive an invitation so that he can go with you. Sir William Cecil knows Thieré well and will be able to point you out to the Queen.'

He sighed and gave a shrug. 'It is not ideal, but when you see the Queen in action, you may well understand a little more.' He shook hands with Jacob, wished him good luck, and then with a gesture inviting Jacob to follow him, led the way to the door.

As the day for his first visit to court drew near Jacob began to have severe doubts about the wisdom of the whole idea. He said as much to Jean who brushed aside his objections.

'You must have no fear that it will be a disaster. The Queen has several reasons to have good opinions of you.' He smiled reassuringly. 'You must say to yourself that you are going to enjoy the experience and I am sure you will. Without any doubt, the Queen has a most imposing presence and her command of languages is as good as, if not better than your own. In any case, now that Walsingham has left for France, I will be with you to help you through. I still recall with pleasure the first time that I went to court and I'm sure that it will be the same for you.'

Jacob was unconvinced, but recognised that it would be impossible to withdraw at this late stage. He made up his mind that Jean was right and he must adopt a positive attitude to the visit. Being by nature a fairly optimistic person he was able to push aside his doubts.

The morning started well with clear skies, little wind and the promise of a beautiful day in store. The trip on the river was pleasant and uneventful. When they arrived at Greenwich Palace, where the Queen generally resided, they had to wait a little while to disembark, as they were only one of a number of boats heading for Greenwich steps.

The orders procured by Walsingham admitted them to the presence-chamber and a gentleman wearing an ornate gold chain over his velvet doublet consulted his list, made a note of their names and then directed them to their places in the large chamber. Jacob took the opportunity to look around as they waited for the Queen to arrive. The chamber was hung with rich tapestries and the floor was covered with rushes. Being a Sunday, there was a great attendance of the nobility in their sumptuous clothes. In the same hall, Jean pointed out the Archbishop of Canterbury, the Bishop of London, and a number of Counsellors of State and Officers of the Crown. Comparing his own clothes to those around him, Jacob felt very dowdy. The brilliance of some of the clothes was amazing and the jewellery worn by many of the nobles looked to be worth a King's ransom. At least he felt comfortable in the clothes now and Walsingham had been most insistent he wore them. With Walsingham's warning in mind, Jacob enquired of the usher if the Earl of Leicester was present. He was relieved to be informed that the Earl would not be present that day, as he'd returned to Kenilworth. Shortly afterwards there was a prolonged fanfare from twelve trumpets and two kettledrums, which made the hall ring. The door to the Queen's private apartments opened and the procession to the chapel began.

The Barons, Earls and Knights of the Garter came first. All of them were bareheaded and richly dressed. Next came the Lord Chancellor carrying the Queen's seals in a red silk purse. Two knights flanked him, one carrying the royal sceptre and the other the sword of state, point upwards, in its red scabbard, studded with fleur-de-lis.

Following behind came the graciously smiling Queen now in her thirty- seventh year. She was as majestic as Jacob had been led to believe. Her face was oblong and fair and her eyes, though a little small by some standards, were black and pleasant. She wore her hair high, with curls of red false hair and wore a small gold crown. She wore two pearls with rich drops in her ears and a necklace of exceedingly fine jewels that accentuated her bosom; uncovered in the fashion of the unmarried ladies of the court.

Her dress was of white silk with borders set with pearls the size of beans. Over it she wore a mantle of black silk, shot with silver threads and her train was so long that a marchioness, wearing an oblong collar of gold and jewels, carried the end of it.

As moved along the line and people were introduced, she spoke graciously to them in their own language. Jacob was able to identify French, English and another language, which Jean later identified as Gaelic, the language of the Scots.

Wherever she turned her face, the person fell to their knees. When it came to Jacob's turn he also fell to his knees and bowed his head. The Queen bade him to rise and smiled sweetly. 'Master Bell, I am indebted to you for saving Sir Francis Walsingham from an untimely death. He tells me that as well as being a talented glassmaker, he has never seen your equal as a swordsman. What say you to that Master Bell?'

Jacob bowed to her again and returned her smile. 'Most Gracious Queen I am overwhelmed by your presence and your kind words. I am delighted I was able to be of service to your majesty. As for the fight, I was somewhat fortunate to survive myself after a rather clumsy parry.'

The Queen laughed loudly and giving him a searching look with eyes that seemed to look deep into him, took off her glove and gave him her bejewelled right hand to kiss. 'There are few men who would have the skill to try and parry a thrown knife Master Bell. I commend you for your modesty. Attend me in my chamber after the service so that I may hear a more detailed account of this fight at first hand. Sir William Cecil will be there to meet you,' she said indicating a thickset man close behind her. He was of average height with a thin face, a moustache and a greying forked beard. The gentleman made a polite inclination of his head and followed the Queen who had moved on, with the ladies of the court following behind.

They too were mostly dressed in white and Jacob's invitation to join the Queen had set them whispering and giggling. As they passed by he was the recipient of a several bold glances.

Jean, smiling broadly, asked him which of the ladies he admired most. 'There are some good catches there Jacob. Several of them are the Queen's wards and would come with quite a dowry.' Jacob wisely refused to be drawn on the topic and watched the Queen's progress.

When the Queen reached the end of the ante-chapel she turned as a loud cry rang out of 'Long live Queen Elizabeth'. She answered it with, 'I thank you, my good people,' and then flanked by her guard of fifty Gentlemen Pensioners with their gilt battle-axes; she entered the chapel for prayers.

While the Queen was at prayers, which took about half an hour, her table was set out with a great deal of solemnity and ceremony. Two gentlemen entered the room, one bearing a rod, whilst the other carried a tablecloth. They both knelt three times with the utmost veneration then spread the cloth on the table. After kneeling again they both left the room.

Two more gentlemen entered, one carrying the rod as before, the other carrying a salt-seller, a plate and bread. Following the same routine they placed the things on the table and left. Next came two ladies, one an unmarried countess the other a married lady carrying a tasting knife, or so they were told. The countess, who was dressed in a white silk dress, curtseyed and then approaching the table, rubbed the plates with bread and salt. Her manner was most respectful, as if the Queen herself was present and when she had done, they both stood to one side and waited.

After a little while the yeoman of the guard entered in their scarlet clothes with a golden rose upon their backs. Some richly dressed gentlemen also appeared and took places by the table. The guard brought in turn twenty-four dishes served in, for the most part, gilt plates. These dishes were placed on the table and the lady taster gave a small piece to each guard to check for any poison. When this ritual had been completed, a number of ladies of the chamber appeared and carried the dishes with particular solemnity into the Queen's inner, private chamber.

Shortly afterwards, the service being over, the Queen made her way into her private chamber. All of the assembled people fell to their knees as she passed and only when she disappeared from sight did they rise and begin to leave the ante-chapel.

Shortly after the Queen entered her chamber, Sir William Cecil appeared at the door and beckoned to Jacob. Promising to tell him everything when he returned, Jacob bid farewell to Jean. Entering the chamber Jacob was just in time to see the last lady of the Court leaving the room carrying some dishes. Apparently the Queen made her choice from all the dishes and the remainder went to the ladies. Following Sir William's lead he bowed low and waited for the Queen to speak. The Queen motioned them to the chairs by the table and bade them to take their choice from the food. This was excellent, befitting the company and Jacob who by now was very hungry, ate with a great deal of enjoyment.

The Queen was obviously in a good mood and whilst they ate, she teased Jacob with relish. 'Methinks you have set the hearts of a number of my ladies all a flutter Master Bell. What thought you of them? There are some very comely unmarried ladies amongst them are there not? Perhaps I should introduce you to one of my wards.'

Jacob answered the question with a disarming smile. 'None of them compare with you your majesty, I confess I paid them little mind because of your presence.' The Queen laughed heartily taking the comment as Jacob had intended. 'He has the makings of a diplomat think you not Sir William?'

'Indeed your majesty, although a little obvious I thought,' he said dryly.

There followed a brief interlude as they concentrated on the food. When they had all eaten well the Queen asked Jacob to tell her about the incident outside the home of Walsingham. As commanded he recounted the tale, describing the action in great detail, whilst playing down his own involvement as much as possible.

The Queen became very involved in the tale with many expressions of delight and commendation, but she also asked many shrewd questions. For the most part Sir William was content to listen, but from time to time, he made some very telling comments.

Despite Walsingham's advice, Jacob did not attempt to flatter, or flirt with the Queen after his first attempt. He was convinced that she would see through it and think the less of him. He was anxious not to convey a false impression to the Queen, even if it harmed his cause.

When his story was finished the Queen looked shrewdly at him. 'You are a man of many talents Master Bell and an educated one at that. I perceive that you have played down the account of your adventures, if I put my trust in Walsingham's account, which I have learned so to do.'

As the expressions on Jacob's face mirrored his thoughts, she smiled broadly at him and laughed. 'Be not discomfited by my comments Master Bell, you have rendered me a good service and I am not one to let it pass without suitable reward. However, Sir William and others persuade me that the matter of the Glass Patent to which you aspire should not be addressed for some time. The Glass Seller's Association also covets them and have been most strident in the request for an Englishman and not a foreigner to get them. Even though Sir Richard Urie is of Scottish descent,' she said with a grin.

She looked shrewdly at Jacob. 'I was more impressed by the little beer glasses sent to me by 'Mr West' than I was by the force of this argument.'

'Mr West?' Jacob enquired ingenuously.

The Queen laughed. 'I can see you are a man to watch Master Bell and I shall do so with some interest, rest assured of that.' She regarded him with an indulgent expression. 'I bid you to attend my court from time to time. You will be most welcome. I will see you receive invitations.'

She rose to her feet and when Jacob knelt in front of her she extended her hand for him to kiss. Motioning him to rise she went on. 'For now I will bid you goodnight, but I wish you to attend Sir William who has a matter of import too discuss, with, I might add, my full approval.' She looked pointedly at her advisor who inclined his head in agreement, and then with a regal inclination of her head to Jacob she moved into her inner chamber.

A short while later seated in his office Sir William explained the Queen's comments. 'I will come straight to the point Master Bell, as you know, Walsingham has been sent to Paris on the express instructions of the Queen. I know you are aware of Walsingham's other role as head of the organisation, which seeks out the Queen's enemies. It was his wish and the Queen now concurs that you should be asked to help him with this task.'

Jacob started to object, but Sir William cut his protestations short. 'Before you commit yourself to an answer, please hear me out. You'll not be asked to spy on people, but simply to gather information of various sorts and send reports to Walsingham. I'm sure you're aware of the need for intelligence of all sorts to build up a picture of how things affect the realm. Venice has one of the finest information-gathering systems in the world and we're trying to improve ours.' He regarded Jacob expectantly.

Jacob was instantly on his guard. Was Cecil hinting about him, or was it simply a comparison he was making? He must tread very carefully. 'Before I give you an answer,' he said at last. 'There are one or two things I'd like to know.'

'By all means I'll try to answer any questions I can.'

Jacob set out his concerns. 'The Queen gave a strong hint that she knew what you were going to ask me. Is that true?'

Sir William smiled broadly. 'If you knew the Queen better there would be no need to ask that question. There is little the Queen doesn't know when it comes to matters that affect the realm. Anyone who didn't keep her well informed would not enjoy her confidence and support for long, of that you can be certain.'

He leaned forward. 'I will take you into my confidence about the Queen's part in this. The private audience was in itself, unusual and was not just to hear about the fight. She has a high regard for men who stand out from the crowd and I was aware that she was intrigued by Walsingham's account of your outstanding skill and conduct during the attempt on his life. This audience gave her the opportunity to meet you at first hand and to make up her mind about you. Whether you like it or not, you have found favour with her, and can expect to be invited to Court.'

'As long as that favour lasts!' he warned. 'Her request for you to talk to me was her way of saying she approved of you.'

Jacob listened to this account with a growing sense of unease. Bearing in mind Walsingham's stricture to flatter the Queen, but not to tread on Robert Dudley's toes he'd tried to avoid any involvement with the Queen. Now it seemed he'd found favour with her. There was also the reference to Venice. Was there anything behind it? 'Why me,' he asked. 'I'm a Glass-maker, not a courtier.'

'The Queen likes to have interesting people around her at Court,' Sir William confided. 'She can't abide the insincerity of a lot of the people at Court, so she tends to invite people she finds interesting. You're not likely to be a favourite in the same way as the Earl of Leicester. So, what else is bothering you?'

'To be honest, I don't know how I'm going to have time for all of this. The glass-works is taking up all of my time at present and my main aim is to make sure it's a success. We've just taken a showroom in the new 'Royal Exchange' and I'm training four Englishmen in glass making. How can I make time for visits to the Court and send reports to Walsingham as well? Let alone decide what information is important enough to be reported on.'

Sir William was not impressed with the argument. 'I'm sure you'll find time to fit it all in. After all, you'll be building up a debt of gratitude with the Queen, which I'm sure will help you with the Letters Patent.'

Getting to his feet he motioned for Jacob to follow him. 'Don't worry about the reports, just send in anything you think might be of interest and we'll decide whether it's important. You may also be asked, from time to time, to find out about a particular person. Does that clarify it for you?'

Recognising that he'd little choice in the matter if he wished to retain the goodwill of the Queen and Cecil, Jacob had no option but to agree. With a promise to be in touch with him in the next few days with details of where to send the reports whilst Walsingham was away, Cecil bade him farewell. Despite the fact that there had been no further reference to Venice, it was an uneasy Jacob who took his leave and made his way to Greenwich Steps and home.

CHAPTER TWENTY - SIX

The morning was bright and clear and Maria was sitting on the veranda of the sala giardino in Giam's villa, which was now her home. It was three months since her marriage to Adrian Ragazoni and at last the gossip seemed to have faded away to concentrate on the latest 'cause celebre.

Before she would set a date for the wedding, she had insisted that she must live at Giam's former villa. The only times she would reside at Adrian's large and ostentatious villa in Venice, was when there was some special occasion. Once each week she joined him for the evening meal. This was usually a bleak formal meal with the conversation only dealing with social events for the coming week.

Of course she still had to spend quite a lot of time at official functions with Adrian since his star had been rising rapidly after his performance in the Giunta during Giam's trial. It was rumoured that he was in line to become an important Envoy and he was very much in demand at both official and social occasions.

As she sat enjoying the morning sun, she made some notes in a diary that she'd started after her marriage. In it she recorded every scrap of information on Adrian she'd found out since then. It was a lot of pages, but unfortunately, nothing of any significance had emerged as yet.

She recorded a note about the two seedy looking men she'd seen at the Adrian's villa the previous night when she and Adrian returned from a social engagement. Normally she wouldn't have thought twice about them if it hadn't been for their furtive manner when the coach had passed them. When she'd asked Adrian about them he'd dismissed them as unimportant, but his exaggerated disinterest struck a discord in her mind and she decided to try to discover more about them.

She also wrote down a careful account of the private dinner

given for the mysterious Count Maldini. He was an extremely witty guest at table, but his pointed avoidance of politics and the clumsy change of subject when Adrian brought up the possibility of being Envoy to London were all fuel for Maria's suspicions. When the meal was speedily followed by a retreat into the private study, the intrigued, Maria tried to get nearer, only for the Count's servants to prevent it. All she could do was to make a note for future reference.

Just as Maria finished writing, Anna Rosso appeared with a tray. Her manner was excited and her face flushed with emotion. As she put the tray down, Maria enquired if there was anything the matter. 'I'm sorry Lady Maria, but I'm all of a dither this morning. I've received a letter from Roberto and he's safe and well and been made a junior partner in the Glass - works in London.'

'Oh! Anna, I'm so pleased for you,' she said. 'It's the first time you've heard from him since he left. What did he have to say?'

'It's mainly about the Glass-works and the wonders of London. He seems quite taken with the place and with that Monsieur Jean Thieré. They've taken on some Venetians from Antwerp and things are going well. It looks as though he's going to stay there for the long time,' she said sadly. She proffered the letter. 'You can read it for yourself if you wish. She passed it to Maria and was so engrossed in showing it to her that she failed to notice the sad look, which showed briefly on Maria's face at the mention of Giam. 'He seems to have become quite a scholar nowadays. He could barely write when he first started working for Master Giam and look at his letter now.'

Recovering her composure quickly, Maria read Roberto's letter with interest. She was glad he was safe and well and making a good life for himself in London. She'd formed a very high opinion of him in the short time she'd known him and wished him nothing but well. She sighed deeply and handed the letter to Anna. Forcing herself to be cheerful she chattered to her for a few minutes then getting to her feet she said it was time for her to change.

'Where is it today Lady Maria? Are you going out with 'your husband'?'

Maria smiled to herself at Anna's use of 'your husband' she always managed to make her feelings about Adrian known to her. To his face, she was distantly polite and willing, but it was exclusively for Maria's benefit. Anna was intensely loyal to her and Maria knew she could trust her implicitly. It was very reassuring to know that. The servants that Adrian had recommended were obviously there to spy on her and she quickly found excuses to get rid of them. All of the new servants were known to Anna and had proved to be well trained and loyal.

Putting her thoughts to one side she smiled fondly at Anna. 'I'm going to see my father and I'll be staying overnight. Will you see to ordering a gondola and before you ask, I'll not need any clothes to take with me to change, as there are still so many at home. And of course, I'd like you to come with me.'

'Very good Mistress, how long will it be before you wish to leave?'

Maria was not at all surprised by Anna's calm acceptance of the upheaval at short notice. She'd only seen her lose this calmness on one occasion and that was when the news of Giam's death had reached them. Not wanting to think any more about that she hurried to reply. 'About an hour I'd think. Will that give you enough time to be ready?'

'Plenty of time Mistress, will 'your husband' be there?'

'Not on this occasion Anna, he's gone to Venice for a few days on some sort of business for the Senate and will stay at his father's house rather than go back and forth.'

'Oh, good! It'll give you chance to spend some uninterrupted time with your father,' said Anna.

Maria laughed openly unable to conceal her amusement. 'Of course Anna I didn't think you meant anything else.' Anna looked at her sharply then hesitantly at first joined in the laughter.

Later that day, sitting in the day room with her father she told him about the letter from Roberto. 'I must admit it upset me at the time, but I've got to put it to one side and get on with my life. One thing did puzzle me though. Roberto didn't mention Giam at all.'

He shrugged his shoulders. 'Perhaps he thought it would upset you if his mother showed the letter to you. It's difficult to say. He would be very upset about Giam too. He thought the world of him and that's probably why he's decided to go to London. I wish he'd come back to Murano. The manager I've put into the Glass-works is not a patch on Roberto despite his youth and I wish he were still in charge. I'm hoping that Antonio Luciano will be able to keep an eye on the new man, he's much better now despite his grief for Giam.'

'I know what you mean about Roberto, father. He'd an old head on his young shoulders and he idolised Giam. I'm sorry he didn't stay in Murano too.'

Maria changed the subject. 'Have you heard anything about Adrian in the Senate corridors lately? He told me he was going to stay with his father for a few days and that he had some Senate business to attend to in Venice, but I've a feeling there's more to it than that.'

'I don't know how true it is, but there's a rumour that he's being considered for an Envoy's post. His father has been pushing his claims and without proof of his part in the plot against Giam, my friends and I have little chance of discrediting him. Either he's being extra careful to cover his tracks, or there really is no truth in his involvement.'

Maria reacted angrily. 'You must never think that father. I know Adrian was behind it,' she cried vehemently, 'and one day I'll prove it.' She took his hands and looked earnestly at his face. 'Please don't be fooled by him. He's cruel, calculating, manipulative and extremely devious. Shortly after we heard about Giam's death he got rather drunk. He was gloating about it and as good as told me he'd planned everything that happened. He also warned me not to interfere in his affairs and to play the dutiful wife or he would kill me.'

Ricardo was aghast. 'He can't be allowed to get away with this Maria,' he stormed. 'The man is a maniac and must be stopped.'

Maria was touched by the instant acceptance of her

denunciation. 'Adrian is so clever. He knows my unsupported word would never be accepted and he's too careful to leave any evidence lying around. We must play the waiting game. Sooner or later he will make a mistake or I will find out who his henchmen are that carry out his orders. I saw two men last night in the drive to the villa. They acted rather suspiciously and Adrian was far from convincing when he said he didn't know them. I'm trying to find out who they were, but I have to be careful. I don't trust the servants so I must be very wary not to arouse their suspicions, they would surely report it back to Adrian.'

Maria was glad her father had agreed to be cautious. She smiled and linked arms with him and they strolled out into the garden. By mutual agreement they changed the topic and chatted about the latest gossip

The following weekend, she was sitting in her bedroom at Adrian's villa, getting ready for sleep. They had been entertaining several Senators and their wives and also Count Maldini, who was apparently returning to England in the next few days. The meal was in the way of a farewell. It came as a surprise, when Adrian who had been drinking rather heavily, made a toast to the Count and linked it with an announcement.

'I would like to make a toast for my friend Count Maldini,' he said with a bow to him. 'He is returning to England the day after tomorrow. Before the toast, however, I have an announcement to make.' He took a drink and then recharged his glass. 'What I have to tell you will be common knowledge soon. The Doge has done me the honour of appointing me his Special Envoy to the Court of Queen Elizabeth of England.'

There were loud cries of congratulations from everyone except Maria who sat frozen in her seat. Adrian ignored her as he shook hands with the men. Maria belatedly gained her self-control and rose to her feet. Adrian put his arm around her shoulders and held her tightly. 'My beautiful wife and I will be leaving Venice in a few weeks time,' he slurred, 'when I have had time to re-order my affairs. Since there is no Ambassador at present, we will take up residence in the Ambassadors house in London.'

For Maria, the rest of the evening passed in a blur. When the others had left, she quickly excused herself, saying she was tired and went to her room. Combing her hair, she was surprised when the door burst open and a drunken Adrian staggered in. He came across and stood behind and then tried to stroke her hair. Maria turned away from him, but grabbing her by the shoulders he tried to kiss her and she struggled to get away from his alcohol-laden breath. She stood up and wriggled out of his grasp, but left behind her robe.

This inflamed him even more and as she tried to escape round the end of the bed he grabbed her round the waist with one hand, fondling her breasts roughly with the other. Pushing her down on to the bed he leered at her. 'It's about time I exerted my rights as your husband,' he said and reached down to rip off her bed gown. Avoiding his clumsy grasp, Maria rolled off the bed and fumbling in the drawer of her bedside table, produced a dagger and held it threateningly. 'Touch me again, Adrian,' she said intensely, 'and I'll stick you for the pig you are.'

Adrian, swaying slightly stood leering at her and then with a little inclination of his head he backed away from her. 'Put down the stiletto Maria, you have made your point for now. But mark my words well; you will be a long way from Venice when we live in London. When my plans with the Count come to pass, I may never return. Then we shall see my beautiful wife,' he threatened. 'Oh yes! Then we will see.'

CHAPTER TWENTY-SEVEN

Spring had been wet and cold and it was not until late April that the blossoms really began to come out in force. In May the talk of London was the flight of Mary, Queen of the Scots to England, after her own peers beat her in battle at Langside in Scotland. The sermon at St. Paul's the following Sunday was full of it and the whole of London could find nothing else to gossip about. Mary was accused of being involved with the murder of her husband Lord Darnley, but nothing had been proved. Elizabeth undoubtedly sympathised with the Scottish Queen in losing her throne, but recognised the threat to her own security by Mary Stuart's presence in England. Mary was transferred to Carlisle Castle and Elizabeth's orders were, 'Use her honourably, but see that she does not escape.'

At the Crouched Friars, everyone was working hard to ensure success, none more so than the English workers who had responded well to Giam's training. It had been hard for them at first. True to his word, Jacob was very strict with them. He was fair and consistent in his dealings with them and they responded favourably.

One of the Venetians, Pietro Tiazoni, was proving to be a fine glass blower. Before long, Jacob made him Senior Glass-blower. The other workers responded well. By September, the Glass-works was highly profitable. Jean was spending more and more time travelling, particularly to Amsterdam and Flanders. Jacob was usually to be found at the Royal Exchange; dealing with the other glass merchants in his room on the ground floor or taking orders in the showroom on the floor above.

Sir Thomas Gresham's Exchange had been an instant success from its opening attended by the Queen. The Queen was impressed by the design, with its stone flagged courtyard surrounded by the colonnaded ground floor and the superbly decorated shops and showrooms above. Gresham had been so determined to make sure it was fully utilised and decorated for the Queen's visit, that he had offered the retailers as many extra shops as they wished, rent free for a year if they stocked and decorated them for the Queen's visit. Jacob had taken on two extra shops and made them into one large showroom and stockroom. The Exchange was a huge success. The Queen gave it the accolade of 'the Royal Exchange' proclaimed, by trumpet by a herald and the shops became known to all and sundry as 'the Pawn'.

Roberto usually held the fort at the Crouched Friars and was also improving his glass-blowing skills. So much so, that shortly after he'd become Senior Glass-blower, Pietro Tiazoni approached Jacob about Roberto. 'Have you seen Roberto making glass recently, Master Jacob?'

'I can't say I have Pietro.' He'd been so busy with the customers at the Royal Exchange, that he'd barely set foot inside the furnace room for several weeks. 'Is there a problem?'

Pietro grinned. 'No problem at all, Master Jacob; but there is an idea I'd like you to consider.'

'What's your suggestion then, Pietro?'

'I'd like you to consider making Roberto a Capo. He's good enough and I think it's a waste of talent to have him foot making.'

'That's excellent news Pietro we can do with another Capo. With all the orders coming in, I think we ought to consider taking on a few more men as well.'

'That was my next suggestion,' said Pietro. 'My cousin is still in Antwerp and if you are agreeable, I'd like to bring him over to London. He's had a couple of years experience in a Glass-Works in Antwerp and he's willing to learn. He recently married a local girl, a Huguenot and he's desperate to get out of Antwerp.'

Jacob agreed to both suggestions, subject to Jean approving Pietro's cousin on his next visit to Antwerp. Roberto was absolutely delighted when Jacob told him he was to be a Capo. 'Thank you Master Jacob, it's what I've always wanted.'

'I know Roberto and I'm delighted for you. But don't thank

me; it's down to your own hard work and to Pietro's recommendation.'

Shortly afterwards, the Glass-Works was producing more glass than ever and a good routine had been established. Today marked a departure from the normal routine. He'd arranged a meeting with the Glass Sellers Association, to try and come to an accommodation with them. The success of the Crouched Friars had cut into their business considerably. Jacob was able to undercut their prices, since he had no expensive transport costs and the introduction of the enhanced cristallo gave the Crouched Friars a better quality than most of the imported glasses. He'd agreed to use the sieved soda method rather reluctantly, but he reasoned that it was already in widespread use in Murano and was not a secret like Cristallo transparente. Indeed Jean had already heard that one of the Glass-works in Antwerp was using a similar process.

Three Needle Street was crowded as Jacob hurried along towards the Royal Exchange. He joined the many traders on the ground floor hurrying to their places to begin morning trading. After a brief word with Roberto who was taking the orders that morning Jacob went up to the meeting room on the floor above.

When he arrived, two men were already waiting there, looking over the balcony at the hustle and bustle of the merchants below. As he approached they turned and Jacob was surprised to see that he knew one of them. 'Are there you are Bell, I was beginning to think you were not coming.' The tone was condescending and Jacob studied the man in the kilt, remembering their first meeting at Court when he'd been singularly unimpressed by his overbearing manner.

Ignoring the comment he addressed them. 'Good morrow to you gentlemen.' He gave a nod of recognition to the speaker and turned to the other. 'Sir Richard Urie and I are already acquainted from Court, but I don't believe I've had the pleasure of meeting you before today, sir,' he said with a slight bow. 'I am Jacob Bell and pleased to make your acquaintance.'

The small ferret-faced man returned the bow. 'My name is

James McFarlane and I have the honour to be the Secretary of the Glass Sellers Association. Sir Richard and I have been asked to represent the Association in this meeting and we are empowered to speak on their behalf. Do you have similar power to speak for your partners at the Crouched Friars?'

The words though moderate, were delivered in a tone that struck a wrong chord with Jacob. 'I do,' he said icily, 'but only within certain strict limits. Should your mission simply be to try and buy us out then you waste your time and the meeting is at an end. I am not of a mind to go over that which has already been discussed and rejected.'

Rather taken aback, McFarlane assured him that he had meant no offence and that they were here to discuss matters of mutual benefit. 'It is no secret Master Bell that your success has been at the expense of our business. Whilst your market is but a stones throw from your Glass-works, we have to bring the glass we sell from Antwerp, or Venice, at prohibitive transport costs and the breakage's...' His voice trailed off and he rolled his eyes heavenwards, in a gesture of exaggerated despair. 'The breakages are crippling.'

'I sympathise with your problems,' said Jacob without any real conviction, 'but how can our Glass-works be of help to you?'

Sir Richard who had been showing signs of exasperation during these exchanges intervened. 'We are suggesting,' he said arrogantly, 'that our interests are so entwined that we should join forces to both our benefits. We would do the selling, leaving you to concentrate on what you're best at, making glass.'

For the moment Jacob was happy to pretend that he was impressed with their suggestion. 'Your arguments have merits, but I'm not sure I understand how it would work. With your greater experience of business, perhaps you could enlighten me.'

Sir Richard smiled not noticing the irony in Jacob's words. 'I envisage with my experience and contacts, both at Court and overseas,' he said expansively. 'I would be the senior partner with yourself and Thieré joining the other partners in the business.'

'What about my assistant who is a junior partner? Would there be a place for him?' Jacob said mildly, although in truth he was feeling far from that state of mind.

'Oh I'm sure we can find something for him to do,' he replied glibly, 'but I don't think a partnership would be appropriate, do you?'

Jacob didn't trust himself to reply at this dismissal of Roberto and taking his silence for acquiescence Sir Richard went on airily. 'By combining our resources like this we will be in an excellent position to obtain the Letters Patent from the Queen and we will all make a lot of money.' He looked expectantly at Jacob who deliberately chose not to answer immediately. Walking towards the balcony he suddenly turned and in a very mild voice enquired if there was anything else Sir Richard wished to say on the matter.

'Only that I urge you to accept this very generous offer as quickly as possible, we don't want this matter to drag on any longer than necessary.'

'Before I give you my opinion there are a couple of matters which I would like to clear up.'

'Of course my dear Bell, I'm only too glad to answer your questions.' Sir Richard was magnanimous now that he thought Jacob was convinced. 'Ask away.'

Jacob paused a moment to consider his words carefully. 'You say that Jean Thieré and I would become partners in the Glass Sellers Association. How many other partners would there be?'

'Three others,' replied Sir Richard, 'plus myself as senior partner of course.'

'Naturally,' said Jacob with an ironic tinge to his voice, which again quite escaped Sir Richard, but which caused McFarlane to look sharply in his direction.

'I suppose you would have the final say if there was a dispute?'

'Of course that is the role of the senior partner.' This was said with such aplomb that Jacob could only marvel at Sir Richard's lack of understanding of the affect that he was giving.

Becoming quite alarmed by the way that Jacob was reacting

McFarlane tried to modify what Sir Richard had said. Full of his own grandiose plans and oblivious to the effect they were having Sir Richard totally ignored the suggestion and sailed on blithely. 'Some men are born to lead and my family have been leaders since the thirteenth century. Who better than I to lead this Association to greater heights?' He sat down and leaned back with the air of a man secure in his self-esteem and in his role in destiny.

Before McFarlane could interpose again Jacob silenced him with a gesture. Keeping a tight control on the anger, he gave his reply. 'Correct me if I'm wrong Sir Richard, but summing up what you've said, you are not offering any money, but simply suggesting Jean Thieré and myself become partners in the Glass Sellers Association?' For the life of him he couldn't keep the sarcasm from his voice as he went on. 'In return of course, Thieré and I would put the production of the Crouched Friars Glass-works at your exclusive disposal? Am I right?'

Sir Richard took the statement at face value. Smiling benignly at Jacob he answered with a statement that caused even McFarlane to look at him with incredulity. 'The Glass Sellers is of course much bigger than your existing business and will give you other opportunities. You can only benefit by agreeing to work under my direction.'

This was the last straw for Jacob and he rose to his feet abruptly and stood with hand on sword, legs apart, and glared truculently at Sir Richard. 'There is only one thing worse than a fool and that's an arrogant fool. Even your own colleague can see that you've totally ruined any further chance of co-operation between us. I came here prepared to deal with you and try to reach a sensible compromise, but you only seem interested in acquiring the Crouched Friars Glass-works for nothing. A plague on you and your partnership, I bid you good day, sir.' So saying, he turned on his heel and started to leave.

Sir Richard who had become increasingly apoplectic as Jacob dismissed his offer caught him by the arm and spun him round. 'You insolent puppy,' he spluttered, 'you can't talk to me like that.' He stepped back and would have drawn his sword had not

McFarlane restrained him. 'Remember the rules of the Royal Exchange, Sir Richard. You would be barred for life for fighting.'

Angry as he was, self-preservation proved the stronger and he thrust his sword back in its scabbard with a frustrated growl. His face ugly with controlled rage and his head thrust forward he spat out his anger. 'I'll not be barred for the likes of an upstart like you,' he spluttered almost incoherent with rage. 'But don't think it's ended. You'll pay for your insults, my word on it.' With that he stormed out followed by McFarlane who shrugged his shoulders giving Jacob a despairing look as he left.

CHAPTER THIRTY

Fate is a fickle mistress as Jacob had come to know over the last couple of years. He well remembered his father's advice on the subject when he was only ten, or eleven years old. 'Beware of putting your trust in fate Jacob,' he'd said. 'She can deal good or ill in equal measures on a whim. You might as well put your trust in the mist that creeps over the lagoon on an autumn evening.' He drew a little nearer to the fire and pulled his cloak around him and the young Jacob sitting on the floor leaning against his legs listened carefully to his father's words.

'You must learn to take control of your own fate Giam, and accept good or ill with equal fortitude. Don't allow yourself to be overly influenced by either. Some things you can't change and they must be accepted or endured. Save your energy for the things you can change. In the long run it's how you respond to the roll of the dice, which makes you the man you are. You must accept good luck gracefully and bad luck with strength. When you master that you'll be the master of yourself.'

He'd not thought about the advice again, until the fateful day he'd been pitched into a cell in the Piombi. Coming only a short while after he'd become famous and engaged to Maria Mula, it had been a struggle to rise above it. None more so than when he'd been sentenced to death, but recalling his father's advice had helped him to survive and fight his way through his doubts and fears.

He'd no doubt that he was stronger for the experience. It had made him more resolute than ever to be the master of his own fate. By determination and dedication he'd become a Master of glass making and he now brought those attributes to bear on controlling his life. In the weeks that followed the meeting at the Royal Exchange, Jacob pushed ahead with his plans for rejuvenating the designs of the Glass-works. By the end of September, he was almost finished. On the last day of the month, Jacob was working late on a new design. As usual Roberto had been called in for an opinion and the two of them were discussing a small change to the design when Jean entered. He was in a jovial mood and chided the pair of them.

'Come on you two, everyone else left ages ago. You might not be hungry, but I'm ready for the evening meal. If I don't eat soon I'll die from starvation.'

'I hardly think that likely Jean. You've become quite the trencherman since you took a liking to Mistress Simpkin's Cumberland recipes.'

'I haven't noticed you holding back either, Jacob. It's not surprising, considering she's such an excellent cook. The more I travel, the more I realise what a treasure she is.' He became serious and asked how long they were likely to be.

'Not too long Jean, I'd like to finish the alterations to this design we've just agreed and it shouldn't take me more than a half-hour. You go with him Roberto; there's nothing more for you to do now. Ask Mistress Simpkin to have the meal ready for then and I promise I'll not be longer.'

'In that case can Jean borrow your cloak Master Jacob? He didn't bring his this morning and it's raining now.' He grinned impishly. 'I'll come back with it in about the half –hour. That way we might have a chance of eating a hot meal for a change.'

'Me! Forget the time! As if I would? Get away with you and mind you bring the cloak back.' Roberto grinned cheerfully at Giam's mock anger and they bid their farewells.

Leaving the Crouched Friars, Roberto and Jean made there way towards Harte Street with the rain starting to become more persistent. Most people had sensibly remained indoors and there were few others about except for one man a little way behind them. Jean was in a good mood and teased Roberto about having to go back with Jacob's cloak in the rain. 'Come on slowcoach,' he said jocularly, breaking into a jog. 'I'll beat you back to Harte Street.'

Roberto laughed and slowed up a little allowing Jean to get a few yards in front. 'You'd better make the most of your start; you're going to need it.'

Jean turned to run, but to Roberto's horror, two men with knives in their hands, sprang out of the mouth of the alley Jean was passing. While one of them grabbed him, the other thrust his knife into Jean's body. As he started to collapse, they dragged him into the alley.

With a shout of rage and fear Roberto drew his knife, but before he could move, he received a stunning blow on the back of his head and sank to the ground senseless.

Once the two of them had left, Jacob quickly became immersed in finishing the design. He had just started to clear away when Roberto staggered into the office. He would have fallen if Jacob had not caught him round the waist and helped to a chair. 'Roberto what's happened? Are you all right?'

His face ashen, Roberto told him about the attack on Jean.

'Where is Jean now, Roberto? Tell me where he is.' He spoke urgently, dreading the answer, but desperate to know.

Roberto simply looked at him too dazed to go on and realising that he was in shock, Jacob went to the cupboard and brought out the brandy he kept for medicinal purposes. Pouring a generous measure into a glass, he gave it to Roberto and told him to drink it. Roberto took a quick gulp and choked as the fiery liquor burned his throat, 'Sip it gently Roberto,' Jacob advised and applied a handkerchief to the cut on the back of his head.

Roberto struggled to his feet, pushing Jacob's hand away. Taking a big drink, he swallowed it, grimaced and then downed the remainder in one go. Placing the glass on the table he walked towards the door. 'We must go and find Jean, Master Jacob,' he said, his voice a little slurred. 'He may be lying injured somewhere.'

'Are you sure you're all right Roberto. You can stay here, while I go and find him. He may have made it back to the house already.'

'I'm coming with you Master Jacob,' he said drawing a knife

221

from his belt. 'I'll be ready for them if they're still there.'

Realising it was futile to argue Jacob led the way. It was raining hard now, but neither of them noticed. Keeping a wary eye out for the attackers, he hurried towards the house in Harte Street with Roberto gamely keeping up. In answer to Jacob's enquiry, Mistris Simpkin said she had not seen Jean since he left to fetch Jacob. Becoming more alarmed by the moment, they searched all the nooks and crannies in the alley, but there was no sign of him. Just as Jacob approached the far end, a figure turned the corner, holding on to the wall for support. As he ran forward Jean, for indeed it was he, took a few staggering steps and collapsed into Jacob's arms.

Jacob sat down and cradled Jean in his arms and Roberto came rushing up. In the feeble light from the lamp at the end of the alley, Jacob could just make out Jean's face. It was ashen and as Jacob tried to mop his brow, a froth of blood suddenly bubbled from his mouth, he gasped once, slumped against Jacob's chest and was still. Jacob moved his hand to support him and realised that it was soaked with blood. Wiping it away on the handkerchief, he felt for a pulse on the side of his neck, and finding none, looked sadly at Roberto and shook his head.

'Oh Master Jacob, they've killed him.' Roberto managed to get out then slumping to his knees beside Jacob, began to cry, his body shaking with grief. 'I should have done more to protect him,' he wailed heartbrokenly.

'You mustn't blame yourself Roberto,' said Jacob, cradling Jean in his arms, rocking the still figure gently, as if to sooth a child and oblivious to the rain streaming down his face. He looked at the distraught Roberto kneeling beside him. 'From what you've told me you were the victim of a planned attack. It's a blessing you're still alive, but it's obvious you weren't the target. Although for the life of me, I can't think why anyone would want to kill Jean. It must have been a robbery.' He shook his head in bewilderment. 'We can't leave Jean lying here; I want to take him into the house.'

Roberto stood up and squared his shoulders. 'I'm sorry, Master Jacob, we must see to Jean. I'm ready now.'

222

'Well done Roberto. You've had a terrible shock and you've recovered well. Lead on and keep a wary eye out in case the attackers are still hanging about.'

Roberto helped Jacob to his feet and drew out a knife. 'I hope they are,' he said savagely. 'They won't have it so easy this time.' With that Jacob lifted Jean into his arms and they set off for the house. Sweeping the things off the table in the entrance lobby he laid the body gently down. He went outside to check if anyone was about and was just about to enter when he heard a scream and a tearful enquiry from Mistress Simpkin.

'Oh! Roberto what have they done to Master Jacob?'

As Jacob stepped into the house her mouth dropped open in surprise. 'Master Jacob you're alive, but who's that on the table?'

Jacob, taken aback by Mistress Simpkin's cry gave a stunned look at the form lying on the table. With his face turned away and the bloodstained cloak with the hood pulled up covering him, it did look like him. Jean may well have been the victim of a case of mistaken identity. No wonder he couldn't think of anyone who'd wish to kill Jean. It was he who'd been the intended victim and he knew who was to blame for the outrage.

His body shook with fury. Sir Richard Urie! He was behind this terrible murder. He could recall his threats as if it was only yesterday. 'It'll be a time of my choosing, not yours.' He'd certainly chosen the time, but his assassins had killed the wrong man because Jean was wearing Jacob's cloak.

As realisation struck him, his anger was replaced with an icy calm. Realising the effect it would have on Roberto, he decided to say nothing for the time being. 'I'm afraid it's Jean, Mistress Simpkin. It would seem that some cut purses or vagrants have murdered him. We'll need to inform the watch. Could you go with Roberto and let them know what's happened?'

With a task to keep her busy, Mistress Simpkin stopped her wailing and became more her normal self. 'I'll go and get my cloak and we'll go straight away Master Jacob, but I'll be glad to have young Master Roberto with me.'

Roberto drew his knife and flourished it threateningly. 'Don't worry Mistress Simpkin. Should we meet those men again, they'll have to answer to me. I'll see you safely to the watch.'

As they hurried off Jacob turned the body over and examined Jean's wound and his purse. There was a single wound in the abdomen. The knife had been slipped in under the rib slanting upwards towards the heart. It was either a lucky thrust, or the mark of a skilled assassin. They must have left Jean for dead, but the thrust had not been instantly fatal. He felt carefully around the wound and above, but there was no sign of a glass blade. It was probably the work of some local villain, which again suggested Sir Richard Urie.

Turning his attention to Jean's purse, he examined it carefully. As he'd suspected it was still attached to his waistband and there was no sign of any attempt to cut it. Drawing his knife he slashed across the purse cutting one of the ties but not the other, then examined his handiwork. He nodded in satisfaction, then, carefully removing his cloak he covered the body. Before covering the face completely, he made a promise to his friend. 'I know who did this my friend and I swear by all the saints that this foul deed will be avenged. This time Sir Richard,' he spat out, 'it will be a time of my choosing, but first, it will be Jean's Crouched Friars Glass-works that will have its revenge. Then and only then will I take mine.'

With this chilling promise he reverently closed the eyes of his dead friend and drew his cloak over the face. Drawing up a chair he sat down and kept a vigil for Jean until the others returned with the 'Watch'. There was little doubt in his mind that the Watch would accept the bungled cut purse theory and so it proved. This suited Jacob perfectly. He knew that Sir Richard would be worried when he found out his assassins had bungled and those fears would be allayed when he learned that it was being credited as just another robbery. He might think that with Jean dead, he could buy the Crouched Friars for a song. Jacob resolved to see that this did not happen.

It was unlikely that Urie would try the same tactic again. Two similar attacks would be far too suspicious. This gave Jacob a little time to plan his tactics, but he would be alert for the slightest sign of any danger.

Once the watch had finished and the body had been taken to the undertakers, Jacob and Roberto sat down to a gloomy meal. Afterwards they started to go through Jean's papers in the hope that they would find some evidence of a next of kin. Jacob was not hopeful since Jean had told them that he had no family after his wife and child had died. Although as expected there was no reference to any kin, there was a reference to a lawyer in the City, together with a bill for drawing up a will. There was no sign of a will anywhere in Jean's room, so Jacob determined to visit the lawyer the following morning. The other letters and notes were all relating to visits to Antwerp and notes of discussions with Merchants, which were for the most part of little interest.

There was one however, that caught Jacob's interest. It was an account of a meeting between Jean and Sir Richard Urie and it was dated about sixteen months earlier. The notes themselves contained nothing new. Jean had passed on all the information to him at the time the partnership was agreed. What intrigued Jacob was a short note at the bottom in Jean's hand, which read 'See Walsingham about RU'. There was no doubt to whom this referred and Jacob made a mental note to ask Walsingham what had been discussed about RU when next they met. When that would be Jacob could only guess.

CHAPTER THIRTY -ONE

S leep was difficult that night and by the time the bells started their morning clatter Jacob was already astir. He sat gloomily picking at the food that a tearful Mistris Simpkin had set out for him. The anger of the previous night had given way to a mood of depression. Just when he was starting to feel optimism about the future, this had to happen.

Roberto came in looking as though he too had hardly slept. Refusing the offered food, he said he was going to the Crouched Friars. Jacob looked up his eyes dull with grief. 'I know I should do it myself, but will you tell Pietro and the other workers, what has happened and say that the Crouched Friars will be closed for a few days as a mark of respect.'

'What are you going to do Mater Jacob,' said Roberto anxiously. 'I'm not sure it's a good idea for you to stay here and grieve.'

Jacob gave a wan smile. 'I don't intent to Roberto. Don't worry, I'm not about to do anything silly.' He indicated some papers on the table. 'I think I'll pay a visit to the lawyer mentioned in Jean's papers. It's quite possible he has the will.'

A little while later they parted and Jacob went off to find the lawyer. Whilst the outside of the chambers used by the lawyer were very run down and seedy, Thomas Pepper most certainly was not. There were several people in the waiting room when Jacob arrived.

Thomas Pepper came out to greet him as soon as his clerk informed him that Jacob was waiting. 'Come in my dear sir, come in; Thomas Pepper at your service.' He said in a very friendly manner, shaking hands and ushering him into his room. Hurriedly moving a pile of papers from a chair he invited Jacob to be seated. 'I assume that Monsieur Thieré has asked you to visit me; he indicated you would be doing so shortly, when we last met. How may I be of service to you?'

He was shocked when Jacob explained the circumstances of his visit and shouted for his clerk to attend him. When the clerk arrived, he was sent to fetch the papers relating to Jean Thieré. He retuned with a large bundle tied up with red ribbon. Untying the ribbon, Thomas Pepper took out a document, secured with a large seal and placed it on his desk. Leaning back in his chair he regarded Jacob solemnly. 'Before I apprise you of the contents of this document, perhaps you would explain the reason for this visit. I had assumed it was some legal matter to do with the Crouched Friars, which I have represented on a number of occasions for Monsieur Thieré, but in view of this dreadful murder I now believe it to be a different matter entirely.'

Jacob nodded and explained how he had found the bill in Jean's papers, but nothing like a will, or any indication of any family who would need to be informed.

The lawyer indicated the document in front of him. 'The will is here and as the executor I propose to open it here in your presence.' Taking a knife from his desk, he carefully broke the seal and opening out the will he began to read.

It was a short document and the provisions were simple. Jean had left everything he owned to Jacob without any other bequests. Jacob was stunned. He'd not expected this at all. In truth he'd never considered what would happen if Jean died. The likelihood of that had never occurred to him.

A discreet cough roused him from his thoughts. Looking up he saw that the lawyer was holding out a letter for him. 'Monsieur Thieré left this letter to be handed to you in private if he was to die suddenly and only after I had read the contents of the will.' When Jacob took the letter he bowed and excusing himself, leaving Jacob to read the letter.

Jacob moved the chair round to the light and began to read.

'Mon cher ami, Jacob,

Greetings from beyond the grave! The fact you are reading this letter is proof that I have met an untimely end. I need to inform you of some circumstances, which may have a bearing on this and some other things, which you need to know.

You will remember that at the time we agreed on our partnership, I apprised you of certain discussions, which took place between representatives of the Glass Sellers Association and myself. What I did not tell you was that after these discussions, in a private conversation with Sir Richard Urie, he made thinly veiled threats as to how dangerous a place London might be if I continued to oppose him. I've had the feeling in recent weeks that someone has been following me. Try as I might though, I've been unable to catch anyone. Beware of Sir Richard Urie; he is a very dangerous man. I suggest you have a word with Walsingham. He knows all about him, but I would be betraying a confidence if I told you directly.

The other thing you must know is that in order to fit out the Crouched Friars as a Glass-works I was obliged to borrow money from John Isham, a leading member of the Mercers Guild, a Merchant Adventurer and an unusual fellow to boot. You will need to arrange to take over the loan and to help you in this I have prepared a letter for you to take to him. He is usually to be found either at the Guildhall, or at the Mercers Hall.

I do not believe you will have any problems over the loan. He's a very honest man who believes in making a deal on a handshake alone and he's not one to demand his money back if you're having problems. In some ways he's a strange fellow, but I'll not spoil your first meeting with him by telling you more.

I've left the details and this letter with Thomas Pepper who is a most trustworthy fellow. I commend him to you and suggest you seek his advice on legal matters. He is very well thought of by Walsingham amongst others and it will serve you well to listen and accept what he recommends when it comes to legalities of any kind.

Finally, a word to you on a personal note, Jacob: I have been very aware that but for my presence in Murano in '69, you would still be one of the most influential glass makers in Venice and if I'm any judge, the world as well.

It is my wish that you should have the Crouched Friars Glass-works as some small recompense for the loss of your own. Make of it what you will. I have no family left and you and Roberto have filled their place for me for which I thank you. I know you will look after that remarkable young man as he looks out for you. I envy you the devotion he shows you. It is a rare thing and needs to be cherished, as I know you will.

Fare you well Mon Cher ami and May God grant you a long and successful life.

Jean Thieré

Signed by his hand on the fifteenth day of May, in this year of our Lord one thousand five hundred and sixty-six.

Jacob put the letter down leaned back in the chair and took a deep breath. Letting it out slowly, he stood up and began to prowl around the room striving to gain control. An incandescent rage, fuelled by Jean's death and his own confrontation with Sir Richard Urie, threatened to take over and lead him down the all-consuming path to revenge. His vow to avenge Jean's death made over the body of his friend was nothing to what he now felt. His immediate impulse was to seek out Sir Richard Urie. 'I'll confront him and call him out!' Jacob raged to himself. 'I'll make him rue the day he killed Jean.' He savoured the thought of plunging his sword into his black heart. Eventually, he calmed down a little, as logic won the battle over his rage. Sir Richard had a lot of influence in London and there were no witnesses to either his, or Jean's confrontation. The letter wasn't proof; it would be dismissed as groundless fears. After all Jean admitted in the letter that he'd not been able to catch anyone following him.

The more he thought about it, the more he realised that fighting was not the answer and that his original idea to ruin Sir Richard by undercutting his glass selling would be the best starting point. He had no compunction about this, as Sir Richard deserved everything that was coming to him and more.

While the Crouched Friars was doing its work he might be able to get another lead from Walsingham in view of Jean's heavy hint and his suggestion to talk to him. If he could attack Sir Richard on two fronts, he might even be goaded into making threats before witnesses, and then he'd better look out. By the time Thomas Pepper came back into the room; his rage had turned back to icy calm, with only the high colour of his cheeks as an outward sign of his struggle.

For the next hour, they went through the various legalities surrounding the will and the transfer of the title. Eventually the lawyer announced that all the formalities had been completed and he would see that the appropriate authorities were informed. Jacob thanked him for the advice and help he'd been given; assuring Thomas Pepper that he would continue to be the legal adviser for the Crouched Friars.

As he made to take his leave the lawyer stood up. 'If you don't mind me saying so Master Bell I would advise you to see John Isham today if possible.' He looked guiltily at Jacob reminding him of a young boy caught stealing apples. 'I took the liberty of sending one of my apprentices to look for him. He's at the Mercers Hall and I'm informed he is likely to be there for the next couple of hours.' That guilty look again. 'I also took the liberty of informing him of Monsieur Thiéré's death; the fact that you were the new owner of the Crouched Friars and of your intention to take over the loan with his agreement. I hope that this meets with your approval?'

Jacob shook his head in amusement. 'Your help is much appreciated Thomas Pepper and as I fully intended to see John Isham at the earliest opportunity, you have saved me a lot of trouble by locating him. Could I impose on you further, by begging the loan of your apprentice as a guide? I don't know London well as yet and I've only the vaguest idea where the Mercers Hall is to be found.'

'Of course Master Bell with pleasure, but a word in your ear, John Isham is a strange fellow in some ways and don't be surprised if he recounts a story of sea serpents, or monsters on some far off shore. He loves telling stories of that sort and quoting proverbs. Don't be fooled though, he is very shrewd and wealthy too, as the result of his investments.' He smiled sheepishly. 'He's also a long-standing client of mine and is always going to court on one matter or the other. Oh and by the way, I've advised him that you would be every bit as safe with the loan as Jean Thieré.'

Jacob was rather overwhelmed by the trouble that his newly acquired lawyer and adviser was taking on his behalf and said as much in unequivocal terms.

For his part, Thomas made light of it. 'I'm only doing what I'd do for any of my clients.' He smiled pleasantly giving a depreciating wave of his hand. 'I like to think that I look after the best interests of my clients and try to anticipate how I can most be of help.'

Completing his business with Thomas, Jacob set off for the Mercers Hall, with the apprentice leading the way. As always, Jacob was amazed at the hustle and bustle of the streets. The noise was deafening and even the broad main thoroughfares were crowded, with the occasional coach putting life and limb at risk as the crowds scattered to make way. The many lumbering carts of produce, whilst not as dangerous as the coaches, severely restricted progress as they trundled along.

Arriving at the Mercers Hall, Jacob thanked the apprentice, gave him a small coin and went into the Hall. He was informed that John Isham was expecting him in the main dining hall, where he was supervising the preparations for a dinner.

Whilst he was waiting for John Isham to finish his conversation with a large florid faced woman Jacob assumed to be the cook, he studied his surroundings with interest. The long oak-panelled room was sumptuously decorated and contained many fine oil paintings. There were two long oak dining tables with trestle forms for seats. At the far end of the room was a slightly raised dais with another table set at right angles to the others. Behind this table were set ten large carved, upholstered oak chairs. The wall behind this table had some extremely fine portraits, the central one being of Sir Richard Whittington, a former head of the Mercers who died in 1423, or so the label informed him.

'A fine portrait of my predecessor is it not?' said a jovial voice from behind him and Jacob turned to see the rather portly figure of John Isham. He was soberly dressed, but his round florid face was creased with many laughter lines. 'Dick Whittington was responsible for many improvements in the City,' he went on chattily. 'He built his famous Long House pissing place on the riverside between Billinsgate and Queenhithe. It can accommodate sixty-four users, equally divided between men and women and is still in use today. I doubt you had anything like that in Venice, eh!, Master Bell,' he said with a smile. 'I do have the pleasure of addressing Master Jacob Bell, have I not?' He indicated the painting of Sir Richard Whittington. 'He's a fine example to us all. He came from humble beginnings to be Lord Mayor of London no less than three times.'

This stream of information overwhelmed Jacob, as without waiting for a reply, John Isham led him over to the table. Pulling one of the chairs round to the end, he motioned for Jacob to sit down. Pulling one of the other chairs forward, he sat facing Jacob and studied him for a moment before continuing. 'Welcome to the Mercer's Hall, Master Bell, although I must say, it's a sad occasion that brings us together. A sad business indeed; I counted Jean Thieré as one of my friends.'

'A terrible thing, Master Isham,' agreed Jacob with feeling. 'I too have lost a friend as well as a partner. I have too few of those, to lose one such as Jean.'

'Amen to that,' was the reply. 'Jean Thieré was good man as well as having a shrewd eye for business. The Crouched Friars has been doing good trade since he persuaded you to join, that is, if the screams from the Glass Sellers are any indication.'

Jacob felt his hackles rising at the reference to the Glass Sellers, but contained his anger. Although John Isham appeared to be kindly disposed towards him, it was too soon to confide in him about the part played by Sir Richard Urie. At John Isham's request, he recounted the events leading up to Jean's death. He simply explained that the watch thought it was the work of cutpurses.

When he'd finished John Isham stood up and held out his hand. When Jacob stood up and took the proffered hand he closed his other hand over the top and regarded Jacob with an encouraging smile. 'Heart and hand, Jacob Bell; heart and hand; you have my blessing for the loan and I trust you to continue in the same fashion as Jean Thieré.' He smiled broadly at Jacob surprise. 'Although I use Thomas Pepper to fight my cases in court, all of my loans are done on the shake of a hand.' His grin became even wider. 'I give Thomas enough money with court work as it is, without adding to it,' he said with a laugh. 'Thomas says that Jean Thieré trusted you and made you his heir. He was my friend,' he said simply, 'so that is good enough for me. I only make loans to people I trust and a handshake given from the heart is all I ask.'

He walked with Jacob towards the entrance and placed a friendly hand on his shoulder. 'I would like you to call me John from now on and I would be honoured if you will allow me to call you Jacob in return.' He smiled when Jacob nodded and went on. 'Should you have any difficulty with the Glass-works, or need more money to expand, you can rest assured that I'll be sympathetic. The Letters Patent you seek will result in a large expansion of your business. Sir William Cecil is well disposed to me and I will add my voice to your supporters. I believe you'll do very well in London, but if you require any assistance with business in Antwerp, I have many contacts. Jean usually handled trade with them and a lot of it was financed by me and went through my warehouse in that city.' He tapped the side of his nose with his finger and grinned like a schoolboy. 'I keep quite a bit of money in Antwerp for just that and other purposes you know.'

This offer was gratefully received and accepted, since Jacob had been worried about that side of the business. Together with the loan, it removed all of the immediate problems and Jacob felt confident that the Glass-works was now on a firm footing. He thanked John Isham profusely, especially for his support with the Letters Patent.

'A small matter Jacob, I am glad to assist you as I would have Jean Thieré. By the way, I would like you to accept my invitation to spend the weekend at the Isham cottage in Tottenham. I like to get away from the City and the countryside is still reasonably unspoiled there. The garden keeps us in fresh vegetables you know. I'll send you an invitation when I've had a word with Mistress Isham, but we'll make it soon.'

Jacob thanked him again, then making his farewell, he hurried away to give Roberto the good news.

CHAPTER THIRTY-TWO

O ver the next few months Jacob, Roberto and everyone at the Glass-works worked hard to establish more trade. The English workers continued to improve with one exception. He'd proved to be a disruptive influence and was not well liked by the other workers. Once he'd left, things settled down well and everyone worked happily together.

Spring was now on them and the trees had begun to burst into new life. It was against this time of renewal, that Jacob received some shattering news. One evening they had finished early for once and Jacob suggested they went to the Three Stars Tavern for a drink. It was one of the most popular taverns in London. While we were waiting for Roberto to bring the drinks, he heard two men talking in Italian at the next table. They were gossiping about Venice one of them having recently arrived in a private trading ship. Starved of news from home, he listened to a lot of small talk until suddenly the new arrival mentioned Lady Maria Morisini.

At first Jacob couldn't believe what he was hearing. There had to be some mistake. Unfortunately, it soon became obvious that it was not. Lady Maria had married Adrian Ragazoni. I know she loves me he thought and she wouldn't marry Ragazoni, not even though she thinks I'm dead. He sat slumped in his seat and tried to imagine why she would do such a thing. It was to his credit that at no time did he think that Maria had betrayed him. He simply couldn't understand what inducement would make her take such a step.

Just then Roberto arrived and put the drinks on the table. Seeing the expression on Jacob's face, he became concerned. 'Whatever is the matter Master Jacob,' he cried. 'You look as though you've seen a ghost.'

When Jacob explained what he'd overheard, Roberto

immediately sprang to Lady Maria's defence. 'He must have forced her in some way Master Jacob; she'd never marry that swine unless she had to.'

Jacob was touched by Roberto's reaction. 'Apparently Senator Morisini had an argument with Ragazoni at the wedding feast,' he told him, 'and Lady Maria is living in her own house and not his.' Suddenly he realised the significance of the description by the man. 'Oh Roberto, I'm so relieved. I realise now that Lady Maria is living in my villa. Now I'm sure that Maria hasn't betrayed me. She'd never have gone to live in my house, which I signed over to her, if she had.' He became agitated again. 'That still doesn't explain why she married Ragazoni though. Perhaps he worked one of his tricks on her as well!'

Roberto shook his head. 'I don't know Master Jacob perhaps she's doing it to try and catch him out. If I was in that position that's what I'd do.' He became angry and his face darkened with emotion. 'She'd never let that scheming swine Ragazoni get away with it, not while she had breath in her body. You can be sure of that Master Jacob.'

He was startled when Jacob gave a sharp barking laugh and clapped him on the shoulder. 'You're a marvel Roberto. You have this God – given ability to get right to the heart of something. I do believe you've the right of it. That's exactly the sort of thing that Maria would do.'

He became pensive again. 'I wish we'd let her know I was safe and not let her keep on thinking I was dead.' He turned to Roberto again. 'I can't let her keep on suffering on my account. I must get a message to her as soon as possible and my father too.'

Roberto frowned. 'I'm not sure that will change anything Master Jacob,' he warned. 'She'll still be married and you can't change that.'

'I can go back and kill Ragazoni and then she'll be free.'

'And you'd really be executed this time, Master Jacob. Like it or not, you're still an escaped galley oarsman and would be arrested as soon as you set foot in Venice.'

Jacob had the grace to look sheepish at his outburst. 'Right again Roberto, I know you're right, but it's so hard to do nothing.' He went over to Roberto and put an arm round his shoulder in a friendly gesture. 'You always manage to find the right thing to say.'

'I'll never be able to repay you for what you've done for me.'

'Don't think that Roberto,' Jacob said. 'Anything I've done for you, you've repaid me several times over. I count you as my friend and I value your way of seeing things.'

By mutual consent, they changed the subject and relaxed and enjoyed their drinks. Both of then had acquired a taste for the local ale, which at first they'd found bitter.

The next morning, Jacob sat in his workroom and contemplated the new situation. There was no denying that the news of Maria's marriage to Ragazoni was a shattering blow. One thing was certain, as Roberto had pointed out, he couldn't change it and if he went back to fight; he would lose everything again and alter nothing. There's only one thing I can do and that's to trust Maria and hope that she can discover Adrian's plots and expose him to the authorities. He grimaced as he thought of the danger she might be in. I hope she's careful though. That viper Ragazoni is just as dangerous as the real snake and it will go hard for her if she's found out. Fortunately she's a resourceful woman and she'll know the danger. He brooded for a while. I wonder what pressure Ragazoni put on her to marry him. It obviously didn't go down too well with Ricardo.

Recognising there was little he could do at present he turned to more immediate tasks, but not before he'd vowed to try and get Lunardo to help when he visited London next.

There'd be a lot to talk about as well. Details of a battle between Venetian and Turkish galleys near Cyprus had been trickling through to London. Only a few days ago he'd heard that the refitted 'Galliano' had been at the forefront, and inflicted enormous damage on the Turkish galleys. Having seen the English long guns in action this was no surprise to Jacob. Lunardo had no doubt returned to Venice as a hero. Well good for him and he hoped his former shipmates had come through the battle safely.

Just then Roberto arrived and for the next hour they concentrated on organising the Glass-works and planning the next stage of their attack on the Glass Sellers. Through one of his apprentice friends Roberto had found out several of the Glass Sellers customers. It was surprising what you could find out from them for the price of a drink. Façon de Venice glasses were being made at the Crouched Friars at a price the Glass sellers couldn't hope to match with their imported glass. The Glass Sellers could of course sell at a loss, but that was almost as satisfactory. The result would be the same, the Glass Seller's would have to meet his terms, or go out of business.

Jacob smiled grimly at the thought. He'd no quarrel with most of the Glass Sellers, only with Sir Richard Urie. Once he'd been dealt with, he could afford to come to a more generous accommodation with the rest of the Glass Sellers.

The information from Roberto's apprentice friends had once again proved to be very useful and Jacob was grateful for it. This set him thinking on other lines and he decided to have words with Roberto about it. Later that evening when they were enjoying that pleasurable feeling brought on by a satisfying meal, he broached the subject with Roberto. 'I have been most grateful for the information, which your apprentice friends have passed on. I know that most of them don't earn a lot. Do you think they would be offended if I offered to pay them for any information they supply?'

He was startled when Roberto burst out laughing. 'Not at all,' he said when he'd calmed down a little. 'In fact I've been giving them a shilling each time and they all want to have the same.'

It was Jacob's turn to laugh. 'You must tell me how much you've paid out and I'll pay you back.'

'There's no need to do that Master Jacob. It was only a few shillings and I can well afford it from what you give me.'

Roberto's answer was as usual direct and knowing from his tone there was little point in arguing, Jacob accepted gratefully. 'In that case Roberto I'm going to give you an allowance for paying for information.' This could be the answer to obtaining the information that Cecil and Walsingham wanted. 'Is there one of the apprentices who can be trusted to act as a go-between with the other apprentices?'

After a moments thought Roberto nodded. 'I think I know the very one. What exactly do you have in mind?'

'When I was thinking how useful the information from the apprentices was this afternoon, it occurred to me that we haven't made full use of them. There must be hundreds of them in London alone.'

'More like thousands Master Jacob,' interrupted Roberto.

'Yes, well what I had in mind was to try to set up a network of apprentices who would bring us information on any topic, which was of interest. They don't get paid a lot and many of them live and work in very poor conditions and they would be glad of some extra money.'

'They get heavily punished as well for the slightest thing in some cases,' said Roberto, his tone became very indignant. 'One of my friends was given a terrible black eye last week by his employer. Just for spilling a drop of ink whilst filling an inkwell. That's all!'

'Is he the one you had in mind as the go-between, Roberto?'

'Yes Master Jacob. He's about a year older than I am and he's in debt to his employer. He gets charged interest for what he owes and gets paid so little that his debt just seems to mount up. He can't get away unless he pays up and his employer keeps threatening to send him to the debtor's' prison.'

'He sounds like a really nice man.' Jacob said without humour. 'Do you know how much he owes?' He asked thoughtfully. 'If you think he can be trusted I could pay off his debts and get him to organise the network of apprentices for us. I would give him a job and pay him, of course.'

Roberto reply was delighted and enthusiastic. 'If you pay of his debts Master Jacob he'd be your man and you could trust him with your life.'

'I hope that won't be necessary,' said Jacob with feeling. 'Get in touch with him tomorrow and bring him to the house if he can come, or arrange a day when it's convenient. I'd like to get this started as soon as possible. Do you agree?'

'I certainly do Master Jacob and if we can help 'Quiff' into the bargain, so much the better.'

'Quiff?'

'It's the name everyone calls him. I don't know his real name. His hair is dark, but he has this tuft of white hair sticking up above his forehead. No matter what he does, it still sticks up. It's very distinctive.'

'It sounds like it,' commented Jacob. 'Get him to come and see me as soon as possible and we'll see what can be done.'

A week later, having met Quiff, Jacob decided that the best way to proceed was indeed to pay off Quiff's debts and to buy out his apprentice papers. 'This sounds like a job for Thomas Pepper,' Jacob informed Roberto and sent Quiff to the lawyer with a note of explanation. Two days later Quiff arrived at the Glass-works and presented Jacob with a letter from Thomas. This contained his apprentice papers duly signed over to Jacob and the Crouched Friars Glass-works had a new worker.

Jacob chuckled when he read the note from Thomas. He recounted his meeting with Quiff's master and described how he'd explained the laws of 'Usury' and its penalties to him. 'For some reason he seemed very glad to accept a reasonable figure for the apprentice papers,' he wrote ironically. 'In return of course, for my assurance that I wouldn't report his transgressions to the authorities.'

With the legalities settled, it was now a matter of arranging a cover job for Quiff, which would leave him free to make contact with the apprentices. There was also the matter of where he should live, as he was now homeless. The latter problem was easily solved. Roberto moved into Jean's old room and Quiff moved into Roberto's old room at Harte Street.

After some discussion Jacob decided that Quiff should be Roberto's assistant and would do all of the errands and special deliveries. This would give him the freedom to move around and keep him in contact with other apprentices. One thing Jacob was adamant about was that the house in Harte Street should not be used for contacting the apprentices. That was to remain completely separate from any type of business, private or otherwise.

Quiff suggested that they use a well-known tavern 'The Swan', which was frequently visited by apprentices from all over the city. 'I know the landlord quite well. He's a bit of a rogue, but he's discreet if paid to be. They have some private booths, which are often used for assignations. For a sovereign I'm sure he'll let me use one of them regularly and would probably take messages as well.'

Jacob thought a moment then agreed. 'That sounds like a good arrangement, but give him three sovereigns with the promise of more to come from time to time. That should ensure his discretion.'

Quiff laughed. 'There's no doubt about that. For that amount he'd kill his own mother!' he said sarcastically. 'But it's not a bad idea. He'll be very anxious to keep the arrangement going. I'll go round tonight and set it up.'

As Quiff had forecast the landlord was delighted to have such a generous agreement and more than willing to take messages. He even arranged for Quiff to use a booth near the private entry at the back so that people could slip in and out without going through the main room.

Within two weeks the group was beginning to expand rapidly and word was spreading among the apprentices. The first target for information was Sir Richard Urie. Knowing his arrogant attitude and quick temper, Jacob was sure that some of his apprentices would be only too willing to provide information and so it proved. By the end of a month, information of all sorts was coming in and Quiff was proving to be an inspired choice. He had quickly gained the confidence of the apprentices and enjoyed the freedom of his role as collator of the information. The reports he gave Jacob in his small, neat handwriting were usually short and to the point. He often added a personal comment on how much trust he put in the report. This helped enormously in assessing its value.

Quiff introduced a regime of leaving the Glass-works about an hour before the normal finishing time to go to the 'Swan'. He'd pick up any messages and then wait in the booth for the rest of the hour, before returning to Harte Street to join the others for the evening meal. All Jacob could do now, was to have patience and wait to see what the apprentices turned up.

CHAPTER THIRTY-THREE

At first the information from the Ring was of too general a nature to be of interest. The first real fruits of the network came from a rather unexpected quarter. On this particular evening Quiff arrived home a little earlier than usual and was waiting in the entrance hall when Jacob came in. 'Can I tell you what I've found out right away Master Jacob,' he burst out excitedly before Jacob had even chance to take off his cloak. 'I've some interesting news about Sir Richard Urie, which I must tell you.'

Seeing how excited he was Jacob took him straight up to the sitting room. Once they'd settled Quiff blurted out his news. 'When I got to the 'Swan' tonight the landlord said two young men had been in a short while earlier asking for me. He'd shown them the back way in and told them to come back in half an hour.'

Jacob expressed his concern. 'I hope the landlord is careful about giving information to strangers like that. He mustn't let everyone know about you and the apprentices.'

'It's all right Master Jacob, don't worry about him.' Quiff reassured him confidently. 'He's no fool and he knew the younger of the two, he's been to see me before.'

'That's a relief,' said Jacob with feeling. 'I don't want this job to put you into any danger. I'd rather forget about it than have you hurt as a result.'

'Don't worry about me Master Jacob; I can take care of myself.' He smiled self-assuredly. 'The landlord can be trusted to make sure it's only apprentices who get to see me in private. He's been paid well for what he does and he isn't going to put it at risk. Besides he's a bit of a rogue and he's no love of snoopers.'

Jacob was relieved to hear it. 'That's all right then. Please go on with your tale.'

Quiff explained that the man was the older brother of the

apprentice he already knew and he was employed in the household of Sir Richard Urie.

'Is he now,' said Jacob with feeling, 'that's very interesting.'

'It is indeed Master Jacob.' answered an excited Quiff, 'and it gets better. He had quite an interesting tale to tell. It seems that Sir Richard has some visitors who come and go by a secret entrance.'

Jacob was surprised. 'A secret entrance, how does he come to know about it?'

Quiff was getting a little impatient to tell the whole story. 'Please don't ask anymore questions Master Jacob, or I'll never get to finish.' Jacob grinned and jocularly told him to get on with it, which he proceeded to do with alacrity.

About four weeks ago, the servant John Noble had been on duty in the house when Sir Richard was at home. Part of his duty that day was to answer the door to visitors and there had been none. An errand boy brought a message for Sir Richard and John took it to his study, where Sir Richard had been for some time. He knocked on the door and not hearing any reply, walked in to find the room was empty. Whilst this in itself was not that unusual, on this occasion however, he'd been within sight of the only door into the study since Sir Richard had gone in and he was certain he'd not come out.

He was about to leave when he heard the sound of voices. It was rather muffled, but he could tell it was people arguing. Curiosity overcame his caution and he searched around to find the source. He managed to trace it to a section of bookcase on the wall, to the right of the fireplace. Noticing that the central section was slightly out of line with the others he looked closer. There was a secret door in the bookcase and a fallen book had caught in the bottom, stopping it from closing completely. His interest being further aroused, he listened at the crack.

Sir Richard was saying goodbye to someone he addressed as Count Maldini and fearing he'd be discovered John fled. He was just closing the door when Sir Richard called out angrily wanting to know who was there. Realising he couldn't get away he decided to brazen it out and went in pretending he was just coming in with the letter. Sir Richard flew into a towering rage and struck him several times with a riding crop he picked up from the desk. He's still got a scar on his cheek from it. He was told that if he ever went into the study again without knocking he would have him whipped and dismissed on the spot. He then hustled him out with further blows and kicks.

'What do you think of that, Master Jacob?' asked Quiff jubilantly.'

Jacob was exultant. The reference to Count Maldini and the secrecy could mean only one thing. Sir Richard Urie was probably involved in the plot against the Queen. His mind raced on a little then he became aware that Quiff was regarding him with a puzzled frown on his face.

'I'm sorry Quiff I was lost in my own thoughts. This is splendid news. It's just the sort of thing I hoped you might turn up.' Seeing Quiff's deepening frown he realised that of course he wouldn't realise the significance of the reference to Count Maldini. 'I'm sorry Quiff I've just realised that you will have no idea what I'm talking about. Let me explain.'

He told Quiff about the plot by Count Maldini and a much watered-down version of his part in thwarting the assassination attempt on Walsingham. 'So you see this can only mean that Urie is involved.'

'He mustn't be allowed to get away with it,' said Quiff fiercely. 'Everyone loves the Queen. She's the best thing to happen to England for years and she'll make things better for everyone if she's allowed to do it.'

Once again Jacob reflected on the loyalty that the Queen commanded, even from lowly subjects. He was about to say more when Roberto came in. He'd stayed to lock up and was really looking forward to the evening meal, but seeing the two of them looking sombre, or so he thought, he wondered what had happened.

'You two are looking serious. What's the matter? Has Quiff had some problems tonight?'

Jacob laughed and Quiff joined in. 'Not at all, it's not trouble at all, it's rather good news.' He quickly brought Roberto up to date and then asked what he thought. As usual he was quick to put his finger on the core of the situation. 'It seems we have two things, first we have a good indication that Sir Richard may be plotting against the Queen and secondly we have an ally in his household. Did this John Noble have anything else to say about this secret passage, or room? There must be another entrance, or John Noble would have seen the men he was talking to come into the house.' He asked Quiff astutely as it turned out.

'As a matter of fact he did although I was saving this up until the last.'

Jacob grinned and looked at Roberto. 'Quiff's another one I'm going to have to watch.' He pretended to be angry, but gave up as both of them grinned. He reminded them that the meal would be ready and suggested Quiff should hurry up and tell the rest.

What he had to say was that John Noble had found out about the secret room and passage, since that's what it was. He'd crept into the study when Sir Richard had gone to a meeting in London and knowing where to look had discovered the secret door in no time at all. A passage led down to the cellars into a secret room. The room was fairly small with only a table and three chairs and a small fireplace with a stack of logs beside it. There were some candles on the table and a low passage led off from the far side. Lighting one of the candles he'd gone along the passage coming out through a bolted door concealed in a thicket at the rear of the house. After a quick look to get his bearings, he went back into the secret room.

As well as the candles on the table, there was some writing material, but no letters. Fearful of discovery he was about to go back into the house, when he noticed some charred papers in the fireplace. When he examined them, he discovered in the middle, one of the papers was only charred around the edges and some writing was still visible. He could see nothing else of interest, so taking the paper, he returned to the study, checked the door was closed correctly and hurried off to his room.

'That's incredible,' said Jacob excitedly. 'What was on the paper Quiff? Did he tell you?'

Quiff made the most of the moment. 'He did better than that Master Jacob,' he said producing a charred letter with a flourish. 'He brought it with him.'

Jacob took the proffered letter and began to read it eagerly, hoping it was not simply a meaningless scrap of paper. His heart leapt as he took in the full import of the rough draft of a letter addressed to no less a person than Mary Stuart, the imprisoned Queen of the Scots. The letter was badly charred at the top and bottom and the middle was scorched. However, it contained one telling phrase near the bottom and the signature of Sir Richard Urie. 'I have consulted with Count Maldini on the details of which your majesty is aware, for the removal of the bastard Queen and find myself in complete agreement with his conclusions and plans.'

Jacob had little doubt what Sir Richard meant by 'the removal of the bastard Queen'. Walsingham had been certain that Count Maldini was plotting to kill the Queen and put the Queen of the Scots in her place. Whilst it was clearly not the final letter, Jacob had little doubt that it would be sufficient to incriminate Sir Richard and Count Maldini.

He congratulated Quiff on the success of his contacts. 'You know Quiff I could hardly have asked for anything better from the 'Ring'. The problem is how best to use this information. What is this John Noble doing now and have you paid him well for the letter?'

'I did Master Jacob, I hope you agree, but I thought it was worth a sovereign.' He looked relieved when Jacob smiled and nodded. 'As for John Noble, he's gone back to the Urie house in Tottenham.'

'Tottenham?' The name sounded familiar to Jacob, but for the moment he couldn't recall why. 'Of course,' he said a moment later. 'I knew I'd heard the name somewhere else recently. John Isham of the Mercers has a cottage there, which he uses at the weekend. He said he would invite me to visit him fairly soon and it might be a useful to have a look at this secret room. Providing Sir Richard Urie is away of course. Will it be easy to contact John Noble?'

'I thought you might want to get in touch, so before he left I arranged that his brother would pass on a message if we wanted to see him.'

Jacob clapped him on the shoulder and congratulated him. 'That's excellent Quiff, you've done very well. I can see you and your apprentice 'Ring' are going to be very useful. Now let's go and have our meal, we've earned it.'

Quiff blushed with pleasure at the praise. He was not used to it, the only contact he'd usually had from his employer was kicks and curses. It is interesting to note that from that day forward, Quiff simply referred to the apprentices as 'The Ring', following Jacob's reference to it as such. Jacob for his part was convinced that the 'Ring' was destined to prove its worth many times over in the years to come.

CHAPTER THIRTY-FOUR

The voyage to England had been long and tedious and Maria was thankful that she'd seen little of Adrian during the journey – she'd shared a cabin with Anna Rosso, whilst Adrian had his own. Since the night that Adrian had tried to make love to her, relationships had been strained. At least he'd not tried again! Adrian made a sort of apology next day; blaming the drink for his actions, but Maria was wary of him even now.

The Ambassador's house they had reached two days earlier was large and built with oak beams and supports between which, were red bricks, laid in a herringbone pattern. It had originally been constructed for a German merchant, in Galley Row, sometimes known as Petty Wales, close to Galley Key, where the Galley to Flanders unloaded its wares. Most of these were stored in the basements at the rear of the house. The house had been rented by the Venetian Republic for several years and had been extensively restored by the last Ambassador, who had used his considerable wealth to good effect. The interior of the house was striking with its extensive floor to ceiling oak panelling in the "lignum undulatum" pattern and the imposing enclosed fireplaces used for burning coal. The plasterwork, especially the coat of arms over the fireplaces, was exceptional.

Maria's favourite part of the house was the long gallery, used for entertaining, for exercise on dull days, and as a portrait gallery. It featured windows on three sides and fireplaces along the fourth, and it ran the entire length of the upper floor.

That afternoon it was raining heavily and Maria was walking in the long gallery, admiring the many fine paintings, one of which was of the Doge in 1567, Pietro Loredano. Stopping to look out of the windows at the far end of the gallery, directly over the living quarters, she was surprised to hear faint voices, one of which sounded like Adrian's. The courtyard below was empty and there were no rooms leading off the gallery. Intrigued, Maria tried to trace the sounds. As she approached the nearby, empty fireplace, the voices became louder. Bending down and putting her head inside the large opening, she was surprised, to hear Adrian's voice, obviously from the study below.

He was talking to his servants and his words could be heard quite clearly as he gave instructions for a meeting to be held at the house the following evening. 'I want you to make sure that we are not disturbed,' Adrian said in his usual arrogant tones. 'There will be Count Maldini, Sir Richard Urie and several other prominent Englishmen. You must make sure that the room is totally clear and secure before the meeting and that nobody, including my wife, is allowed access without my express orders. Do I make myself clear?' The rest of what he said was almost inaudible, presumably, he had moved to the far end of the room. In case he came upstairs, Maria hurried down to the other end of the long room and sat in one of the comfortable chairs. There was no doubt that her husband was up to no good. She had her suspicions about the meeting with Count Maldini in Venice, and now this!

One thing Maria knew from bitter experience, when Adrian was plotting, someone was going to get swindled, hurt, or worse. If only she was able to overhear what went on at the meeting in Venice. Suddenly a thought struck her and she smiled. She didn't succeed in Venice, but here was a different matter now she knew about the fireplace. It might not be possible to hear all of the conversation, but she would be able to get an idea of what was going on.

The following evening Adrian warned her about snooping. 'I will not tolerate you interfering in my affairs again,' he said. 'You will not escape so lightly this time if you do. My men will be on the look out so stay in you r room.'

When the meeting had started in the study, Maria cautiously slipped out of her room and went up to the long room.

Fortunately, the back stairs were at the end nearest her room and not near the study. When she arrived at the fireplace, she was dismayed to find that all of the fires had been lit. Luckily they had not been lit too long and the coal had not burned through. There was a fire screen with an ornate Chinese pattern nearby and by putting this to one side of the fireplace and crouching down, Maria found she could listen without getting burned,

As she settled down, she heard Adrian propose a toast. 'Gentleman the toast is Mary Stuart, Queen of the Scots and rightful heir to the throne of England. May she soon be restored to both thrones.' There was a loud cry of Mary, Queen of the Scots from all present and then a loud voice called for attention. Maria was certain the voice belonged to Count Maldini who had visited them in Venice.

'Gentleman, I thank Envoy Ragazoni for the toast and I tell you all that if we play our parts well, that day will not be long delayed. The bastard Elizabeth will be no more, Mary Stuart will be released and with the backing of the Catholic Lords, will take her rightful place as Queen of England.' This brought loud approbation, which went on for some time. He then called for Envoy Ragazoni to outline his part of the plot, which was to assassinate Queen Elizabeth.

She listened with mounting horror as the full scale of Adrian's involvement enfolded. The plot had been worked out in Venice with Count Maldini and was dependent on Adrian becoming the Venetian Envoy to England.

Once he had presented his credentials to Elizabeth, she and the court would be invited to an elaborate reception at the Ambassadors residence. Knowing Elizabeth's love of dancing, an orchestra would be set up at the end of the long room with curtains behind them covering the back stairs. The two assassins dressed in Adrian's distinctive livery of gold and black, would be on guard in the corridor leading to the private apartments. When the orchestra began tuning up, they would don hooded cloaks hidden behind the door leading to the basement and go up the back stairs and conceal themselves behind the curtain. Once there, they would unfold the small crossbows from there doublets and when Adrian led out the Queen for the honour of the first dance, she would be shot with quarrels dipped in an opium based poison, provided by the Spanish.

At a range of less than fifteen feet, they should both hit the target and even if she were not killed outright, the poison would finish the job. The assassins would rush down the stairs, throw the cloaks down the stairs to the basement and rush up to the long room by the front stairs to join in the search for the assassins. The back door to the basement would be left unlocked and if pursuit went that way, an accomplice would say that two men dressed as sailors had come out of the door and headed towards Galley Key.

They were sure that Elizabeth would take the bait. Like her father before her, Elizabeth was sympathetic to the Venetian cause, but the Signory had preferred to avoid conflict with its fellow Catholics countries, by remaining neutral and not sending an Ambassador. Elizabeth's support of their dispute with the French, had changed their mind and led them to send an Envoy to carry out negotiations with Elizabeth, with a view to restoring full diplomatic relations. Letters sent prior to Ragazoni's appointment had signalled their intent. The Signory was of course unaware of the plot against the Queen and Ragazoni's part, once he had been named as Envoy.

Maria who all this time had been craning forward to hear all the details of this dastardly plot, became aware of a burning sensation on her arm and a strong smell of scorching. Realising that the fire had been burning up and the sleeve of her dress was now almost in flames, she jumped back. In her haste, her knee caught the screen and it toppled over knocking down the firedogs with a resounding crash. Beating at the smouldering sleeve, Maria fled in panic down the back stairs and rushed to her room. Ripping off the dress in such a hurry that the top of her chemise was torn, she hurriedly looked for another day dress.

The door burst open and Adrian appeared his face distorted with rage. Without a word he rushed up to her and smashed his fist into her face sending her crashing to the floor. Standing over her, he sniffed the air then went to the dress over the chair and brandished the badly scorched sleeve. 'I assume you overheard the conversation from the room below at the fireplace. You stupid fool,' he snarled. 'I warned you not to interfere in my affairs.'

Reaching down as the still dazed Maria tried to get up, he grabbed hold of the torn chemise ripping it from top to bottom. He launched a flurry of blows on her, which left her sprawling half senseless on the bed. Taking off his belt and removing the sword and scabbard, he wrapped the buckle in his hand. Ripping off her silk drawers, her turned her over and began to lash her with the belt, raising weals across her back and buttocks. Ignoring her cries for mercy, he gave her a dozen strokes, punctuating each with a threat. When at last he stopped, there was still no release for the barely conscious Maria. Turning her over, he removed his tights and spreading her legs he savagely violated her. When at last he'd finished, he dressed and sat down beside her, stroking her hair and caressing her breasts.

Maria cowered away from him as the nightmare continued, his relentless voice seeming to come from the end of a long tunnel. 'My dear wife,' he mocked. 'I told you in Venice that things would be different in London. From now on you will be confined to your room and only my men and that women of yours will attend you.' He smiled evilly. 'Except for the nights of course; you'll have my visits to look forward to. I want to make sure, that before long; you're pregnant with my child. Your father will never refuse to cut off his heir.' He chuckled evilly. 'We'll have so much fun trying for a baby. I confess I've never felt so virile.'

Mercifully for Maria, she must have fainted at this point. Some while later, she felt the soothing touch of a cold cloth on her face. Opening her eyes, she saw Anna Rosso bending over her with tears coursing down her cheeks. When she saw Maria had come round, she sobbed, 'Oh! Thank God, my Lady, I thought he'd killed you. Your poor face and back. I've done the best I can with the weals and although you have the start of a black eye, it's not too bad. You'll be fine when the swelling goes down.' Maria tried to speak but her mouth was swollen and her throat was dry. Unable to tell what she'd said Anna gave her a drink of water, which Maria drank greedily.

Sitting up with a groan, she clutched Anna's arm. 'Fetch me my writing material and a pen,' she cried urgently, ignoring the pain from her bruised mouth 'I must write a letter.'

'Just rest, my Lady, you're in no fit state to be writing letters.'

'But I must Anna; this may be the only chance I'll get. They'll not suspect it, especially if you play up how bad I am. Just do as I ask,' she said fiercely, wincing at the pain from her back. 'Where is my husband?'

'That fiend,' spat Anna, 'he's gone off with that Count Maldini. Laughing and joking they were.'

'Good,' said Maria, 'now tell me what was said to you.'

Anna explained that she had been told that Maria had been chastised and was to stay in her room and that Anna was to attend her and do what was necessary to see that she recovered. Adrian had warned her that she'd suffer the same fate if Maria didn't get better. The two guards had been told to make sure that Maria didn't escape, but that Anna was to be given anything she needed to treat Maria. Anna was to remain in the house, but they were to ensure that Lady Maria was treated for her injuries.

While explaining all this, Anna helped her to put on her nightdress and propped her up in the bed with extra pillows. Fortunately for Maria, her hands and arm were not hurting and so long as she held her body as still as possible, the pain was tolerable. Taking the pen, she thought for a moment and then began to write a letter to Sir William Cecil. She knew from what Adrian had said that he was the Queen's Senior Advisor. She also knew he was at Greenwich Palace because that is where Adrian had been told to reply to the invitation to present his credentials.

Keeping the letter as brief as possible, she explained about the plot she had overheard. She also told him about Giacomo Bellini and how Adrian had plotted against him. Finally, she begged him to take the letter seriously, or the Queen would be assassinated. Before sealing the letter she called Anna to her side and read it out to her. She then signed it Maria Morisini-Ragazoni and applied her seal.

Anna's eyes widened in surprise at the letter's contents, but only a small gasp came from her. 'That husband of yours is truly the devil,' she said, when it was finished. 'What must I do with the letter?'

Maria thought quickly, she knew that it was not going to be easy to get it to Cecil. Suddenly an idea came to her. 'We must persuade the guard that I'm seriously ill and that it's necessary for you to go to the Apothecary for a potion. They will insist that one of them goes with you.' She paused a moment and wrote on the outside of the sealed note, "To Sir William Cecil - A matter of Life or Death. In the Queen's name, pay the bearer five gold royals." Give this note to the Apothecary when you get the potion and give him this gold royal. Impress on him the need for secrecy. We can only hope he delivers it.'

Turning on one side she gave a groan and Anna looked at her back in horror. 'My Lady, your nightdress is soaking with blood. I'll have to get you another and try to dress the wounds.'

'Not yet Anna,' she said with a tight smile. 'We have to convince the guards I'm very ill and that will help. Now, fetch me my toiletry and we'll try to give a more realistic impression that I'm at deaths door.'

A short while later the guards were shocked as Anna threw open the door and cried hysterically that her mistress was dying and needed a physician. One of the men came in while the other remained on guard. Maria lay on the bed, her breath coming in little gasps and moans and her face was deathly white. The sheets and the back of her nightdress were soaked in blood and her limbs twitched in violent spasms.

One look was enough to convince him. 'The master will kill us all if she dies! He cried panic stricken at the thought of what Ragazoni might do.

Anna played her part well. 'If only we could get a physician or a potion from the Apothecary, I'm sure we can make her better.'

The guard hurried to the door and held a whispered conference with his fellow guard. After a short time they both came in and looked at Maria who was shaking and moaning piteously. 'We must act, or it will be too late,' cried Anna.

There was another hasty conference and then the guards came back. 'No physician, it's more than our life's worth to let one in. I will take you to the Apothecary for a potion,' he indicated the other guard. 'He will stay here on guard and see she doesn't escape.'

'Escape!' scoffed Anna, 'can you really see her escaping in the state she's in?'

Half an hour later, Anna came back with the potion and a salve for her wounds. She gave the potion to Maria under the watchful eye of the guard. After a while, Maria began to stop shaking and her breathing became more normal. Anna took a damp cloth and wiped Maria's face removing some of the toiletry from her cheeks. As Maria pretended to sleep, Anna called the guard over. 'It's working,' she said. 'My Lady is sleeping and she has more colour in her cheeks.' She gave the guard a smile. 'Thank you for saving her life; it would have gone hard for all of us if she'd died.' Anna regarded him slyly. 'Are you going to say anything to the Master? I don't want him to do that to me,' she said indicating the blood stained nightdress.

The guard shook his head and shuddered. 'Neither do I. We've both agreed it would be best to say nothing. You didn't go out and Lady Maria is getting better.' He glared at her. 'Make sure, you clean up her wounds and use the salve. Say nothing about the apothecary and we'll all be alright.'

With that, he went out and when the door closed, Anna gave a sigh of relief. When the key turned in the lock, Maria sat up, not without some difficulty. 'Did you give the letter to the Apothecary,' she asked urgently.

'Yes I did, my lady. He looked at the inscription and his eyes lit up at the thought of five gold pieces. I impressed on him the need for secrecy and gave him the gold royal. He bit it and said he would see the letter was delivered as soon as possible.' She held Maria's hand and regarded her earnestly. 'I'm sure he will, my Lady.'

'Let us pray he does,' Maria said fervently with a sigh of relief, 'for all our sakes.'

Now that she had done all she could to warn Queen Elizabeth, the energy that had galvanised her into action deserted her. She sank back on to the pillow; pain and grief etched on her face and tears streaming down her face. When Anna had gently cleaned the wounds, applied the salve and covered them with strips of clean linen torn from a chemise, she helped Maria into a clean nightdress. She hugged her, talking gently and wiped away her tears until the potion did its work. Anna began to sing softly; a lullaby she had sung to Roberto when he was a child. Eventually Maria went to sleep and Anna continuing to cradle her gently, settled herself as comfortably as she could.

CHAPTER THIRTY-FIVE

The urgent summons to go to Walsingham's house in Seething Lane came as a surprise to Jacob and not least because the signature was that of Sir William Cecil. Hastily arranging for Roberto to look after things for him, he hurried to the house in Harte Street to change. As he entered Quiff was just coming out. 'What are you doing here?' Jacob enquired in surprise. 'I thought you'd gone to the Royal Exchange with a message.'

Quiff smiled depreciatingly. 'Oh I've done that already I and thought I might as well get changed ready for going to the 'Swan'. I put on my old working clothes when I go there so as not to stand out too much.'

'Very sensible idea,' agreed Jacob. 'I'm also getting changed, but for the opposite reason. Sir William Cecil wants to see me straight away so I'd better look presentable.'

'You're moving in exalted circles Master Jacob,' teased Quiff. 'It'll be the Queen next.'

A broad grin crossed Jacob's face and his comment contained more than a little irony. 'The way things are going Quiff that could be a lot more likely than you might think. I've had two invitations to court recently, but I declined because of the death of Jean Thieré. I'll probably get the imperious invite next time, which is really a polite 'I expect you to attend.' type of order. '

Quiff was embarrassed. 'I'm sorry Master Jacob; I didn't know you went to court.'

'Think no more of it young Quiff. You weren't to know and it amazes me sometimes when I stop to think about it. I'll tell you the story sometime.' He smiled at Quiff and then taking his leave, hurried off to keep his appointment with Sir William.

When he arrived at the house he was shown up to the study. Sir William was seated at Walsingham's desk and Jacob intent on him, failed to notice the figure in the large chair partly in shadow to the right. He bowed and sat down in the chair, which Sir William indicated without speaking and waited for him to begin. He was startled when the familiar dry voice of Walsingham spoke from the shadows. 'I trust you are more observant when out and about on my business Master Bell.'

Jacob turned towards the speaker. 'I'm sorry Sir Francis, I didn't expect to see you here; I thought you were in Paris.'

'And so he should be,' interposed Sir William, 'but he's been quite ill and was brought home secretly to recuperate. Fortunately he seems to be on the mend now. But that's why we are meeting here not at Greenwich Palace.' He wagged a cautionary finger and said. 'We don't want his presence known for several reasons, which I won't bore you with, so please keep it to yourself.' Turning to Walsingham he enquired. 'Shall I explain what this is about Walsingham?' When he inclined his head in agreement Sir William continued. 'You are acquainted with Sir Richard Urie, are you not?'

Jacob was a little surprised at the rather inquisitorial tone of the enquiry and decided to be circumspect with his replies. 'Indeed I am my lord, what has he been up to now?' Despite himself, Jacob couldn't keep the loathing out of his voice.

'That is exactly what we'd like to know,' said Sir William, 'and since you are likely to meet him in the course of your business, we'd like you to find out what you can about his movements and contacts.'

'I can do better than that,' retorted Jacob a little smugly. Drawing the Urie letter from his doublet he passed it to Sir William without further comment. When he'd read it Sir William sprang to his feet with an oath, strode across to Walsingham and gave him the letter. 'By all the stars Walsingham, read this.' Turning to Jacob he swore again. 'There's something of the warlock in you Jacob Bell. How came you by this letter? I can see you've no love lost for Urie. I trust it's not a forgery.'

'Not at all my lord, it comes from a secret room in Urie's house in Tottenham.'

'A secret room!' Sir William spluttered again. 'Now I'm even more convinced you've been using the black arts. I think you'd better explain,' he said sitting in his chair again.

Walsingham waved the letter at Sir William. 'Magic or no, I care not. This is more than we could have hoped for and more than enough to confirm our suspicions about Urie.' He looked at Jacob and gave one of his rare smiles. 'You've done extremely well Jacob Bell and I too would be interested in your story on the matter of this secret room and the letter.'

Jacob was delighted to have caused a stir with his revelation as he usually felt more like an errant schoolboy in their presence. He'd the feeling though that he was missing something. There appeared to be some sort of undercurrent in the questions, which had preceded his disclosure. However it seemed to have gone now so he intended to make the most of the moment.

He explained how the 'Ring' came to be set up and Quiff's part in it and told them how the letter came into his possession. 'It owed nothing to magic my lords; it was a combination of a little forethought and a large slice of luck.'

Walsingham smiled again. 'I think you are being somewhat modest, Jacob Bell. I believe you've a natural talent for intrigue that can be most useful to us in our fight against the Queen's enemies. Your idea of using the apprentices to gain information is inspired.' He was wracked by a fit of coughing, which interrupted his flow of words and Jacob jumped up and went across to him with a drink he'd picked up from the desk. 'I fear this is taxing your strength Sir Francis. You should rest more.'

Walsingham accepted the drink gratefully and sipped it slowly as his coughing subsided. 'Thank you for your concern Jacob Bell, I am recovered.' He gestured to Sir William. 'Perhaps it would be better if I retired.' When Sir William indicated his agreement he went on. 'Will you explain to Bell why this letter is important while I away to my bed?' His tone became almost conspiratorial as he continued. 'There is also the matter of the letter the Queen asked you to pass on. You will forgive my presumption in reminding you,

I trust.' Struggling to rise he gestured to Jacob. 'Lend me your arm Bell I fear I am not as strong as I thought.' Then with a nod to Sir William he leaned heavily on Jacob's arm and they went out into the hall.

Once they were out of earshot, Walsingham stopped and regarded Jacob with what for him was a kindly expression. 'Thank you for your concern Jacob Bell, I leave you to Sir William.' His voice became conspiratorial. 'But remember, things are not always what they seem.' Jacob was puzzled by this remark, but Walsingham did not explain further and went off to his bed with two servants helping him.

Once he had seen Walsingham safely on his way, Jacob returned to the study, where Sir William awaited him. His tone was quite jovial as he handed Jacob a glass of mead. 'I trust you'll join me we have a lot to discuss and we might as well be comfortable.' He indicated for Jacob to sit in the chair recently vacated by Walsingham and sipped his mead until he was settled.

'I think we'll dispose of the matter of the Queen's letter first.' He handed a heavily sealed letter to Jacob and gave a wry smile. 'I would hazard a guess from your expression that you've guessed the contents?'

'I expect it's an urgent summons to attend the court,' said Jacob in a resigned voice. Sir William tutted at this and shook his head in mock disapproval. 'The Queen merely thinks it's time for you to resume your appearances at court after the understandable absence following the death of your friend and partner,' Sir William replied with an ironic grin. 'One of the penalties of being popular with the Queen is that she likes to have her favourites around her at court. You won't disappoint her this time, will you?'

Jacob bowed to the inevitable and asked Sir William to pass on his acceptance to the Queen. Cecil nodded and said that Jacob would be receiving the formal invitation in a few weeks when arrangements had been made. Changing the subject, he explained the background to the Council's concerns relating to the activities of Count Maldini. He left Jacob in no doubt that there was already sufficient evidence to convict him many times over for plotting against the Queen. 'The only reason he's still at large is because Walsingham wanted to find out the names of his fellow plotters. It nearly cost him his life, as you know better than most. A few days ago one of Walsingham's men intercepted a letter from the Count to Sir Richard Urie.'

He sipped his mead thoughtfully for a moment as if debating what to say, then choosing his words carefully, continued. 'The letter itself was innocuous being simply a business enquiry about some glass. Unfortunately for the Count, Walsingham employs Thomas Phelippes, the best encrypting expert in the world and he was able to break the cipher and read the real message, which was much more revealing.'

'I assume that's the reason you wanted me to find out about Sir Richard Urie and why the letter I brought was interesting.'

'It was indeed and very revealing it was too. Without any doubt this draft is Urie's response to the letter I referred to and links him directly to the plot. In due course he will pay for it, along with anyone else involved.'

'I look forward to that day.' The heartfelt comment just slipped out before Jacob could stop it and Sir William regarded him curiously. 'That was said with a lot of feeling Jacob Bell. I noted your dislike of the man earlier, but I suspect that it goes a lot deeper than I first thought. I think you'd better enlighten me. It's important I know these things so I can assess whether it is likely to cloud your judgement.'

'Begging you pardons my lord, but this is a personal matter and has nothing to do with my efforts on your behalf.'

Sir William smiled grimly. 'I'm afraid that State security takes precedent over any personal considerations and I must insist on knowing what has kindled your wrath against Urie.'

Jacob was still minded to defy him, but mature consideration led him to believe that this would be counter-productive. Reluctantly he explained about the threats Urie had made to him and Jean's posthumous letter. 'I believe that Sir Richard Urie was the architect of my friend and partners death. Either as a case of mistaken identity because Jean was wearing my cloak, or in order to remove Jean as a rival and destroy the Crouched Friars Glass-works.' His face became grim as he continued. 'Whichever it was I intend to see that he pays. I am already hitting him in his purse and eventually I hope to see him pay the ultimate penalty. Whether by my hand, or by the state, I care not,' he finished defiantly.

Sir William chose to ignore this and simply said mildly. 'Have a care my impetuous young friend. It is pointless to ruin your life for a traitorous dog like Urie, whatever the provocation. You can rest assured that he'll pay for his crimes against the state and you have my word on that.'

The way he emphasised this left little cause to doubt neither his sincerity, nor his concern. 'Don't do anything precipitous Jacob Bell; it could interfere with our plans. For now, find out what more you can, but be cautious. This group would think nothing of snuffing out a life to further their cause.'

Getting up from his chair he motioned for Jacob to follow and went out into the hall. Acknowledging the information from a servant that his coach was waiting outside he turned to Giam. 'Farewell Jacob Bell, we will meet again at court and with Walsingham too, before he returns to Paris as I fear he must very soon.' Then with a friendly wave of his hand to Jacob he drew his cloak around him and went off to his coach.

Jacob accepted his own cloak from the servant enquiring if Walsingham was in bed. He was informed he was asleep now and had left instructions not to be disturbed. There was nothing more Jacob could do for the moment, so he headed for Harte Street.

CHAPTER THIRTY-SIX

The evening meal had just finished, and Jacob brought out the letter from the Queen and showed it to Roberto and Quiff. Quiff was taken aback by his swift comeuppance and apologised again. Jacob made light of it and told him to forget all about it. 'I assume you've heard about the fight in Seething Lane, everyone seems to know about it?'

'Of course Master Jacob, it was in the 'broadsheets'.

Jacob nodded and went on with his story. 'The fact I saved the Queen's Assistant Secretary seems to have made me one of the Queen's favourites at present and I'm expected to attend court when she sends for me. The fact I've missed the last two times because of Jean's death, made it likely that I'd be expected to attend the next.' His grin widened. 'Take note, Quiff, Queen's don't like to be turned down.'

'Perhaps the Special Envoy will be there this time handing in his credentials, Master Jacob.' said Roberto who'd been enjoying the exchange. 'Quiff has heard that one has come to London, although the informant didn't know which country he was from.' He grinned cheekily. 'You'll have to put on your best clothes if so.'

Jacob replied in vein. 'It's always best clothes at court.' He sighed extravagantly. 'They're like a lot of peacocks trying to outdo each other with the latest fashion and the most expensive jewellery!' He gestured and continued depreciatingly. 'They must bankrupt themselves spending vast sums on clothes and jewels like that and I for one have no intention of joining them. Do you know it's rumoured that the Earl of Leicester spent over nine thousand pounds on clothes last year.'

Quiff was incredulous. 'Nine thousand pounds! You could cloth the whole of London for that.'

Whatever he might have said on the matter, the next day Jacob put on his best court clothes and took great care with his toilet. Arriving at the palace, to his surprise, he was shown into the main presentation chamber where Sir William Cecil waited at the front.

Sir William acknowledged his arrival with a grim, distracted smile and then, with a brief apology, moved to a small group nearby. Jacob was puzzled by his manner, he'd been so friendly when last they'd met, but now he seemed very distant. He was sure it was not his doing; perhaps the Queen had been throwing one of her well-known temper tantrums?

Left to his own devises, Jacob looked around with interest. He was standing only a little way to the side of the throne, which was set on a raised dais with a backdrop of sumptuous draperies. The court in all its finery was spread out on both sides of a clear corridor leading to a pair of imposing doors at the opposite end of the room to the throne. Intent on his perusal of the scene, he failed to notice that Sir William had returned until he attracted his attention.

'It should be interesting for you today, Master Bell; a Special Envoy is presenting his credentials. It will be fascinating to see how a new man gets on with the Queen.'

'Gets on?' Jacob was puzzled by Sir Williams's tone. 'Isn't it just a matter of form?'

Sir William gave a tight grin. 'You have much to learn about the Queen, Master Bell. Nothing is just a matter of form for her. She's been known to have a real temper outburst if she's not treated with the respect due to her,' he shuddered dramatically. 'I remember the time when she refused to accept the credentials of the new Spanish Ambassador because of his haughty arrogance. It was three months before she forgave him, even though he apologised the next day.'

Realising that there was indeed a lot to learn about this regal Queen, Jacob made a vow to try and avoid upsetting her. He was about to ask about the Envoy when Cecil gave a signal and to a prolonged fanfare of trumpets, the Queen and her entourage entered. The Queen was magnificent in a richly embroidered white dress, with a huge pearl and jewel-encrusted collar, which set off her white powdered face. Her red hair was piled up and was richly decorated with pearls and jewels, woven into the elaborate hairstyle.

Two gentlemen pensioners preceded her, bearing velvet cushions on which, were the symbols of state, the orb and sceptre. As they processed towards the dais the court bowed deeply to the Queen as she passed. Reaching the dais the gentlemen moved to stand each side of the throne. The Queen mounted the dais and stood in front of the throne while her attendants arranged her dress. Her honour guard of gentlemen pensioners with their ceremonial pikes arrayed themselves around the dais and faced the court. The Queen with a gracious nod towards the court sat down.

When she had composed herself she nodded to Sir William who had moved to the foot of the dais and he turned and signalled to the gentlemen pensioners by the doors. There was a short fanfare of trumpets and the door was opened. Jacob craned his neck to see over the courtiers, but could only see the tops of the pikes of the honour guard of gentlemen pensioners as they escorted the new Envoy in stately procession towards the Queen.

Realising he would get a very good view when they reached the dais he made no move to come forward. The Envoy had his head turned away acknowledging someone on the other side of the court. There was something familiar about him, but Jacob couldn't make him out. The Envoy mounted the first step and stopped. Just then the Envoy's wife came into Jacob's view. She turned towards the side of the dais where Jacob was standing and Jacob's heart stood still. An involuntary cry was wrenched from his lips when he saw who it was.

'Maria!'

The cry contained all the loneliness, loss and despair of the past few months.

Looking up, Maria saw the man she believed to be dead. 'Giam!' She gasped and her hand flew to her breast at the shock of seeing him. 'How can this be? I...' She got no further before the colour drained from her face and she slumped in a dead faint at the foot of the dais.

Adrian Ragazoni, the Special Venetian Envoy, turned at the cry of his wife's name, just in time to see her slump to the floor. Seeing Jacob standing by the prone figure, his face blanched, and with a foul oath he drew his sword. 'Bellini,' he spat out. 'I should have killed you myself instead of trying to be too clever,'

Before he could make any further move, he was surrounded by the pensioner guards, with a ring of pikes at his throat. Cecil rushed forward. 'Throw down your sword Envoy,' he shouted urgently, 'or you'll be butchered on the spot as an assassin. You should know better than to draw a sword in the Queen's presence.'

Thwarted in his murderous attempt and unhinged by shock and anger at seeing Jacob alive, Ragazoni shouted wildly at the Queen, as he was disarmed, 'You must arrest that traitor Bellini,' he screamed pointing at Jacob. 'He...' Before he could utter another word, the Queen who had risen to her feet as the drama unfolded took a step forward her face flushed and her eyes blazing with anger.

'Must!' She screeched in disbelief. 'Must! You dare to come to my court and tell me what I must do.' She gestured to Sir William. 'Remove this arrogant fool from my court and place him under house arrest until I send for him. Perhaps by the time I do, he will have learnt some manners.' Turning on her heel she stalked imperiously to the throne and sat down every inch the regal, insulted Monarch. A contingent of the guard hustled the still raving Ragazoni from the chamber as the courtiers craned their necks to get a better view.

Jacob meanwhile had reached Maria's side where two of the Queen's ladies were already trying to revive her, but to little avail. Seeing how hemmed in they had become, Jacob shouted at the courtiers crowding round her to move back and give her some air. Bending down he picked up Maria and cradled her in his arms, looking round for Cecil to ask if he could take her somewhere to recover. At that moment the crowd started to back away bowing low as they did so and Jacob found himself confronted by the Queen herself.

Jacob bowed as low as he could without dropping Maria and held his position. The Queen standing with her hands on her hips looked at Jacob's awkward stance. 'Oh for goodness sake,' she said in an exasperated voice. 'Get up from that ridiculous stance before you drop the poor lady.' When Jacob straightened up gratefully, the Queen glared at him. 'What have you got to say for yourself Jacob Bell, causing uproar in my court like this?'

Although the words were admonishing, the tone was much milder than Jacob had expected and he was astounded to see a gleam of amusement in her eyes. Before he could answer, Sir William appeared at the Queen's side and suggested they should retire to somewhere more private.

'An excellent suggestion Sir William,' the Queen agreed. Turning to her guard she rapped out a series of instructions. 'Take the Envoy's wife to my chambers and instruct the ladies of my chamber to look after her. Send for the Royal physician and have him attend her at once.'

She turned and regarded Jacob again with that small secret smile again. 'As for you Master Bell, or is it Bellini, I think it's time you explained what has prompted this unseemly scene. Bring him to my private audience room Sir William,' she instructed, 'and we shall get to the bottom of this.'

Jacob had the feeling that events were totally out of his control. He was bemused by the Queen's attitude. He had expected her to be incandescent and have him thrown in the Tower. Instead she seemed to be finding the affair rather amusing. It was as if it was all part of a game. One in which only she knew the rules. He struggled to make sense of it, but by the time he was standing in the Queen's presence, he was no more enlightened than before.

When he entered her audience chamber she was sitting in her high-backed chair with Sir William at her side. They were talking urgently in undertones to a lady in waiting who, after nodding in understanding, curtseyed and went into the inner chamber. As the Queen turned, Jacob dropped on to one knee with head bowed and waited for the onslaught. When this failed to materialise he looked up uncertainly and started to explain.

Before he had said more than two words the Queen interrupted him. 'Be quiet Jacob Bell and get up from that absurd pose. Just sit down and listen to what we have to say to you.'

Jacob obeyed with alacrity and sat in the indicated chair. When he had done so, the Queen spoke to Sir William. 'I suppose we had better put him out of his misery. Will you explain please Sir William?'

'Certainly your majesty,' he agreed with a bow. Then proceeded to give Jacob the shock of his life. 'This whole scenario has been carefully arranged to bring you face to face with Special Envoy Ragazoni.'

Jacob gasped at this revelation. He tried to speak, but Sir William motioned him to be quiet. 'I think it would be better if you heard me out and then we will listen to what you have to say.' Receiving a nod of approval from the Queen he continued. 'Envoy Ragazoni arrived in London almost a month ago, somewhat earlier than expected. He explained this to the Queen in a letter, by saying that since this was his first visit he wanted to become more familiar with London and the English before he took up his post. He also advised us that his dear wife had been injured by a fall, during the bad weather the galleass encountered after leaving Calais. A not unreasonable explanation and one which would have been accepted, had it not been for the letter I received from Lady Maria, the Envoy's wife.'

This was certainly a day for surprises. 'From Maria; why did she write to you?'

Sir William gave a bleak smile. 'She wrote to inform us that her husband was involved in a plot to assassinate the Queen and put Mary Stuart in her place.'

Jacob gaped as Ceil continued. 'You were also mentioned. I'm sure you can guess at least some of the contents Jacob Bell.' He smiled. 'I confess that at first we didn't realise the connection between Giacomo Bellini and Jacob Bell. Until that is I was apprised of an entry in the Foreigner Return showing that a Giacomo Bellini had lodged in Candlewick Street, the day after the Galliano docked at Galley Key and some weeks after his reported demise in a galley fight. Shortly afterwards a talented glass-maker called Jacob Bell appeared from nowhere that we could discover and revived the fortunes of the Crouched Friars Glass-works. It was only then that we realised the significance of the name.'

His smile grew a little wider at Jacob's expression. 'It appears the Lady thought you were dead, which explains her fainting fit when she came face to face with you. She also blamed her husband for your demise and made some serious allegations about him perverting the course of Venetian Justice.'

He smiled even more widely at Jacob's reaction to this and passed on the information that Jacob had been dreading. 'Oh and she mentioned in passing about your trial and sentence in case you were wondering.'

Before he could continue, or Jacob could think up a suitable reply, the exasperated Queen interrupted. That's enough Sir William,' she admonished with a frown. 'Stop teasing Bell and tell him what we decided. You know I don't like this sort of baiting.' A sly grin came to her face. 'Unless of course, it's being done by myself to the Spanish Ambassador, but that's understandable.'

Sir William smiled his appreciation and continued the tale. 'Today's little performance was to help us to obtain confirmation of what we believed to be the truth.'

'So that's what this was all about,' retorted Jacob angrily. 'You could have found some other way to let Maria know I was still alive.'

'You do Sir William an injustice Jacob Bell. Although I can see it might seem like that from your viewpoint,' interposed the Queen. 'The real reason was much more complicated and if you listen, I'm sure Sir William will explain.'

'I will indeed your majesty. The real reason for this charade was to do with the other allegations made against Envoy Ragazoni by his wife. Together with Sir Richard Urie he is planning to aid Count Maldini in his plot to kill the Queen. The two assassins in his entourage masquerading as servants, were going to assassinate the Queen at a reception given in her honour.'

Jacob found this was too much to take in and sat there trying to

270

come to terms with the implications. He roused himself as Cecil continued. 'It is now clear to us, that you were telling the truth at our recent meeting and that the letter you brought was genuine. It seems that Ragazoni was less careful on his arrival in London and his wife was able to overhear the details of a meeting at which Sir Richard Urie was present. Our own men confirm that Sir Richard visited Ragazoni on that day. It would seem that Ragazoni has been acquainted with Count Maldini for some time and in return for supplying money and political support he has been promised some rich pickings when the Queen has been deposed.'

'As if foolish bunglers like Count Maldini could depose me,' the Queen snorted in disdain.

'Foolish they may be your majesty,' agreed Sir William, 'but nevertheless, they should not be underestimated with professional assassins in their employ.'

She smiled rather bleakly at these words, but her tone was still conversational. 'I do not believe for one moment, you would allow me to do that Sir William. I am not usually foolhardy where my own safety is concerned. I would not be Queen today if that were the case.'

Knowing the way the young princess had managed to survive after her father's death, Jacob had no doubt that this was true. It was one of the things that had forged her personality and made her such a charismatic figure.

'I think it is time we took Master Bell fully into our confidence Sir William,' said the Queen. 'I must attend to other things, so please see that you do so, while I take my leave of you.' She acknowledged Sir William's bow of compliance and as Jacob also bowed low, she showed her approval. 'Do not fear for the Lady Maria, Jacob Bell.' She smiled kindly. 'I confess, I cannot think of you as Giacomo Bellini. Lady Maria will remain as my guest for her protection. Ragazoni will be informed she is too ill to be moved and he will not be allowed to leave his house.' Having delivered this information she turned on her heel and with an imperious swish of her skirts went into her inner chamber.

When she had left, Sir William explained to Jacob the reasons for the events of the past few hours. He told him that at first Maria's revelations of his conviction had gone against him and the request for information on Sir Richard Urie was in the nature of a test. The letter he'd produced had been a masterstroke since it confirmed their suspicions of Sir Richard and together with Maria's information had shown that Ragazoni was the Envoy referred to in the Count Maldini letter.

'I'm afraid that we had to keep Lady Maria in the dark, since it could have alerted Ragazoni if she gave it away. This way we could test his reactions and it succeeded beyond our wildest dreams.'

'I see what you mean Sir William. Ragazoni has been put in a difficult position by his house arrest. Visitors will be monitored and he is not free to meet anyone outside.'

'Exactly. And since he has not presented his credentials, there can be no reception.' he said smugly. His tone became more serious as he explained further. 'It does however place you in some jeopardy. Ragazoni will surely try to have you killed; if I read his character correctly. He rather gave the game away to those in the know with his outburst and when he drew his sword.'

'I am grateful for the warning, Sir William. I will be glad to entertain his assassins. You can rest assured that I will be on my guard.' He touched the hilt of his sword in a meaningful gesture. 'I hope they do try, I will ensure that it will be for the last time.'

Sir William grinned rather bleakly at this then added a suggestion. 'It would be more useful if you could capture them instead. We could obtain a lot of information from them.'

'My way is a lot cleaner,' said Jacob with feeling. 'As I told Walsingham, I'm not fond of the idea of torture,' he said. 'I will bear it in mind if the chance comes, but I won't put myself or my friends in any danger to do it.'

CHAPTER THIRTY-SEVEN

Once back at Harte Street Jacob lost no time in making his preparations against the assassins. His first task was to get the Ring alerted to find the assassins. He would have found out from Sir William in due course, but the Ring was likely to be quicker. When he had finished, his thoughts turned to Maria and her marriage to Ragazoni. It was obvious that she'd been spying on Ragazoni and her marriage was to make this easier. This came as a huge relief, since despite his confident words to Roberto; his defence of Maria had been based on trust rather than facts. Reassured now, he sat down with Roberto and Quiff, to plan their tactics. One thing Jacob was determined on and that was that he was not going to wait for them to act.

The 'council-of-war' went on for some time. Mistress Simpkin had long gone to her bed with the instruction to exercise extreme care if there were any callers and to admit no one at all without checking first. At the moment, Roberto and Quiff were arguing as to who should stand guard through the night. Jacob was forced to intervene. 'I think it unlikely that anything will happen during the night. However, it would do no harm to be sure, so we'll take it in turns. I'll stand the first guard of two hours, then Quiff and finally Roberto. That way we will all get at least four hours sleep.'

Knowing that this would provoke an argument, he sought to forestall it. 'And before you object, there will be no argument on this.' Then a thought struck him. 'Oh and by the way, no thinking you know better. I'll expect you to stick to these times.' He looked meaningfully at Roberto who made a gesture as if to say 'who me?'

Having disposed of the argument, Jacob ordered Quiff off to bed and asked Roberto to stay behind for a short while to discuss the Glass-works. When Quiff had said his goodnights and departed, Jacob talked to Roberto about promoting one of the glass blowers to the post of Senior. 'I think Peter Tyzack would be my choice. Do you agree?'

Roberto considered a moment then nodded. 'Yes I do Master Jacob. He's come on a great deal working with you and since he anglicised his name, he's shown a great deal of commitment to the Crouched Friars. He's marrying an English girl too next month so he'll be grateful for the chance.'

'Good,' said Jacob, 'then it's settled. I'll tell them tomorrow and he can start straight away. We've got to make some more time for ourselves. I want you to concentrate on the customers and the Royal Exchange and I will travel around more.'

That settled, Roberto went off to his bed. Jacob made himself comfortable as he kept watch and thought about Maria. He hoped that he would be allowed to see her soon. Still he consoled himself, at least she's in England and won't have to go back to that swine Ragazoni.

There were no alarms during the night and next day he went to the Glass-works as usual. He'd just finished explaining to the men about Peter Tyzack's promotion, when a messenger arrived with a summons to attend Walsingham at his house as soon as possible. Since the message gave no reason for the summons, Jacob decided to go round to Seething Lane straight away. Sir William had said Walsingham's health was improving, but he hoped that he'd not had a relapse. Roberto insisted on accompanying him for safety and after an uneventful walk, they were shown into the study.

'So this is your redoubtable young assistant, Bell,' said Walsingham when Roberto was introduced. 'Perhaps he could wait outside while we discuss our business.'

'I'd like him to stay Sir Francis, you may not agree, but I have taken him fully into my confidence.' When Walsingham showed his displeasure, Jacob argued his case. 'I trust Roberto with my life Sir Francis. He is completely trustworthy and my confidant and I want him to stay.' He smiled as he continued. 'He's also the most accomplished knife thrower you're ever likely to meet.'

'I'll take your word on that Jacob. As to Roberto staying,

perhaps it wouldn't be such a bad idea after all.' He motioned them to sit down then sat on the corner of the desk facing them. 'Firstly I have a message from Sir William. He says to tell you that the Lady Maria is now recovering well and that she is asking to see you.' When Jacob tried to speak he waved him to silence. 'He also says that it would not be a good idea as the men who are described as assassins are no longer at the Envoys residence.' He shrugged apologetically. 'Apparently the men sent to guard Ragazoni had no orders concerning any other person and they were allowed to leave.' He made a wry smile. 'I think it more than likely that you will be having visitors in the near future.'

'You're probably right Sir Francis although they might try to see Lady Maria using the Envoys name.' He was quite concerned about this and his anxiety was not lost on Walsingham.

'It's possible I suppose, not that it would do them any good. The Queen has ordered that no one is to be to be admitted to see Lady Maria, without her permission. The Lady Maria is to be watched at all times and given the same protection as if she was the Queen.'

Jacob was relieved and pleased at the Queen's orders, but disappointed that he couldn't see her for now. He thanked Walsingham and then broached another matter. 'Do you have a description of these men? I'd like to pass word around to the Ring so that they can try and locate them.'

'An excellent suggestion, but I only have a very brief description. One is said to be tall and thin and the other is shorter and thicker set. They both have short black hair and the only other thing that was noticed, was that they both wore black cloaks over a livery of black and gold, which is probably, that of Ragazoni.'

'As you say Sir Francis, not a lot to go on it could be almost anyone.' He was about to continue when he recalled the incident when he was attacked outside the home of his fencing master. As he pictured the scene, the two men came into focus. 'I think I may know who they are,' he exclaimed excitedly. 'I do believe they've tried to kill me once before in Murano.'

Walsingham looked puzzled, but when Jacob explained the circumstances Walsingham agreed he might be right. 'It would be useful if they were the men, it would make it easier for you to identify them.'

'That is so Sir Francis, but in view of what I did to them on the previous occasion we met, they are not likely to risk my sword again. I fear that if there is an attempt it will be from hiding.'

'You could be right, but that will make this even more appropriate in the circumstances,' he said producing a garment from the cupboard behind him. The 'this' he referred to was a velvet tunic. The sleeves were made up of what, on closer inspection, turned out to be a very fine chain mail. He handed it to Jacob who was surprised at its weight.

'What on earth is it?' He exclaimed examining it closely. He felt the front and back and exclaimed in surprise. 'Why it has what feels like metal plates inside it. Look at this Roberto.

When the young man had looked at it closely he turned to Walsingham. 'I suppose this is to be worn under a doublet, as protection?'

'Indeed it is Roberto,' replied Walsingham. 'It is a present for Jacob from the Queen and was made in her armoury at Greenwich. Her father set up the armoury and though it declined for a while after his death, the Queen has maintained it to the same standards used during his reign.' He turned to Jacob again. 'She is aware that our charade at the court has placed you in a lot of personal danger and ordered that an existing brigandine be altered to fit you. You should be honoured Jacob, this brigandine is one of only three that have been made, and all for Royalty. There are overlapping metal plates inside, which I'm informed will not only turn a rapier point, but will also stop a crossbow bolt, or a pistol ball.'

Jacob was impressed. Although it was fairly heavy, it was remarkably flexible and shouldn't restrict him too much. He was very flattered by the Queen's gift and accepted it gracefully. When he tried it on he was delighted to find that it fitted under his doublet without difficulty.

'Try using your sword,' suggested Sir Francis. 'You'll soon see if it restricts you too much.'

Jacob demonstrated his agreement by drawing his sword and going through several of the standard exercises he used for practice. He was elated to find that there was little restriction of his moves. With practice he would soon come to terms with the rigid feel of the plates around his chest.

Sheathing his sword in one fluid movement, he thanked Sir Francis for the gift again. 'It's much more flexible than I thought it would be,' he commented, 'but then it would be no use in battle if it made it impossible for the wearer to defend himself.'

'Quite true Jacob. I would strongly urge you to wear it at all times until this matter of the assassins is resolved.'

'Thank you, I will do as you recommend. In the meantime, I presume you have something else on your mind,' he asked perceptively.

'I think I am becoming too predictable,' said Walsingham with a brief grin. 'I must watch myself with you Jacob Bell. Few men seem to read me as well as you appear to do.'

Jacob inclined his head in acknowledgement of the compliment and asked about his health.

'I am much recovered and I wanted to tell you I will be leaving for Paris on the early morning tide.' He made a grimace. 'I would much rather remain in London, there is much to do, especially with these assassins on the prowl, but her majesty requires me to continue my negotiations with the French.'

His tone became more conspiratorial. 'I hope to conclude an agreement shortly and then I am promised a return to the court and a place on the Privy Council, but that is confidential and not to be talked about.' He went and sat down again and Jacob went across to sit in the chair at the side of the desk. It proved to be a little awkward because of the brigandine, but he found that be sitting up straight he could manage quite well.

'I swear this vest will improve my posture somewhat,' he commented with a grin as he settled.

'No doubt' was the dry reply, 'but we must get on. I have another appointment this morning and a lot of correspondence to deal with, so no more interruptions,' he commanded. 'This matter of Count Maldini concerns me,' he confided. 'It is more complicated than it first appeared. The addition of Ragazoni to the plotters leads me to worry about the likelihood of Venice herself being involved. What are your thoughts on this?'

Jacob nodded. 'I too have thought about this, but I don't think it is likely to be official policy unless things have changed very dramatically since I left.' Choosing his words carefully he went on. 'Because of the affect that your ships are having on trade, England is not popular with the ruling class of Venice. However, despite this, they see the English as a foil for the territorial ambitions of Philip of Spain, who they have good reasons not to trust. For this reason, I cannot believe they would sanction involvement in a plot against the English monarch.'

Walsingham smiled bleakly. 'The advice received from our former Ambassador confirms what you've just outlined. In fact, he believes that the Signory have sent Ragazoni to discuss restoring full diplomatic relations. Our support for Venice against the French has been much appreciated. I must conclude therefore that Ragazoni is acting in his own interests, either for financial gain, or for power and influence.'

'Based on what I know of him, I would think the latter,' confirmed Jacob. 'He seems to be obsessed with power and is prepared to go to any length to achieve it.'

Roberto who'd been sitting quietly throughout these exchanges was fascinated by the conversation. He was also conscious of the confidence shown in him that he'd been allowed to stay to hear it. He was surprised and flattered when Walsingham addressed him directly with a question. 'What do you know of this Ragazoni young Roberto?'

Taking a lead from Jacob he answered without hesitation. 'He's a dangerous man, Sir Francis. From what I've seen and heard he would use and sacrifice anyone for his own ends.'

Walsingham nodded. 'That seems to make it unanimous.' He commented getting to his feet. Putting his arm round Jacob's shoulders he surprised him with the warmth of his concern. 'You must take care, Jacob Bell. A clever assassin could easily attack you in a crowded street without you spotting him. So keep your eyes open when you're out in the streets.' He tapped the plates under the doublet. 'Wear this at all times, it will protect you from such a cowardly attack.'

Jacob thanked him again. 'I am overwhelmed by this gift from the Queen, Sir Francis. It shows a care for me that I did not expect.'

Walsingham smiled. 'Her majesty can be most generous at times; at others she can be ruthless. Do not think that personal feelings will interfere with what she sees as her duty; England will always command her first loyalty.'

Jacob nodded. 'I understand that, Sir William. Is there anything else you wish me to do?'

'You could see if your informant at Urie's house at Tottenham can keep you informed of Urie's movements, but tell him to make sure he's not discovered. He's far too valuable to risk. He can be of great help to us.'

'Don't worry Sir Francis I've already told him that. He's to play the trustworthy servant and keep well away from the secret room. Only if there's a matter of the utmost urgency must he risk being found out. He's been told not to visit Quiff again and only to see his brother who will pass any messages to us and visit him if we have an urgent message.'

'Excellent,' said Walsingham ushering them out, 'and now if you will excuse me, I must attend to some urgent documents. Fare you well until we meet again.'

CHAPTER THIRTY-EIGHT

After leaving Walsingham's house on Seething Lane, they hurried off to the Glass-works, keeping a wary eye on the passers-by for any sign of the assassins. The next couple of hours were spent in discussions with Peter Tyzack to organise the new procedures for the Glass-works. When Quiff arrived a little later, they asked him to organise the Ring in a search for the two assassins. Working on the basis that it was the two men he'd met in Murano; Jacob was able to give a good description.

As he left the Crouched Friars that afternoon he stopped at the gate to look around. Deciding it was safe, he stepped forward, just as a crossbow bolt passed through the spot he had just occupied and thudded into the gatepost. Springing back inside, he crouched behind the gate and using the crack for the hinges, he looked around for signs of the assassin. Seeing a vegetable cart lumbering along Harte Street towards him, he waited until it was level, then dashed out and walked along behind the rear wheel, keeping a careful lookout.

About fifteen yards down the street was a narrow alley leading to Tower Hill. When he came level with it, sword at the ready, he was just in time to get a glimpse of a man in black and gold hurry round the corner at the far end. Knowing it would be foolish to run down the narrow alley in case the man was waiting, he continued behind the cart until he reached his house and darted inside. He rushed up to the living room and looked out through the windows, but there was no sign of anyone.

About an hour later Roberto arrived home and came up to the living room. 'I don't suppose you know anything about this, do you, Mater Jacob?' He said brandishing a crossbow bolt. 'It was sticking in the gatepost at the Crouched Friars.'

'Really,' said Jacob, 'how peculiar. I wonder how it got there.'

Roberto gave a sigh of exasperation, so Jacob explained what had happened, admitting that he'd been fortunate as the brigandine would not have saved him. The bolt had only just missed his head. If he hadn't moved at that moment! Well, he'd been lucky and the sooner they caught the assassins the better. Next time he might not be so lucky!

They discussed the assassin's next move. All they could do was to be extra vigilant, and hope that the Ring would locate their bolthole. Only then could they take any positive action.

The following afternoon following his visit to the Swan, Quiff arrived back at the Crouched Friars, in a high state of excitement. 'I think we've found the assassins for you Master Jacob. One of the apprentices lodges in Mincing Lane not far from here. Two men answering the description we put out have recently moved into lodgings next door and the landlady says they're Italians.' He gave a huge grin. 'What do you think of that then?'

'Well done, Quiff, that's an excellent piece of work. Your apprentices are really proving their worth. I think an extra bonus is due if this turns out to be correct. What say you Roberto?'

'I agree Master Jacob they'll have earned it. What do you want to do about it now?'

Jacob thought furiously as he considered the news. He'd not been happy waiting for them to make a move, but now the hunters could become the hunted, if it was indeed the two assassins. The first thing was to establish if it was the right two men.

Hurrying to the house in Harte Street, Jacob changed into some older clothes, but made sure he was wearing the brigandine underneath. Roberto made his own preparations; as well as the two knives in his belt, he had two more in the sleeves of his doublet. He was determined to go with Jacob and he was prepared to kill if necessary.

When their preparations were complete, Jacob had words with Roberto. 'I don't want you to be in danger. The main aim is to find out if these are the two Venetian assassins. If the opportunity presents itself, I intend to capture them and hand them over to Sir

William.' He grimaced with distaste at the thought, and then went on grimly. 'I don't like the idea, but in their case I'm prepared to make an exception. They'll know a lot about Ragazoni's plots and may even be able to clear me of the charges in Murano.'

'Amen to that Master Jacob, but it would be unwise to take any risks with them if they are assassins.'

Jacob nodded. 'I don't intend to Roberto they'll get short thrift if needs be.'

With that they set off for Mincing Lane, which was only a short distance away. Quiff's informant had done an excellent job of describing the place and they had no difficulty in finding it. Taking up a vantage point in the mouth of an alley almost opposite the lodgings, they took it in turns to keep watch. An hour passed with no sign of them. It was a very warm day and Jacob in his doublet and brigandine began to feel very uncomfortable. He was considering removing his doublet when Roberto stiffened and tugged his arm to attract his attention. 'Two men have just come out Master Jacob. Are they the ones?'

Jacob peered cautiously round the corner and spotted the men merging into the street. It was indeed the two ruffians who'd fought with him in Murano!

By now the men had turned to the right and were heading towards the river, so Jacob spoke urgently to Roberto. 'Follow them on this side of the lane, but just keep them in sight. I will follow you and do the same so they don't see me. They've never met you, so they'll not recognise you even if you get close. Just be casual and try not to look directly at them.'

Roberto nodded and immediately sauntered out in pursuit of the men. Keeping them well in sight, but stopping to look at wares offered by street traders, he contrived to follow them without any problems. It soon became obvious that they were heading towards Tower Bridge and as the streets became busier, he was forced to close up.

Tower Bridge was thronged with people as usual during the day. Its many shops and fine buildings attracted shoppers and sightseers alike. As the human tide flowed back and forth across the bridge the apprentices kept up a running banter as they tried to attract custom for their master's wares.

Jacob fearing he would lose sight of Roberto began to close up and was just in time to see him pulled roughly into a narrow passage between two shops. Cursing under his breath he ran as quickly as he could and after a quick look entered the passage. A little way along, there was a corner and as he approached it he could hear the sound of an altercation. Roberto was shouting at someone to take his purse, but spare his life,

Taking a deep breath, Jacob drew his sword and dashed round the corner. Suddenly a man appeared and fired a pistol at point-blank range. Jacob felt a hammer blow in his chest as a piston ball hit him over the heart. The blow winded him and threw him to the ground where he lay still too dazed to move. The man shouted in triumph and walked slowly towards him, while Roberto gave a cry of despair.

Just before the assassin reached him, Jacob jumped to his feet clutching his sword. The assassin's jaw dropped in amazement. Recovering, he drew out a dagger and threw it at Jacob. The point struck Jacob in the chest and the glass blade shattered into pieces against the brigandine. Too late he tried to run, but Jacob was on him like a tiger and killed him with one skilful thrust.

Struggling to withdraw his sword, there was a warning cry from Roberto, followed by a loud cry of pain. Fearing the worst, he dragged his sword free and turned his attention to the other man.

He was relieved to see it was not Roberto in pain, but the assassin. He was on his knees trying ineffectively, to pull out a dagger, which protruded from his upper arm. By his side lay a small crossbow.

'He was about to fire it at you Master Jacob. I had to throw at him.' Roberto said apologetically. 'I didn't realise he had it until he unfolded and cocked it. It's lucky he didn't find the knife in my sleeve.'

Jacob strode over to the man who was groaning loudly. 'You're fortunate the knife's only in your arm,' he said pulling it out none too gently and wiping it on the man's sleeve. Ignoring his whimpers of pain he dragged him to his feet. There was a box by the wall and Jacob instructed the man to sit on it while Roberto held a knife threateningly.

'Aren't you going to do something about this arm, I'm bleeding to death,' bleated the man querulously in Italian, as he sat down.

'Be quiet and do as you're told and I will,' said Jacob replying in the same language. Stepping to his side he tore the shirtsleeve and exposed the wound. Wrapping the torn sleeve tightly round the wound he stood back and drew his sword. Holding it at the man's throat he called to Roberto. 'Fetch his little toy Roberto and don't be afraid to use it on him if he tries to escape.'

Roberto did as he was bid and fitting the quarrel he cocked it and aimed it at the man.

'Be careful with that crossbow, young sir,' cried the man anxiously. 'It doesn't need much pressure on the catch to set it off.'

'In that case you'd better not make me nervous, or my finger might twitch,' said Roberto. 'I wouldn't want to shoot you accidentally you murdering scum.'

Jacob regarded the man with a steely look. 'You had better think carefully before you answer my next question,' he said. 'You can either give me the answers I need, or I'll turn you over to the authorities. They will not be so friendly. Do you understand?'

The man nodded sullenly and Jacob began to question him. It soon became apparent that he wasn't going to co-operate, denying any involvement in the plot against Jacob, or anyone else. Reluctantly, Jacob decided to hand him over to Sir William. 'Go and get the watch Roberto, we'll see what a spell in the Tower will do for him.'

Roberto darted off and in a short while came back with two watchmen. Jacob instructed them to take the man to the Tower and hold him there until Sir William Cecil sent instructions for his questioning.

'Keep him safe my friends he's involved in a plot against the Queen. Sir William Cecil will want him delivered to him in good condition.' The watchmen, searched the man for weapons and marched him away.

Jacob clapped Roberto on the back and congratulated him on his coolness. 'You did well, watching my back.'

Roberto grinned. 'It was nothing Master Jacob; it wasn't as if the crossbow was going to hurt you. The other rogue must have had a huge shock when his ball and knife failed to stop you. I was worried when you lay still.'

Jacob smiled grimly. 'You could say that it was such a shock that it killed him.' He indicated the body still lying there. 'It might be a good idea to search him thoroughly. We forgot to do it with the other except for weapons. They set about the grim task and apart from some money; the man appeared to have little else on him.

Jacob was puzzled. 'I was sure he'd have some instructions, or at least a note.' He shook his head in disgust at his mistake. 'The other man must have them and he will probably have disposed of them by now.'

'I don't know about that Master Jacob, but I think we should check his boots and hat. I'll look in his boots while you check his hat.'

Jacob agreed and picking up the hat inspected inside it. There was nothing to be seen, but when he ran a finger round the lining he could feel something underneath. He fished out a small square of paper and gave a broad smile when he read the note.

'Look at this Roberto.'

The note read 'Meet RU London Bridge Wed., or Thurs aft. Three o' clock E side Nonesuch House. Password: Luceo – Reply: Non Uro. It was signed with an elaborate capital R.

'RU is surely Sir Richard Urie and he's meeting them today in about an hour's time,' said Jacob triumphantly. 'We must go and keep watch so that we can be sure.' He looked round anxiously. 'I hope these watchmen are not long, or we must leave the body as it is. Did you find anything else?'

'I didn't finish looking Master Jacob, but I'll do it now. There may be a letter since they were meeting this RU.' He looked in the boots, but found nothing. Neither did a further search of his clothes and belt. A careful search of the alley, turned up nothing. Jacob was just about to give up, when picking up the remains of the glass dagger he saw that the top of the hilt was loose. Examining the hilt, carefully, he discovered that the top was hinged and released by a concealed spring. The hilt was hollow and, carefully rolled up inside, was a letter.

Jacob examined it. 'It's too well sealed to try and open it, which is a pity. I'd like to see what it says.'

'Perhaps Sir William has someone who can do it?' suggested Roberto.

'I'm sure he has, but the note said to meet Urie today if he is RU.'

'And tomorrow,' reminded Roberto. 'The note said Wednesday and Thursday.'

Jacob looked at it again. 'You're quite right Roberto; it does say Wednesday and Thursday. That gives us a whole day, but first we must confirm that RU is Sir Richard Urie as we suspect. I wish those watchmen would hurry up, it must be nearly three of the clock.'

Fortunately, a few minutes later, the watchmen arrived and Jacob and Roberto hurried off towards Nonesuch house. Taking up a position overlooking the East Side they settled down to wait. Half an hour passed, and Jacob was beginning to think they were on a wild goose chase. It was past three and not a sign of anyone waiting outside.

'We'll give it a short while longer and then..' His voice tailed off as a familiar figure appeared and stood looking around. 'It's him!' He hissed triumphantly to Roberto. 'I knew it would be. We must wait until he leaves, before we make any move, just in case someone else is keeping watch.'

A short while later his caution was rewarded. A tall, dark man emerged from a doorway close to where they were hiding and went across to Sir Richard. From their gestures, it was obvious they were surprised by the fact that the messenger had not arrived, but they didn't appear to be unduly alarmed. After a short conversation and a final look around they set off in the direction of the City.

Once they had been gone for several minutes, Jacob and Roberto emerged from their hiding place and cautiously made their way to the quayside, keeping a lookout in case their quarry doubled back. Seeing no sign of them Jacob moved to the edge of the quay. 'Oars!' he called loudly and one of the many boatmen plying for custom pulled in. Sending Roberto off to check the Glass-works, Jacob set off for Greenwich Palace.

CHAPTER THIRTY-NINE

At first, when Jacob arrived at Greenwich Palace he was refused entry. Showing the Queen's ring, he requested to see Sir William and was soon escorted to his study.

Sir William was obviously displeased with the interruption. 'Come in and state your business Master Bell.' He said curtly. 'You said the matter was of some urgency, but be brief. I have a great deal to do this afternoon, as well as an audience with her majesty to contend with.'

'I have some important news for you my lord, which relates to the matter of Sir Richard Urie and the Venetian Envoy.'

'You'd better sit down then and tell me your news.'

Jacob explained the events of the afternoon and produced the note and the letter with a flourish. Reading the note with mounting excitement, Sir William swore quietly under his breath. 'By the Lord Harry we have him. This password is the Clan Mackenzie motto. The Urie family are associated with the Clan in some way. He told me about it once at court. He had a brooch with a stags head and the motto, fastening the tartan 'brat' he was wearing across his shoulder.'

'Not only that, but he was at the appointed place shortly after three,' rejoined Jacob with some satisfaction. 'Roberto and I saw him there, with another man who I didn't recognise.'

Sir William got to his feet and picking up a small hand bell from the table rang it vigorously. A man entered and bowed waiting for instructions. 'Take this letter to the usual place and have it opened and copied. Make sure that there is no sign it's been opened.' He warned sternly. 'I want it back here within the next couple of hours, or so.'

'Very good my lord,' said the man and with a bow left the room. 'I must also leave you for now Master Bell,' explained Sir

William. 'I have a number of matters of state to take care of and I must make arrangements for this assassin you captured to be questioned.'

He smiled thinly at Jacob. 'I know that the methods used in the Tower are not to your liking Master Bell, but they are a necessary evil in our fight against the plotters who would harm this realm.' His voice took on a zealous tone as he continued. 'I will do everything in my power to protect my Queen and England. I've no doubt you'll be pleased if some of the information proves to be of use to you personally,' he concluded waspishly.

Jacob wisely refused to be drawn and simply nodded. Regaining his good humour, Sir William made to leave. 'I will arrange for some company for you while you wait. I'm not sure how long I will be, it depends on her Majesty and as you will know by now, she can never be taken for granted.'

Jacob smiled and made himself comfortable in the window seat, which looked out over a formal garden. Admiring the view he was not aware that someone had entered the room. He started with surprise when a familiar voice enquired. 'You sent for me, sir.'

Turning round he saw Maria making a deep curtsy with her head lowered demurely. Walking quickly towards her he enquired. 'Do you not know me Maria, my love?

With a glad cry she flung her arms round his neck and hugged him tightly while tears flowed unchecked down her radiant face. Jacob embraced her fiercely and kissed her wildly as all the pain of many months flowed away. Realising that they might have visitors at any moment, even perhaps the Queen, he disentangled himself enough to lead her to the window seat.

He gently wiped her tears away with his kerchief and spoke softly to her. 'Maria my love I cannot say how sorry I am that you've suffered so much sorrow on my account. I wanted to let you I was alive, but my friends persuaded me that Ragazoni would find out and cause you and our families harm to make me return.'

Maria put her finger over his lips with a tender gesture. 'Say no more, Giam, I am over that now. The important thing is that you are alive and that Ragazoni is in disgrace. I feared he would send his assassins after you, but you are safe.'

'Indeed I am my love and the assassins are no longer a threat. One of them is dead and the other will shortly be put to the question, by Sir William's men, in the Tower of London, God help him.'

Maria shook her head. 'I cannot find it in me to feel sorry for him. He and his foul master have been responsible for so much grief.'

Jacob quickly changed the subject and time fled as Jacob held Maria in his arms and made up for lost time. Jacob explained about the galley fight and how he came to be in London. Maria asked him about the name Jacob Bell. She said she like Jacob, but she was not sure about Bell. However, it was agreed that for the present, it would be diplomatic for Maria to use Jacob.

They talked about many other things, although fearing his reaction, Maria left out the terrible events at Ragazoni's hands. More than two hours had passed when they were interrupted by a discreet cough from behind. Startled they turned round to see a steward setting out some food on the table. He bowed and informed them that Sir William had arranged for the food and would join them later. He bowed again and left the room.

The smell of the food quickly made them realise how hungry they were and in no time at all they were enjoying the rich repast. Just as they were finishing the door opened and Sir William appeared.

'The Queen has spared me a long meeting today,' he said with a brief smile. 'She was not really in the mood for long discussions on the latest missive from Parliament urging her to marry and secure the succession.' He shuddered dramatically. 'She became quite vitriolic at one point, but fortunately it didn't last.'

He now addressed Maria. 'I mentioned to the Queen that you were here with Master Bell and that I had business to discuss with him. She asked me to request that you attend her in her private apartments.' He gave her an encouraging smile. 'Her Majesty has taken quite a liking to you, my dear Lady Maria.'

Maria blushed with pleasure and excusing herself she gave, Jacob's arm a tender squeeze and then with a loving smile for Jacob, and a curtsy to Sir William, she left the room.

'I envy you Master Bell.,' said Sir William as he watched her go. 'You are a fortunate man indeed to have a woman as attractive and plucky as Lady Maria so obviously in love with you. It is unfortunate that she was forced to marry a man such as Ragazoni, who used her so ill. Perhaps we may be able to remedy that situation.'

Although Jacob asked him to explain further, Sir William refused to expand on his cryptic remark and changed the subject.

They discussed the capture of the assassin and Sir William promised to keep him informed of any information that he obtained. He then produced a letter from his doublet and passed it to Jacob. 'That's the letter, which you obtained from the dead assassin. Ragazoni has agreed to go to Tottenham for a meeting next Saturday.' He grimaced in annoyance as he went on. 'Apparently he is confident he's found a way to get out of the house without being detected by my men and suggests a meeting about eleven of the clock.' Then he smiled. 'On the other hand, it may be to our advantage to allow him to join the others.'

He handed the letter to Jacob. 'I have a copy and I want you to arrange for this letter to be passed to Sir Richard Urie tomorrow when the second meeting time is due.' He frowned. 'We can't risk sending the other assassin and I wondered if your assistant, Roberto could take it. What do you think?'

Jacob thought carefully. 'I'm not sure about this idea at all. I agree we can't risk sending the other assassin that would be far too risky.' He frowned in concentration. 'I don't think we can risk Roberto either, for two reasons. Firstly, it is possible that Sir Richard has seen him at the Royal Exchange. Roberto has been there quite a lot recently. Secondly, although his English is improving, he still has a pronounced Venetian flavour to some of the words he pronounces and that might give the game away.'

He paused, as another thought struck him. 'On the other hand,' he conceded. 'It's possible that with a little bit of disguise he could pass for one of the assassins. From the need for a password, it's obvious that they've never met. His accent would be an asset in that case.'

'I do believe you're right,' agreed Sir William, 'but we must make sure that he's not in any danger.'

'I agree,' said Jacob. 'I think it might be an idea for Roberto to carry the other glass dagger that we found on the dead man and the folding crossbow. The dagger is a sort of badge of office for assassins and he might be asked to show it as proof of his identity. I'll also check to see if he's ever met Urie, if he has, we'll have to think again.'

'An excellent idea Bell, I'll also put some of my best men at your disposal just in case there's any trouble. They can be hiding nearby waiting for a signal.'

Having made the decision, they spent the next half-hour making detailed plans for the hand over and signals if help was needed. Jacob decided that if Roberto had any qualms at all about doing the hand over, they would simply hire an apprentice to take it to Nonesuch House. They also agreed to have another meeting the following evening at Walsingham's house to discuss the hand-over and what should happen for the meeting at Tottenham.

There was little more that could be done for the present, so Jacob said his farewell and returned to the Crouched Friars. Everything seemed to be running smoothly, so he and Roberto went to his office where Jacob brought him up to date with events.

Roberto was sure that he'd never met Sir Richard Urie, although he had seen him and was keen to take on the mission. It was agreed that Roberto would play the part of one of the assassins. Roberto then informed him that Thomas Isham had called about an hour before Jacob returned.

'Did he leave any message?'

'He asked me to remind you of his invitation to join him at his home in the country and said he would be there for the next two weekends if either was convenient. He also included me in the invitation, which was very kind of him.'

'It was indeed,' rejoined Jacob, 'but I can't make any arrangements until this business with the Maldini plotters is settled.' He sighed in disappointment. 'It's a pity really. He's an intriguing fellow and good company. It would also do us good to have a break from work. Perhaps I'll have a better idea after this meeting with Sir William tomorrow at Seething Lane and by the way, he wants you to be there as well. He will want to know if the hand-over went according to plan.'

So it was that the following afternoon, promptly at three o clock, Roberto approached the East side of Nonesuch House. Despite his confidence in playing the part of the assassin successfully, he was surprising nervous as he approached Tower Bridge. The bridge was crowded as usual and Roberto waited with some anxiety for his contact. Fortunately for his nerves, he had only a short time to wait. The tall, dark man they had seen the day before approached him. There was no sign of Urie.

'I am Luceo,' said the man, 'you have something for me.'

Roberto gave the reply 'Non Uro' and after showing the glass dagger as his credential, he passed him the letter. The man accepted it, handed over a purse of money, turned and walked quickly away, while Roberto did the same.

The following evening Roberto was able to report to Sir William that the meeting with Urie's man had gone very smoothly. 'It was a good idea to take the glass dagger. Once I'd shown that, it was plain sailing. He even gave me a purse of money.' He held it out for Sir William.

'Excellent. That was well done young Roberto.' When Roberto made to put the purse on the desk, he waved it away. 'Keep the purse, Roberto, you've earned it.'

While Roberto put the purse away, Sir William sat looking thoughtful. Eventually he turned to Jacob. 'We must decide what is to be done about this plot. I am not of a mind to allow it to continue in case we lose touch with the plotters.' He paused.

'Assuming Ragazoni escapes from house arrest and goes to the meeting, I believe it is the right time to strike whilst all of the conspirators are in one place.'

He smiled without humour at Jacob. 'You'll be interested to know that the assassin you captured has been most co-operative. I now have enough evidence to convict them all. There was no need to torture him, he owes Ragazoni no loyalty and couldn't wait to tell us all he knew about him and his friend Count Maldini.'

'Did he mention anything about Ragazoni's plot against me,' Jacob enquired hopefully.

'Not so far, but he was still talking to my men when I left. I would imagine, if he knows anything, he will tell us.'

'That's a pity,' replied Jacob. 'I was hoping that he would be able to clear up that matter for me.' He sighed wistfully. 'Perhaps he wasn't involved.'

'All in good time Bell, but for now we must concentrate on the Maldini plotters.' He rubbed his hand against his temple deep in thought before he went on and then said decisively. 'We'll send a troop of soldiers to Tottenham on Saturday and arrest all of the people at Sir Richard Urie's house.'

He hurriedly scribbled a note, sealed it and then rang the bell. When the steward entered he instructed him to take the message to Colonel Young at the Tower and to give it into his hands only. 'Make sure there is no delay. I want Colonel Young here at Greenwich within the hour.'

When the steward had hurried off they settled down to discuss the details of the raid. 'I want you there, but I don't want to give the game away by having you meet up with the Colonel's men, just in case they are watching you; have you any thoughts on the matter?'

'I've been thinking about that, Sir William. I have an invitation to go to John Isham's house either this weekend or next. By a fortunate coincidence his house is at Tottenham, less than two miles from that of Sir Richard Urie, or so I believe.'

'Fortunate indeed,' agreed Sir William. 'It should be easy to slip away and join Colonel Young in time for the meeting. Isham is most trustworthy and well known to me. He has provided us with much useful information from his overseas contacts as well as being a source of money to pay some of our foreign agents. I would have no objection to you taking him into your confidence,' he gave his characteristic wry grin, 'but don't burden him with too many details.'

He leaned back in his chair with a satisfied expression on his face. 'I'm not an overly superstitious man Jacob Bell, but I have a good feeling about this venture. I certainly feel happier that the assassins are out of the way, thanks to you and young Roberto and if we can arrest all of the plotters at one fell swoop, it will bring this Maldini affair to a satisfactory conclusion. What say you?'

Jacob agreed wholeheartedly. The time was ripe for bringing Ragazoni and Sir Richard Urie to account. He was anxious to have the matter settled so that he could concentrate on Maria. They had a lot of time to make up.

When Colonel Young was shown in, Sir William introduced Jacob and Roberto and outlined the operation to arrest the Maldini plotters at the meeting in Tottenham the following Saturday. Much to Jacob's surprise he then informed the Colonel that Jacob was acting as his representative and would be in overall charge of the operation.

The Colonel who had carried out a number of similar operations simply nodded his agreement. Jacob made no comment as Sir William continued. 'We have discovered that a passage leads from the study in Urie's house, to a secret room in the cellars and then through a hidden door to a grove at the rear of the house. It will therefore necessitate a rather larger force than might at first seem necessary.' He looked at Jacob for confirmation.

'I think you are right,' confirmed Jacob. Turning to the Colonel he enquired how many men he would normally take on a mission of this sort.

'It entirely depends on the amount of opposition we are likely to meet. Do you know how many men will be there?'

'I'm afraid not, but if we assume that all of the people we know to be involved in the plot will be present, there will be at least nine, or possibly ten.'

'I see,' mused the Colonel, 'a sizable number if they choose to fight. We must make sure that we have superior numbers.'

Jacob, who'd been considering the problem while these exchanges were going on, had come to his own decision on a strategy. 'I think we will have surprise in our favour. They will not be expecting us, nor are they aware we know of the secret room and its bolthole.'

'That's true,' agreed Sir William, 'what had you in mind?'

'I think the Colonel and about ten men should ride up to the front door and make a big show of coming to arrest Sir Richard and his fellow plotters. This should cause them to make a general exodus via the bolthole. A second larger force will be waiting and will arrest them as they emerge.' He gave a grin. 'If we are really lucky, they will come out singly, or a few at a time, and make our job easy.'

Cecil was enthusiastic, but had a question. 'What if they hide in the secret room?'

'The first force will keep a guard on the study, round up all the servants, and search the house for other plotters. Having done that, most of them will go through into the secret room and come up behind anyone who tries to turn back.'

The Colonel was enthusiastic. 'An excellent plan, Jacob: a classic pincer movement if ever I saw one. However, I would prefer it if my Captain led the force at the front. I like to be in at the kill.' He gave a grin. 'I think I'm going to enjoy working with you.'

Acknowledging the compliment with a smile, Jacob went on to explain about the help he'd received from John Noble, the steward at the house. 'We must make sure that the servants are not arrested unless they try to fight,' he explained to the Colonel. 'The other servants are not to know that he's helped us.'

'Agreed,' said the Colonel nodding his approval, 'he could well be useful again and it would be foolish to give him away. I'll see my men are given careful instructions to round up all of the servants, but not to mistreat them in any way.'

Having satisfied themselves that the plans were as fool proof as possible, they said their farewells and went their separate ways.

CHAPTER FORTY

John Isham had given them very detailed instructions how to reach his house, although Tottenham was difficult to miss, lying directly on the main road north from London. Collecting their mounts from the livery close to Aldgate, Jacob and Roberto turned left outside the gate on to Houndsditch, until they reached Bishopgate Street Without. Roberto was not an experienced horseman, but the mare he'd been given was very docile. This was just as well, since it was about ten miles to John Isham's house.

Once past Bethlehem Hospital, the houses began to thin out with only occasional ones, with gardens, on either side of the road. Soon however, these were left behind with the road keeping to the high ground to avoid the marshes; they had lovely views to both sides. The ride turned out to be very pleasant, although Roberto had one near fall. In the end, they arrived at the Isham cottage without further mishap. The description of the Isham's weekend home as a cottage, had led to certain expectations in Roberto's mind. It turned out to be a huge surprise. True, it had a thatched roof and the look of a cottage, but it was considerably larger than the town house in Harte Street. There was a large garden at the front and an even larger orchard at the side.

They were overwhelmed by their reception; John Isham met them in the courtyard at the front, with all the family and servants lined up to meet them. He introduced Jacob and Roberto to his wife and two daughters; Rebecca, a widow of ten months and Elizabeth the youngest daughter; Roberto was quite smitten by Elizabeth. Mistris Isham invited them to join the family for a cool glass of freshly made lemonade and led them round the side of the house, where a large table had been set up in the shade of the orchard trees. There were large pitchers of stoneware and platters containing apples, pears, and other fruits from their garden.

Roberto found himself sitting next to Elizabeth, while Jacob was next to Rebecca. Elizabeth chattered away in a very friendly manner as though they'd known each other for years and Roberto responded. When he mentioned the canals of Venice, Elizabeth begged him to tell her more.

'I have heard that in Venice, there are no roads at all. Surely that cannot be true Mater Rosso?'

Roberto smiled. 'It is true that all of the main routes throughout Venice and the islands such as Murano, where I was born, are either canals, or part of the lagoon that surrounds the islands of the Republic,' Roberto explained. 'But there are streets and alleyways that go between the houses.'

'Is it like London, then?' Elizabeth said eagerly.

'I suppose it is, if you can imagine London, with the main streets as canals, the rest is very similar, although the houses look different and many in Venice are built of wood, as are the bridges. There are some magnificent stone buildings, like the Basilica and Doges Palace in the Piazza San Marco. The Doge is the elected ruler of Venice,' he explained when Elizabeth enquired what a Doge was. 'He's a bit like your Dukes, but he's the head of the Republic.'

Elizabeth sighed. 'It sounds so beautiful. I wish I could go there.'

'Maybe you will, one day. I would be pleased to show you around.'

'Would you, Roberto,' she said, impulsively giving his hand a squeeze under the table. 'That would be lovely.' She made no move to remove her hand and with a swift glance at her mother, she leaned a little closer and asked if he would like to see the garden. When he quickly agreed, Elizabeth asked her mother if she could show Roberto round the garden. Her mother agreed without much protest and they strolled into the garden with Elizabeth pointing out her favourite flowers, comfrey, foxgloves, golden rod, wallflowers and lavender. After a little while, she led him to a rose covered arbour out of sight of the orchard and sitting close to him asked him to tell her more about himself and Roberto told her about his life as an apprentice and how he came to be in London, carefully omitting about Jacob's trial.

Jacob and John Isham, meanwhile, were enjoying a pleasant drink and chat with Mistris Isham. When she excused herself saying she had work to attend to do and they were left alone, Jacob explained his sudden acceptance of John's invitation. 'I must apologise for the fact that our visit here is not simply to enjoy your company. There is a matter of the utmost importance, which I must attend to in Tottenham tomorrow. It's on Sir William Cecil's behalf and I have his permission to disclose some of the details.'

He explained and John Isham gave one of his hearty laughs. 'I'm willing to bet, Sir William told you to tell me as little as possible, if I know him at all....' His grin grew even larger as Jacob looked rather sheepish.

'I'm afraid he did John, but he did say he considered you to be most trustworthy and that you had been of great service in the past.'

'What I have done has been little indeed and simply because of certain disposals of money at my command.' He became serious for a moment. 'If I can be of any service in defeating the Queen's enemies, then the whole of my resources are at your disposal.'

They stood up and started walking around to the front of the house.

'The sentiments are well said, John, but if you will simply help us to slip away tomorrow without any fuss, I hope to complete our business and return before too much time has elapsed.' He gave a broad grin and looked impishly at John. 'Besides it would never do to deprive your daughter of Roberto's company for too long, they seem to be getting on famously,' he said, indicating the couple in the garden seated in an arbour deep in conversation.

John gave a hearty laugh. 'By heavens you're right, they do seem to be getting on rather well; my wife will be delighted. Elizabeth doesn't often get the chance to meet people of her own station here in Tottenham and my wife tends to worry that she'll finish up an old maid even though she is but sixteen.'

With a grin Jacob assured John that there was little chance of that. 'She's an attractive young girl and I can't imagine her being left on the shelf,'

Just at that moment the young lady in question, oblivious to being observed and the subject of speculation, rose to her feet took Roberto's proffered arm and they strolled happily away into the garden and out of sight.

That evening before the meal, Jacob presented John with a fine set of goblets that he and Roberto had made. As they sat sipping a glass of sack, John insisted that they must use the glasses that evening. They enjoyed a most satisfactory repast complete with Bourgogne and Anjou wines from France, which John insisted on using to compliment the new glasses. It was the first time Jacob and Roberto had tasted these wines and they found them excellent.

Following the meal the men went into John's study. 'I know you can't tell me too much about the affair,' John said, 'but I will do all I can to assist you.'

Jacob thanked him and explained about their rendezvous the next day. He briefly explained to John about the plot and also that he had a personal stake in the affair because of the involvement of Adrian Ragazoni. 'I don't want to say any more on this John. All I will say is that my future happiness is at risk, as well as the security of the Queen. Either one would be enough for me to be involved.'

Jacob could see that this intrigued John, but thankfully he refrained from asking any further questions. John was fast becoming a firm friend and Jacob did not wish to tell him any lies. 'What will you tell your wife and family?'

'They are used to comings and goings at this house, my friend. I shall say you have some business nearby and that you hope to conclude it for the midday meal.'

Jacob couldn't help but grin. 'Ay, and a funny business it is too, but with God's help, we will prevail.'

'Amen to that,' said John with feeling and raising his glass called for a toast.

'Here's to the downfall of all the Queen's enemies.'

'To the downfall of the Queen's enemies,' they chorused as they drank deeply and drummed their hands on the table in approval.

Later that evening, Roberto knocked quietly on Jacob's door. For once he felt out of his depth and needed some advice. When Jacob invited him to sit on the bed next to him, Roberto felt strangely hesitant. He found it difficult to explain what he wanted, so Jacob told him to take his time.

'It's Mistris Elizabeth,' he eventually blurted out. 'I haven't had any experience with girls and I wanted to ask your advice.'

'I'm not sure I'm the best person to ask,' said Jacob kindly, 'but I'll do my best. What do you want to know?'

'I've never felt this way before,' said Roberto earnestly. 'I've never been with a girl, you see,' he admitted self consciously, 'but I get such a warm feeling when I'm with her. She's very young - even though she does behave as though she's older and I don't want to cause offence to the Isham's.'

'She's not so young in fact,' replied Jacob, 'less than two years younger than you. As for the Isham's, I wouldn't worry about them. John told me they were glad for Elizabeth to have company of her own age. I would suggest you let things take their course. A few genuine compliments might help to smooth the way, but from my limited experience, you will soon know if Elizabeth doesn't find your company to her liking.'

Roberto was happy with this advice. 'Thank you Master Jacob I will try to take your advice and I'm sorry for disturbing you.'

Next morning after a sound night's sleep, birds welcoming the morning sunshine and the pleasant voice of a girl singing a traditional air greeted him. Going to the casement Roberto looked out into the garden. Elizabeth, with a basket containing eggs on her arm, was strolling towards the house.

He called out to her. 'Good morrow, Mistress Elizabeth that's a lovely tune you're singing, even the bird's fall silent to listen to your voice.'

Elizabeth flushed with pleasure and giving him a warm smile

waved and then went into the house. Roberto put on his riding clothes and set off in search of breakfast.

John Isham and Jacob where already seated at the large oak table in the lovely half-panelled room. The side cupboards were covered in platters with ham, salt beef, fruit and preserves, but it was the aroma of freshly baked bread that attracted Roberto. John Isham greeted Roberto with a friendly smile. 'Come in, come in, my boy, you are most welcome. The others have already eaten and Jacob and I are about to start. I hope you won't mind if I chatter? I know many people like to eat in silence, but it's not in my nature to keep quiet for long.'

They sat down together and Roberto soon felt very at ease. The bread was wonderful, and when he said as much to John, he was delighted. 'I'm glad you think so, Roberto. My wife will be pleased. Although we have a cook, of course, she still likes to get up early and make the bread when we have visitors.'

While they ate, John talked about many things and they were highly entertained by his banter and fanciful tales. John was careful not to mention the real reason for their visit, but seemed to be happy to get to know them. Jacob told him about his background and how he came to be in London, without going in to a lot of detail.

'I was aware of some of your story,' said John, 'both from what you've told me yourself and from Jean.' He gave a slightly embarrassed grin. 'I may look a happy go lucky person, but I only lend money to people I know and trust. You'll find me willing to listen if you have any problems over the loan or, get into difficulties.' He smiled a little sheepishly. 'I don't pester the people who borrow money from me. I've found over the years it's best to trust people to do the right thing and mostly they do.'

He was obviously a little embarrassed by this confidence and before Jacob could reply, he put an arm round his shoulder and suggested they all took a walk round the property before it was time to leave.

Roberto hoped that Elizabeth might be somewhere around, but

to his disappointment, she was not in sight. He decided to excuse himself to see if he could find her. John, guessing what he was about said teasingly, 'I think Elizabeth may be in the vegetable garden if she's not in the kitchen. It's her job to pick the vegetables for dinner.'

'I might have a word before we leave,' said Roberto and then hesitated. 'I thought it must be about time for us to be getting ready for our trip.'

Jacob was amused by the slight hesitation, but simply observed that they would need to set off in about an hour. 'I'll just have a walk round the house with John and then I shall go and get ready. We may see you in the vegetable garden,' he said with a smile. 'Meet me downstairs on the half hour and we will pay our respects before we leave.'

With a small bow to them both, Roberto departed into the house and after a brief walk around Jacob went to his room to make ready for the journey. A little while later, they were standing outside the house saying their farewells. John Isham advised them to take the track along the crest of the hills, since there were some very bad marshes in the valleys. Jacob agreed and John, passing up a parcel wrapped in cloth, said to open it later.

It was heavy and Jacob passed it to Roberto to put into the leather panniers they had used to bring the glasses. Promising to return as near to midday as possible, they set off, with the waves and goodbyes of the Isham family to send them on there way.

When they had gone a little way and out of sight from the house, Jacob reined his horse to a stop and told Roberto to open the package. Roberto did so with alacrity, for he had been dying to know what was inside. To his great surprise, it contained a beautiful pair of matched wheel-lock pistols together with spare powder and shot. There was also a brief note. 'Godspeed in your mission and I hope this gift is useful in defeating the ungodly.' It was signed, your good friend, John Isham.

Jacob examined them with interest. 'I'm not too familiar with this type of pistol I believe they are mainly used for sport, but I don't trust that wind up wheel-lock, it's too cumbersome.'

'Well they're no use to me Master Jacob,' said Roberto, handling them with care. 'I've never fired a pistol in my life and I don't suppose I'd hit anything if I did,' he observed with a grin.

'I can't say that I favour them either,' rejoined Jacob with a frown. 'I suppose they're fine for hand to hand work, but you'd only get the chance to use them once.' He looked thoughtful for a moment. 'Mind you, they'd have come in handy during that business with Maldini's men outside Walsingham's house,' he said passing them back to Roberto. 'Put them away Roberto it's time we went. We don't want to be late for the rendezvous with the Colonel, so we must press on.'

CHAPTER FORTY-ONE

The ride was uneventful and John Isham's directions proved excellent. Having examined the house from a distance, they set off round the side towards the copse where he hoped to meet Colonel Young. A little while later they cautiously entered a wood, which Jacob hoped, would lead them to the hidden exit from the tunnel. When they reached a small glade, they were both surprised when a uniformed man stepped out from behind a tree.

Jacob reached for his sword hilt then stopped with a laugh. 'Good morrow Colonel, you gave me a surprise; I didn't see you there behind the tree.'

'You missed my men too,' he said with a grin indicating three men who had fallen in behind them. 'I can see you're more at home in the city than in the countryside. We've been tracking you ever since you entered the wood.'

Jacob got down from his horse and strode over to the Colonel. 'You're right about that Colonel,' he answered with a grin. 'I've spent almost all of my life in Venice, so this is very foreign, not a canal in sight.' His smile became broader as he went on. 'Mind you, I'm probably more at home in a boat than you, Venice has canals for roads.'

'So I'm led to believe,' said the Colonel. 'I've never been, but I've heard it's a very beautiful city.' He became the soldier again. 'Forgive my abruptness Master Bell, but I think it's time we set out our men. It won't be too long now before Captain Green and the other detachment start knocking on doors. I gave him the signal to proceed as soon as you arrived.'

Jacob nodded his agreement. 'Have you had time to look for the hidden exit?'

'We have indeed and I'm bound to say that your informant was most accurate in his description. We found the door exactly as he said and several of my men have been keeping guard and setting up ambush points.' Leaving the horses with some of his men he led the way deeper into the wood. After a little way, he put a finger to his lips to indicate they should be quiet and gave an imitation birdcall. He listened intently and when a reply came to his satisfaction, he led them forward slowly and carefully. A sergeant met them and led them through a tangle of undergrowth until they reached the door.

'All the men are settled into ambush positions Colonel and I've checked the door and it's locked, or bolted. With your permission I'll stay by the door to listen for them unlocking it.' He indicated a crevice in the rock to one side of the door. 'When I hear them I can slip in there and deal with anyone who goes that way. Otherwise if they come out en masse, I'll be able to attack them from the rear if they resist.'

The colonel nodded in approval and turned to Jacob. 'That sounds like a sound plan to me do you agree?' Jacob thought a moment and then went to have a look at the crevice.

'I think the plan has merit, but I'm concerned that the sergeant would be overwhelmed if several of the plotters went that way.'

Striding forward the colonel examined the crevice. 'You could be right Jacob have you a suggestion?'

Jacob thought for a moment. 'Have your men searched the area to determine if the plotters have any horses nearby?'

He nodded. 'There are no horses in the wood, but just to the west of here there's a farm with a number of horses in a paddock. It would only take a few minutes walk to get there.'

'In that case colonel can I suggest we deploy our forces to allow them to get away from the door and ambush them as they come through that dip, which is out of sight of the door.' He indicated the area they had passed through shortly before they met the sergeant. 'We may be able to secure them without alerting any of the others.' He paused briefly to look back at the crevice. 'If we cut some branches and arranged them by the side of the crevice, we should be able to hide a couple more people there.'

The colonel signified his acceptance of the plan and in a quarter of an hour, they were all in position. Jacob had volunteered to stay in the crevice to take charge near the door and the colonel went to supervise the ambush. Despite Jacob's misgivings, Roberto also insisted on being with him in the crevice. Having made sure that there were no signs of the area being disturbed, they all settled down to wait.

Time went by slowly and after what seemed like an hour, but was really only about half that, the sergeant come scuttling towards the crevice giving the low bird cry they had heard before. Drawing his sword he made ready and the others did the same. Peering cautiously through the branches hiding the crevice he saw a man with drawn sword come out of the doorway. He was moving with extreme caution, looking round to see that the coast was clear. Seeing nothing to cause alarm, he turned to face the doorway. 'We're in the clear,' he called, 'lets hurry up and get the horses from the farm and we'll be away before that stupid captain is any the wiser.'

So saying he set of at a trot and disappeared from view, followed by two other men. Several minutes went by and no other men appeared. The sergeant was about to emerge from hiding when Jacob placed a restraining hand on his arm and shook his head silently.

The silence was intense, broken only by the buzzing flies, which they tried to ignore. Jacob was just about to say they could come out when he felt the sergeant tense. A man had emerged cautiously from the doorway and stood just over the threshold with a pistol in one hand and a sword in the other. He spoke to another man over his shoulder, but it was impossible to hear what he'd said. Moving slowly forward the man stopped about three paces from the door.

Jacob recognised Sir Richard Urie immediately, but had been so intent on the figure that he had not realised that the sergeant was creeping forward. Suddenly there was a sharp crack as the sergeant stepped on a fallen twig. Sir Richard turned round and fired hurriedly, crying out a warning to alert his friends. The sergeant was hit in the shoulder and dropped his sword with a curse. Sir Richard sprang forward towards the groaning sergeant and would have run him through if Jacob had not dashed out and parried his blow.

'Bell,' screamed Sir Richard in disbelief, 'what trick of the devil is this?'

He backed away and then regaining his composure a little he moved cautiously towards Jacob his sword at the ready. 'I'll teach you to meddle in my affairs again Bell,' he snarled, 'and this time there's nobody to stop me from killing you.' With that he launched a vicious attack, which needed all of Jacob's skill and resources to thwart.

Thrust followed thrust; riposte followed riposte as the battle ebbed and flowed across the small glade and the ringing clash of blade on blade resounded through the wood. Roberto had crept out of the crevice and while checking to see if the sergeant was badly hurt, he kept a wary eye on the door.

The duel between these two skilled swordsmen was difficult to follow, but Jacob was putting all the long hours of practice with his mentor to good use. Despite being under intense pressure, he was very calm ignoring the attempts by his opponent to taunt him into an indiscretion. As the minutes fled by Jacob realised that the long hours of work in the Glass-works had better fitted him for a long duel.

Sir Richard seemed to sense this, raised the level of his attack and drove Jacob back towards the door. Suddenly Sir Richard sprang back and shouted.

'Shoot him now Ragazoni before anymore of them are on us.'

Before Jacob could move there was a warning cry from Roberto. Knives appeared as if by magic in both hands and he threw them at the shadowy figure in the doorway.

There was a scream of pain and a shot rang out. To Jacob's horror, Roberto slumped to the ground with blood pouring down his face. Sir Richard seeing that Jacob was distracted launched a murderous thrust. Some sixth sense warned Jacob of the thrust, which had been made with an overextended arm and the trick his mentor, had taught him flashed into his mind. Desperate to attend to Roberto he put the risky move into effect.

Swaying to one side he allowed the thrust to go past his left side where it pierced his doublet, but nothing else, being deflected by the metal plates. Clamping his left arm firmly to his side he held the blade tightly and at the same time delivered two hard blows into Sir Richard's face with the hilt of his sword. As the second one struck home he released his arm and Sir Richard staggered backwards completely off balance. Without a moments thought Jacob ran him through and as he fell stricken to his knees he turned without a glance and rushed to Roberto's side.

Wiping away the blood from his face with his kerchief he was relieved to see that the ball appeared to have only grazed the side of his head. He was unconscious, but when he checked his pulse he found it strong and steady. Just then, the Colonel and several men burst on to the scene and Jacob indicating the still figure of Sir Richard brought him up to date with what had happened.

'The corpse is Sir Richard Urie and I think Ragazoni is still inside. It was he who shot Roberto, but I don't know about Count Maldini, I haven't seen him.' He shook his head in sorrow. 'I was the target you know, but Roberto distracted him and threw his knives just before he was shot.' His smile was one of grim satisfaction as he continued. 'At least one of the knives found its target and I can only hope that his wound is not trivial. I suggest you send some men in to bring him out.'

'I've already done that and he should be trapped between the two parties by now.'

A few minutes later, the Captain came out and reported to the Colonel. 'Everything is now secure at the house. We arrested Count Maldini and two of his men before they could get to the passage. They thought they were safe in the secret room and we were on them before they realised. The servants have been told to carry on looking after the house and the secret room and passage are clear.' He gave a broad smile. 'We also found a lot of papers and the Venetian Envoy trying to destroy them. He's taken a knife in each arm Colonel and he needs some attention. My men are patching him up now and then they'll bring him out this way.'

Shortly afterwards Ragazoni was brought out of the tunnel between two soldiers. He still had enough fight left to curse Jacob. 'You think you've won Bell, but you'll still pay for this. You'll lose your precious Glass-works just like you lost Maria and I hope your little knife throwing urchin is dead too.' He winced with pain as the soldiers led him away none too gently and he soon disappeared from view.

The colonel watched him depart and shrugged his shoulders. 'I don't think he knows we've have his tame assassin talking his head off in the Tower. I think the former Envoy is in for a few surprises before very long. Incidentally, it seems young Roberto managed to hit both arms Jacob, he must be quite some adept at knife throwing.'

'He certainly is Colonel, but he's a lot kinder than I would have been in the circumstances, I'd have killed him if I could.' His icy tone left no doubt as to the truth of that and the Colonel thought how glad he was that Jacob was on his side. Changing the subject, he enquired about the body. 'What happened here?'

'Sir Richard Urie left me with no alternative, but to kill him. It was lucky for me that Roberto distracted Ragazoni, who was about to shoot me in the back, as I was busy with Sir Richard at the time. Fortunately I was able to dispatch him and see to Roberto.'

'It's saved the executioner a job anyway,' said the Colonel. 'There was already enough evidence to convict him of treason and no doubt we'll find more from the papers in the secret room, or the house.'

Just then, Roberto stirred and tried to get up, but sank back with a groan. Jacob was at his side in a flash and sitting down cradled his head on his lap. 'Stay where you are Roberto, you took a nasty graze from the pistol ball and I think you'll have a headache for a while.'

'What about Ragazoni and Sir Richard and are you all right Master Jacob?

'I'm fine Roberto, not even a scratch, which is more than you can say for the two you mentioned. Sir Richard is dead and Ragazoni is nursing two knives, one in each arm.' He grinned fiercely. 'I think you might know a thing or two about that.'

Roberto gave a wan smile. 'I thought it was best to go for both arms in case he'd another pistol. It's more difficult to aim with a knife in your arm.'

The colonel who had been listening to the conversation gave a snorting laugh. 'I wish I had both of you with me on a regular basis. Not only are you good fighters, but you'd keep us amused as well.' He became serious for a moment as he noticed how pale Roberto had become. 'I think this young man could do with some rest and recuperation. Don't worry about this end we'll tidy everything up.' He winked conspiratorially at Jacob. 'Besides apart from Ragazoni and Sir Richard Urie, nobody knows you were anywhere near here except my men and none of them will talk. Sir Richard can't and Ragazoni will be in the Tower, so what do you want to do Jacob?'

Jacob thought for a moment then turned to Roberto. 'Do you think you could ride as far as John Isham's with some help?' Roberto nodded and with the help of two of the colonel's men, they lifted him on to his horse. The colonel told the men to ride with them and to say that footpads had waylaid them and that Roberto had been injured. Your arrival scared them off and the rest of the troop is hunting them down.

'That should do the trick for the family,' said Jacob, 'although John Isham will know differently. I'll put him in the picture later in private.'

The colonel saluted Jacob and bid him Godspeed reminding him about the pre-arranged meeting with Sir William at Walsingham's house on the following day. 'I hope Roberto recovers quickly and I will see you on the morrow. Until then fare you well.'

CHAPTER FORTY-TWO

His arrival with the injured Roberto at the house of John Isham sparked off a flurry of questions and activity. The soldiers had departed after passing on the agreed story of footpads; Roberto was hailed as the hero of the hour for saving Jacob's life and taking the pistol ball intended for him.

The local doctor was sent for and Roberto was pronounced to be in need of rest and nursing for a week when he would be fine. He had been packed off to bed and Elizabeth had announced her intention to ensure Roberto's full recovery, even if it meant constant nursing. Roberto had gone to bed with the first smile since he'd been shot.

After a belated meal, John took Jacob into his study and enquired as to the real story. With his usual modesty Jacob glossed over his part in the raid and simply said that the Queen's enemies were now on their way to the Tower. He also told him of the death of Sir Richard Urie in a sword fight.

John looked at him shrewdly; indicated the hole in Jacob's doublet and gave a broad grin. 'And I suppose that was simply where you caught it on a thorn too?' he said.

Jacob had the good grace to look sheepish and gave John a brief account of what had taken place. 'I have to admit it was touch and go for a little while. Roberto's intervention turned the tide. Had it not been for him the outcome could well have been very different for me.'

'Ah, but in your case Jacob Bell, God and the Right were on your side,' said John with conviction. 'He would not let the defender of the faith be defeated so the ungodly were vanquished.' Jacob was not at all sure about this explanation, but wisely let it go. They talked at length for a further half hour then spent the rest of the day relaxing, followed by an early night.

The smell of fresh baked bread greeted Jacob when he awoke next morning. He stretched luxuriantly and lay back enjoying the sense of peace and well being that comes after a good nights sleep. After a quick wash Jacob took his time dressing and packed his things ready for his departure. On his way downstairs, he popped his head round the door of Roberto's room. He was fast asleep in bed and in a chair at his side, his hand firmly clasped in hers, Elizabeth Isham was also asleep. Smiling to himself at this charming scene, Jacob quietly made his way downstairs. He found the Isham's ready to break fast and joined them for a meal of fresh bread and home cured ham, washed down by some delicious elderflower cordial.

'I will join you on your ride to the city,' John informed him. 'I suggest that Roberto stays here until the end of the week when you are welcome to join us for the weekend again.' He pulled a comical face and smiled. 'That is if you aren't planning any more business trips,' he concluded in a mildly sarcastic tone.

'Not at all,' Jacob assured him with a laugh. 'I'll be delighted to share your hospitality again; I haven't felt so happy in a family atmosphere since I left Venice.'

'It's settled then,' said John with some satisfaction and they arranged to meet on the Friday afternoon for the ride back to Tottenham.

The journey back to London was enjoyable. Jacob left his horse at the livery near Aldgate and saying farewell to John Isham, made his way towards Harte Street. Turning the corner to the Crouched Friars he was greeted by chaos. A pall of smoke hung over the Glass-works and the workers were scurrying too and fro. Running into the yard, he could see that the huge stack of timber, which had stood against the wall, was mostly a pile of ashes. There had been almost fifty thousand billets of beech wood in the pile and apart from some that had been dragged to one side it had all gone.

The fierce fire from the burning timber had also spread to the roof and at least part of it was burnt out. Fortunately, the walls of the former abbey were almost six feet thick and had suffered little damage. As he walked towards the main entrance, Peter Tyzack and Quiff came out of what was left of the door, coughing and looking exhausted. Peter his face blackened with smoke and his clothes scorched, was talking earnestly to Quiff. That worthy had a large bloody bandage round his head and was very pale.

Seeing Jacob, their faces reflected their relief at seeing him. 'Thank God you're here Master Jacob it's a terrible mess,' said Peter in tired despair. 'We've been fighting it all night, but it's out now.'

'What on earth happened here? How did it start?' Not giving them time to answer he launched into his next question. 'And what's happened to Quiff?'

'It was deliberate, Master Jacob,' said Peter, 'that's what it was. Two men set on Quiff while the rest of us were at St. Olaves for the evening service and set fire to the billets. Fortunately Quiff managed to stagger to the church and raise the alarm.' He put his arm round Quiff who was looking rather embarrassed. 'Thanks to him, Master Jacob, we managed to save some of the billets, but most of the glass in the store has been melted. The roof is a mess too; the fire from the billets was so intense it spread to the roof in no time. It was well alight by the time we got here. Fortunately there's not too much damage inside the furnace room apart from roof debris.'

'What about the furnace Peter? Is it still workable?' asked Jacob anxiously. He knew that if it was not too damaged there was a chance of getting back into production in weeks instead of months. The roof could be repaired without too much trouble; the main problem would be in replacing the beech billets. Most of the beech woods in private hands close to London had been cut down already and they had been transporting the timber from Northamptonshire for some months.

'Come and see for yourself Master Jacob, we'll need a new roof, but once we have cleaned up inside it'll not be too bad.'

About an hour later, Jacob was sitting in his office, when a weary Peter came in and sat down. The office at the far end of the Glass-works reeked of smoke, but thanks to its separate roof and very thick walls it had not been touched at all.

'We've done about as much as we can for now,' Peter said wiping his face. 'I've sent Quiff home to get some rest. He's been working right through the night with us despite the knock he took from the villains who set the fire.' He cursed them roundly then apologised to Jacob for his language. 'I'll bet it was some of those thugs who work for the Glass Sellers. It'd suit them to have us out of production.'

Not wishing to say too much on that score, Jacob changed the subject. 'I'll want someone to go to the Mercers Hall for me to take a message to John Isham and before you ask I can't send Roberto.'

'Where is he then?' said Peter. 'I'll bet the lazy beggar is lying in bed while we've been here slaving away.'

'As a matter of fact, that's exactly where he is with a pretty girl holding his hand the last time I saw him.' Peter looked puzzled. 'In fact he's still in Tottenham at John Isham's house,' explained Jacob, 'He was hurt when we were set on by some footpads, but fortunately not too seriously,' he hurried to reassure Peter. 'It's not too bad at all and with any luck he'll be back in a week chasing everyone about, if Elizabeth Isham lets him leave.'

'I can't wait for that,' said Peter, 'and what's all this about Elizabeth Isham?'

'That's another story and one you'll have to wait for until Roberto gets back,' he teased when he saw the look on Peter's face. He enjoyed the strong bond, which had been growing between all of the workers. The light-hearted repartee, helped to cement this bond and he liked to join in from time to time.

Before he could continue, one of the workers came in. 'Excuse me Master Jacob, but there's a Colonel Young outside asking for you.'

Jacob sprang up from his seat in some haste. In all the furore of the fire and its consequences, he had completely forgotten his meeting with Sir William Cecil.

'Damn bad business this fire Jacob, I've just come from Sir William and as you might be sure, he's heard about the fire. He says to tell you to come to Greenwich Palace on Wednesday about noon and he will see you then. Give you time to get things organised. In the meantime, he has asked me to put some of my men at your disposal for guard duty. They'll make sure that the villains don't come back to finish the job.'

'Thank you Colonel that will be a load off my mind, I'll tell the men they can go home and get some rest and that your men will be on guard. How's your sergeant by the way?'

'Oh he'll mend; his wound ain't too bad at all. It'll teach him to watch where he puts his big feet in future though.' They laughed and Jacob invited him back to the house in Harte Street. 'I want to check up on Quiff and you can bring me up to date with what's happened since we parted on Sunday.'

'I'll be glad to do that as I've some good news for you from Sir William.' He gave a wry smile and indicated the Glass-works. 'I dare say you could use some after this mess.'

'I wouldn't disagree with you on that,' said Jacob with some feeling, 'but it can wait until were settled at the house.'

A little while later when they were sitting at their ease Colonel Young informed him of Sir William's message. 'He asked me to tell you that the assassin has made a signed confession about everything that Ragazoni has been up to.' He grinned. 'Apparently the sight of Ragazoni in chains in the Tower worked wonders in loosening his tongue and he couldn't wait to tell the inquisitors everything he knew.' He paused dramatically before he continued then seeing Jacob's impatience, went on. 'Including my friend, how Ragazoni was able to make the Venetian courts think you were a traitor when you were completely innocent.' His smile was one of immense satisfaction. 'I told you it was good news.'

Jacob could barely take it in. Could his nightmare really be over? Doubts began to creep insidiously into his mind. It was one thing for this man to confess in the Tower, it was another for him to do the same in Venice, especially with Ragazoni's family connections.

Colonel Young looked puzzled. 'I thought you would have

been more excited by the news. What ails you Jacob?

'Ragazoni is so devious and he has powerful family connections,' Jacob explained. 'I fear that he'll be able to wriggle out of it when he gets back to Venice.'

The colonel looked thoughtful. 'I see what you mean Jacob, but there's also a little matter of plotting against the Queen to consider. That will weigh against him as well.'

'Not as much as it would here,' explained Jacob sadly. 'There are many in Venice, who see the English as enemies out to steal their markets in the Levant. Trade is necessary for the continued existence of Venice and English ships are threatening their major market for Venetian trade.'

Again, the colonel looked thoughtful. 'You know the system Jacob; do you think there's a real chance he could get away with it in Venice?'

After a long pause to consider, Jacob was forced to admit that it was a real possibility. 'I'm probably being too pessimistic. I have some friends and family connections of my own who would dearly love to bring Ragazoni down.' He grimaced as he thought about them. 'He's manipulated things before, and he might do so again.'

Colonel Young got up and stretched. 'I think it's time for me to get back. I'll call in at the Crouched Friars to ensure the men on guard know what to do and I'll see you at Greenwich Palace on Wednesday, if not before.'

The following day, Jacob sat in the office feeling very despondent. He had just received the estimates for the repairs and they made very depressing reading. The replacement of the roof was far more expensive than he had at first thought. Because of the campaign he'd been waging against the Glass-Sellers, he had been making little profit for some time and the loss of the glass in the store, meant that they would not have any money coming in until the works was back in production. The repairs and replacement of the beech wood would take all of his reserves and a lot more.

The one bright spot was that John Isham had been to the Crouched Friars, and offered to extend the loan. Although welcome, it was a mixed blessing. It was going to be difficult to pay the instalments with no money coming in. John had been most sympathetic and true to his word had promised that he would not press Jacob for repayment if he found things difficult. However, at this stage, Jacob could not rule out having to sell all, or part of his business to the Glass-Sellers. At least there was no Sir Richard Urie to contend with. He was fairly sure, that Urie had been acting on his own in firing the Crouched Friars, possibly encouraged by Ragazoni. Realising that there was nothing to be gained by brooding about it, he put the papers in the drawer of his desk and strode out into the Works.

By Wednesday things had gone from bad to worse. Although work to clear the site was progressing, the replacement of the beech wood was proving to be a problem. Careful checks on the billets saved from the fire, showed they had only enough for about four days full production. So far, he had been unable to locate any supplies that could reach London in time for the estimated reopening of the Works. Worse still, the prices being quoted were much higher than usual. He was reluctant to ask John Isham for more time to pay the loan, but if he didn't, selling might prove to be the only option.

Jacob was still wrestling with these problems when he set off for Greenwich and his meeting with Cecil. To his surprise not only was Colonel Young present, but Walsingham too. 'Good morrow Sir Francis,' said Jacob. 'I didn't know you had returned from France, I trust you are now fully recovered.'

'I am indeed Jacob Bell and pleased to be back in England, which I may say is a safer place after the good work you and the Colonel put in this last few days.' He nodded cordially to the Colonel and Sir William added his thanks.

'How are things at the Glass-works Bell?' Sir William was most cordial. 'I've heard about the fire and from what the Colonel tells me, it seems you have the late Sir Richard Urie to blame for it.'

Jacob nodded. 'It wasn't clear at the time when we took Ragazoni, but his remark about me losing the Glass-works came

319

home to me when I stood amidst the wreckage of the Crouched Friars.' He shook his head sadly. 'It'll cost a pretty penny to put right there's no doubt, but it's the loss of the beech wood, which is likely to be the biggest problem at least the men managed to save some of it. Fortunately, there was only minor damage to the furnace. It's built to withstand heat after all. It needs cleaning of course, but we've removed all the debris. The roof is the major building problem, the walls are so thick, that there's no structural damage. '

Sir William nodded. 'You seem to be more worried about the wood than anything else.' He indicated Walsingham who was giving the best impression of a warm smile that Jacob had ever seen. 'I will let Walsingham tell you what we have been up to while you have been busy sorting out your Glass-works.'

Walsingham seeming to regret his show of pleasure now reverted to his normal dry self. 'You may not have realised it at the time Bell, but you did the Crown and yourself a good service when you sent Sir Richard Urie to meet his maker to answer for his crimes.' The grim smile was back and he gave a dry cough. 'Although it's not common knowledge as yet, on Monday, the Queen's Council declared the late unlamented knight to be a traitor to the Crown, for treason against the Queen.'

When he saw that Jacob was looking puzzled he went on to explain. 'The decision by the Council means that all of his land and possessions are forfeit to the Crown. I have spoken to the Queen and since it is certain from our investigations that Sir Richard was directly involved in the fire; we feel that it is poetic justice for his estate to provide the means to repair it. In addition, it was discovered that there are some large beech woods in his estate to the south of London, and the Queen has granted permission for them to be felled.'

Jacob was stunned. This would remove all of major hurdles in rebuilding the Crouched Friars. He stammered his thanks, but he was waved to silence. 'There is no need for thanks Bell; you have rendered the State a great service at no little cost to yourself and your assistant. In recognition for this, you have also been awarded the house in Tottenham, which was the scene of your recent action and all of Sir Richard's interest in the Glass Seller's Association.'

Jacob was speechless as he was treated to Walsingham's wry smile again. 'I particularly like the latter part, which was Sir William's suggestion. It will be the final irony that this will make you the senior partner in that organisation and therefore its head.'

Before Jacob could comment, Sir William interrupted. 'We are also mindful of the part played by your assistant Roberto and as some recompense for his help and the injuries he sustained. We have decided he can choose one of several town houses that Sir Richard formerly owned. They are currently let out to members of the House of Commons and others and should provide the lad with a steady income. And before you ask, the Queen's treasury is still doing very well from this, as Urie was a very wealthy man.'

Jacob shook his head in disbelief. 'Her Majesty has been most generous and I am delighted to accept for both of us.' He felt that something further was required. 'Neither of us came into this business seeking reward, but to avenge the death of my friend and partner Jean Thiéré. At least Sir Richard had the courage to cross swords with me whilst Ragazoni skulked in the shadows and tried to shoot me in the back.'

His voice trailed off and he shook his head. 'Forgive me my lord I'm somewhat overcome. I thank you for your help and for the generous gifts, you have bestowed on Roberto and myself. Can I be of any further service to her Majesty?'

Sir William smiled broadly. 'I was hoping you might offer. I will leave it to Walsingham to discuss with you how you might be of service. For now, I would suggest you get on with the task of repairing the Glass-works. I will speak to my staff and make arrangements for the payment of the repairs from the Treasury. A letter of authority to fell the beech wood will be sent to you shortly.'

Before he could continue, there was a knock on the door and a secretary came in. He reminded Sir William that he and Walsingham were due to attend a Council meeting shortly. Taking their leave they went off to the meeting and Colonel Young walked with Jacob to the quayside.

'This has been almost too much to take in,' said Jacob plaintively. 'It's certainly been an interesting week.'

'You must be feeling happier about things?' The colonel asked sympathetically. 'Although the Glass-works is a mess now, you can build it up even better than before. I'm sure that since it's coming out of the Urie estate the Treasury will pay any reasonable bills.' He grinned mischievously. 'Not to mention a certain young lady who is likely to be free in the not too distant future.'

He was dismayed by Jacob's negative response to this quip. 'That's where your wrong my friend. It could take years to settle this matter through the courts in Venice. It's a great pity that Roberto didn't put his knives in his lying throat.' His manner was so fierce and unforgiving the Colonel was taken aback.

'I wish it had been Ragazoni that had died instead of Urie,' Jacob retorted sadly. 'It would have left Lady Maria free to remain here with me. Now she'll have to go back to Venice and I may never see her again.'

'Perhaps it will not be so bad,' said the Colonel reassuringly. 'It could be all over in a few months and you could be reunited with Lady Maria.'

'You don't understand half of the problem, Colonel.' Jacob had only just realised the full implications himself. 'Until the time my conviction is overturned my family can be thrown into goal and they could send the state assassins after me now they know I'm still alive.'

Colonel Young was astonished to hear this. He became thoughtful for a while and then as they reached the quayside he shook Jacob's hand. 'Don't despair Jacob the matter is not finished yet. We may obtain sufficient information to clear you completely and for that matter, it is not clear if the Queen will even allow Ragazoni to return to Venice. I will pass on your thoughts to Sir William and I'm sure he will not bet impressed at the thought of Ragazoni being able to wriggle out of things on his return to Venice.'

'I hope you're right,' said Jacob.

CHAPTER FORTY-THREE

The following morning Jacob was standing in the Glass-works stripped to the waist wiping the sweat from his face. Already the main timbers of the new roof were in place and he'd spent the last few hours helping to get the furnace ready for relighting. He was just about to carry on when there was a loud commotion in the street outside. Hurriedly putting on a shirt Jacob rushed into the yard to see what was happening. He was astounded to see the Queen and a large entourage bearing down on him. Hastily trying to straighten his dress, he gave a deep bow and dropped on to one knee.

The Queen stood in a pose, which Jacob was later told was so like her father; legs apart and hands on hips, she surveyed Jacob searchingly. 'Oh do get up Jacob Bell you look a sight with your face all black and your shirt out of your breeches,' she said with a wry smile then laughed heartily at Jacob's woeful expression. A ripple of laughter swept through the courtiers as her entourage took up her mood. 'What have you to say for yourself this time Master Bell you always seem to be in some mess, or other when we meet.' Her words were bantering, but her eyes were smiling and indulgent.

Recovering his composure and realising he could do little about his clothes except to tuck his shirt in, which Jacob did so, he gave a deep bow. 'Welcome to the Crouched Friars Glass-works, or what's left of it, your majesty. It's a pity you see it for the first time in such a state of disrepair.' He gave her his most disarming grin. 'Perhaps your majesty will come again when the new Glass-works has emerged triumphant, like that mythical bird the phoenix.' Bowing again, he indulged in a little flattery. 'I'd be delighted to be favoured by your presence once more and I assure you I would be more appropriately dressed to meet England's most magnificent and beautiful Queen.'

The Queen laughed and turning to her entourage, she waved one of them forward. 'I can see why you were attracted to this glassmaker Lady Maria, he has a way with the ladies, think you not.'

'I do indeed your majesty,' said Maria with a mock frown, 'but I thought he reserved them for me alone when we were in Venice. It would seem he has learned some new tricks at your court, your Majesty.'

The Queen roared with laughter and Jacob who had started to move towards Maria stopped as he realised it would be inappropriate with the Queen present. Instead, he bowed to Maria and emulating her light tone retorted. 'I most certainly did Lady Maria, especially the last time we were together in Venice.'

Maria's blushed as she remembered the night in Jacob's house those many months ago. Turning to the Queen, she curtseyed low and asked for leave to stay at the Glass-works with her companion when the Queen departed. 'She is anxious to learn of news of her son Roberto whom she has not seen for a long time,' she explained.

The Queen gave a knowing smile. 'Of course Lady Maria, stay as long as you like. Perhaps you might have some catching up to do yourself as well, my dear.' She smiled benignly at Maria and turning to Jacob, gave him a smile of approval and exhorted him to look after Maria.

Maria made a deep curtsy in acceptance and the Queen with a final smiling caution to Jacob to treat Lady Maria according to her rank, she held out her hand and Jacob bowed and kissed it. Then turning on her heel the Queen swept imperiously out of the courtyard to the cheers of the Glass-works workers and onlookers.

At first things were very awkward between them, for Maria found it difficult to tell Jacob about her ordeal at the hands of Ragazoni. It was the rapes, for that is how Maria saw them that were the most problematical. Not only was it traumatic to talk about them, but also she dreaded what Jacob's reaction might be. The first night Maria slept in Roberto's room, but after seeing how much Jacob wanted her, she went to his bed the following night.

First of all, she showed him the scars on her back. They were healing well, but the physician had warned her that she would have some scars for life. Then, seeing the rage burning in his eyes, she went in to his arms and said he must be prepared for worse, making him promise to hear her out. When she told him how Ragazoni had forced her after the beatings and on several other nights, Jacob face was bloodless and grim. For a moment Maria feared he was going to reject her, then suddenly his face changed and the look of compassion and love he gave her, sent her crying with relief into his arms.

After that first revelation of the rapes and the beating, Jacob had shown only compassion. Oh, he'd raged about Ragazoni, but when Maria explained that she wanted to forget Ragazoni and make the most of every minute with him, Jacob reluctantly agreed.

The next few weeks were the happiest that either Maria or Jacob had known. It was a period when they began to get to know each other again and to feel comfortable in each other's company. Their lovemaking was tentative at first, but the ardour of their first meeting soon became re-ignited and reached new heights.

They both knew they had to part again; Maria was to return to Venice on the next available ship, or if one was not available, on the galley bringing the new envoy. It was enough for now that they were together and they refused to let the thought of parting, ruin their remaining time together.

That night after their first frenzied lovemaking they lay in each other's arms and Jacob said it was time to turn their thoughts towards the future. 'I know it will take time to sort out our affairs in Venice, my love. Despite the confessions of his assassin and the evidence of his plotting against the Queen, it will not be easy to overcome Ragazoni.' He grimaced as he thought of the trial, which Maria had to face. 'Much as I'd like to come back to Venice with you, I have been advised by Walsingham that if I do so, I am likely to be executed as an escaped prisoner, before I can establish my innocence. He's urged me to stay in London and I think he may be right, although he may have an ulterior motive.'

'Have you decided to do so,' asked Maria anxiously. 'I think he's probably right, my love. Adrian has powerful friends in the Senate and it's by no means certain that he'll ever be brought to trial for what he did to you.' She gave Jacob a hug. 'I'll be loath to leave you here, but at least I know you'll be safe. The Queen has promised that she wouldn't send you back to Venice, even if they demanded it.'

Jacob assured Maria that this was true; but he knew that Elizabeth would send him back if it was in the best interests of England, even though she might be reluctant to do so. The Queen was loyal to her friends, but only as long as the safety of her realm was not threatened. She would defend her friends with all her considerable fire and passion, but in the end, the security of England was paramount.

The days passed in a blur as they got to know each other and explored the great City of London and some of the surrounding countryside. They were both entranced by the huge tracts of countryside only a short ride from the city and spent some of their time exploring. Jacob also took the opportunity to spend some time at his new house in Tottenham. The former home of Sir Richard Urie was a lovely house of honeyed stone, set in several acres of its own grounds. The ivy covered walls and the unusual Dutch gables added to its charm. It had no formal gardens as such, but there was a large orchard at the side, containing a large variety of fruits. On the other side was a long narrow lawn, which the John Noble informed him was used for bowls. The estate surrounding the house encompassed a number of tenant farms and there were some quite extensive woodland stocked with game. These together provided much of the food for the house.

The house had been left in a poor state by the attentions of Walsingham's men, but was quickly restored to order with some hard work. Maria enjoyed the task of helping to restore the house and loved the chance to play the role of mistress. John Noble had been rewarded for his help and was now Head steward. He proved to be excellent at his job and soon had the place running smoothly.

Content that the house was safe, Jacob told Maria it was time they accepted the invitation to call on the Isham's. 'It will be wonderful to see Roberto again,' enthused Maria. 'I expect he's had a poor time with his injuries and will be glad to get back to London.'

'You couldn't be more wrong Maria,' he laughed. 'A certain young lady, the Isham's daughter has seen to that. I think that Roberto is greatly smitten by her.'

'In that case it will make the visit even more interesting,' Maria exclaimed in delight. 'I shall look forward to meeting her.'

Roberto was now well on the way to recovery. Indeed, he was in a very happy frame of mind. His mother had taken to Elizabeth at first sight and they were already more like mother and daughter.

'I think that Roberto's single days will soon be over.' Maria remarked laughingly to Jacob as they were strolling in the garden shortly before they left. 'He might have stood a chance if it was just Elizabeth, but with both mothers as well, I think he will soon be betrothed.'

'I'm sure you're right Maria, but I don't think he'll struggle to avoid it very hard.' He smiled indulgently at the young couple a short distance ahead. 'Elizabeth set her sights on him from the first time they met and he thinks the world of her.'

'Do you think the Isham's will approve?'

'I know they do,' said Jacob. 'John told me this morning that they are both delighted with the match.' He grinned and went on. 'He's quite a good catch now you know. With his partnership in the Crouched Friars and the town house from Urie's estates bringing in rent, he's quite a well off young man.'

They turned into a nearby arbour and sat down. Jacob put his arm round her and kissed her soundly and they were quiet for a time. Eventually Jacob said reluctantly, 'I'm afraid that it's time for me to leave. It has been a wonderful few days, but I must get back to London to sort out my affairs.' He gave her a long loving look. 'Will you stay here, or will you come back to Harte Street with me. I'm afraid I'll have to work, but I'll still be able to see you each day if you come.'

Maria pulled a face at him in mock anger and said. 'Don't think you can discard me for your London doxies so easily. Of course I'll be coming with you.'

Jacob laughed in delight. 'I'd better tell all my ladies to give me a miss for now on then,' he remarked with a sly grin. 'It'll be a sacrifice, but I suppose there will be some compensation!' On that note, Jacob suggested it was time to say their farewells to the Isham's.

CHAPTER FORTY-FOUR

In a dark, damp cell in the bowels of the Tower, Matio Arzento, the surviving assassin started to tremble with fear as the sound of the measured tread of the guards stopped at his cell door and the key grated in the lock. He crossed himself feverishly as he contemplated the torture, which had been threatened and which would shortly become a reality.

Two of the guards entered and seizing his arms, dragged him to his feet, ignoring his pleas for mercy. They marched him away with a fierce warning to be quiet, or be gagged and to his surprise they took him up a stairway and away from the dreaded torture chambers below. After many twists and turns, he was eventually brought into a small antechamber where a richly dressed figure was waiting; looking out of the arrow slit, which served for a window.

Sir William Cecil turned round and surveyed the trembling figure before him. Advancing towards him, he seized his cheeks in a vice like grip with his left hand and thrust his face within inches of the terrified man. 'You will listen to me Matio Arzento and you will do exactly as I tell you, or I will send you to the rack at once,' he hissed. 'Nod if you understand and agree, but say nothing.' He smiled in grim satisfaction as the man nodded vigorously. Releasing his grip, he walked to a chair, sat down and studied the assassin intently.

'You will shortly be taken to a secret room where you will be able to see and hear the persons in the room without being seen,' he explained. 'Two guards will be with you at all times and if you attempt to cry out, or try to escape, they have orders to kill you immediately. Do you understand?' Arzento nodded and Sir William continued. 'You will be brought back to this room afterwards and we will then have further conversation.'

He signalled to the guards and they led the assassin away.

Giving them time to get into position, Sir William got up and left the room.   A short distance down the corridor, two guards stood outside a door.   They sprang to attention as he appeared and one of them opened the door.   As he entered the room, the man seated at the desk turned round and smiled evilly at Sir William.   'What fairytales have you come to tell me this time Sir William,' he demanded.   'I keep telling you I know nothing of the accusations against me and I insist you release me immediately,' he demanded.

Sir William smiled briefly.   'I trust that you are comfortable Envoy Ragazoni.   I have just come from a meeting of the Council where they have studied the evidence against Count Maldini and yourself.   The decision of the Council is that both of you are guilty of the crime of treason against the State.   Count Maldini has been sentenced to be hung, drawn and quartered.

Your own case is more involved.   Although you did not actually present your credentials to the Queen, the legal view is that you have the status of an Envoy and therefore have diplomatic immunity.   In view of this the matter was referred to the Queen.   After due consideration, she has ordered that you and your wife are to be returned to Venice as soon as the replacement envoy is in place.'

Ignoring Adrian's attempt to speak he went on.   'You will be taken to the Venetian ship bringing the new envoy and will leave England on the first tide after the galleass has been re-provisioned. You are declared to be persona non grata and are forbidden on pain of death from returning to these shores.   In addition, you will be required to sign this confession, which will be kept in case you return.   Should you do so, you will be sentenced to death by being hung, drawn and quartered.'

Adrian tried to bluster and refused to sign at first, but when he received an assurance that it would not be used against him in the enquiry that would take place on his return to Venice, he agreed. Carefully sprinkling sand over the signature Cecil folded it and regarded Ragazoni with distaste.   'I will keep my promise to refrain from using this document unless you come to England again. However, I suspect it will not be needed.'

He waved away Adrian's attempts to question him. 'There is one more matter, which must be settled. With regard to your servant who is also confined in the Tower, it has been decided that you may take him with you if you grant him diplomatic privilege.'

Adrian looked at Sir William as if he was deranged. 'Take him with me,' he screeched in disbelief. 'He can rot in hell for all I care. It was thanks to his failure I am here in the first place.'

Sir William smiled benignly. 'I thought you might feel like that,' he retorted dryly as he moved towards the door then turning abruptly on his heel he said icily. 'You will be informed when it is time for you to leave, but in the meantime you will remain here at the Queens pleasure.' Without giving time for Adrian to reply he swept out of the room and the door closed behind him.

Returning quickly to the antechamber, he was seated at the desk, with a loaded pistol close to his right hand, when Arzento was brought in. Sir William regarded him shrewdly. He was still frightened, but now his eyes burned with anger and Sir William smiled in grim satisfaction. 'You heard and saw my meeting with the envoy?' Arzento nodded, still afraid to speak from the previous meeting. 'Then you know what is to be your fate?' Again, Arzento nodded his face sullen with anger. Sir William leaned back in the chair and contemplated him astutely. Coming to a decision he opened a drawer in front of him, took out a glass dagger and placing it on the desk in front of him, regarded the assassin impassively.

Arzento looked down at it in surprise then back again at Sir William, with hope dawning in his eyes. Sir William said nothing and continued to regard the man quizzically. After a short while, he sighed deeply and pushed the knife towards the man. 'I think we can be of service to each other,' he remarked his voice heavy with meaning. Arzento's face was impassive as he nodded in understanding and picking up the knife placed it carefully out of sight under his doublet.

Sir William gave a brief smile of satisfaction, but his eyes remained cold and expressionless. He had decided what must be done when Colonel Young advised him that Jacob thought there was every chance that the Venetian Courts would clear Ragazoni. Turning to the guards he instructed them to take the man to the Envoy. They were to wait outside while he paid his visit and then bring him back to the antechamber. The guards at the door were to be informed that after this visit, the Envoy was not to be disturbed until the morning.

Ragazoni was sitting at the desk writing when the door opened and Matio Arzento came in. 'What are you doing here,' Ragazoni sneered. 'Come to plead for your miserable life I suppose. I assume you have been told what I said.'

Arzento nodded with his head bent down and Ragazoni laughed sarcastically. 'I don't know how you persuaded them to let you see me, but you might as well turn round and leave.' His face darkened with rage and getting to his feet, he strode across to Arzento. 'You pathetic worm,' he taunted him. 'I wouldn't take you to Venice, not after your failures have led me to this,' he said pointing around his cell. 'You can stay here and rot for as long as they let you live and I hope they torture you every day.' He lifted up Arzento's face to gloat some more and then recoiled in horror as he saw the sheer hatred in his eyes and the smile of satisfaction spreading across his face. Too late, he made to jump back, opening his mouth to call the guards. He felt his doublet being lifted and a sharp pain in his chest, then blackness. With a sigh he slumped to the ground; dead before he reached it.

Arzento bent down and carefully moved the shirt out of the way, pushed the blade of the glass dagger in right up to the hilt, and then snapped off the blade, rubbing away the tiny drop of blood that wept from the now closed wound. Putting his arms under Ragazoni's, he dragged him across to the bed and laid him down, face to the wall. Carefully adjusting Ragazoni's clothes, he covered him with a blanket, stepped back to the door and surveyed the scene. With a nod of satisfaction, that a casual observer would think he was sleeping, he put the hilt in his doublet and banged on the door for the guard. As the door was opened he bowed to the figure in the bed and was led away.

A short while later the guards returned Arzento to Sir William. He instructed them to wait outside until they were called. Arzento placed the hilt of the glass dagger on the desk. Indicating the missing blade, he spoke for the first time. 'It is done.'

Sir William nodded, picked up the hilt and locked it in the drawer. 'We shall not meet again before you leave,' he said. 'Make sure you tell the full story about the plot against Giacomo Bellini and against Queen Elizabeth, to the courts in Venice.' He sighed. 'Your signed deposition will be handed to the Venetian authorities, via diplomatic channels; so don't even think about trying to intercept it. If you carry out my instructions exactly, you will be well rewarded and I may have other work for you. Fail me and my spies will kill you as painfully as possible. '

With that final chilling warning, he ordered the guards to return the assassin to his cell, looking on impassively as they took him out.

Jacob meanwhile had returned to London and was inundated with problems from all sides. He soon decided that he was not prepared to tackle everything on his own and delegated the refurbishment of the Glass-works to Peter Tyzack. He was proving to be a tower of strength.

The matter of the Glass-seller's Association caused him a lot of heart searching, but a visit from James McFarlane the secretary soon resolved the matter. Sir William Cecil had acquainted McFarlane with the fact that Jacob was the successor to Sir Richard Urie and that he must now be accepted as the senior partner. Since this request had the Queen's blessing, there was never any doubt that it would be challenged. In any case, the chance to be involved with the most successful Glass-works in the country was too good an opportunity for the Association to miss. With the Antwerp Glass makers in disarray following the occupation of the Netherlands by the Duke of Alva, the Crouched Friars had enormous potential for exporting their glass.

The remaining legal matters resulting from the patronage of the Queen had been left in the capable hands of Thomas Pepper. The wily lawyer had promised to handle dealings with the Treasury over the bills for repairing the Glass-works. Jacob was sure then that he would have every reasonable expense repaid.

Four days after his return to London, most of the problems were solved, or well on the way to being so. Enjoying a quiet moment with Maria in the comfort of the living room of Harte Street, Jacob felt very much at peace. He knew that it would still be many weeks before the new Venetian Envoy could arrive and he was enjoying the chance to get to know Maria at a more leisurely pace.

They had become very close in the days since the Queen's visit to the Crouched Friars. For her part, Maria had no qualms about the fact that she was the wife of another man, she was still committed to Jacob and it was he who was her husband in her mind. Although she would have to return to Venice without Jacob for now she was content to live from day to day making as much of their time as possible.

Things soon settled down into a routine. Maria was content to play the mistress of the house leaving Jacob to get on with ordering his affairs. They both looked forward to being together in the evenings and were content to stay in the house enjoying the simple pleasure of just being together.

Once his problems were sorted out, Jacob decided to take a few days off to spend more time with Maria. After a lazy morning, they were just about to go out when Mistress Simpkin announced that Colonel Young was asking to see them. When he came in Jacob could see that he was rather ill at ease. Refusing the offer of some refreshment, he turned to Maria and bowed.

'I am sorry to be the bearer of bad news my lady, but I'm afraid that I must inform you that your husband the Envoy was taken ill at some time last night.' He seemed unsurprised that Maria was not distressed by this news and continued. 'He was attended by the Queen's personal physician this morning, but to no avail and he was pronounced dead.'

Maria was totally taken aback by this statement. She had expected that Adrian was asking for her to attend him and the news of his death came as a shock. 'Dead?' she said at last. 'How can that be? Are you sure?' When the colonel nodded, her legs gave way and she sat down suddenly and held her head in her hands. Jacob rushed to her side and put his arm round her shoulders and she buried her face against his chest and began to cry.

Jacob did his best to comfort her. Suddenly she looked up at him, her tear stained face radiant as she whispered. 'It's over, my love. The nightmare is over. He can't hurt us any more,' she ended, relief tingeing her voice and then she fainted. Jacob lifted her in his arms, carried her to the settle, and put her down gently. Colonel Young who had been an anxious onlooker through these exchanges, dashed off to find Mistress Simpkin. She came bustling in with some damp cloths and herbs and began to attend to Maria.

The Colonel led Jacob to the side of the room and whispered to him. 'I'm sure that Lady Maria will soon be recovered, but I have a private message for you from Sir William Cecil.'

'What does he want this time,' said Jacob in some exasperation. 'I trust he doesn't expect me to attend him at a time like this?'

'Not at all,' said the Colonel with a faint smile. 'He simply asked me to show you something then I am to return it to him. He said you would know what it means, although for the life of me I can't imagine why you should.' He drew out a small parcel wrapped in cloth and passed it to Jacob. Wondering what it was all about Jacob opened the cloth to reveal the contents.

He recognised it at once and looked at the hilt of the glass dagger in amazement. It was several seconds before the implication sank in and he recognised the significance of Sir William's message.

'Those who live by the sword shall perish by the sword,' he muttered to himself.

'What was that?' queried the colonel.

'It doesn't matter,' said Jacob, 'I was just thinking aloud.' He handed the hilt back to the colonel and bade him return it to Sir William.

'You know what it means then Jacob; it's a mystery to me.'

'Oh yes, I know what it means, but you're better off not

knowing.' He said and glanced round at Maria who was still being fussed over by Mistress Simpkin. 'I would be obliged if you did not let Maria see it,' he said anxiously, 'it might upset her. Put it away, don't mention anything about it and let Sir William know I will be seeing him shortly.'

The colonel did as he was requested. 'Don't leave it too long Jacob, Sir William is about to leave for a meeting with Walsingham in France and will not delay his departure much longer.' He looked across towards Maria who was showing signs of recovery under Mistress Simpkins ministrations. 'I think it would save questions if I left now. Give the Lady Maria my felicitations.' With that, he bowed and strode off.

Hardly had he left when Maria sat up with a groan. She looked round in confusion and Jacob hurried over to her. She held out her arms and Jacob falling to his knees held her tight. 'Is he really dead Jacob? She questioned disbelief tingeing her voice. She looked anxiously to Jacob for reassurance. 'Are we free of him at last?'

'Yes he's dead Maria and he can't hurt us any more with his plots.'

'He'll still affect us from the grave though my love, said Maria bitterly. 'I won't be able to stay with you and you won't be able to go to Murano until I can get the charges against you lifted.'

Jacob shook his head. 'I'm afraid that it's worse than that,' he said sadly. 'By setting up the Glass-works in London, I'll still be a traitor in their eyes and my family will suffer unless I return for sentence.'

Maria shuddered at the thought. 'You could be sentenced to the galleys again?' she gasped as the reality of the situation dawned on her. 'I couldn't let that happen now I've found you again.' She walked around in agitation then sitting next to Jacob she clutched his arm tightly. 'I'll stop here in London with you and forget all about Venice,' she said wildly. 'The Queen is my friend and she'll let me stay.' Her voice trailed off and she put her head on Jacob's shoulder and began to sob heartbrokenly.

Jacob held her for a while until she became quiet then putting his fingers gently under her chin lifted her face up and kissed her. 'I think you know you must return to Venice,' he said kindly. 'There will be much to sort out with Ragazoni's death.' He caressed her cheek lovingly. 'You are the bravest person I know and you must be brave again.' He looked at her affectionately as she gave a tremulous smile, sat up and wiped away her tears.

'You're right Jacob and I knew it all the time, but I just couldn't bear to think about leaving you.' She smiled. 'I'm fine now my love, we must be sure to make the most of the time left to us.'

They certainly did this and in later life Jacob looked back on this period as one of the most tranquil of his life. There was a wedding in September at Tottenham, when Roberto married Elizabeth. The young couple moved into the town house given to him from the estate of Sir Richard Urie. It was only a short distance from Harte Street and Elizabeth and Maria soon became firm friends. Anna moved in with Roberto and Elizabeth and a short period of domestic bliss descended on both households.

All too soon, however they were gathered at the quayside to bid Maria farewell. Maria and Jacob had just returned from Hampton Court where the Queen had bade Maria a fond farewell and told her she would be welcome at court when she returned to England. Indeed, she commanded her to return as soon as her affairs were settled. Her parting gift was a priceless pearl necklace as a token of her regard and admiration for Maria's courage in sending the warning to Cecil. Jacob had hoped to see Cecil and Walsingham, but they were at the Tower on official business.

Now it was time for the final farewell they had both been dreading. The captain was pressing for them to come on board as he did not want to miss the tide and Maria was trying hard to keep a brave face. There was quite a crowd at Galley Key and the new Envoy had just left, having paid his respects to Maria and passing on a letter from her father. Jacob was just about to lead Maria to the gangplank, when there was a commotion at the end of the Key and a coach with several outriders drove along, scattering the onlookers. It pulled up nearby and Jacob was surprised to see Walsingham alight. He came over to them and proffered a sealed envelope to Maria.

'What is it, Sir Francis?'

Walsingham gave his cold smile. 'Something I hope you will find useful. At the insistence of Sir William Cecil, your husband, the late Venetian Envoy, made a signed confession of treason, as the price for being sent back to Venice. On the understanding of course, that it would not be used to bring him to trial in Venice, but as surety for his promise not to set foot on English soil again. Since he can't be brought to trial, I thought it might be useful in your fight to clear Jacob Bell.'

Maria made a deep curtsy. 'I am most grateful to you for bringing this and to Sir William for obtaining it. It could make a lot of difference.'

'I trust so Lady Maria. You are welcome to come to England at any time and I can also tell you, in strict confidence that Jacob Bell will be named Glassmaker to the Queen in the not too distant future.' Brushing aside their thanks, with a final farewell, he turned and strode back to his coach.

'Giam, that's wonderful news. I am so proud of you,' said Maria giving him a hug.

Meanwhile, Roberto's mother had just told him she was returning to Venice with Maria.

'But we've had so little time together, Mother. You could stay with us,' protested Roberto. Taking Elizabeth's hand, she placed it in Roberto's. 'You have someone else to look after you now and my lady has no one. I must go with her, but I know she will return to be with Master Jacob and I will come with her.'

Maria whilst embracing Jacob whispered in his ear. 'I will come back my love, have no fear of that. There is nothing to keep me in Venice now I know that you're alive.' She held him at arms length and looked deep into his eyes. 'Do not forget me Giam.'

'Forget you? I could no sooner forget you than I could forget to breath.' He released her hands as the captain gestured once more for them to go on board. 'You must go my love before the captain has apoplexy. I will keep you in my heart until you return.'

'And I you,' replied Maria and turning on her heel she went up the gangplank accompanied by Anna.

Once the galley was out of sight, it was a sombre party that made its way back to Harte Street. They had no sooner set foot in the house, than Peter Tyzack came hurrying in. 'Master Jacob, we have a problem over the beech billets. The woods that you were given by Queen have been felled, but we can't get a haulier to bring them to London.'

He had no sooner finished his tale, than Quiff came rushing in. 'Master Jacob, there's a messenger arrived from the Glass-Sellers. He says it's most urgent. He's waiting at the Crouched Friars for an answer. I'm sorry, I didn't know if you had returned, or I would have brought him with me. Can you come with me right away?'

Jacob looked at Roberto and a rueful smile passed between them. 'Come on Roberto,' Jacob said in a resigned, but more cheerful voice, 'there's no time for regrets and what might have been, we have a Glass-works to run.' With that, the two partners set off for the Crouched Friars with purposeful steps. Peter Tyzack and Quiff followed behind. For the first time in weeks, they had beaming smiles on their faces.

EPILOGUE

The celebrations had been going on for some time and Jacob tiring of all the backslapping wandered outside. The memories of the ceremony at the Queen's investment earlier in the day were still fresh in his mind. Glassmaker to the Queen! He still found the sound of his new title strange to his ears. Not only that, but the Queen had granted him a monopoly for twenty-one years.

Jacob shook his head in wonder. What a year this had been. There were times when he couldn't begin to understand his changes of fortune. Not that the monopoly was going to make life easy. Sir William had seen to it that there were clauses in the letters patent that would require some changes to be made.

He took out the document and read it again. He looked at the two main clauses.

'A monopoly is hereby granted to Jacob Bell formerly of Murano, for a period of twenty-one years, for the makynge of drinking glasses such as be accustumblie made in the towne of Murano and he hathe undertaken to teache and bring uppe in the said Arte and knowledge of makinge the said drynkyng glasses our natural Subjectes.

The drynkyng glasses are to be as cheape or rather better cheape than those commonly broughte from the citie of Murano, or other parts of beyond the Seas.'

Jacob smiled to himself as he thought of the implications. The first part was the most difficult, because teaching English workers how to make glass cut across the secrecy imposed by the Venetian state. It was a crime punishable by death. However, since he had already been falsely convicted for this 'crime', he had no qualms about it any more. When he'd agreed to take over the running of the Crouched Friars he'd faced that hurdle and put it behind him.

When he considered the clause in detail it shouldn't be too difficult after all, since he'd already taken steps to train some English workers. However, it would be a long time if ever, before the Crouched Friars could supply all of England's demand for quality glass and some would still have to be brought in from Murano, or Antwerp. On mature consideration it was a wonderful opportunity, especially now he had a controlling interest in the Glass Sellers Association.

The second part was easy. It was the shipping costs and breakages that made Murano glass so expensive. He could make it just as cheaply as the glassmakers could on Murano and there were no shipping costs, so there would be more profit. He smiled in satisfaction as he folded up the document again, the extra profits would certainly please the Glass Sellers Association and Murano would have to come to him if they wished to continue to sell glass in England. The thought occurred that he might be able to use this fact to come to some accommodation with Venice, but now was not the time.

Putting the letters patent away in his doublet Jacob's thoughts turned to Maria. He was worried that she would be safe on the journey back to Venice. It was not the best time to be travelling and he hoped that she had arrived safely.

As the sails of the Galleass were lowered and the oars run out, Maria was standing by the stern rails having just been very sick. They we're just entering the Venetian lagoon and the buildings could be seen clearly through the heat haze. Thank goodness for that thought Maria; the journey was bad enough, but to have morning sickness as well has been almost too much to bear.

It wasn't the thought of the baby, she welcomed that; it was the vexed question of who was the father. Ever since she realised she was pregnant, it had been the one thought on her mind. At least she had at last come to a decision, but not one that pleased her. She was going to name Ragazoni as the father; everyone would expect it anyway. She would be ostracised by society if she did anything else.

She trembled, but only partly due to the cold wind blowing across the lagoon and drew her shawl more closely around her shoulders, as she thought about what the decision involved. As a Ragazoni, the child will inherit all of Adrian's estates and even eventually all those of his grandfathers. It will be a suitable revenge and a fine irony for Giam's child, to be Adrian's heir: she was sure in her own mind that it was his. The thing that bothered her most of all, was how was she to tell Giam. He knew about the rape, but could he accept the baby being brought up as a Ragazoni? It was going to take a lot of courage to tell him. Perhaps after the trial might be the best time. Especially when Giam was found innocent, as she believed he must.

She turned round as Anna came bustling up with her cloak and looked towards the superb skyline of the city coming into view. Even against the dull, cloudy sky it looked as magnificent as ever. Sending Anna to finish the packing, she watched the imposing bulk of San Giorgio come into view. Resting her hand on her stomach she thought of Giam. You'll know about your child as soon as it is safe to tell you, she promised him silently. I miss you so much and I wish you could be here with me. Take care of your self my dear, she thought and sent her love winging across the long miles to London.

Jacob who was still outside, shuddered as if a cold breeze had blown through him. He pulled his cloak more tightly around him, turned and strode purposefully in the direction of the Crouched Friars. As he approached the Glass-works, now buzzing with activity, its chimneystacks belching white, aromatic smoke into the grey London sky, he suddenly felt light- headed with relief and happiness. He wasn't sure how he knew it, but he was certain that Maria was safe and well, although hundreds of miles away across the sea.

AUTHOR'S NOTE

The Glassmaker series was inspired by the life of Jacopo Vercelline, a Murano glass blower working in Antwerp. In 1570 he was brought to London by a Frenchman, Carré to run his Glass-works at the Crutched Friars, part of a former monastery in Aldgate, behind the Tower of London. One year later Carré died, cause of death unknown and Vercelline took over the Crutched Friars, bringing in Venetian glass blowers. Four years later, he was producing glass to rival Murano. Falling foul of the Glass-Sellers Association, his glass-works mysteriously caught fire while his workers were at church. He pleaded with Lord Burghley for protection and became the first Glassmaker to Queen Elizabeth on the 15th December 1575. He was given a monopoly for twenty-one years and the original Letter Patent is still to be seen today as part of the National Archive. By the time Vercelline, retired in 1592 a rich man, the Crutched Friars employed twenty glass-blowers and their assistants, some 150 men in total and Vercelline had prepared the way for England to develop its own distinctive glass-making industry to rival Murano.

Giacomo Bellini alias Jacob Bell is purely a fictional character and his life, adventures and the Maldini plot are also fictional. These were turbulent times in England's history and throughout her reign, plots that threatened her life plagued Elizabeth. In order to suit the purposes of the book, some historical dates have been altered i.e. the award of Glassmaker to the Queen. Wherever historical figures have been used, I have tried to ensure that they have behaved in a manner consistent with my research. Giacomo's glass-making discoveries are purely fictional, but are certainly possible from the state of knowledge at that time. As such, they would have proved equally as important as suggested in the book.

Today, everyone owns some glass, but few know much about

this strange solidified liquid and indeed how glass is made. I have tried to give some idea of the techniques used in glass making, which have changed little, in 400 years, apart from the furnaces, now electric. I hope the readers' find this as fascinating as I have during my long-held love of glass and that it enhances their enjoyment of the book.

Peter Cooke, Yorkshire, 2005.